MAGIC, THE FINAL INGREDIENT

"Am I your kind of woman, Nate?" I murmured as I crushed the walnuts for the batter. "I'd like to be. I'd like to make those green eyes of yours go dark with desire."

I tried to think of the last time I'd felt special. Sexy. Spectacular. Beautiful. How sad was it that I couldn't remember?

Setting the oven to preheat, I chose a large wooden spoon. I like my muffins a bit dense, so I tend to hand mix the batter rather than use my electric beater. My skin grew hot at the idea of Nate in my bed.

"Nate, I want you to see me as the woman I am. I want you to desire me. I want you to *want* me." I whispered my thoughts out loud, still stirring.

Almost instantaneously, a hard shiver rode my body from my feet to my scalp and then straight down my arms to my hands. A spark zapped from my hand to the spoon to the batter to the bowl. The spark turned into a soft glow that I could almost hear. It crackled and buzzed and sizzled in my ears.

Last I checked, wooden spoons don't run on electricity.

a Taste of Magic

Tracy Madison

LOVE SPELL NEW YORK CITY

To my great-grandmother Verda.
You helped me see that anything in life is possible
and you always, no matter what, believed in me. I miss you.

LOVE SPELL®

March 2009

Published by

Dorchester Publishing Co., Inc.
200 Madison Avenue
New York, NY 10016

ISBN 10: 0-505-52810-X
ISBN 13: 978-0-505-52810-0
E-ISBN: 1-4285-0617-9

The name "Love Spell" and its logo are trademarks of Dorchester Publishing Co., Inc.

Printed in the United States of America.

10 9 8 7 6 5 4 3 2 1

Visit us on the web at www.dorchesterpub.com.

ACKNOWLEDGMENTS

From the moment I decided to write this book, many people helped it along. Thank you to my best friend and sister of the heart, Lisa Mondello. Your steadfast support, friendship, and love make every day brighter. Thanks, also, to my equally as wonderful friend, Natalie Damschroder, who's an expert at "big stick" motivation. Thanks, Nat!

To my incredible critique partners, Dale, Deborah, and Traci; to MVRWA for the laughs, encouragement, and information that is freely passed from one to another; and to David Brown, for pushing me along the promo trail. My gratitude is endless.

To my parents and my brother, who stand beside me in the best and worst of circumstances; to my uncle, who sets the bar high, and expects me to meet it; to my husband, who always has more faith in me than I have in myself; and to my children, who are the reason I wake up every day. I can never thank you enough.

a Taste of Magic

Chapter One

"You married a lemon, Elizabeth," said Grandma Verda, as if that explained everything.

Interesting concept. I'd never compared my ex-husband to a piece of fruit before. Unless you counted the time I likened a certain appendage of his to a banana. "Assuming that's true, even lemons can be satisfying. With a little water and sugar, you have lemonade."

Grandma Verda wrinkled her nose. "You add sugar to a bad lemon and all you get is a nasty aftertaste. And Marc Stevens is about as rotten a lemon as any I've ever seen."

We were sitting in my office at A Taste of Magic, the bakery I co-own with my best friend, Jon Winterson. When I'd arrived at the crack of dawn, I'd found Grandma Verda, hot pink sneakers and all, waiting for me.

I kept my voice light. "But Grandma, when I married Marc, you thought he was perfect for me."

"That was ten years ago. I didn't know. He was still ripening—he could have turned into an orange. Oranges make decent husbands."

"I see." Well, not really, but her train of thought was interesting. Maybe someone should write a guide on how to know you're marrying a lemon. I mean, you get an instruction manual in three different languages when you buy a toaster, so why not when you're committing your life to another person?

I liked that idea. It could be given out after the *I do*s and right before the kiss. Hmm. On second thought, it should happen before the *I do*s. That way, either party can hotfoot it out of the ceremony before it's too late.

Even so, I don't think it would have changed my mind.

I'd been pretty set in my decision to become Elizabeth Stevens.

"You were too good for him. I knew that much." Grandma Verda sipped her tea. "I don't know why you agreed to do it."

She wasn't talking about my ill-fated marriage any longer. *This* subject was one I preferred not to discuss. "I'm fine. Really. It's not that big of a deal."

I'd just told my first lie for the day, and not even an acceptable one at that. While I tended to be an honest person, there were two things in life I figured all women had the right to lie about: chocolate and headaches. Neither of which was the case here. And I never lied to my grandmother. Well, hardly ever. It didn't sit well with me that I just had.

She stared at me with her never-miss-anything blue eyes. You know how when the quiet stretches on too long you feel forced to talk? To fill in the gap, I said, "I'm sure I'm not the only woman in the same situation. Besides, I'm just baking a cake. It's not like I don't do that every day, anyway." Crap. I was overexplaining.

"Uh-huh." She smacked her teacup down, a wave of Earl Grey sloshing over the side. "Let loose, Lizzie. You've been holding back for a year under a blanket of 'I'm sorry,' and 'I'm fine,' and 'It's no big deal.' Tell me how you really feel."

Her words hit me dead center.

I sopped up the tea with a paper towel and ignored the pressure in my chest. "What do you want me to say? That I'm crushed Marc left me for his blond Barbie-doll receptionist? That my marriage fell into the worst stereotype ever? Okay, yeah—it sucked. But it was a year ago."

Last year was supposed to be "our year." Marc and I were finally going to start a family. I'd wanted a baby for a long time, but he'd kept giving me reasons to wait. Only, instead of having a child, he'd decided to marry one.

My eyes welled with tears. One blink and the charade would be up. "I'll be right back, Grandma. There's something in my eye." Second lie for the day. My grandmother might be tough, but she was still eighty-five years old. She didn't need to see her granddaughter cry.

In the restroom, after the tears subsided, I turned the cold water on full blast and splashed my face. I was pale. Too pale. And the dark circles spoke of too many sleepless nights. I put a little color back by pinching my cheeks. As I stared at the woman in the mirror—a stranger—I realized it was time to quit deluding myself. I wasn't okay. I hadn't been for twelve long months. And what I had to do today might make me ill.

Scratch that. What I had to do today could kill me. I could even see the headlines in the *Chicago Tribune*:

DEATH BY CAKE!
Highland Park Baker Chokes to Death Swallowing Every
Last Vestige of Pride
While Baking Ex-Husband and Mistress's Wedding Cake!

Yep, that's right. My job today was to create a culinary work of art for the next soon-to-be Mr. and Mrs. Stevens. *Marc and Tiffany*. Otherwise known as my cheating ex and the young, beautiful woman he'd left me for exactly one year ago. And if that wasn't hell enough, it also happened to be my thirty-fifth birthday. Now, for the second birthday in a row, Marc was front and center in my mind. Something just wasn't right about that.

I pulled in a deep breath, pinched my cheeks again for good measure, and returned to my grandmother. "Sorry about that," I said, avoiding her gaze.

Grandma Verda squeezed my wrist. "I want you to be happy."

Blinking, I said, "I know. I'll get there. Why are you here so early, anyway? Won't you be at Mom and Dad's tomorrow night?"

My family was celebrating my birthday the following night, since it was a Friday. It was easier for everyone to get together.

"Of course I will. I never miss a chance to see all my grand-kids. But this is nice. A few minutes alone with my grand-daughter on her actual birthday. We haven't done that for years."

This was a better subject. "I miss those lunches, but I'm glad you came by."

A smile wreathed her face. She pulled two envelopes out of her purse, one purple and one white. Holding one in each hand, she looked at them. She looked at me. Finally, she tucked the white envelope away and handed me the purple card.

"Open it now." She clapped in excitement, much as a child would.

Curious, I slid my nail under the flap and lifted the card out. Glitter flew up at me, and the heaviness in my chest dis-appeared. I laughed. "You've been putting glitter in my cards since I was little."

"Birthdays are about magic. Magic is fun. So is glitter."

She'd always said that. Always told me that on one of my birthdays, she'd have a very special gift for me. I glanced up and saw her pink cheeks and sparkling eyes. Maybe it was this birthday?

I turned the card face front and laughed again, this time at the picture of a bikini-clad woman wearing a birthday hat popping out of a cake. Maybe more apropos for a man, but after all, I did bake cakes for a living.

I opened the card, and a twenty-dollar bill swirled to the floor. Inside, my grandmother's flowing handwriting said:

> *It's time to believe in magic, Elizabeth.*
> *Open your heart wide and be true to yourself*
> *so the gift can find you.*
> *Happy Birthday, my darling girl.*
> *Love, Grandma.*
> *P.S. Have fun!*

The writing seemed to shine brightly for a second. Bizarre. I blinked and rubbed my fingers along the ink strokes. Whatever I thought I'd seen was gone. Chalking it up to the early hour and my insufficiently caffeinated system, I knelt down to retrieve the twenty.

"This is great, Grandma. Thank you," I said, tucking the money back into the card.

Her eyes narrowed, and she glanced from the card to me. "How do you feel?"

"Fine. Why?"

"Oh, just wondering. I'm your grandmother. It's important to me that you're happy."

Hmm. Something wasn't quite right, but I couldn't put my finger on what. A glance at the clock told me I had no time to figure it out, either. "Come with me to the kitchen. I need to start work."

"Oh, well, I should probably leave."

Grandma Verda grabbed her coat. After I unlocked the door, she gave me another hug. "Sweetie, I want you to have *fun*. I want you to think about the things you really want, what you really wish for, and then—you never know—they might just come true."

"Life doesn't work that way," I mumbled.

"You're wrong. Life *can* work that way." Amusement flitted over her features. "You'll see. Your time is here, Lizzie-girl."

And then she was gone.

My mind played over the conversation as I returned to my office, and it still didn't make sense. Grandma Verda had her own way of doing things, not to mention her unique outlook on life. And, most peculiar, the things she wanted always seemed to come true for her.

And, at times, for me.

I twisted my shoulder-length brown hair into a knot on top of my head and secured it with a band. Smiling, I remembered a summer I'd spent with her as a child. Even though I knew better now, I still considered that summer magical.

It began when I lost my favorite doll. I carried Molly everywhere with me—not so different than Cindy Brady and her Kitty Karry-All doll. Except I knew for sure I'd left her in the park. When we returned to the park, she was gone. I'd cried all night, and the next morning Grandma Verda gave me a card. Seeing as I was too young to read, she read it to me. She told me to close my eyes and wish really hard that I'd find Molly. Later that day, I'd discovered my doll squished behind a couch cushion. Grandma Verda said it was magic.

As an adult, I knew she'd just replaced it with a new one. But then? Yeah, I'd believed her tales of magic and wishes. That entire summer had been filled with unexplained things.

When I told my mother, she got really upset. She told me not to listen to my grandmother. That Grandma meant well, but I should know the only magic you got out of life was made from hard work. And yeah, that was pretty much the truth of it, wasn't it?

Even so, my grandmother's obsession with magic must have made some sort of an impact on me. When Jon and I had decided to open a bakery together, the only name we'd agreed on was A Taste of Magic.

Pouring a cup of coffee, I checked the time again. Marc's cake could wait ten more minutes. I gulped the first sip too fast and burned my throat, but I didn't care.

Grandma wanted me to let loose and quit holding back. That petrified me almost as much as baking the stupid cake. If I faced how I really felt, it would hurt too much. I was an expert at running away from my feelings. From confrontations. From anything that meant anything to me.

I didn't want to hide anymore, but I didn't want to feel, either. And, if I was honest with myself, I knew what I'd become: a woman filled with remorse, confusion, sadness, and yes—a huge amount of venom. I was the coiled-up snake waiting for the perfect millisecond to attack. I was also the timid house mouse that ran and hid at the first sign of trouble. Snakes normally ate mice, but in my case, the mouse won hands down, time after time.

If I could be the snake, just once, maybe I'd have a chance.

My ten minutes were up, so I grabbed the file on the Stevens wedding and focused on that. Marc and Tiffany's order was for a standard three-tier with two additional sides. Any other day, I'd breeze right through. Today, I just wanted it over.

I took my coffee and the file to the kitchen. My business partner's significant other, Andy, was an interior designer, and he'd created the most workable kitchen possible within our limited dimensions. With overhead bins and cupboards for storage, wide surfaces for mixing, kneading, and decorating, along with two ovens and a commercial refrigerator, it should feel cramped. Because Andy was exceptional at his job, the space seemed larger than it was.

Of course, that didn't stop me and Jon from dreaming about the day we'd be able to upsize. Something that seemed more out of our reach now than ever before. We'd lost several high-profile jobs recently to competition, and because of that, we weren't picking up new business as fast as we'd like.

Just one more thing to worry about—but not now. I had enough stress at the moment, so the fate of A Taste of Magic would need to wait until another day.

My gaze flipped through the room and, as pleasant as it was, all I wanted to do was run back home and watch the first season of *Buffy the Vampire Slayer* again. Mature? Probably not. But at least I had good taste. Plus, those men—even the bloodsucking ones—were about as hot as they got.

"Stop," I whispered. I placed the ingredients for the cake-from-hell on the counter.

When everything was ready, I cracked and separated the eggs, measured in the milk, citrus oil, and vanilla into a large bowl. I swallowed. I forced myself to breathe. In. Out. In. Out. And then—out of nowhere—a vision of *my* wedding cake slipped into my mind. It had been far too grandiose for our wedding, but it was beautiful. Jon's gift to us, the sweetie.

I'd saved a slice, just like you're supposed to, and Marc and I meant to eat it on our first year anniversary. For good luck. But he'd been away on business, and it just hadn't happened. Ever.

Maybe that's what went wrong: we ignored tradition.

Anyway, it never got tossed. And I knew if I'd left it at the house, Marc would have disposed of it without a second thought, so I'd dragged it with me to my apartment and gave it a home in my new freezer. Somehow, as silly as it sounds, I wasn't ready to get rid of it yet. That stupid piece of frozen cake represented a life that didn't happen. A life that part of me still yearned for, still mourned.

"You're here early," Jon said.

I jumped at the sound of his voice and then turned to face him. "And you're not?"

He came closer, his jeans hugging his hips like they were painted on. "I wanted to be sure you were okay." Simple statement, but it conveyed a lot. Just like Jon.

"Of course I am."

He gave me a look with his baby blues that shone with pity. I hated that look.

"Stop it. I'm fine."

"No. You're not. You should have taken the day off. For crying out loud, it's your birthday."

"So? You're taking me out tomorrow night to celebrate. This is work."

"You shouldn't have to be here. It's my fault we even have the order."

And it was. Jon had only noticed the consultant's name and the date of the wedding when the order came in. By the time I discovered the identities of the bride and groom, it was too late to pass on the job. If we had, we may have jeopardized our future business from this wedding consultant. Business was business, and A Taste of Magic was too new to chance it. Besides, we'd lost out on enough jobs lately.

"You didn't do anything wrong." And then, to change the subject, I said, "You cut your hair. It looks good."

Jon grinned and ran his hand over his cropped, dark blond hair. "I found this great salon in the city. You should check it out."

"Maybe." For some reason, my stomach roiled, and I fought to quell the queasiness. Getting sick would be bad. Jon would send me home. While part of me wanted to run and hide, another part of me was committed to seeing this through. Possibly, it would give me closure.

Okay, closure was doubtful, but it was worth a shot.

Jon glanced at the counter, his gaze taking everything in. "Want some help?"

"I'm fine right now. But if you don't mind, how about taking over the decorating portion? I won't be in the mood for rosettes and fondant tomorrow any more than I am today. And then I can stay home tomorrow. Is that cool?"

"Absolutely." Jon pulled me into his arms, squeezing tightly. "You know I love you, right?"

I closed my eyes and hugged him back. My cheek rested on his shoulder, and I could smell soap, shampoo, and his newest aftershave. This man, not just my business partner, but my friend, had been my rock for the past year. "I love you, too," I mumbled.

We stood that way for a minute. Then, we both stepped away at the same time, disengaging ourselves. His eyes held worry, but he smiled at me. "You're not going to wiggle out of tomorrow night, are you?" he asked, referring to our plan of karaoke and margaritas after my birthday celebration with my family.

"Nope. Maddie would kill me. She's bringing her new man for our approval." Maddie Sinclair was my other best friend. She lived in the apartment above mine. Actually, it was because of her I'd even found my apartment. And having her so close had made the move that much easier on me.

"Sounds good. I'm going to get started on the monthly accounting. Call me if you need anything."

"I will."

After Jon left the kitchen, I returned my focus to finishing the damn cake, which—somehow—had become synonymous with moving on with my life. I turned on the mixer and added some egg whites, along with some milk. I tried to think of something else, tried to push back the sadness. "Snap out of it," I muttered.

Grandma Verda asked me to think about what I wanted, so

I decided to concentrate on that. If I could have anything I wanted for my birthday, what would it be?

A vacation in Maui would be sweet. Or maybe a new car, one with a functioning radio. My little Volkswagen bug wasn't nearly as cute as it used to be.

But there had to be something better. Something bigger.

I mentally thumbed through the possibilities, and suddenly, my mind latched onto the perfect one. I wanted retribution.

"Revenge is sweet; payback is a bitch," I said. Yeah, I wanted both. Revenge *and* payback. Closure was nice and all, but the snake in me wanted to come out. Since I had to make the damn cake, it would be nice if I could inflict some sort of legacy to go along with it.

Oh, I didn't want to poison the bride and groom. That wasn't me; and besides, jail didn't appeal in any way. So totally not worth it. If I could do anything, it would have to be something personal. Something subtle. But also, something that stuck.

As I added the remainder of the egg white mix, the perfect payback hit me. Mirth bubbled up inside, and I giggled. I couldn't help it. Wedding nights meant sex. Honeymoons meant more sex. What if Marc's body refused to cooperate? What if—on his wedding night with his new bride—he couldn't get it up?

See, I knew Marc inside and out. He, like most men, was paranoid about his sexual performance. I'd never complained about it, but it's not like I had anyone to compare him to. He'd been it for me, in more ways than one. But if this happened, he'd be mortified. Tiffany would be hysterical. And yet no one would be *hurt*—not really. And the situation would be temporary. It really was the perfect payback.

Yeah, I liked the idea. A lot. It didn't even bother me that it was the bitchiest thought I'd had in a long, long time. Hell, if I could wish that upon him—if I had any power—I'd do it. In an instant. It was subtle, but in a big—or in this case, limp—sort of way.

I increased the speed of the mixer, my movements automatic. Gradually, I added the dry ingredients I'd measured earlier, the bowl rotating smoothly.

I didn't feel queasy anymore. Without understanding why, I whispered, "See how you like this, Marc. No sex for you until after your honeymoon, because you won't be able to get it up. No matter what you do, no matter what your wife tries. Soft and limp. Even if you have Viagra, it will do you no good."

I laughed again, and curiously, felt a strange buzz around me, kind of like static electricity but stronger. It bounced through me, and off me, and prickles coated my skin. A shiny glow moved from my hand to the mixer and then to the bowl. Then the entire thing lit up in faint pulsing shots of light.

"What the hell?" The lights kept bobbing around, getting stronger as the energy flowed through me. I dropped my hand and leapt back to unplug the mixer. I was pretty sure I'd been an instant away from electrocution, because nothing else made any sense.

A few seconds later the buzzing stopped, the tingling subsided, the glow faded. I examined the plug and the mixer. Both looked fine. I pulled on some thick rubber gloves and shoved the plug back in the outlet. The mixer just whirred away. No sparks, no sizzles.

"Weird," I said.

All I wanted to do was finish up, so I got back to work. Once the batter was ready, I prepared the pans and filled them. After they were in the ovens and I set the timer, I cleaned up my area and then just stopped.

And breathed.

I looked at the mixer, anxiety churning in my gut. Jon was going to flip when I told him we needed a new one, but no way in hell was I using that one again.

As I left the kitchen, mug in hand—because I needed more caffeine—I realized something had shifted inside of me. Maybe it was my imagination, but I felt stronger than I had in a year.

Weird.

Chapter Two

"Lizzie, glad you're here," said my mother. Isobel Raymond stood in front of the fireplace, hands on her narrow hips, directing traffic. Her perfectly coiffed hair framed her face, and tiny gold earrings added a bit of sparkle. "Go sit next to your father."

"Um, okay." Obviously, something was up. I'd find out what soon enough, but for now, I was happy to be with my family. While I'd taken the day off, it had mostly been spent staring out my bedroom window in depression. Marc's wedding was the next day, and I couldn't seem to get my mind off it. Luckily, my mood brightened the moment I entered my parents' house.

My dad, Marty, was sitting on the couch we'd had for a hundred years. The orange monstrosity was indestructible, and your skin stuck to it if you were wearing shorts. But my mother refused to replace anything, ever, no matter what. She figured a staple gun and hot glue could fix anything.

I grabbed the blanket from the floor and laid it on the cushion next to my dad before sitting down. Even though I was wearing jeans, the memories of raw legs were too strong to chance. Naugahyde scared me. Enough said.

"Hi, Dad." I leaned over and gave him a smooch on his stubbly cheek.

Raising his gaze, he smiled briefly, blue eyes bright behind his glasses. "Happy birthday, kiddo." His attention immediately returned to the sports page. That was fine by me; we never had much to talk about, but if I ever needed anything, my father would move heaven and earth to get it to me. To any of us kids.

"As soon as Scot gets here, we need to decide what we're going to do about Grandma," my mother announced.

My grandmother seemed to be dozing in the rocker, but with her, you never really knew. She played possum a lot.

"I already told you she can't stay with me," my sister Alice said.

"Wait a minute. What's going on?" I asked. "Why does Grandma need a place to live?" As far as I knew, she was happy in her condo.

My mother crossed her arms. "If Scot would get here, I'd explain it to you."

I glanced at Alice. She shook her head and made the crazy sign with her finger. I resisted the urge to giggle. Most people thought Alice and I were twins, as we shared the same shade of brown hair and eyes. That's where the resemblance stopped, so those people were blind, nuts, or both. She was easily two inches taller than my 5'6", thinner by at least ten pounds, and younger by almost three years. I loved her anyway.

My younger brother, Joe, with his blond hair and blue eyes, was the only member of the family that resembled my father. Of course, my father's hair had receded to the point that he was almost never without a hat.

"Why's everyone so glum?" asked my older brother, Scot, finally making his entrance. He looked fit, healthy, and tanned. In February, that's saying something.

"You're late." My mother pointed. "Go sit with Alice. We need to have a family conference."

Scot knew enough not to argue, so he took his place as requested.

My mother strolled across the room, her navy house dress swishing around her legs. She sat down on the other side of my father and snatched his paper. "Pay attention, Marty. Everyone's here now."

"I've heard it already, Isobel. Tell them." He retrieved the paper.

My mother stared at him. The rest of us watched. We'd seen

this power play our entire lives, and the outcome could go one of two ways. After about a minute, my father released his hold on the paper. "Fine, I'm listening."

One point for Mom.

"Thank you. You can go back to it in a minute." Turning to us, she said, "Your grandmother needs a new place to live, and she refuses to move in here." Her eye twitched. "She says I'll cramp her style. That means it's up to one of you to take her in."

Alice pushed a strand of hair behind her ear. "I don't have room. Otherwise, I'd love to have her."

I suspected Alice was more concerned about the man living with her, unbeknownst to our parents, than she was about finding room for Grandma Verda.

"Joe has plenty of space," I interjected. It wasn't that I didn't want Grandma to live with me, but I *really* didn't have the space. My tiny one-bedroom apartment was barely big enough for me and my unpacked boxes. Not to mention my half-finished latch-hook rugs and paint-by-number kits.

Plus, as much as I loved her, Grandma Verda had some oddities that, while endearing from a distance, probably wouldn't be as cute up close on a consistent basis.

My mother scowled. "Joe?"

My younger brother shook his head and frowned at me. "Last time Grandma stayed with me, her cat stayed hidden the entire time. She wouldn't agree to it."

I'd forgotten about Shirley. Only my grandmother would name her cat after her deceased husband's mistress—whom she hadn't even known about until the day of the funeral. *Twenty years ago.* As she'd only had that cat for about two years, I'd say she was still carrying a grudge.

Scot stood and shoved his hands in his pockets. "Why does she need somewhere else to go?"

Ha, smart man. Changing the topic before all fingers pointed to him.

"She fell asleep the other night while heating up soup. It

wasn't a huge problem . . . this time. But there's more." Fear resonated in my mother's voice.

I didn't have to hear more. Grandma could stay with me. I glanced at her, and I saw her squinting out through one eye. Yep, playing possum.

My father rustled the paper on his lap. "Tell them the rest, Isobel."

"Your grandmother has been calling 911 nearly every night. Esther, from my bridge group, told me." She crossed her legs, bobbed the top one up and down. "Esther's daughter works in the call center and recognized the name." Heaving a breath, she continued, "So I called around and found out about it. In the last month, she's called asking about the weather, for synopses of her favorite shows, and twice to inquire if an officer could bring her beer."

Just like that, everything I'd worried about that day vanished. Was my grandmother lonely? That's what it sounded like to me, and I hated that. Hated thinking of her alone, late at night, reaching out to strangers instead of family.

The deal was cinched. "She can stay with me."

"Did they bring her beer?" Joe asked.

My mother huffed. "I have no idea, Joe. What does that have to do with anything?"

I stole another look at Grandma, and she was sitting upright now, eyes wide open. She winked at me. I winked back.

"So I wanted a beer, who cares? And yes, those nice fellows brought me a six-pack and a bag of Cheetos." She stood up and put her hands on her hips, just like Mom had earlier. "I don't need to move in with anyone. I can take care of myself just fine."

"Mom, you can't call 911 because you want a beer. When did you start drinking beer anyway?"

Grandma shrugged.

"I want you to stay here, with me and Marty. I'm worried about you," my mother pushed.

Brushing at her purple sweatpants, Grandma Verda said,

"Thank you, but no. It's a nice offer, and I appreciate it." She looked at me. "We're here for Lizzie's birthday, and I'm hungry." Swiveling on her heel, she dashed for the dining room.

"We'll talk about this later," my mother whispered.

My grandmother had great ears. "No, we will not. The discussion is over."

"Honey, don't worry about it. We'll start checking on her more," my father said to my mother. "We can all do that." He whipped his gaze to each of us. "Right?"

"I'm usually over by her place a couple times a week," Joe said. He was a salesman and was on the road a lot. "I'll start stopping in."

The rest of us worked out a system so that someone would be calling or visiting every day. That would have to be enough for now.

After dinner and presents, I found my mother in the kitchen. She was drying a dish and to most people would probably appear calm. But her spine was a little too straight, her wiping at the plate a little too fast. "Mom, can I help?"

"Don't be silly. It's your birthday, no dishes for you. Do you like your gift?" She'd purchased me a year membership at a fitness club, along with the services of a personal trainer.

"It's very thoughtful."

Snapping the dishtowel on the counter, she said, "I know what that means. If you don't want it, give it to a friend."

"Mom, no, that's not it. I do like it." I just wasn't sure I'd use it. But, knowing my mom, it was probably a nudge to pretty up and find a man. She wanted grandbabies, and none of her kids had yet procreated. Seeing as we were all over thirty, her chances seemed to decrease each year.

Pushing that thought away, I smiled, hoping to lighten the mood. "You're not going to let Grandma go home by herself tonight, are you? I think she should stay here, or with me, at least for a couple nights."

"*Let* her? She'll do what she wants. She always has. I can't tie her up and force her to stay. Maybe you can talk some sense into her."

"I can try." After a moment I added, "You know it's not you she doesn't want to live with, right? It's giving up on her independence."

My mother's shoulders sagged, and I saw defeat in her eyes. "I'm just scared. She's eighty-five years old, and I don't know how to handle this portion of her life."

I gave her a hug, and the scent of gardenia she wore reminded me of my childhood. In a flash, I was ten years old again, hugging her before going to bed. "Thanks for dinner and the present. Jon, Andy, and Maddie are taking me out tonight, so I need to run home and change."

She squeezed again, tight, and then let go. "Have fun, but don't drive if you drink."

"I never do, Mom."

She turned back to her dishes, and I went to find Grandma. Only she and my father remained in the living room. "Where did everyone else go?"

My father, who was now watching the television, said, "They had dates."

"All of them?"

"That's what they said."

I tried to ignore the longing that hit me, despite the fact that I was going out with friends. I wanted a date. I wanted to feel attractive to a man again. I pushed the wish aside and focused on my grandmother. "Grandma, you look tired. Maybe you should stay here tonight and go home tomorrow."

"No." She didn't look at me, just sat on the couch, watching out the window. "I'm waiting for Vinny."

"Who's Vinny?"

"My beau. He's taking me to the movies."

That caught my father's attention. Briefly. He must have thought he'd heard wrong, because he quickly returned his gaze to the repeat of *Magnum P.I.*

"Beau? You have a boyfriend?" The question barely left my mouth when I heard a *toot-toot* from outside.

Grandma Verda stood and straightened her sparkly sweatshirt. Her eyes found me. "Remember what my card said?"

"Well, yeah. You gave it to me yesterday."

"Good. Have fun, but be careful. That's all I have to say on that." With another wink, Grandma Verda sashayed off, leaving a dusting of glitter in her wake.

Me? I was speechless. Quickly, I jumped on the couch and pressed my nose to the window. Yep, it was definitely a man opening the passenger door of an older model car—don't ask me what kind—for Grandma Verda. He was elderly but in a healthy sort of way. He settled her in and helped her with her seatbelt. I was still staring out the glass when they sped off to parts, or a movie, unknown.

Maybe she wasn't as lonely as I thought. I needed to think about this. Each and every one of my siblings had a date on Friday night. Even my eighty-five-year-old *grandmother* did. But not me.

Somehow, karaoke and margaritas didn't sound as appealing as they had earlier that day.

When had my ass gotten so big? Or maybe it was my hips. Oh, hell, maybe it was both.

Groaning, I shoved myself harder to no avail. Now I could barely breathe. And to make matters worse, every time I pushed forward, my skirt inched down. The damn thing was caught on something, and if I wasn't careful, not only would I be stuck, I'd be stuck without a skirt.

Pleasant thought. Anyone passing by would see my pink-pantied rear hanging out the window. My stomach twisted at that image, and I swallowed to keep from retching.

Oh yeah, in addition, my bladder was so full that I thought it would burst. Why had I had one last margarita before taking the cab ride home? Rhetorical question. I knew why—the mix of relief, celebration, and hoping for a better future. But now I just felt stupid.

I held still for an instant, using the power of positive persuasion over my bladder. If I didn't think I had to pee, I wouldn't have to pee, right?

Wrong. So very wrong.

I shivered as a cold breeze rolled over me, and I realized suddenly that my previous concerns were short-sighted. If I didn't get out of there, I might actually freeze to death. It was time to figure this out, and fast.

Maybe I could back out? Hell, it was worth a try. Slowly, I eased myself in reverse and felt the wood of the windowsill scrape against my belly, but I was still wedged tight. Come on, my bathroom window was small, but it wasn't *that* small. I might seriously have to reconsider the personal trainer and the gym membership thing.

And of course, that would prove my mother was right once again.

Heaving my weight completely forward, I hoped the pull of gravity would send me tumbling into my bathroom. Instead, I heard the tearing sound of fabric.

Damn! I loved that skirt. It was one of the few articles in my wardrobe that made me feel sexy. Of course, why *wouldn't* my birthday end like this?

In reality, the evening had been great until I'd misplaced my keys. Which left me locked outside, at one in the morning, in the cold February rain.

At least it wasn't snow.

Normally, Maddie would have helped me out, but she'd gone home with her new boyfriend. I should have called one of my brothers, but no. I hadn't done that because I'd "had an idea."

This is a good place to mention that any ideas arrived upon after consuming multiple alcoholic beverages will tend to equal stupidity. The position I was currently in proved that point. I'd seriously believed I would be able to crawl into my ground-floor apartment through my bathroom window, which I'd left open by accident. I'd considered it a friendly twist of fate. Of course, that twist hadn't gone exactly as planned. Things couldn't get any worse.

"Stop right there." A deep voice came from behind. So

that meant, he (whoever *he* was) was pretty much *at* my behind. With a perfect view of any cellulite hanging around on my thighs. I'd been wrong about things not getting worse.

"I'm f-fine. You can go. This is a l-little embarrassing," I said through chattering teeth. Immediately, I recognized my mistake. I needed help, no matter how humiliated I was. Hopefully, he wasn't a burglar—or, God help me, a photographer. "Actually, I could use some help. But you don't have a camera, do you?"

"Breaking and entering is a crime. Unfortunately for you, you chose the wrong window. Not only am I a cop, but I live in this building. So, what you're going to do is come down from there so I can read you your rights and take you into the station." He sounded annoyed. As if I had somehow ruined *his* night.

"Don't you think I'd come down if I could? Or do you think I like having strange men look up my skirt? And I'm not breaking in, I *live* here." Police officer, huh? I thought I knew every occupant in my building, and there weren't any cops.

"Ma'am, you need to come down now. I don't want to use force."

"Please, use force."

"I'm going to count to three. You have that long to get out of that window."

"Wait! I can prove to you who I am if you can get me out of here. My ID is in my purse!" Did I sound desperate? Probably. I didn't care.

He sighed. What sort of a man sighs? "Where's your purse?"

"On the other side of this window. I dropped it in before I tried to climb through."

"Why are you breaking into your own home?"

Was this guy an idiot? I mean, seriously. "Because I lost my keys." I enunciated each word slowly.

I heard footsteps and then a click. His body brushed against mine as a bright light swooped into my field of vision, presumably from a flashlight. Maybe he *was* a cop? I turned my head, trying to catch a glimpse of his face, but couldn't quite see that far behind me.

I really had to pee.

"I don't see a purse. You'll have to show me your ID when I get you out."

"Yeah. Sure. I'll need to see yours too, *Officer*."

Another click, and all was dark again. I felt hard warm hands on my thighs. In other circumstances, I might have enjoyed such a feeling, but not these circumstances, despite the tingles traveling the length of my body. "Watch where you grab, fella."

"You want out or not?"

"Yes, please." No one would ever know about this. *Ever.*

He tugged and then he pulled and then he yanked, his grip tighter on my thighs with each attempt. Next, he stood right behind me and moved his grasp up to my hips and pulled harder. This was an entirely new form of humiliation. I just knew my face, and all my other body parts, were as red as a fire engine.

At least it was dark.

The cop abruptly let go. "This is a really small window. How did you think you'd get through it?"

Was that a joke about the size of my ass? "One too many margaritas," I quipped, trying to cover my anxiety.

"Oh. You've been drinking." He sounded disapproving.

"I was out for my birthday. People drink; it's not a crime. Just get me out of here. It's freezing, if you haven't noticed."

"Yeah, well, that's not happening. I'm going to have to get some help, I think. We might have to remove the window bracing for enough give."

"No! Don't do that!" I think I whimpered. The thought of more people viewing this spectacle would make any red-blooded woman whimper. Trust me. Even though the rain had stopped, I didn't need my neighbors running outside to see what the commotion was. If that happened, I'd have to move. To another state. "Just try again."

"You're not coming out this way. I'm going to radio in for assistance."

"No! I have an idea." Hopefully, I was sober enough to have a good one. "Will you try something first?" I begged.

The man hesitated. I could hear his intake of breath. I'm sure he wanted this over with. Well, guess what? So did I.

"You said you live in this building?" I prayed he hadn't been lying.

"Yeah."

"So you have a key to get into the building then, right?"

"That's how it works when you live in a building." Nice, not only could he see my panties, but he was sarcastic, too.

"I have an extra key to my apartment underneath the plant outside my door. Maybe if you let yourself into my apartment, you can pull me in from the other side."

"You keep a key hidden outside your apartment? That's not safe."

"Yeah, well, I'm pretty darn happy it's there now," I growled. Oops, wrong tactic. No need to piss the guy off. "I mean, I know, and you're right, and I promise I'll move it if you'll just get me down."

"Whatever, lady. We'll try it your way. If it doesn't work, I'm calling for help." As he walked away, the mutter "Why do I meet all the crazy ones?" met my ears.

Right back at you, buddy.

The wait seemed excruciatingly long, but that possibly had more to do with the intense discomfort I was in rather than the actual number of minutes the cop took to get to me. When the bathroom light blazed on, I winced. Because the window was above the bathtub, all I could see was the fifteen-dollar white shower liner I'd bought at Wal-Mart almost a year ago. I probably should replace it; it was kind of dingy.

"You there?" He really had a great voice. Deep and rumbly. I still had to pee.

"Where would I go?"

The curtain whipped back. I sucked in a deep breath—which wasn't that easy due to my current predicament.

The stranger was in uniform, so it appeared he'd been honest with me and really was a police officer. Kudos for him. His black hair was in a military cut, and his eyes were a shade of green I hadn't known existed. Not romance novel handsome, but I definitely wouldn't toss him out of bed—if he managed to find his way there. With the way my year had gone, that wasn't likely.

His gaze took in my appearance, and I couldn't help but wonder exactly what he saw. I suspected it was better I didn't know.

"Let's get this over with. What's your name?"

"Elizabeth."

"Hi, Elizabeth. I'm Nate Sutherland." As he spoke, he grabbed my purse and flipped it open.

"What are you doing?"

"I'm ascertaining you are who you say you are."

"Can't you get me out first?"

"No."

Jerk. Stupid, sexy jerk.

"I have to pee."

"Shouldn't have had so much to drink."

I watched as he opened my wallet and scanned my driver's license and then raised his gaze to my face. "Sorry about that, Elizabeth." He tossed my purse to the floor.

Stepping halfway into the tub, Nate grasped underneath my arms. Right at my armpits. I hoped my anti-perspirant hadn't stopped working. Wow, he smelled really nice. Sort of woodsy and manly all at once. I'd have to ask him what cologne he was wearing.

"Ready?"

"God, yes."

"I'm going to pull you out now." Nate's grip tightened and then he yanked. When I barely budged, he tugged again with far more force. I fell forward, and by reflex, I wrapped my arms around his neck. Moving his hands down to my waist, he pulled slower this time.

This cop was strong; even with the majority of my weight in his arms, he stayed upright. Gotta like that in a man.

"I'm just going to step backward and bring you the rest of

the way—" Before he could finish the sentence, my skirt gave up its fight. The piece of fabric that had been caught let loose. I tumbled into Nate, he tumbled backward, and in no time at all I was free. Free!

I was also in the arms of, and on top of, a fairly sexy guy—a sexy guy who, naturally, didn't appear very pleased. More's the pity.

I stood up, fast, and tried to right my ruined skirt as much as possible. Its destruction saddened me, as it had been a long eight-hour day of shopping to find the dang thing to begin with. And I *hated* shopping.

Wrapping my arms around myself, I rubbed my arms in an effort to warm up. "Can you give me a minute?"

As he righted himself, Nate frowned. Fortunately, he didn't argue—just backed out of the bathroom and closed the door behind him.

I wasn't fast, but after I completed the necessities, I checked the mirror. Horrid wouldn't begin to describe my appearance. Washing my face helped. Brushing my hair only gave me a nestlike style, but at least it was no longer rain-plastered to my head.

After slipping off my totaled skirt, I grabbed my robe from the hook on the door and slid it on. Opening the door, I went to face the music.

Nate leaned against the wall outside the bathroom, his legs stretched out in front of him. Silently, he offered me my key.

"Thank you. For your help and everything. When did you move in?"

"Yesterday. I'm your next door neighbor."

Oh, that was solid information. Maybe things were finally turning around.

He walked to the front door. "I don't need to file a report. I found you hanging out the window after my shift ended."

"Oh. Good," I said. Nothing in writing to prove the night ever happened. Couldn't argue with that.

The cop stopped in the hallway, the open door between us. "Don't keep your key outside. It really isn't safe."

I nodded. "I'm sorry to—"

A small smile and a tip of his head cut me off. "Things happen. Be more careful in the future."

Nodding again, I tightened the belt on my robe.

"Good night, Elizabeth. Happy birthday."

Silly, but I stayed in the doorway for probably five minutes or so after he'd let himself in to his own apartment. Nate. I really wished I'd met him under better circumstances.

Chapter Three

I had cotton in my mouth. Rolling over, I squinted at the clock. The glowing blue numbers read 8:30 A.M. Earlier than I'd intended, but no way would I fall back asleep now. The older I got, the harder it was to sleep in. Even on Saturdays.

Reaching for the water bottle I kept on my nightstand, I took a hefty swallow. *Better.* My head seemed a little foggy but not too bad considering the previous night. Other than the complete and utterly embarrassing way I'd encountered my new neighbor.

"Don't dwell." I swung my feet to the floor and stretched my arms wide. My muscles pulled a bit, probably from being stuck in a window, but a hot shower would relax the kinks. After that, I wasn't sure how I'd spend my day. It wasn't like I had a pressing schedule to adhere to. I could finish one of the latch-hook rugs I'd started months ago, or I could unpack a few boxes, or I could even go shopping to replace my skirt.

Yes, my life was exciting.

It wasn't until I stood in the shower, rinsing apple-scented shampoo out of my hair, that I remembered it was Marc's wedding day. Pain sliced through me quick, and the air around me grew heavy, making it difficult to breathe normally. I wished I hadn't remembered. Closing my eyes, I leaned against the shower wall. Today, the man I'd believed I'd spend the rest of my life with would vow to love and cherish another woman for the rest of *her* life.

I didn't cry, which surprised me. I felt like I *should* cry, because how could something hurt so much and not bring forth tears? Maybe I'd finally cried myself out. Did a person only get so many tears, and once shed, that was that? I didn't know, but I didn't really care, either.

I couldn't believe I'd forgotten—well, that it wasn't the first thing on my mind when I'd woken that morning. But maybe, just maybe, that was the good news?

Opening my eyes, I grabbed some conditioner. I poured a glop of it into my hand and tried to think of something else. Anything else.

Nate's face popped into my head, along with a possible plan. To thank Nate and to (hopefully) alter his first impression of me, I could bake him a thank-you-and-welcome-to-the-building treat. It couldn't hurt, and it gave me something to do. The longer I thought about it, the better I liked the idea. Before I knew it, I breathed easier, and the knot in my shoulders eased. I could do this.

Thirty minutes later, dressed in jeans and a yellow sweatshirt, hair pulled back, I put on ABBA and went into the kitchen. Maybe it *was* Marc's wedding day, but that didn't mean I had to be miserable, right? Today could be as good or as bad as I chose.

I chose "good." And with that, everything about the day became a little brighter—a little happier. Singing "Take a Chance on Me" along with the CD, I gathered the ingredients to make banana-nut muffins. I enjoyed baking. It was a process I could control from beginning to end, and I liked making food that other people found pleasure in.

My tiny kitchen didn't compare to the kitchen at A Taste of Magic, but it suited me. Though, it could definitely use a fresh coat of paint. An actual color, perhaps, instead of the standard off-white. I'd planned on painting when I moved in, but hadn't gotten around to it. Someday, maybe, I'd find the time.

I mashed the bananas up in a bowl, my thoughts wandering to the prior night. Up until losing my keys (which were in my jacket pocket the entire time), my birthday had certainly been acceptable. Karaoke was always fun, and I'd met Maddie's new boyfriend. I kind of thought she'd keep him for a while. She'd had that look.

Just once, or maybe twice, I'd like to be on the receiving

end of smoldering gazes from a sexy man. Maddie might be used to it, but I wasn't.

That hunky cop, for instance. "Am I your kind of woman, Nate?" I murmured as I crushed the walnuts for the batter. "I'd like to be. I'd like to make those green eyes of yours go dark with desire."

Odd that this man who'd seen me in the most awkward of circumstances could make my blood run hot. Especially after the crappy year I'd had. It was something in his smile, though, something in those eyes. And hey, it didn't hurt that he lived right next door—and was a cop to boot.

A man in uniform. Need I say more?

Setting the oven to preheat, I chose a large wooden spoon to stir the remaining ingredients together. I liked my muffins a bit dense, so I tended to hand mix the batter rather than use my electric beater.

I tried to think of the last time I'd felt special. Sexy. Spectacular. Beautiful. How sad was it that I couldn't remember?

I'd have to change that. I was divorced, not dead. You know what they say about women in their mid-thirties, right? Yeah, well, it's true. Being at your sexual peak with no one to ride it with (literally and figuratively) was an extremely frustrating experience. If you can possibly avoid it, do so. Otherwise, you'll end up with a drawer full of toys branded with very interesting names. Names such as "Bunny Rocket" (my favorite), "Pure Paradise" (regrettably, not so much), and "Velvet Touch" (no comment). And then, of course, there was "Sultry Lights," which, yes, actually had colored strobe lights running up and down the shaft. Not my smartest purchase. But what's a girl to do?

I'll tell you what. You thank God for the Internet and plain brown packaging.

Well, I had to thank Maddie, too. After all, she was the one who—after several drinks one night—showed me *her* collection of toys. We laughed for hours over the names, colors, and added accessories someone, somewhere, came up with. As best friends, I couldn't let her one up me, so now I had my own collection.

What I really wanted, though, was a man. A standing up, walking around, totally male *man*. And for whatever reason, I couldn't get the cop out of my thoughts.

I stopped. Was I overreacting? I didn't know, but it was so nice to feel happy I decided to go with the flow. Grandma Verda had said to let loose, so why not?

Returning my attention to my task, I tossed in the chopped nuts and slowly mixed them into the banana batter. My skin grew hot at the idea of Nate in my bed. Or me in Nate's bed. I wasn't too picky on the actual logistics. Silly, I guess, dreaming about a man who'd seen my rear in about the worst imaginable position, but I couldn't help it.

Maybe I'd go for it. Oh hell, why not? I wanted a new life. I wanted to change. I wanted something different for my future. And I was already baking the guy muffins. Sure, it was under the guise of a thank-you, but that was a thinly veiled excuse. At least I recognized that. Could I flirt with him? Did I even know how to flirt?

I just wanted it to happen. I wanted *him* to do the work. Keep dreaming, right? Maybe if last night hadn't occurred, it could be a possibility.

"Nate, I want you to see me as the woman I am. I want you to desire me. I want you to *want* me." I whispered my thoughts out loud, still stirring.

Almost instantaneously, a hard shiver rode my body from my feet to my scalp and then straight down my arms to my hands. A spark zapped from my hand to the spoon to the batter to the bowl. The spark turned into a soft glow that I could almost hear. It crackled and buzzed and sizzled in my ears.

"You have got to be kidding me!" I dropped the wooden handle. Fast. Stepping back, I forced a breath. My arms were shaking, my legs were weak, and my heart was pounding. This reminded me of the mixer at A Taste of Magic. But last I checked, wooden spoons didn't run on electricity.

So if the problem hadn't been the mixer, then it had to be me. I was the only common denominator in both situations, correct? But that didn't make any sense. I sucked in another deep breath as the tingles slowly dissipated. Again, the light died down, and all that remained was a very normal appearing bowl with a spoon. No sparks. No sizzles. Nothing.

I tried to find the answer as I finished the muffins and slid the pan into the oven. Nothing I came up with equaled a reasonable explanation. Static electricity, maybe? Like when you rub your stocking feet on the carpet and shock someone with your finger?

Possibly.

Okay, doubtful.

But until a better solution came to mind, I was sticking to that one.

An hour later, I stood outside of Nate's apartment, freshly baked muffins in tow. I used to hate the expression "The way to a man's heart is through his stomach," but now I sort of hoped it was true. Or, at the very least, I hoped it was the way to his libido. Because while I was hungry for sex, I—definitely and without a doubt—had had my fill of love.

Rapping on the door, I waited and tried to stay calm. I'd never done this before. Marc had chased me. I'd never needed to chase anyone. Ripples of nervousness coated my skin. My palms were moist. I forced my feet to stay put.

It's not like Nate could read my mind. He'd see what I wanted him to see, simply a neighbor thanking him for helping her out. One thing I *had* learned over the years was that most of the time, people saw what they expected.

The door swung open, but it wasn't held by Nate. A boy— don't ask me his age, because while I loved children, unless they were in diapers, I didn't have a clue—grinned up at me.

"Hi, are you a friend of my uncle's?" Nephew, not son. Aww, he had dimples. They were totally cute.

"Sort of. Is your uncle here?"

"Yeah, he's cleaning the juice I spilled. It was grape."

"Grape, huh?"

The boy stuck out his chin. "Uncle Nate says it's probably gonna stain, but it's okay cuz he likes purple a lot."

And that was completely sweet.

"Sam? Who's at the door?" I heard the yell from a place I couldn't see. Probably the living room, if his apartment was the mirror of mine.

"Elizabeth," I called. "You know, from last night?"

"Oh, window girl?"

Swiveling my head quickly, I checked to be sure no one else roamed the hallway. *Window girl?* I would have preferred something like "Oh, that sexy chick from last night?" But all I said was, "Yes."

A second later, Nate appeared. "Hey. Anything wrong?" He wore navy sweats and a white T-shirt with a bright purple wet splotch on the front. This made him all the more endearing.

"No. Not at all." Hesitating, I thrust the plate out in front of me. "Here, I baked them. As a thank-you."

Sam stood up on his tiptoes, obviously trying to see for himself. "Is it chocolate? I love chocolate!"

Nate glanced at me inquisitively.

"Oh, no, sorry. They're muffins. Banana."

"Can I have one, Uncle Nate? Please? I'm starving."

Nate accepted the offering and nodded to Sam. "Go sit down, and be more careful with the juice this time. I'll be there in a minute." He returned his attention to me as Sam ran off. "You didn't have to do this. I'm glad I could help." His mouth twitched. "I do have a question, though."

"Sure." *Yes, I'll go to bed with you.*

What was wrong with me? I hadn't felt like this in years.

"What would you have done if I hadn't shown up?"

"I'd still be there, probably, with a gaggle of onlookers laughing at me while I cried." I cringed at the mental image. It honestly could have turned out that way. Or worse.

He waved a hand in dismissal. "Nah, someone would have helped."

"I'm just glad you didn't have a camera."

Nate shook his head, the skin around his eyes crinkling as he laughed. "Well, I'm going to start carrying one around with me. I realized this morning I could've made a bundle off that picture."

"You think? Who would you have sold it to?" I was beginning to doubt my taste in men.

"*You.*"

Ah, a tease. I liked being teased. My faith was restored.

"Uncle Nate! I'm hungry!"

Nate looked into his apartment; then he looked at me and said, "He's getting antsy. I should go feed him." Did he seem regretful? Or was that wishful thinking?

Nodding, I backed up a couple of paces. "Have a good day. Thank you again." God, this was it; he was going to close the door. I needed to say something. I needed to remember how to flirt. *Now.*

"Um, Nate?" My brain fumbled around, trying to find what to say, something that would draw his attention so that he'd feel compelled to, I don't know, ravage me.

"Yes, Elizabeth?"

"Um . . . you never did show me your ID." And this, my friends, is what happens when you blurt without thought.

"You want to see my ID? Now?"

"No." Come on, be smart, be charming. "Why would I need to see that now? You live here, like you said you did, and you were wearing a uniform. I'm good. I don't need the ID." Everything came out in a rush. An idiotic, blathering rush.

Nate tipped his head and examined me silently. Examined was the correct verb, by the way, as he could have been looking through a microscope at an unknown species of larvae. Did larvae have species?

"Did you bang your head last night?"

Great, now he was concerned. About my head.

Well, I *was* acting a bit crazy. I tried to look normal. "You know what? Maybe I did. I can't remember. Anyway, I have to finish my rug."

"Uncle Nate," Sam said, back at the door, tugging at his uncle's pants.

"It's okay. You know . . ." I broke off.

Nate nodded. "I know. You have to get back to your . . . rug, was it? Well, thank you for the muffins."

"Uh-huh, I hope you like them." I turned on my heel and tried to walk naturally back to my apartment, which wasn't that easy on rubbery ankles. Plus, I could feel him watching me.

After I was securely inside my door, I crumpled to my knees in defeat. The pounding of my heart filled my ears. My stomach sloshed with nervousness. I was *horrible* at flirting. It possibly would be a good plan of action to get some more information—so I'd be better at it next time.

Flirting for Dummies, perhaps? Did they make a book like that? They had to. I couldn't be the only woman in the universe who needed it. Other women got divorced. What did they do?

I could stop at the bookstore near A Taste of Magic on my way home on Monday. This was my new plan until the image of purchasing such a book, with such a title, in public, brought me to my senses. Which was when I remembered the Internet was a far better choice. You could buy everything from a toothpick to a new house to "Sultry Lights" online. Gotta love it.

Standing up, I looked—really looked—at my apartment. I didn't like what I saw. A tiny dining room opened into the living room on one side, the kitchen on the other. A narrow hallway led to my bedroom and the bathroom. My life was encapsulated into less than 800 square feet. And not even an attractively furnished 800 square feet, at that.

When I'd moved out of the house Marc and I shared for so long, I couldn't have cared less about furnishings. I just wanted it over with, and I didn't want to drag along any physical reminders. One quick trip to Valu-Mart had done the trick. A cheap black couch set, fake wood end tables, no-frills lamps, a bed minus a headboard, a wood-composite desk, half-opened boxes, and the laundry baskets I kept my clothes in rounded out my furnishings. I hadn't even bothered to buy a real dresser. I'd been living like this for nearly a year, and it hadn't bothered me once in that entire time. I mean, I had food, a place to sleep, a roof over my head—what else did I need?

I sat on my bed and hugged a pillow. Why I hadn't seen this before, I didn't know. I hadn't been living. Not really. More like existing: just getting from one day to the next as quickly as possible. My chest grew tight and heavy. The room swam as my eyes filled with tears. It seemed the entire year of misery bombarded me at once.

No. I didn't want this. I needed to learn how to breathe again. To see in color again. And yes, I had to figure out how to live again. I was ready for a change.

No, more than that. I *needed* a change. Merely existing could kiss my ass.

"I want to dye my hair," I told Maddie the following Wednesday. We were eating lunch at the deli down the street from A Taste of Magic. Maddie had Wednesdays off. And for me, Wednesdays tended to be slow at the shop, so it was the best day of the workweek for us to meet. Not that we needed to arrange a certain day to see each other. After all, Maddie's apartment was directly above mine, so we pretty much could visit whenever we wanted. But these lunches had been habit long before my separation from Marc.

"What color?" she said over a bite of her sandwich.

"I'm not sure. What do you think?" Maddie was an expert when it came to flair and fashion. If anyone could help me, she could.

Maddie sat back in her chair and appraised me. She'd pulled her blonde hair up into what appeared to be an effortless style. Tendrils framed her face, making her smoky eyes large and luminous. And, as always, regardless of the time of day, her makeup was perfectly applied. As strange as it sounds, in all the years we'd known each other, I'd never seen her with a bare face.

"Hmm. Well, red highlights would be awesome on you.

But everyone does auburn. You have beautiful hair anyway. Why mess with it?"

"I want something different." I licked the mayonnaise from my chicken salad off my lips. "I'm ready. I want to make a few changes, though nothing drastic."

"Really? What brought this on?"

"Marc. The wedding. The cake. I don't know. I'm just ready. But I don't know what to do." As much as I trusted Maddie, what occurred in my bedroom was private. Realizing I'd barely been living the past year had startled me, changed me, and it still weighed too heavy inside to share. I felt like someone had erased me and I had to learn to draw myself all over again, only I didn't know which pencil to use. Or where to begin. And now I was talking like my sister Alice, the artist.

Realizing I wasn't going to offer up more information, Maddie grinned. "I'd stick close to what you have. Maybe lighten the base shade a couple of degrees and then add some blonde highlights. Not too blonde. Go for a dark honey tone."

Before I could respond, my cell phone rang. Flipping the cover up, I saw my sister's name on the Caller ID. "Sec," I said to Maddie. Speak of the Devil.

Alice rarely called me during the day. Worried, I clicked the button. "Hi, Alice."

"Oh my God! Elizabeth, I'm so glad you answered. You are not going to believe this. I still can't believe it, and I heard it with my own ears."

"Is something wrong?"

"No, something is great. I am about to make your day. In fact, this might make your entire year." The sound of a horn honking came through the connection.

"Are you driving?" *Yes,* I chided. One of my pet peeves was people on the phone when they should be focusing on the road. Especially when that person was my baby sister.

"No. I'm in the parking lot at the club. You need to listen to me."

The club was the Brookhaven Sports Club, a rather pricey gym that offered racquetball and tennis courts, hot tubs, and both indoor and outdoor swimming pools as added perks for their clientele. I had no idea why, but the club seemed important to Alice. And I knew she gave up on a lot of other extras to fit the fee into her finances, especially since she didn't even have a real job, just a series of part-time ones that kept her afloat so she could devote her time to painting. "So, tell me already."

"I was changing into my swimsuit when I heard Ginny Lewis on the other side of the lockers talking to someone. You know Ginny, don't you?"

"No, Alice, I don't know Ginny. Who is Ginny?"

"She's Tiffany's best friend. She was her maid of honor at the wedding on Saturday."

Yeah, now I remembered. Not that I'd ever met Ginny, but Alice had talked about her ever since Marc and Tiffany announced their engagement. Apparently, Ginny had made several derogatory comments about Marc, which, for some reason, Alice felt compelled to pass on. I'm sure she thought it made me feel better.

"You know what? If this is another one of those 'she said this' things, I'm not interested." I couldn't talk about Marc anymore.

"I promise you will want to hear this. You have to let me tell you, Elizabeth."

I sighed. I knew better, but time was running short and I still wanted to chat with Maddie before getting back to work. Probably easier to give in, listen, and then forget about whatever the newest gossip was.

I hate gossip. It always finds a way to wrap itself around you and cause you, or someone else, pain.

Relenting, I said, "Fine. If you're going to freak out, just tell me and get it over with."

"Good. So, anyway, apparently Tiffany called Ginny at, like, two in the morning last night. *From her honeymoon.*"

This piqued my curiosity. Who called their best friend from their honeymoon? Aren't there, well, more exciting things to be doing? I could think of a few.

"This part may sting. Tiffany is pregnant. She just found out before the wedding, so she's kind of frantic." Alice rushed the last sentence out, as if the momentum would gloss over the impact.

It failed, by the way.

Marc had refused to have children with me. His excuses about the timing not being right still rang clearly in my memory. It never mattered to him what I wanted; it was always about him. This was more than a sore spot. It was pure agony. I tried to breathe, tried to stop the pain from bubbling over. This was not the time for it.

"Are you there? Did you hear? Tiffany is pregnant."

"Stop. I don't need this. I really don't."

"You stop. I told you that part may sting. But listen to the rest. Marc couldn't get it up. Not on their wedding night, not at all so far. And they're on their honeymoon! Tiffany thinks it's because he's upset about the baby, but the important part is—he *couldn't get it up*. Isn't that awesome? I think it's perfect. The perfect payback for that asshole."

Her words forced themselves through the haze of shock. As soon as they did, goose bumps sheathed my skin and my breathing hitched. I think I mumbled I had to go, but I know for sure I disconnected the call. Staring at the phone, I sat there and rehashed the conversation.

Holy crap.

The perfect payback.

All that weird stuff that had recently been happening dashed through my head. You know, the glowing and the buzzing and the static electricity. Then, my mind centered on the birthday card from my grandmother and the message that I swear had sparkled. What had it said? Something about believing in magic . . . or something about it being the time for magic? I wasn't sure. Not exactly. But then, I thought of the last thing Grandma Verda said to me in the living room at my parents' house right before going on her date.

"Have fun, but be careful," I murmured, repeating it.

Next, the magic moments from childhood tumbled into

my memory. Grandma Verda had been in the center of every unexplained incident.

My heart rate jumped a zillion notches as the unbelievable, the entirely ridiculous yet somehow right pieces floated together. "Crap. No way." Had I somehow caused this to happen?

"What? You're white as a ghost. Drink some water." Maddie offered me my glass, but I shooed it away.

"Tiffany's pregnant," I mumbled.

"Oh, honey. Why did Alice tell you that?"

"And Marc . . . he couldn't—"

"Marc couldn't? What's going on?"

I cycled through the conversation again. "I have to find her. Now." Standing up, I shoved my cell phone into my purse and snatched my jacket.

"Who? What? Where are you going? You're too upset, sit back down."

A new thought occurred to me: *Oh, no. The muffins. Nate.* What had I said? I closed my eyes, trying to think. I didn't recall the words, but I did remember my mood, the want, the desire. Any semblance of calmness I may have had skittered away. Bam. Gone.

"I have to go, Maddie. I'll explain later." Not waiting for a response, I left the deli, the cold air biting my skin, and aimed toward A Taste of Magic. I needed to see my grandma's card again—it was still on my desk. I had to ask Jon to handle the afternoon business, and then I had to search the entire Chicago area for a crazy old lady who believed in magic.

"Grandma Verda, what have you done?"

I was an emotional woman with practical beliefs. But somehow, somewhere inside, a click had fallen squarely into place. It didn't matter if the click made sense (it didn't), because I knew some freaky stuff was going on. Either I was the loony one or Grandma Verda had cast some sort of a spell on me.

Chapter Four

I rested my chin on my steering wheel and stared at Grandma Verda's Shady Pines condominium. Not only was my grandmother absent, but there weren't any shady pine trees, either. This, I guessed, was an example of marketing. Make something sound more attractive than it is and someone will buy into it.

My stomach rumbled, a not so gentle reminder that it was almost dinner time. I'd left A Taste of Magic almost four hours ago and headed straight to Grandma's, only she wasn't home. When I called my parents and siblings to see if they knew where she was, no dice.

Unclenching my hands, I flexed my fingers to try to work out my nerves. This was crazy. Even if my imaginings from earlier were right on, waiting around wasn't giving me any answers. I fastened my seatbelt and headed out. Surely she'd be home later. I'd try calling. Until then, I pushed the questions away.

Keys in hand (no more window climbing for me), I unlocked the door to my building, stopped to grab the mail, and beelined it for my apartment. A bright yellow Post-it was stuck to my door. Written in a nearly illegible scrawl were directions to go to Nate's place.

A shiver rolled down my spine. Interesting, but also a little unexpected, especially after my weird day. What did he want? And . . . what if it had something to do with magic-spiked muffins? Could he arrest me for that? If he could, would it be considered a crime of passion?

I laughed. This must be what losing your mind felt like. I looked at the Post-it again and another shiver hit me. Who knew paper could be so alarming? Ripping it off, I marched to Nate's and knocked on the door. Easier to get it over with than just stand and fret.

The door opened almost immediately. Nate held a can of soda and smiled. Somehow, he was even better-looking than I'd remembered. Romance novel heroes had nothing on him. As an added bonus, he still smelled terrific.

"There you are. We were beginning to wonder," he said, motioning for me to come in.

"We?" Hesitantly, I entered the lair of the cop, stopping on the threshold. Nate's apartment was the same as mine, except in reverse. Only, for someone who'd moved in less than a week ago, his place appeared lived-in. Actual pictures graced his walls, and not one unpacked box anywhere.

"She should be out soon." Nate nodded toward the hallway. I assumed he meant the bathroom. He wore another pair of sweats (red) and a T-shirt (black). No grape juice stain this time.

"We must be talking in different languages. I have no idea who 'she' is." I edged over by the table, taking cover behind a chair.

He grinned, and my heart tumbled. "Your grandmother. She's been hanging out with me until you got home."

Grandma Verda was here? I'd been searching for her for hours, and she'd been tucked up with Nate? Little spiders crawled across my skin at the thought of what she may have said to him. After all, with Grandma Verda, you really never knew. "How did she end up here?"

"We walked in together. It's cold in the hallway, so I invited her in." Nate set the soda can down and stepped toward me. "Let me take your coat. Sit down. Relax. We can talk while we wait."

I slipped my coat off, switching the mail from one hand to the other while I did. Part of me thought it was chivalrous he'd saved my elderly grandmother from standing around in a breezy hallway. Another part of me wondered why she'd come into a stranger's home. "That was nice of you. I'm just shocked she agreed."

The corners of his lips twitched. "Why?"

"She doesn't know you. You could be a madman." I wasn't really worried about that, but come on—Grandma Verda wouldn't have known. I needed to give her the strangers talk.

"Ah, you're a worrywart. That's kind of cute." He reached over, his fingers brushed across mine as he took the mail out of my grasp. Setting the stack on the table, he said, "Sit down, Elizabeth."

"It's not cute, it's common sense," I blurted, still recovering from his touch. "There are crazy people in this world. As a cop, you should know that."

"But your grandmother and I know each other. No reason to worry."

They knew each other? I wanted to ask him how, but I kept the question to myself. I'd ask Grandma Verda later. In private. "What's taking her so long? You sure she's okay?"

"I'm swell. I've been eavesdropping. It's one of the few perks of being old." Grandma Verda waltzed into the room as if she were a queen—which isn't easy in fluorescent sneakers, but she pulled it off. "Glad to see you, Lizzie. We were just talking about you."

"We should get going." I wanted to get her to my place so I could question her about the birthday card. Then, what she said hit me full force. "Talking about me? What do you mean, talking about me?" I saw a twinkle dance into Nate's eyes. The cop seemed to be enjoying my torment.

A frisson of something passed between us. I wasn't sure what, exactly, but it could have been attraction. Maybe. Or not. I was pretty clueless on that stuff.

"Nothing to concern yourself over," Grandma said, pulling the recliner up and out and leaning back. As if she planned on staying awhile.

Not if I could help it.

"She asked me if I was a lemon, an orange, or a pomegranate. But she didn't tell me how I should know," Nate said, a teasing lilt to his voice. "Or why it was important. Why don't you explain it to me, Elizabeth?"

My face flushed. I stayed behind the chair. "I don't understand Grandma's fruit versus men comparisons, either. So I wouldn't be much help."

"It's important to know before you start dating again," Grandma said.

I needed to get her out of there. Now. "I'm sure Nate has better things to do, Grandma." I looked to Nate for confirmation.

"Nope. You're welcome to stay. I'm enjoying myself."

I frowned at him. "Don't you have unpacking to do?" He couldn't be completely done. I mean, there had to be boxes to be dealt with—somewhere.

"Nope," he said again. "All done."

"You moved in less than a week ago. You can't be done."

"I am. I'm organized that way," he teased.

"Organization is a mighty fine trait in a man," Grandma piped in.

Nate nodded. "It is."

I was being double teamed.

"Quit standing there with your mouth hanging open." This came from Grandma Verda, who, honestly, appeared as comfortable as a cat on a sunny windowsill.

I snapped my mouth shut. I wanted to learn how to flirt. And I wanted to flirt with Nate, but not with my grandmother in the room. "I'm going home. I'd like it if you came with me, Grandma, because I need to talk to you."

"Can I stay for dinner?" she asked.

"Sure. What do you want?" Anything to get her out of that chair.

"I don't care. Nate, do you want to join us?"

Had she just invited him to my place for dinner? My brain scanned the contents of my freezer. I thought there were a couple of frozen burritos left. I could feed him those and my decade-old wedding cake for dessert.

Nate laughed but shook his head. "Thanks for the invite, Verda, but I work the late shift tonight. I should take a nap soon."

Okay, so he'd let me off the hook. Good. Except I was disappointed. So yeah, I guess I'd wanted to feed him a meal. Another time, perhaps. Without Grandma and when my questions were answered. Preferably before I committed any further culinary crimes.

My mind went back to those muffins, and I relaxed slightly. After all, if they'd been magical, I'd have noticed something—wouldn't I? Probably.

But then Nate winked at me, and I felt it. Electricity. Attraction. Interest. Oh, hell. I stepped backward and bumped against the wall.

"Maybe another time, Nate," said Grandma Verda, pushing herself to her feet. "Be careful tonight. There are a lot of bad folks out there."

Nate opened the door. "I'll be careful." He raised a brow at me. (How did he do that? I couldn't raise an eyebrow. I knew this because I'd tried.) "I even found someone trying to crawl through an apartment window the other night."

The brat. I grabbed my coat and mail. Scowling at him, I pulled Grandma's sleeve. "Come on, Grandma, let's go."

"I'm coming. What's your hurry?" she complained. But at least she followed.

"Thanks for taking care of my grandmother, Nate. I appreciate it," I said. Grandma and I stepped into the hallway.

"You're welcome, Lizzie," he replied.

Ah, so he'd figured out one of my nicknames. Better that than any of the names my brothers used to call me.

In my apartment, I deposited my stuff before making a quick meal of soup and sandwiches for me and Grandma. Afterward, we sat at my dining room table. I tried to think of how to ask about the possibility of my wreaking havoc with Marc's sexual prowess on his honeymoon. Nothing I thought of sounded right. I mean, while it certainly had a cool factor, it was still just a little too out there for me to comprehend.

But because I needed to understand, and because I knew deep inside that something had happened—was happening—

I had to ask. "I want to talk about the birthday card you gave me."

Her blue eyes went opaque, and her gaze hit the wall behind me. "I don't think so. I told you I wasn't going to say anything more about it. At least, not yet."

"But you haven't said anything at all."

"I said a lot. You just weren't listening. Think about it, Lizzie-girl, and then trust your instincts. You'll know the truth, and when you do . . . we can talk then." She twisted her wedding band, a gesture I recognized as nervousness.

I weighed her words and decided to forge ahead. "Something has happened. And I think I do know the truth. But I need to hear it from you."

A tremble passed through her. She shifted her gaze so it rested on me. But she stayed quiet.

"I think I did something that interfered—changed— someone. I'm not sure, though, which is why I need you to explain that card to me," I said.

"Tell me exactly what happened." Her voice was soft but insistent.

I crossed my arms. I knew my grandmother well enough to know I'd have to act tough to get the information I wanted. "Not until you tell me everything."

Indecision played over her face. A current of energy passed between us. She wanted to tell me; the truth of that was in her eyes, in her expression. At that moment, I knew I wasn't crazy.

My arms shook, just a little, as I reached across the table to grasp her hand. "Come on, Grandma. Spill the beans. What did you do?"

"You're asking the wrong questions. It's not what I did— it's what *you* can do and *why* you can do it." She pulled her hand out of mine. "I don't know. When I told your mother, she didn't take it very well. This time, I decided to take it slow. I really want it to work for you."

"My mother?" What did she have to do with this?

"Do you promise to consider everything I say? And to not make any rash decisions?"

"Yes. I can do that."

"Say it." Her chin was set.

I sighed. Semantics, you know? "Yes, Grandma. I promise I will think it through and not make any rash decisions."

She wagged a finger at me. "I'm going to hold you to that promise." She waited a beat, probably to be sure her words had meaning to me, and then continued. "How much do you know about your great-great-great-grandmother? Her name was Miranda Ayres."

"I know nothing. You talked about her once, a long time ago, when I was little, but I don't remember anything but her name. Why?"

"It started with her. It's because of her. So you need to understand who she was and what kind of woman she was before you can understand the answers to your questions."

"Fair enough."

"Miranda's family came from Romania, but she was born in this country. She was a gypsy. And I mean a *real* gypsy, Elizabeth. Complete with magic, curses, and trickery."

"Magic isn't real," I blurted.

"You're wrong. But you already know that, or we wouldn't be having this conversation."

She had a point, even if I wasn't ready to admit it. But come on—magic?

"So, my great-great-great-grandmother was a gypsy. Go on."

"Miranda and her mother traveled with a large group of other gypsies. Some were blood family, others weren't. It was a tough life back then. When Miranda was a teenager, her mother passed away. I don't know how, and I don't know why, but it left Miranda in a precarious situation. A lot of the other gypsies were envious of her—of her power."

"How old was she when her mother died?"

"Sixteen or seventeen, I think. But she was young. Too young."

"Did she have any brothers or sisters?" My heart went out to the young girl who'd lived so many years before. I hoped she'd had someone on her side. Someone who loved her.

"None. She was surrounded by people who should have been her family. Who should have protected her and watched out for her. Instead, she was alone."

"I know that feeling," I mumbled.

Grandma Verda frowned. "You have family and friends who want the best for you. You've felt alone, but you really aren't. There's a difference."

"I know. That's not what I meant. I just . . . understand, I guess."

Her eyes remained on me, her expression both sad and thoughtful.

"What did she do?" I asked.

"She did what any young woman would do. She met a man, and she fell in love."

"Well, that's good, right?"

Ignoring my question, she said, "For some reason, the other gypsies decided to stay in one place for a while, rather than moving on as quickly as they normally did. Maybe they recognized that something was happening with Miranda. Maybe they hoped she'd leave. We'll probably never know. But Miranda took advantage of the opportunity and spent every minute she could with her new love."

At those words, something opened up inside of me. It was as if I could feel this woman's happiness. Strands of hope, love, and joy wove through me. And, as strange as it was, it felt right. It felt real. And I felt a connection to Miranda that I'd never been aware of before but somehow realized had been there all along.

Grandma seemed to notice, because she smiled. And in that smile, I saw the young woman she once was. Lines in her face softened, almost disappearing. Her faded blue eyes deepened in color to the rich hue of a ripened blueberry. Mischief sparkled, and her skin glowed with youth.

I didn't want to lose this picture of my grandmother, but when I blinked the vision vanished. The room was eerily silent. I wanted her to continue, to finish Miranda's story, but I didn't want to rush her, either. Finally, when the quiet didn't seem as if it would ever end, I said, "What happened? Did she live happily ever after?"

Grandma Verda's lips curved downward. "What happened? She fell in love with the wrong man. He wasn't a pomegranate, I can say that much for sure. She became pregnant, and her wishes and hopes were tied to the man who'd fathered her unborn baby. Only, when she told him, he rebuffed her. He was already married. She was nothing but a plaything."

My hands shook. I clenched my fists to make them stop. "What did she do?"

"I'm not done. Later, the man returned with his wife. They wanted Miranda to stay with them until the child was born. And then, they wanted her to give the child to them."

As fast as a breath of air, Miranda's agony became mine. It grew inside of me until I could hardly bear it. This mysterious woman I'd never met, whom I'd known nothing about before that night, somehow became intertwined with me. Anger, fear, and loneliness flashed inside of me so fast that, when it passed, I wondered if I'd imagined it.

"Don't cry. This was a long time ago."

I wiped the dampness from my cheeks. Did it matter how long ago it was? I mean, pain is pain. It felt as real today as it must have felt for Miranda then. "She didn't give in, did she?"

"Of course not! What she did was talk the gypsies into moving on, and she went with them."

An almost overpowering scent of roses saturated the room. I breathed it in, and if I hadn't known better, I'd have sworn I was standing in a rose garden. The music from the show *The Twilight Zone* echoed in my ears. Kind of apropos, really, considering the circumstances. "Grandma? Can you smell that?"

Little lines crinkled around her eyes in confusion. "Smell what?"

"Flowers. Roses, I think."

A tiny smile. "No, I don't smell that. But the fact you do tells me you're ready for this. That you're the right one for the gift. My mother talked about smelling flowers, but I never have. I don't know what it means."

Seriously strange, but I could almost see velvety red roses stretching their petals to the sun. The scent was so intoxicating. I set it aside, for now. I wanted to hear the rest of Miranda's story. "Finish, please."

Grandma Verda closed her eyes, her soft voice weaving around me. "Miranda kept to herself throughout the early months of her pregnancy. One night, in a temper, she decided to use her powers to curse the father of her child. But before she did, she felt her baby kick for the first time." Opening her eyes, Grandma clasped my hand. "In the flutter of that soft, sweet kick, Miranda's sixth sense told her she was carrying a daughter. Your great-great-grandmother. *My* grandmother. And so she didn't."

"She should have cursed him." I scowled. "I would have."

Grandma regarded me silently for a moment, but then she said, "Maybe so. Maybe Miranda would have if she hadn't felt her daughter at that instant. But, if she had, it may have cursed us all, as we have as much of his blood in our veins as we have of hers."

"Good point," I realized.

"What she did instead was cast a spell in the form of a gift. This gift has been handed down daughter to daughter, and now it's your turn. It's only skipped one generation, and that was your mother."

"Why did it skip her?"

"I passed it to Isobel when she was your age. I don't know what happened, but it didn't take hold. I got it back." Grandma tipped her head, eyes on me. "I think because she doesn't believe in magic. Even as a child, your mother had no affinity for anything make-believe. Even the Tooth Fairy was nonsense to her at an age when she should have been pure enchantment. Too much of your grandfather in her. Practical to the core."

Reaching over, she stroked my cheek. My face warmed at her touch. "Open your heart, Lizzie. You are the descendent of a powerful gypsy. I gave you Miranda's gift on your birthday. It's your turn now. You have magic at your fingertips!"

"How does it work?"

"Well. It's different for each of us. But simply speaking, it's all about wishes. My magic has always been in my writing, which is how I passed the gift on to you—through your birthday card."

Ah. The glowing writing. I hadn't imagined it.

"And my grandmother was an artist, just like Alice, and that's where *her* magic came through. What about you?"

If what my grandmother was saying was true, I knew how my magic manifested. Seeing as I baked for a living, this could pose a rather large problem for me in my day-to-day life. I thought again of Marc and the honeymoon wish. "Fuck," I whispered.

"Lizzie! Watch your language."

"Oh, sorry Grandma." My mind flipped through the conversation we'd just had, trying to find holes and gaps. Anything to put my worry to rest. I couldn't have really done that to Marc, could I?

"You said something happened. What was it?" Grandma asked.

I conjured up the scene at A Taste of Magic and whispered, "I was baking Marc's wedding cake. I was upset." Everything I'd experienced came back at me. The anger, the hurt. My whispered wish. I'd never thought in a million years I would share that moment with anyone, let alone with my grandmother. "And, well, I wished he wouldn't be able to have sex on his honeymoon." I rushed the words out, not sure how she would take it.

"Why do you think it worked?" Her matter-of-fact tone settled me.

"Alice said. She heard it from someone else. Or, at least, the same thing I wished for happened." I peeked at Grandma. She was smiling, so I figured she didn't think I was too small-minded for the wish I'd made.

"Did anything happen when you were making the cake that was odd or different?"

"There was this energy in the room and kind of a static

electricity thing I can't explain. I didn't know. I thought the mixer was acting up."

"That's it! I knew it. I'm so happy you're able to carry on the gift."

Inhaling a breath, I pushed the surreal feeling away. As out-there as this was, I'd experienced too many unexplained in-stances with my grandmother to doubt her story. Plus, I couldn't deny the truth. Not when it sat inside of me and was as clear as day. I had brown eyes. I had freckles on my nose. I had magic.

See? That simple. But also, more than a little scary.

"So, when I bake wedding cakes, I can cast a spell? Or is it with anything I bake?" Kind of a rhetorical question. The glimmering wooden spoon proved that.

"Anything, probably. Baking is your specialty. You'll have to practice to be sure, but my guess is that's where your mag-ical energy is."

"So, if I wish it, it will come true?"

She shook her head quickly. "Not everything. Magic is powerful, but it's also unpredictable. You'll have to practice. There were many things I wished for that never came to pass. I think it has to do with your emotions and how they affect the energy."

"Do I have to say it out loud, or can I just think it?"

"I've never said my wishes while I wrote them. Be careful of what you think when you bake. And you need to under-stand that as wonderful as this gift is, it doesn't come without hazard." She hesitated. It was obvious she didn't want to say anything that might dissuade me from accepting the gift, but come on—hazardous?

"What hazards, Grandma?"

She shifted in her seat. Her gaze, once again, hit the wall behind me. "It's not a big deal, not really. You just need to be very clear in what you wish for. You need to be positive of the words you use and the outcome you want."

"Or what?"

"Well. As I said, magic can be unpredictable. And where there's the chance for unpredictability, there's the chance that something negative will occur. Of course, how bad the possible negativity is depends on the wish itself, what's at stake, and a whole lot of other things I still don't really understand."

"Grandma! If I need to be careful, shouldn't you have told me about this from the beginning?" I mean, come on, I bake almost every day. And, mostly, my mind wanders while I do. What type of damage could I have done? A chill overtook me, and I rubbed my arms to stave it off.

"I was afraid you'd turn it away, like your mother did. So you needed to experience it first. Besides, in all my years of wishes, I've only had one truly negative result. I figured you'd be safe enough for a little while."

"And what was the negative result?"

She shifted again. "I don't know if I want to share this with you."

"I'm trying hard to believe everything you've said to me, but I need to hear all of it. Otherwise, I'll wish the gift away. I can do that, right?"

"Why would you want to? It's your legacy."

"Because if I don't know the ramifications, it's not worth it."

She pouted. And then, in one huge burst of words, she said, "Years ago, when your grandfather was still alive, he'd lost interest in sex. I wanted him to have that interest again, so I wished that he would."

Oh, no. I already knew where this was heading. "Shirley?" I asked.

Grandma Verda nodded. "His interest was revived, but with someone else. I wished again, over and over, hoping to bring him back to me. Out of her bed and into mine. Into ours. Only, it never worked."

"So you knew about her before Grandpa's funeral?"

"Of course I did. Your grandfather may never have asked for a divorce, but he left me just as surely as Marc left you. The difference was I had to live with it, every single day."

"You don't know your wish did that. You can't be sure of it."

The sheen in her eyes told me she was holding back tears. "I know. In my heart, I know."

"Then why did you name your cat after his mistress? I've always wondered that."

"To remind myself that I needed to be careful with the magic. While your grandfather was alive, that was all the reminding I needed. And even after he died, for a long time, I was fine. And then one day, the pain left. That scared me, because without the pain . . . how would I remember? So I bought Shirley."

We were quiet for a few minutes. I knew she needed time to pull herself back to the present, and I was still considering everything that had been said. Then I said, "Can you show me? Write a spell now so I can see it work. Something simple."

"I can't. I don't have it anymore. I gave it to you. This is why I'm so pleased you can use it. I thought it might die with me, which would be a travesty. It's our heritage; it needs to stay alive."

"You're not dying." I loved my grandmother. I didn't want to think about her being gone.

"Right now? No. But someday."

"There's always Alice," I pointed out, changing the topic.

"You needed it more. She's doing just fine right now."

Exasperated, I asked, "What if I don't want magic?"

"Why wouldn't you want it? It's a gift. Think of how you could change your life!"

And that was the problem. I couldn't stop thinking about the *what ifs*. "I didn't say that. But if I don't, what happens?"

Grandma's expression relaxed. "That's simple. You can either pass it to Alice or back to me." She snorted. "Or you can try your mother, for all the good that will do."

I grinned. Mom was Mom. I loved her the way she was.

"What do you want?" Grandma asked.

"I'm not sure." Maybe I *was* crazy, because I wasn't sure I wanted this gift. While I knew my grandmother meant well, it sort of seemed like cheating to me. Not to mention the supposed possible hazards.

But then I looked around my living room at the remnants of a half-lived life. Memories of Marc's betrayal came next, along with the pain of the past year. Then Nate's sexy face popped into my head, along with images of Maddie and her new boyfriend, Jon and Andy, and even Vinny and Grandma. I thought of all the dates I'd never gone on, all the men I didn't know, and all the possibilities I'd let pass me by.

All because I'd married a man who was now married to someone else.

"What do you want?" Grandma asked again, a glint of hope in her gaze.

I wanted to make her happy. But my decision couldn't be based on that. It had to center on me. On what I wanted.

I closed my eyes. All that stuff floated right there in front of me, so close I could touch it. Did I want the next year to be more of the same?

No, I didn't. It couldn't be.

There was only one thing I could do. Only one thing I *wanted* to do. Like I'd said earlier, it was time to live again, to have some fun again, and hey, if the process took a bit of gypsy magic to get me going, why not? After all, it was mine to use.

"I'm going to keep it, Grandma." The decision made, I opened my eyes and smiled at her. All the anxiety dissipated, replaced with pure anticipation for the future.

I, Lizzie Stevens, was about to learn exactly what I was capable of.

"So long, Miss Mouse," I whispered.

Chapter Five

I looked at the list I'd written and focused on number one. While another dose of retribution at first sounded appealing, it probably wasn't the most practical way to begin. Think about it. I didn't yet know enough about how the magic worked. Anything I did to Marc needed to be done correctly, and I couldn't get my mind off some of the things my grandmother had shared with me. Possible repercussions and all that.

In all honesty, it was a fairly pitiful list I made. You'd think creating magical goals would be easy, but it wasn't. For one, the fact that whoever I enchanted would need to eat whatever I baked—well, that limited what I could realistically accomplish. For two, the whole concept, while exciting, was more than a little panic-inducing.

Before I could give it any further thought, the office door opened. I tucked the paper away and smiled at Jon.

"I'm out of here, Lizzie. Are you all set for the day?" he asked, his tired gaze taking in the notepad on my desk, the stacked files, and the order on my computer screen.

"Almost, but I'll be in early tomorrow to finish up the samples for the wedding show." Each year we participated in several wedding expos throughout Chicago. This weekend was the largest of them all, and in order to have enough samples ready, Jon and I had been on a baking blitz. Tiring, but fun, too. Plus, we needed the new business.

"I'll meet you here at six, then." He turned to exit but stopped and faced me again. "Lizzie?"

"Yeah?" I asked absently, still thinking about magic.

"Do you believe in true love? The ever-after kind?"

Both the question and his tone of voice startled me. It wasn't like Jon to sound so melancholy. Probably, he was still worried about me. "I don't know. For some people, maybe. Like you and Andy. You two will be together forever. But not everyone's that lucky, you know?"

"Yeah, I guess." I thought I saw sadness flicker over his face, but then he grinned and I was sure I'd imagined it. "You want to walk out together? I can wait," he said.

"I don't want to hold you up. I'm not sure how long I'll be. Andy's probably wondering where you are by now, so go home."

He hesitated, as if he wanted to say something else. After a moment, he said, "I'll see you in the morning, then. Don't stay too late."

When the bells jangled at the entry, signaling his departure, I grabbed my list out of my pocket and ran to the kitchen. But then I stopped. I thought about the question Jon had just asked me, and I recalled the sadness I'd seen in his eyes. Had I mistaken the reason he'd asked about love? Could he and Andy be having problems?

But, no. They were the happiest couple I knew. I set my worry aside. But I also promised myself I'd pay closer attention to Jon. Just in case.

Spreading the list on the counter, I tried to decide what I wanted the most. Okay, strike that. I already knew the answer to that question, but what I *really* needed to do first was test out the magic, see how it worked and figure out the rules. Which meant it would be smart to start with the easy stuff. I had to be somewhat responsible, after all.

I flipped on some music, grabbed my apron, poured myself a glass of wine, and washed my hands. I'd baked all day and had to concentrate to keep my mind empty so that I didn't accidentally cast a spell. I'd spent the time repeating the recipes over and over as I measured and mixed, because I didn't want any other accidents until I'd practiced it a little.

Tonight was a different story. This baking was personal,

and I was going to test my limits—find out exactly what I could and couldn't do. In baby steps, of course. It would be rash and ill-fated to jump in with both feet otherwise. Right?

Yeah, that's what I thought. So, while plenty of ideas swarmed through my brain, I forced myself to let them float away for now. Payback could wait a bit longer. Unfortunately, so could crazy sex. Instead, I was going to use the magic for something simple and small, but something good.

Maddie would never know what hit her. If it worked.

I focused on exactly what I wanted to accomplish in Maddie's chocolate chip cookies, going light on the magic. I thought about the outcome I wanted, just as Grandma had instructed me to do, and I worded my wish accordingly.

When I finished with her recipe, I moved on to brownies for me. This recipe was almost more important, because while I'd been cautious in what I'd wished for Maddie, I could be far freer with myself. Scary.

I thought about the wish I wanted to make. How I wanted my life to be different and exciting. How I wanted to go out and do things and not be stuck at home all the time. Decision made, I measured out the ingredients and dumped them into a bowl. When I was ready, I closed my eyes, and said, "My wish is to have men find me alluring and interesting and to ask me out on dates, so I can see what I've been missing. Oh. Not just any men, but sexy, handsome men."

The energy began at my toes, moving through my body, and swirling around me as I stirred the brownie batter. I repeated the wish a second time—just to be sure—and then I poured the batter into a pan. After sliding the pan into the oven, I paced the kitchen, not able to settle down. I wanted the wish to work. I wanted it more than I'd wanted anything in a very long time.

When the brownies were finally done, I hovered over them as if they would jump out of the pan and bite me. Carefully, I sliced a chunk off. I blew on it to cool it down. It looked like any other brownie I'd ever made.

"Here goes nothing," I said, and popped it into my mouth.

The dark fudgy confection melted on my tongue and slid down my throat. I waited for a magical zing, something to tell me the die had been cast and sexy men would be flocking to my door.

"Hmm," I muttered. I took another bite.

Still nothing. Weird. You'd think enchanted brownies would somehow taste different, but they didn't. I ate a couple more before wrapping them up to take home with me. Maybe by the time I saw Nate again they'd have taken effect. One could always hope, anyway.

A sizzle of desire had me stopping to catch my breath. I shivered. I couldn't wait to see if my magic worked, if everything I wanted was only a wish away. No time like the present, right? Besides, I needed to get going if I wanted to see Maddie. And then maybe I'd give myself a little "alone" time— with Nate in mind, of course.

As I headed out the door, excitement and happiness put a smile on my face. Things were about to get better. I just knew it.

I was still smiling an hour later. I'd dropped the brownies off at my place before taking the steps to Maddie's apartment. She had a little more real estate than I, with around 1,000 square feet to call her own. And she'd taken the time to paint *and* decorate. While the pastel colors and ultra-feminine furnishings weren't my style, they suited her perfectly.

"I can't believe you brought me chocolate. I'm so glad you're my best friend," Maddie said, choosing one of the cookies I'd baked for her. Her blonde hair swung loose around her head, glimmers of light bouncing off it as she moved.

"Just a thank-you for helping me through the past year." This wasn't really a lie. I *was* thankful for her support, even if that wasn't the reason I'd baked the cookies. And really, if I told her the truth, she'd think I was crazy.

She took a large bite. I watched her carefully, waiting for a sign that the magic was doing what I'd bade it. Nothing happened. Just like with me. Maybe it was too soon.

"Here, you want one?" Maddie nodded toward the plate.

"I've had several brownies already. Besides, those are yours." She brushed imaginary crumbs from her flowing black slacks before standing. After she straightened her sparkly blouse, she grabbed the plate of cookies. "I'm going to put these away and get some milk. You want anything?"

"No, I'm fine. Thanks, though."

She took the cookies into the kitchen.

"Maddie," I called. "Are you going out tonight?" I mean, come on, she was wearing clothes I'd wear to a social event.

"No way, I'm staying in and relaxing."

"Is someone coming over?"

"No one but you. Why?"

"Just wondered," I replied. Even at home, at night, her makeup was expertly applied. Glamour could be her middle name. If someone dropped in on me at nine o'clock on a weeknight—okay, a weekend, too; who was I kidding?—they'd be lucky to see me in real clothes. I basically had my pajamas on within an hour of coming home. This, actually, was one of the perks of not being married. I could dress how I wanted, when I wanted.

Maddie returned with a glass of milk and another cookie. I should have quizzed Grandma Verda more on this, because I didn't know how many Maddie would have to eat for the magic to work. You'd think just one bite, wouldn't you? But this was the test phase, and I didn't really know anything yet.

"Knock, knock! Anyone in there?" Maddie squeezed my arm. "You seem really out of it. Are you still thinking about Tiffany being pregnant?"

"Nah, that's old news now," I said, ignoring the spasm of pain that hit. "I'm just tired. Long day today." Until the words were said, I hadn't realized they were true. But, all at once, I was exhausted. My late night with Grandma Verda combined with my early morning was to blame. Not to mention all my obsessing over Miranda, magic, and casting actual spells.

"You shouldn't have baked these then." Maddie put the last bite in her mouth. "But I'm really glad you did."

Suddenly, my stomach churned with nerves. What if I, with the best intentions, inadvertently hurt Maddie when something went wrong? Just minutes ago, I'd wanted her to eat more. Now, I was seriously considering forcing ipecac down her throat. What was I doing even wishing good things for my friend when I didn't know how all this magic would work?

"Maddie? Wait until tomorrow to eat more cookies."

"Why? Do you think I've gained weight?" Rising to her feet, she swiveled her hips and tried to get a view of her rear. "Is my butt bigger? I thought my jeans felt a little tight the other day."

"That's not what I meant."

She put her hands on her hips. "What did you mean then? Just tell me, Liz. You're my friend. If I'm turning into a Moo Moo Cow, it's your job to tell me. No. Not just your job, it's your *obligation*. It's like a rule of friendship."

"A Moo Moo Cow?" My anxiety fled. I pursed my lips so I wouldn't laugh.

"Forget it. If you refuse to answer my question then it must be true." She crossed her arms and stared at me, her lips twitching.

"If you keep squinting at me like that, you'll get wrinkles around your eyes," I teased. "Wrinkles age you, so watch it."

Her eyes widened. "You're a brat, Elizabeth Stevens."

"This brat is tired. You're not gaining weight. You look terrific. There's a lot of sugar in the cookies, and you know how sugar affects you. You'll be awake all night."

"I'll just come wake you up then."

After a hug and a good night, I took the stairs to my apartment. It was going to be fine. I'd only wished for Maddie to relax and not feel like she had to be a walking cover model every second of the day. To have a little self-confidence, to not be so self-conscious all the time. How could that hurt her?

In front of my apartment, I knelt down and reached under the nearby plant to pull out the key I'd hidden there earlier.

"I told you to move that." The now recognizable voice

came once again from behind me. At least this time my cellulite was safely hidden beneath denim and my rear wasn't hanging out of a window. Good news on both accounts.

Still crouching, I flipped my head to get a look at the cop. Kinda cool, running into him. "Hey there, you."

"You really can't keep your key there. What if I was a major lunatic? Or, as you said, a madman? I would now know how to get into your apartment whenever I wanted. I could hurt you," Nate said.

"Lucky for me you're not a major lunatic." I stood and tilted my chin so I could look him in the eye. I hadn't remembered him being so tall. "Or a madman." He was in uniform again. The pants, while not tight, easily accentuated his taut, muscular legs. My stomach quivered—just a little—as I took in his full appearance.

Nate rubbed his hand over his face. "Tonight I responded to a rape call. Please, do not keep your key out here." His voice carried through the hallway, anguish and maybe a little anger evident in each abruptly spoken word. But it was his expression that really got to me. More than tired, he looked beaten down.

"Is that why you're home early? I thought you were on the late shift."

"They needed me early tonight, but don't change the subject. This woman's life is forever altered. It's not her fault what happened, but hell . . . if she'd been more aware of her surroundings, she might have stayed safe." Slowly, he stepped toward me, his gaze even. "If you don't make sure of your safety, you won't be safe. It's really that simple. So much of what I see could be avoided by taking precautions."

Stopping, he held out his hand. I dropped the key into his open palm. He unlocked my door and pushed it open. I didn't know what to say, didn't know how to react.

"Go inside. Take this key and lock your door. Take my advice." He voice was clipped and sort of cold, more like the cop I'd met that first night than the man I'd started to get to know.

"Look, it was just for a few minutes while I ran up to see my friend Maddie. It seemed simpler to leave the key here because my hands were full, that's all."

Nate frowned. "That's not a good enough reason. It's too easy to feel safe in a locked building. You don't know all of your neighbors, and you don't know who they might have coming to see them. Trust me on this."

"This woman, will she be okay?"

"Physically, probably. Mentally? Who knows. It depends what type of help she gets and how strong she is. This job . . ." He broke off and shook his head. "It's rough sometimes."

"Do you want to come in? I can make coffee. We can talk." My heart reacted to the stiff way he stood, the washed out color in his face. If a cup of coffee and some conversation would ease his tension, I was all too happy to offer.

He hesitated, and I thought he was going to say no. But then he said, "Yeah. That would be nice. Let me go get out of uniform and I'll be right back." He started to step away but said, "Lock your door. I'll knock."

Once inside, I locked up as he'd requested and went to the kitchen. I barely had the coffee brewing when there was a light rap on my door. Even though I knew it was Nate, I checked through the peephole just to be sure. I couldn't stop thinking about the woman he'd told me about. Sliding the chain off, I said, "Come in."

"Please tell me you didn't open this door without seeing who it was."

"I looked. And I saw it was you," I said softly. "Come on, you need to relax."

He exhaled. "I'm sorry. It usually takes me awhile to clear my head after a bad night. I don't mean to be taking it out on you."

"I can't imagine the things you've seen."

He followed me into the living room and sat on the couch, his long legs spread out in front of him. I curled up on one of my ugly chairs. This was the first time I'd seen him in anything other than his uniform or sweats. He had jeans on, along with a soft-looking flannel shirt the color of a worn teddy bear. His eyes were a dark jade.

More than beat, he appeared empty—as if what he'd witnessed had reached down inside of him and jarred everything loose. I wondered how often he had bad nights. After all, we didn't live in small-town USA. And then I wondered how long it would take for the pieces to settle again. For him to have that amazing smile I'd seen so often in such a short time frame.

"Why do you keep doing it?"

"Because I can't do anything else," he replied.

"What do you mean?"

He cleared his throat, and I didn't think he was going to answer, but then he said, "When I was a kid, my mother was attacked. A police officer saved her life. That's why I do it, to help keep people whole." And then, in an obvious attempt to change the subject, he asked, "How long have you lived here?"

"Almost a year." Everything in me softened as I looked at him. Somehow, I'd met a really cool guy. In today's world, that's not so easy to do.

A slight grin tipped the corners of his lips, and I was happy for it. "Really? That long?" He chuckled. "I wouldn't have guessed."

His teasing tone vanquished any embarrassment I might have felt. "I haven't unpacked much yet."

"How come?"

Such a simple question. Unfortunately, I didn't have a simple answer. The beeping of the coffeemaker saved me. "How do you take your coffee?"

"Black."

"I thought I was the only person to drink coffee at night," I said when I returned to the living room. Handing him his cup, I had the impossible desire to brush my fingers across his cheek. To wipe the strain away from his expression. To somehow offer him comfort.

"I drink it all hours of the day." Accepting the cup, he patted the cushion next to him. "Sit. Let's talk."

He didn't have to ask me twice. I sat down and angled my body toward his. "What do you want to talk about?"

"Anything other than what I did tonight. Tell me about you."

"Me? There's not much to tell. I'm divorced and I work in a bakery. Oh, and I suck at follow-through. That pretty much sums it up." Well, that and I was the descendent of a gypsy. And I could spell people with baked goods. But really, he didn't need to know that.

"Follow-through? What do you mean?"

"Take a look around. I start crafts, but I don't finish them. I start unpacking, yet it's never really done. I make myself promises and rarely keep them. I'm sort of stuck between here and where I want to be."

His body tensed. Not in a negative way, but in a *I'm-really-paying-attention-to-you* way. "Where do you want to be?"

"I don't know. That's probably why I'm stuck." I laughed, trying to lighten the suddenly serious moment. All the focus on me was a little uncomfortable. "Happy, I guess."

"Why aren't you happy?" He smelled so good, and all I wanted to do was crawl onto him and lay my head down on his chest. Partially to give him comfort, but I'd be lying if I said it wasn't to gain a bit of comfort myself.

Instead, I set my cup down and twisted my hands together. "Long story. Let's talk about something else. What about you? How do you know Grandma Verda?"

Good humor zipped into his eyes, chasing out the desolation of earlier. "I thought you were going to ask me about follow-through. I excel at follow-through." He scooted closer to me, put his cup on the table, and leaned in. And in that second, everything changed. The atmosphere in the room became charged. Tickles of awareness dotted my skin. I couldn't breathe, he was so close.

"Do you know how sexy you are, Elizabeth?"

"No," I whispered, my belly doing all sorts of weird flip-flops.

"You are. I haven't been able to stop thinking about you since I found you hanging out your window."

"Not my finest moment."

"Nah, I remember it as being an excellent moment."

And then, his hand was on my chin, tipping it upward. His eyes changed again, from humor to something else. Desire?

His lips touched mine, softly at first, as if testing the waters. I sighed, allowed myself to fall forward slightly. His other arm wove around my back, pulling me tight to him.

"I want to taste you." His rough and tumble voice made my heart skip a beat in anticipation.

"Okay," I said.

His hand moved from my chin to my cheek, guiding my face closer to his. The flip-flopping in my belly disappeared, replaced by searing heat that slowly inched from nerve to nerve, muscle to muscle, until my entire body flushed with warmth and I shivered from the pleasure of it.

Yes, this was exactly what I wanted.

What I craved.

What I'd wished for.

His mouth took mine as if we'd kissed before. No hesitation, no doubt. Just stark desire and needy want. It had been so long since a man touched me like this, kissed me like this, that I thought I would explode. I moaned as his lips left mine, afraid what had barely started was already over.

I shouldn't have worried.

"Come here," Nate said, pulling me onto his lap.

"I'm here."

For once, I did what I wanted. *I* took *his* mouth this time. Tasting, exploring on my own, while he held me, one hand on my back, the other in my hair. My tongue slipped into his warm mouth, and I tasted coffee, heat, and yes, desire. I wanted him to touch me. No matter how fast this was, whether it made sense or not, I acted on my want. I pulled back and slid my sweater off, tossing it on the ground.

"Liz," Nate groaned, as I began unbuttoning his shirt.

"I want to feel your skin against me. Help me," I whispered. "Please."

"Please?"

"Yes, please."

In mere seconds, his shirt met mine on the ground, and he unhooked my bra and dropped that, too. His mouth came back to mine, and he took control. My nipples hardened beneath the stroking of his fingers, and all I wanted was Nate. Just Nate. Every coherent thought left my brain.

Trailing kisses from my lips to my cheek to my earlobe, he said, "You're beautiful."

"No, you are," I argued.

A small chuckle. "No more talking."

"Okay, no more talking."

I moaned as his mouth found my breasts. Arching back, I closed my eyes and just experienced the moment, the hot flash of his tongue as it brushed over each nipple, the suction of his mouth as he brought them to hard peaks, and the press of his erection through his jeans, pushing against me, making me even wetter. I had never wanted a man as quickly as I'd wanted this man.

"You need to lie down," Nate muttered. "Right now."

"Right now?"

"Yes." He stood up, holding my weight easily, and turned, laying me down on the couch. Straddling me, he leaned over and began kissing my breasts again, moving down to my belly, leaving a trail of wet fire wherever his mouth touched.

He unsnapped my jeans, then looked at me. "Is this okay?"

"Yes." My belly quivered again. "Hell, yes."

I lifted my hips so he could pull my jeans down my legs, and those, too, met the ever-growing pile of clothes on the floor.

"You're wet," he groaned, his hand inside my panties, rubbing, feeling, teasing me. His fingers stroked, starting an entirely new burn, one I hadn't felt for far too long.

I pushed his head closer. "Kiss me again."

His mouth came back to mine. His fingers entered me, thrusting deep inside. With a gasp, I raised my hips. I wanted more than his fingers, but before I could pull away long enough to say those words, the burning grew hotter, and my mind numbed to anything but sensation.

It traveled through me in a hot rush, setting off tiny explosions as it went from the core of my body. I ground against his hand, needing to find the release only Nate could give me.

"That's right, Liz, come on, baby," he whispered, moving his fingers to the rhythm of my movements, to the sound of my moans. I pulled his face back to mine. I wanted my tongue in his mouth when I came. At that moment, I would have swallowed him whole if I could.

I whimpered, pushed against his hand again, and suddenly everything exploded in a burst of light, sensation, and pleasure. "Oh my," I murmured, riding the crest, still moving my hips against him as my entire body melted from the release, from the heat.

Nate kept his hand there, but laid his head on my chest, playing with my breast with his other hand. "This should feel odd, but it doesn't," he said quietly. "Are you good?"

"I'm good. I'm very good." Though, I must admit, I was now a bit shy. Crazy, but there you have it. "I feel kind of bad, though. What did you get from this?"

"More than you know. This was exactly what I needed tonight. Thank you."

"Whenever you feel that particular need, let me know," I laughed. A few minutes passed, with neither of us speaking. A little while later, I asked, "Are you doing better now?"

Lifting his head, he kissed me slowly. "Yes. You could say I'm a new man."

I stroked his cheek, like I had wanted to earlier, and soaked in his gaze. "I'm glad."

"Hey, Elizabeth?"

"Hmm?"

"I don't think you should say you suck at follow-through anymore," Nate said with a chuckle.

"I don't know. You were the follow-through that time."

Another laugh, and then his head came back to my chest. I closed my eyes, enjoyed the weight of him, the feel of his body against mine, the solidity of it, and simply relaxed.

Tired, I yawned, and began drifting off. Then, the banana muffins came to mind, followed by the brownies, and I had to wonder if the night's magic was real or simply the result of Miranda's gypsy magic.

At the moment, I wasn't sure I cared.

Chapter Six

"Sit up, back straight, legs even, knees out. Pull your arms slightly to the back and slowly push the weights in toward you, but not too close. See how my feet are flat on the floor? This is the posture you want when you're using this machine," said Kevin, my hunky trainer, as he demonstrated.

It looked simple enough. Even better, it wasn't hard on the eyes watching him work out. With his rippled physique, chocolate brown eyes, tawny complexion, and almost-to-his-shoulder chestnut hair, Kevin had it going on. In fact, there were plenty of muscle-bound gym guys at Steel Bodies. There were also numerous women with, well, yeah—steel bodies. I fit in about as well as a carrot in a box of donuts. Well, I wasn't the carrot, but the analogy is still valid.

I couldn't help but wonder what my mother thought when she came in to get the gift certificate. The gym was close to A Taste of Magic, and my mother was well aware of my innate laziness, so it probably seemed a perfect fit. But it wasn't a polished and pretty gym. The people there were definitely serious about fitness.

"Your turn, Elizabeth," Kevin said. He adjusted the machine and waited for me to hop on. As if.

"Could you show me one more time? I'm not exactly sure I understand how to use it."

He smiled, and his dimples appeared again. I loved dimples.

"It's easy. I'll help you." He put his hand on my hip and pushed me toward the machine. Hesitantly, I slid on the seat and tried to take the position he'd just shown me.

"This can't be right. It feels as if my shoulders are going to pop out of joint," I said, my arms stretched behind me.

"You're holding them too far back." He gently repositioned everything. "There, like this. Slowly push forward. There you go. See, you're doing great." He moved directly in front of the machine. "We're only going to start with two sets of twelve reps. It'll be a breeze."

"You have no idea how completely wrong you are." I pushed the weights in and then slowly released them. The muscles in my arms began to burn, but it wasn't really unpleasant. At least not at first. After I'd done a few, I could definitely tell the difference, and yeah, it pretty much sucked.

Why did I need hot-looking arms anyway? I lived in Chicago, so I didn't have twelve months of short-sleeve weather to contend with. I wasn't really concerned about my arms. I needed to focus on my midsection, flatten my tummy, tighten up my rear, and pull in the hips. Kevin said we'd focus on a core workout, so why the arms? "How many more?"

"Five."

"Really? I've done that many?"

"I told you! Just a few more and you'll have the first set of repetitions done. Doesn't it feel great? Do you want me to add more weight for the second set?"

"No," I huffed. "Make it lighter."

"That's twelve. Rest for a second, drink some water if you need to, and we'll do the last set."

"Make it lighter," I said in between gulps of water. I was going to die. I didn't realize how much of a wimp I was. Pitiful, I know, but facts are facts. "Please. My arms are going to fall off."

"Good! That's how it's supposed to feel."

I didn't think he looked so hot anymore. He was torturing me, and he was smiling while he did so. No way would I come back. Forget it. It wasn't worth it. Not for anything.

But then I thought of Nate. A week later and my body still buzzed with the memory. Maybe a few more sessions wouldn't hurt. I hadn't seen him again since that night. The fact that I hadn't, well, it worried me slightly—but not too much. He did work odd hours, after all.

The rest of the training session went pretty much the same way. By the end of the two hours, I couldn't decide if I wanted to slap Kevin or thank him. Because, while I was certainly exhausted, I also felt really good. Though, I stunk. And the mirrors surrounding the entire damn gym didn't make me appreciate my appearance any.

"This was the first half of your workout. Tomorrow, same time, good for you? If so, we'll go over the second half," said Kevin the torturer, as he bent over to pick up his water bottle. I had never seen butt cheeks as firm as his. Forget what I said earlier, the man was definitely hot. Working out eight hours a day will do that, I guess.

"Elizabeth?"

Oh yeah, I was supposed to answer him, not stare at his drool-inducing body. Silly me.

"First half? You mean I'll be doing twice this much every day? I can't do that. You're crazy."

"Stop saying you can't do something. That's the number one rule here. You can do anything, Elizabeth! But no, you'll have two different sets of workouts, so you can switch things around. Then, after six weeks or so, we'll change them again."

"Why would we do this?" His enthusiasm should annoy me. The intelligent part of my brain knew this, yet it was weirdly endearing. As if he'd become my personal cheerleader.

He laughed. "Because our bodies fall into a habit, and once they're used to something, they get lazy. They find ways to cheat so your muscles don't get everything out of it they should." He tapped his finger to his temple. "But we're smarter than that."

"I see." I didn't really see, but he was the expert, not me. "Well, I can't come in tomorrow morning. I work until five."

"What time do you go in?" Kevin asked.

"Early. Why?"

"We open at six. You could get your workout in before the day started. What a great way to wake up, Elizabeth!"

Yeah, right. Sure, that would happen. Before coffee. "I don't think so, Kev."

He sighed. "That's too bad. I won't be here tomorrow evening. Let's see who we can hook you up with. When can you be here?"

"Um. I don't know. Six, I guess?"

"That's Ellen or Joy. Have you met either one?"

I didn't really want to meet a new trainer. I hated this so much anyway, I figured I should at least enjoy looking at my torturer. "No, but what about lunchtime? Can you see me at eleven? And can we make it shorter? Like an hour or so?"

"That will work, and yeah, you'll have a heavy and a light day, so that's perfect."

"Okay. I'll see you then. Thank you for being patient with me." This was odd. I almost felt as if we'd been on a date, because let's face it, we'd just gone through a fairly intimate process. All the groaning, sweating, and swearing created an interesting bond I hadn't expected.

"We'll weigh and measure you tomorrow, so wear something more formfitting than those baggy sweats. You don't want to add extra inches on because of too-loose clothes."

"I don't think so," I said, aiming for the door. He was nice and all, but wow, a little too overwhelming for the first day. I wanted a shower. And I was ravenous. I'd planned on a healthy salad for lunch, but now I wanted a huge burger, complete with all the trimmings, and maybe some dessert. Screw salads.

"Elizabeth! We need to know where you start so we can celebrate each accomplishment! It's exciting," Kevin called after me.

Sure, exciting. I didn't bother replying as I made my way to my car. This exercise stuff hurt. My muscles were already curling up into tight little knots. I wondered if I could wish myself to a better body. Yes, I liked that idea. Smiling, I decided it would be the perfect experiment when I got home. I mean, I couldn't bake a salad, now could I?

What is it they say about best-laid plans? On my way home, Alice called crying so hard I couldn't begin to make any sense of what she said. So now, instead of standing in the shower contemplating what words to use for the steel body spell,

I was pulling into the parking lot of my sister's apartment complex.

Alice didn't get upset often. Well, wait a minute. She gets upset, but usually it's the fearsome, get-out-of-my-way-before-I-clobber-you type. Nobody was as scary as my little sister when she was pissed off. But crying hysterically? No, that had been my niche for the last year, not hers. Luckily, I seemed to be growing out of that, which made not only me, but everyone around me, all that much happier.

Climbing the last flight of stairs to her fourth floor apartment wasn't easy. My legs almost gave out. My entire body hated me. Tomorrow would be fun, adding insult to injury.

I arrived at Alice's door and found it hanging open. This on its own didn't alarm me. Though, in hindsight, it probably should have. Walking into her apartment scared the crap out of me. My eyes took in the mess, and even though it was right there, right in front of me, I could still hardly believe it.

My sister's place was normally perfect. Anyone from *Home Beautiful* could literally stop by at any moment with a camera and snap amazing pictures. Well, not at *that* moment. But that's what terrified me.

Broken glass pieces were strewn all over the dark wooden floor of her entryway. The cloudy green of her drinking glasses, the head off her white-as-snow porcelain cat, other various pottery pieces, and her black dishware—all were smashed in a trail from the entry to the kitchen to the dining room.

"Alice?" I yelled. "I'm here, honey. Where are you?"

Carefully, I stepped over the chunks and splinters of glass, every now and then crushing a piece beneath my feet, and moved to her bedroom. Maybe she was in there.

She wasn't. I shoved my trembling hands into my coat pockets. The mess hadn't come this far. Whatever had happened hadn't touched her bedroom, as it was as neat as a pin.

"Alice! You're scaring me. Where are you?" I yelled again. I knew it was useless; she wasn't there. I could tell I stood in an empty apartment. You get a specific type of feeling when you're alone.

Grabbing my cell phone out of my purse, I tried to ignore the panic building. I clicked her cell number in my directory. It rang, not only through the phone, but from somewhere inside the apartment. I set my phone on her bed and followed the melodic sound of ringing. It took me to the living room, and I had to step over more broken glass as I made my way to the other side.

My eyes darted around, trying to find it. *There.* Her little blue phone was sitting on an empty bric-a-brac shelf above her leather couch.

I clicked the END button on the phone. My mind sifted through the possibilities, and I didn't like any of them. Most people thought they knew exactly how they'd react in situations like this, but it was as if my mind had shut down and I had to remind myself to call 911. I pushed the numbers in as fast as I could and hit the SEND key.

"911. What is the nature of your emergency?" the operator's voice came through the line.

"My sister is missing. Well, maybe she isn't. I guess I don't know. But her apartment door is open and there's broken stuff all over, and she's not here." I rambled as I tried to make sense of an unimaginable situation. I stopped, took a breath. She was fine. There was probably a perfectly reasonable explanation.

"What's your name?" the operator asked calmly.

"Elizabeth. Elizabeth Stevens."

"Elizabeth, are you in danger?"

"What? Me? No."

"You're safe?" she questioned again.

"Yes! I'm safe. I'm worried about my sister."

"Is your sister a child, Elizabeth? And what is the address, please?" the operator asked, enunciating each word slowly.

"No, she's an adult. And, I don't know. She's in the Vale Apartments on . . . oh hell, what is the name of her street." I closed my eyes and tried to envision the street sign. "I thought you could tell by the number I called from," I snapped, my mind blank.

"Are you on a cell phone?"

"Shit. Yes. Wait—she's on Edmonton Street. The Vale Apartments on Edmonton, number 4521."

"We'll send a car over. Stay on the line with me until the officers get there."

"But I'm safe. No one is here. I have a friend who's on the police force. I don't know if this is his jurisdiction or not, or even if he's on duty today, but can you contact him? His name is Nate Sutherland. Please have him come."

"One moment. I am not putting you on hold. Do not hang up."

I paced the living room, my heart pounding like crazy, my feet crunching on bits of glass. "Where are you, Alice?" I murmured.

"Elizabeth? Did you say something to me?"

"No. I'm sorry. Is Nate coming? Please tell me Nate is coming," I blubbered.

"I don't know. I'll try to get a hold of him for you, but I can't promise anything. The important thing is for you to stay calm until the officers arrive."

Stay calm? I inhaled deeply and tried to stop trembling. "It's not working."

"As soon as the officers get there, they'll need you to be calm enough to take your statement so they can find your sister. What is your sister's name?"

"Alice. Alice Raymond."

"That's a nice name. Is she younger than you?"

"Look, I know you're trying to make me feel better, and I appreciate it, but I don't need to have a conversation right now. I need to find my sister. But there's no one here, so there's no reason to stay on the phone. I'm going to disconnect and wait for the police." I clicked the END button and set my sister's phone back down on the bric-a-brac shelf.

Both sick at heart and sick to my stomach, I closed the door to the apartment and then retraced my steps through each room. This time, I opened every closet and cupboard door. I looked behind the shower curtain and under the bed. I even opened her bedroom window to make sure she wasn't on the fire escape. Silly, because obviously if Alice had been anywhere near, she'd have heard me by that point, but that didn't stop me. I had to be one hundred percent positive. And I really wanted her to be there.

I was still in Alice's bedroom when I heard the knocking on the door. I ran at top speed—well, as quickly as I could amid the glass and clutter. Of course, it couldn't be Alice, she'd just let herself in. But it might be Nate.

My heart dropped when I opened the door to two strangers.

"Hi, I'm Officer Thomas," said the older, gray-haired man with a slight paunch. "And this is Officer Neuman." He nodded to the tall, slender, black-haired female cop next to him. "We're responding to a 911 call. Are you Elizabeth Stevens?"

"Yes. I am. Please come in." I stepped back to give them room to enter. I shuddered. Seeing the police made the situation all too real.

They followed me in, and the woman, Officer Neuman, took charge. "Let's you and I talk while my partner checks the apartment out," she said softly, with a reassuring smile.

We went into the living room, and I sat down. I was beginning to comprehend how serious this could be. I looked at the door again, willing Alice to come through it with her goofy grin.

Officer Neuman flipped open a notepad. "Can you tell me what happened? All the way through. I'll probably ask you to repeat things."

I related the events to her the best I could. As I did, my eyes kept drifting back to that damn door. My intuition didn't tell me anything. You'd think if my sister was hurt in some way, I would know. That somewhere inside, I'd feel it. While I wanted to hang on to that, I couldn't quite allow myself. After all, I didn't have a history in ESP or precognition.

Gypsy magic, yeah. Freaky see-into-the-future stuff? Nope.

Officer Thomas returned. He tried to walk around the glass, which was nice of him. "Does anything appear to be missing?"

"I don't know. I'm honestly not here enough to answer that. Alice keeps to herself, mostly."

"Does she have a husband or a boyfriend? There are some men's clothes hanging in her bedroom closet."

"A boyfriend, but I've never met him. He's been under wraps. It's a fairly new relationship, I think." The shakiness in my voice pissed me off. How could I help Alice if I couldn't remain calm?

"Do you know his name?"

I shook my head. How stupid that I didn't know the name of the man my sister was involved with. Let me tell you, that one fact made me realize, like little else had, how much I'd pulled away from the people I loved in the past year. Alice and I used to share everything. What a rotten sister I'd turned out to be.

"Elizabeth? I asked you if anyone in your family would know his name," Officer Thomas said.

I refocused. "Oh, I don't know. I'm not sure anyone in my family has met him. She hasn't been dating him for long."

"How long?" This came from Officer Neuman.

"Um, maybe a month? No more than two, I think." Damn, I couldn't remember for sure the first time Alice mentioned the mystery man. I thought it was at least a good month before my birthday, which probably meant she'd known him longer. "Do you think he had something to do with this?"

"We have no way of knowing that. Right now, we're just trying to get a little information about your sister," said the female officer. "When you talked to her, did she sound scared?"

"Not scared. Sad. Like something really awful had happened." Another shiver of cold fear struck me.

I hated this.

A knock on the door made me jump. I shot to my feet, but Officer Neuman laid a hand on my arm. "Let us get that," she said, with a nod to her partner.

Officer Thomas checked through the peephole before opening the door. "Hi, Nate. We were told you might stop in. You're a friend of Elizabeth's, right?"

Nate stepped into the entryway, his eyes taking in the broken glass, and then moved on, searching. When his gaze landed on me, my composure fled. Every bit of what I'd been holding myself together with went flying out the window. He wasn't in uniform, which meant someone had contacted him at home. I'd have to find out who the 911 operator was and send her a thank-you card. Or maybe some flowers.

I started to cry, slowly at first. As Nate came toward me, my tears came faster. He didn't say anything, just opened his arms and I walked into them. They closed around me, and I buried my head in his chest, my cheek rubbing against the rough grain of his sweater.

"I don't know where she is," I mumbled.

"We'll do our best to find her," he murmured in my ear, stroking my back. "Have you called your family?"

I lifted my head and clenched my jaw, trying to stop the tears. "No. I was hoping I wouldn't have to."

"Maybe she's with your parents or your grandmother or your brothers? Could that be the case?"

I shook my head. "No. She called me and asked me to come over. Why would she do that and then leave? Without letting me know." I pointed to the cell phone. "She didn't take her phone with her either, and she never goes anywhere without it."

"Does she carry a purse?" Officer Neuman asked.

"Yes. Of course she does. Don't all women?"

"Look at me, Elizabeth." I focused on Nate's steady green eyes. Thank God he was there. "Did you see her bag anywhere in the apartment?"

I mentally went over my frantic search. "No . . . but I didn't look for it either. I was looking for *her*, not her purse."

"Do you want to do that now? If it isn't here, that may be a good sign. It's easy to leave in a hurry and forget a phone. After that, you should call your family. Before we send out the search dogs, let's make sure she isn't sitting at your grandmother's place drinking tea."

It was useless to argue with him. The last place Alice would go in a crisis was to any of our family. Maybe she'd call her best friend, Chloe. But I didn't think so, because she'd called me. I just hadn't gotten there quick enough.

Because Alice was such a neat person, it didn't take me long to ascertain her purse was not in her apartment. Which meant she had her car keys. Returning to the living room, I saw Nate in deep conversation with the other two officers. He turned to look at me. Concern flickered over his expression.

I cleared my throat. "It's not here. And I realized that means she has her car keys. Should I go downstairs and see if I can find her car in the lot?"

Officer Neuman came forward. "Give us the make, model, and color, and my partner and I will take a walk outside. That way, you can have some privacy while you call your family."

"Alice drives a Mitsubishi Eclipse Coupe. It's red."

"How old is it?" Officer Thomas asked.

"Um, a couple of years, at least. I think it's a 2005, but I could be off a year or two."

Officer Neuman wrote the information down. "We'll go look. Fill Nate in and then call your family."

When they exited the apartment, I collapsed on the couch. "I don't want to call my parents. They'll flip out. And Alice is probably okay. So why worry them for nothing?" I needed to believe this.

Nate sat down next to me. "You need to call. But you can start with your brothers if you want."

"How do you know I have brothers?"

"Your grandmother told me."

I kept forgetting they knew each other. One of these days, I'd have to find out how. "This will not be easy." I heaved myself up and walked toward the bedroom.

"Where are you going?"

"I left my phone on Alice's bed. I don't think I want to call my family on her phone to tell them she's missing."

I retrieved my phone. I held it for a minute, delaying the inevitable. Calling them made the situation even more real, and this was real enough as it was. Another minute passed.

I sat on the edge of her bed, put my head between my knees, and cried some more. When I felt I could talk clearly, I went back to Nate.

"Here goes nothing," I said, punching in the first number.

Nate squeezed my knee and offered up a smile. It didn't help, but I appreciated the effort.

Grandma Verda wasn't home when I called. But I got through to everyone else. I told my parents and then my brothers that I didn't know where Alice was. I explained the condition of her apartment and that the police were there. I told them she'd called me upset and asked me to come over.

Nate spoke to each of them as well, asking the same questions I'd been asked. He impressed me, this cop I'd met so unexpectedly. His voice was warm, reassuring, and stabilizing as he talked to my family. Before he hung up, he asked everyone to stay at home, in case Alice showed up or contacted them.

On a different day, for a different reason, I would have laughed at this. Telling my family to stay put was, for lack of a better phrase, a complete waste of time. I gave it thirty minutes, forty-five on the outside, before the entire Raymond clan barged in the door at Alice's.

"They're not going to stay home. They'll be here within the hour."

Nate frowned. "We don't want people trampling over possible evidence."

"So you *do* think something happened to her, don't you?"

"It's not that, but we have to preserve the scene—" He broke off, a flustered expression crossing his features.

"The scene of a crime, right?" My chest tightened again and another tear rolled down my face. "I can't comprehend this. It doesn't make any sense. Who would want to hurt Alice?"

"We don't know she's hurt, Lizzie. Worrying about things that might have happened isn't going to help. Focus on the facts. That's all you can do right now."

I excused myself and went to the restroom. I washed my face and used Alice's brush to comb through my hair. I looked around the small blue-painted room and tried to find a reason to stay. Going back out *there* meant seeing the remnants of whatever happened again. I didn't want to.

But because it was expected, I went back out. I'd barely sat down when the door opened and Officers Thomas and Neuman entered. And then, right behind them, a bedraggled Alice followed. Everything shifted back into focus as soon as I saw her.

Bolting off the couch, I ran to her and hugged her tight. "Where were you? Are you okay?" I demanded. "I've been frantic, Alice. Tell me you're not hurt."

She hugged me quickly and then pulled herself free. Her eyes were rimmed in red, and her pale face was blotchy from crying. "I'm fine. Why did you call the police?" she whispered.

"I was so scared when I got here and found your apartment like this. You left the door open and all this broken stuff. Where were you? What happened?"

"I've already explained to the officers," she said, her voice stiff. "You shouldn't have called them. This is private. I called you."

"But you weren't here. What was I supposed to think?"

Alice opened her mouth to say something, but before she could, all hell broke loose. My parents entered the apartment with a bang. The tension emanating from my sister amplified instantly. They made record time; they must have left the second they hung up the phone. My mother took one look at Alice and started to cry, so that made three of us. The expression on my father's face went from fear to concern. Next, Scot ran in, and, right after him, Joe. The only person missing was Grandma, and I suspected that was only because she hadn't been at home when we'd phoned.

With a shaking hand, Alice tucked her hair behind one ear in a nervous gesture. Her eyes questioned me as my mother exclaimed over the shattered glass and my father spoke to the police. Nate came up behind me and put his hand on the small of my back, as if letting me know he was there, supporting me.

It helped. A lot.

"I'm not sorry for getting the police involved. I didn't know where you were. I didn't know what happened. You were supposed to be here. You called me and wanted me to come to you. What was I supposed to think?" My voice quavered with emotion.

Averting her gaze, Alice said, "As you can see, there's nothing wrong with me. I'm sorry I worried everyone, but now I'd just like to be alone."

"Not until you explain what happened," my mother said.

"Did someone hurt you?" Scot asked.

"Where were you?" my father interjected.

"What's the deal?" Joe asked.

"Your sister was just worried," Nate added.

I didn't say anything. I didn't feel bad for calling 911, but I felt lousy as I observed my sister trying to take everything in. Whatever happened had shaken her up, and then coming home to an apartment filled with people while she dealt with it couldn't have been easy.

Alice burst into another round of tears and raced out of the room. Her bedroom door slammed shut, followed by the unmistakable sound of a lock turning. She wasn't normally one for melodramatics. I was scared all over again.

"Can you explain what's going on?" my father asked Officer Thomas.

The officer shook his head. "She hasn't been hurt, and she's not filing a complaint, but what happened should come from her."

Officer Neuman added, "I gave Alice my card. She knows how to reach us if she changes her mind."

They said their good-byes and left.

My family reverted back to their normal positions. My mother got a broom and started cleaning up the mess. My father and brothers went into the living room to hash things out. I had a feeling none of them would go anywhere until Alice rematerialized with an explanation.

I wanted one, too, but I needed a break.

"I'll be right back." I went outside. I needed fresh air.

I needed to come down from the tension in the apartment. And I needed to dispel the horrific images that had started forming in my mind before Alice finally came home.

I sat down on the step outside of the building and wished I hadn't quit smoking three years previously. I really wanted a smoke. Biting my lip, I leaned against the railing and rubbed my arms against the chilly air. I'd left my coat on the couch upstairs.

Nate came through the door and knelt next to me. "How are you doing?"

"I'm not sure yet."

"She's home and she's safe."

"Thank God," I said. "She's mad at me."

"She'll get over it. Once she's calmed down enough to realize how it looked, she'll get over it."

"Promise?" I asked.

"I promise."

And when I looked into those green eyes, I believed him, so I exhaled all the pent up frustration in one whoosh. "Thank you."

"For what?"

"You know, just being here."

"Anytime, Liz. Anytime."

How's that for a guarantee?

Chapter Seven

The now familiar electrical buzz swept through my body, casting an odd glow from me to the mixer to the bowl. I didn't jump away from the energy; I basked in it, opening my body to the power swirling thickly around the room. When the last tingle disappeared, I switched off the mixer and poured the batter into the prepared cupcake tins.

"I thought everyone left, and then I heard you banging around." Alice padded into her kitchen, opened a cupboard, and pulled out one of the few glasses that were still in one piece.

"Everyone else took off, but I wanted to stay. Even if you don't want to talk yet, I didn't want you to be alone." After sliding the pan into the oven, I noticed her eyes were still a little puffy but not nearly as bad as before. "Do you mind?"

Sipping the orange juice she'd poured, she shook her head, and her eyes narrowed. "You're wearing my clothes."

"I came here straight from the gym. When everyone left, I grabbed a shower. These were in the dryer," I said, motioning to Alice's lime-green polka-dotted pajamas.

"They're too long on you."

I wanted to hug her, but by the way she held herself, it was fairly obvious she didn't want to be touched, so I resisted the urge. "Are you hungry? I have cupcakes baking for dessert, but I can make us some dinner if you want."

"Pizza. I want pizza with everything on it and regular soda. No diet." She looked at me as if I would argue. Not likely, I love pizza.

"Where do you usually order from?"

"Vito's. I'll get the number." Swiveling on her heel, she

gave me a hug. "I acted like an immature brat. I'm sorry I scared you."

"You should be. I'm relieved you're okay. You'll need to call the folks tomorrow, you know."

She frowned. "Yeah, I will. That will be fun."

"Feel like talking about what happened yet?"

"Nope. You order the pizza, and I'll find a movie. You're staying the night, right?"

I'd already called Jon, and he'd ordered me to take the next day off to hang with Alice. "I planned on it, but if you'd rather I leave, you can kick me out."

"Stay. I could use the company. Just no nagging. Deal?"

"I never nag."

"Yeah, right."

The next several hours passed quickly. We watched an older Steve Martin flick, ate pizza, drank sodas, burped from the sodas, and laughed at Steve Martin and Martin Short. When the credits rolled on the movie, Alice clicked the TV off and angled herself on the couch so she could face me.

"I feel really silly," Alice said.

"Why?"

"Because I'm a fool and, when I tell you this, you'll know I'm a fool."

"*Now* you're being silly. Look at who you're talking to. Like I haven't made a complete idiotic mess out of my life with some of the choices I've made?" I squeezed her hand. "I'm the one person you don't have to worry about coming off as a fool to."

A smile skimmed across her expression, quickly gone. "Well, that's true."

"Hey! You didn't have to agree so fast!"

"You said it." Some of the tension dissipated. If she could smile, it couldn't be too horrible.

"I'm listening." I curled my legs beneath me and leaned back against the cushion.

"You remember when I told you I met someone? And that he was staying here for a while?"

"Yes. You didn't tell me anything else, though. I wish I'd pressed you more for details."

"It sounds stupid now, but I thought I was protecting something special. I didn't want to bring in the craziness of our family until we had a chance to settle a bit." Alice's eyes glazed over. "It all happened so fast."

"He?"

"His name is Troy. I met him at the club almost a year ago."

"That long?"

"Well, that's when things started becoming serious. But we dated for six months before he started staying here a lot. You were having a rough time with Marc, and I didn't want to make you feel worse because I'd found the love of my life." Alice fidgeted. "What a joke that is."

"I don't understand. Where does the broken glass come in? And your phone call to me today?"

"I'm getting there. Be patient. This is hard for me."

"Take your time." I mimed zipping my lips shut. "No more interruptions."

"While we were dating, things were really great. Troy made me happy. And I felt special to him. It was incredible. So, when he told me he'd lost his job and needed a place to stay, I naturally said he could stay here."

"Naturally."

She glared at me.

"Sorry."

"Then he needed money to fix his car so he could look for a job. He needed money to pay bills. He needed money to pay his club dues. He never asked me for money, but I wanted to help him. I loved him. I thought we were going to have a life together. Anyway, I gave him my savings," Alice admitted.

"Oh honey, no."

She held a hand up. "Wait. It gets worse. Then, he said his ex-wife was coming down really hard on him and he had to come up with some extra money." Averting her gaze from mine, she added, "To pay for stuff for his kids."

I bit my lip to keep from exploding. Instead of shaking

her by the shoulders, or pulling her into my arms (I simultaneously wanted to do both), I simply nodded for her to continue.

"Liz . . ."

"You can tell me."

"I took out a loan. And I gave it all to him."

Exhaling deeply, I asked, "How much?"

"Only five thousand."

"Only?!" I tried to think about it from her point of view, but I couldn't really get a handle. I mean, none of us had even met this man, and she was bending over backward to fill his pockets. It pissed me off.

"I know. Stupid. But Troy was so happy about it, and he promised he'd pay me back. I was smart enough to ask him to sign a contract stating he would, once he found work."

"Did he?"

Mutely, she shook her head no. "He said he was going to. Maybe he just didn't get around to it."

"Then why did you give him the money?"

"Told you. Stupid. But I've picked up a few extra hours at work and managed to sell one of my paintings last week, so I figured no big deal. You know, once we were married, it would be our money, anyway."

"Married? He asked you to marry him?"

"Not exactly, but he talked about it all the time. Not that he could have married me, it turns out." Her voice broke, and her eyes began to well up.

"What do you mean?"

"Today, I got home and walked into an argument between Troy and this strange woman. There was broken glass everywhere, and she was really laying into Troy. So I asked what the hell was going on."

"And?" I prodded.

A tear rolled down her cheek. "The woman—it was his wife, as in current and not ex."

Pain sliced into me. "The bastard! Oh honey, I'm so sorry." I squeezed her hand again, little good though it did.

"So this woman was in my home arguing with her husband, who barely came home anymore, and was throwing all my stuff at him. When she saw me, she came after me. Called me a home-wrecker and a slut and honest to God, Liz, it was horrible." Alice shuddered and wiped the tears from her eyes.

"She didn't believe I didn't know. Told me I could keep his sorry ass, that he'd drained all of their money and left her penniless with a houseful of kids and bills to pay." Alice slumped, as if the weight of her words was too heavy to handle. "She stormed out."

"What did you do?"

Alice's brown eyes darkened to almost black. "I kicked the jerk out and told him never to come back. Then I called you."

"Good girl. Why didn't you wait for me?"

"I got overwhelmed. I didn't plan to be gone for so long. I just couldn't deal with the broken glass and everything else. I couldn't sit in here and wait for you. I figured I'd go for a quick drive and then come back to talk to you, which is why I left the door unlocked. I lost track of time."

"The door wasn't just unlocked. It was hanging open."

"I thought I closed it, but I wasn't exactly rational at the time. I still can't believe he's married and I gave him so much. And that I believed every word he ever told me."

The tears fell harder, and I opened my arms. She crawled into them, and I held her while she cried. It reminded me of when we were kids and she'd sneak into bed with me at night after having a bad dream.

After a while, she pulled herself away and once again wiped the tears from her cheeks. "Do you hate me?" Her voice wobbled with the question.

Startled, I replied, "No. Of course not. Why would you think that?"

"Because I slept with another woman's husband, just like Tiffany did with Marc."

"Are you serious?" At her nod, I said, "Sweetie, there isn't a comparison. Tiffany knew Marc was married, and she didn't care. That isn't what happened here. You were deceived and betrayed by a man you love."

"I had to make sure. I couldn't live with myself if you hated me."

"Of course I don't. But what are you going to do about Troy?"

Her expression went blank. "It's over. There's nothing to do about Troy."

"You should press charges. He stole money from you."

"No, he didn't. He didn't even ask me for money. I naively just gave him money when he said he needed it. Elizabeth, he never once asked me for a dime. *Ever.* Which makes this entire situation even more ludicrous." She stood and then began pacing.

"You still might be able to press charges. I'll look into it for you." Nate might know. If not him, the attorney I used for my divorce maybe would.

Shaking her head vehemently, Alice said, "Even if I can, I don't want to. I want to forget this mess and move on. That's it."

I sighed. "Are you sure? I'll help you in any way I can."

"I'm positive."

"What about your lock? Does Troy have a key?" A shudder whipped through me at that thought.

"Shit. Yes." Alice blinked as the implications took hold.

"Don't worry! That one's easy. We'll call for a locksmith tomorrow and get it fixed. And, until it is, we won't leave."

"Thanks, Liz."

"You feel like one of my super duper double dark chocolate cupcakes?"

"Definitely! I even have milk, which is a rarity. But Troy liked it, so I tried to keep it on hand." Alice pulled me up.

Hopefully, the spell I'd cast when baking the cupcakes would work, and quickly, too. Alice could use a little magic right now. Of course, now that I had all the facts, I could think of another batch of cupcakes I'd love to make in the near future.

Peeling the paper wrapper off mine, I asked, "Hey, Alice, what's Troy's last name?"

She popped a bite of cake into her mouth. "Bellamy. Why?"

I shrugged. "Just curious, that's all."

"How horrible!" Maddie exclaimed. "I hope Alice goes for the jugular."

"She won't, but I might. You think you can get some information on him with just his name?" Maddie and I were at the mall. I was shopping for a new skirt to replace the totaled one, and she'd come along because . . . well, because she's Maddie. Maddie loves to shop.

"Of course I can! Who do you think you're talking to? An amateur?"

Maddie also loves to snoop. With men constantly after her, she'd learned how to find almost anything out about anyone. She said she did it to ascertain that she wasn't dating any fugitives from the law. My take on it was a little different. I thought it gave her confidence to know a few basic facts. It's a harsh world out there, so more power to her.

"Hey, while we're here, maybe I should see if the salon can fit me in. I still want to color my hair," I said.

"I've been thinking about that. You shouldn't bother. Your hair looks great. Why would you want to put all those chemicals in it?"

I glanced at her. "You dye your hair."

"Not anymore. I read an article that said hair dye might cause brain cancer in lab animals. I'm tired of the upkeep, anyway. Hair, makeup, clothes—it doesn't make me happy. And it feels like a stupid rat race every morning."

A tingle of excitement teased at me. Now that she'd mentioned it, I noticed that while she did have makeup on, it wasn't the full glamorous war paint she usually wore. Plus, she had on a plain old pair of jeans and a sweater, nothing like her normal fashion-plate ensembles. And guess what? She still looked beautiful.

We continued to window shop, neither of us seemingly in the mood to actually venture into any of the stores we passed. Not so unusual for me, but for Maddie? Again, this was a different side than I'd ever seen. Interesting, and more than a little cool. I was feeling quite smug about the spell I'd cast on her. No negative side effects to be seen.

"Want to get a latte?" Maddie asked, nodding toward the Starbucks we were approaching.

"Definitely." My nose perked up at the aroma as we made our way in. After we purchased our beverages, we chose a little table near the back of the shop.

For fun, I like to people watch and guess facts about strangers. Where they live, where they work, stuff like that. Maddie and I had even made a game out of it.

My attention centered on an older couple at a table across the room from us. The woman's hair was so pristinely white it almost glowed. It was the sort of do she probably had washed and set once a week at a beauty salon, possibly the same salon she'd gone to for years.

Her partner was just as striking, but in a distinguished professor sort of way. I guessed them to be in their sixties, maybe their early seventies. I had a difficult time tearing my eyes away from the couple.

"Do you think they're married or just friends?" I asked Maddie, nodding toward them. She located the pair and tipped her head to get a better view. The man covered the woman's hand with his. She smiled tenderly and said something we couldn't hear.

"Second marriage. Six kids between them, eight grandchildren." Maddie sipped her cappuccino but kept her eyes on the couple. "No. That's not right. Eight grandchildren and a great-grandchild on the way. It's your turn now. What do you think?"

"Hmm. First marriage, four kids, three grandchildren and no great-grandchildren."

She appraised them again. "Maybe, but I'll stick with my guess. Go ask them. I did it last time." Her lips twisted into a grin.

I hated this part. I'd barely scraped my chair back when a recognizable voice hit my ears.

"Elizabeth! I hope that's a sugar-free, fat-free cap you're drinking!"

Oh my God. *Him. Here.* I twisted toward the sound of the voice and focused in on my torturer—er, trainer—as he strode over.

"Who is that? He's hot! You've been holding out," Maddie whispered. "You *will* tell me everything later, won't you?"

"Shh! He'll hear you."

Kevin reached our table and sat down in the remaining empty chair. Jeans had never, and I mean never, fit a man as well as they fit this man. Well, Nate's body was exceptional in jeans. But this man's body was made for denim. Tightly fitted, faded denim around a perfect physique.

"Hey," I said. Suddenly, I found it a little difficult to breathe.

"I'm glad I ran into you! You missed your last appointment and haven't been in since. You're not giving up already, are you? No pain, no gain!" Kevin unscrewed the top of his water bottle and took a long swallow.

What the hell? He bought bottled water at Starbucks? Wasn't that a sacrilege? The man was insane. I ignored his question and gestured to Maddie. "This is my friend Maddie. Maddie, this is Kevin, my trainer at Steel Bodies." If I knew men, and I definitely knew Maddie, she'd have him wrapped around her little finger in seconds, and I wouldn't have to comment on the missed workouts.

Of course, for once, Maddie didn't seem interested in conversing with a hot man. She just sat back in her chair, smiled at Kevin and then widened her eyes at me.

"You are coming back to the gym, right?" Kevin asked.

"I don't know. Probably. It's been a crazy week."

Leaning back in his chair, Kevin cradled his muscular arms behind his head. "I'd really like to help you meet your goals, but you have to do your part."

The man *was* insane, wearing short sleeves at the end of February. No snow, but let me tell you, it was dang cold outside. Not that I didn't appreciate the view. "I've just been really busy." I didn't like being put on the spot, no matter how cute he was.

"Busyness is no excuse for not keeping your body in tiptop shape. Tomorrow is Sunday. I'm not on the schedule, but I'll be happy to make an exception for you. What time is good?"

Maddie chuckled. "Yeah, Elizabeth, what time is good?"

Cornered, I sipped my coffee to give me a little breathing space. It's not that I didn't want to work out again. I just didn't want to do it tomorrow. My plan for Sunday involved more baking and inviting Nate over. We hadn't seen each other since the fiasco at Alice's. I definitely wanted to see him again, for more than one reason. "I don't know if I can tomorrow," I finally said.

"I guarantee your body will thank you if you do."

I was all set to say "no," but then he smiled at me, dimples and all, and my willpower took a nosedive. "If you're making a special trip for me, you can choose the time."

"Perfect! Let's get started early, and then we can go out for breakfast afterward."

"Breakfast?" Had the gym hunk asked me out on a date? Nah, no way. He was just being nice.

"You know, Lizzie, the first meal of the day, often with bacon and eggs and orange juice?" Maddie teased.

I kicked her under the table. "Breakfast sounds great. What time should I be at Steel Bodies?"

Kevin stood, and my eyes took in the length of him. The tight abs showing through his equally tight black shirt, the skin-like denim, and his long muscular legs. He really was a handsome man, in a buff bodybuilder sort of way. And even if his excitement for fitness was a little over-the-top for me, it was also a little endearing.

"Bright and early, Elizabeth! I'll see you at seven." Without waiting for a reply, he picked up his water and left as quickly as he'd arrived.

"Seven? As in, the morning?" I muttered. "On the weekend?"

"Oh my. He was flirting with you," Maddie said, a tinge of humor in her words.

"You're crazy. He was not. How is going for breakfast flirting?"

She held up a finger. "One, he is coming in on his day off to train you. Two, he damn near begged you to agree. Three, he asked you out for a meal. Four, his eyes barely flicked over me." Another grin. "Want me to continue?"

"No, but I still think you're wrong." I mean, come on, why would Mr. Perfect Steel Body be interested in me? And besides, I'd never in my life had to choose between more than one man.

But then I remembered the brownies I'd made the same night I baked cookies for Maddie. My wish for myself had seemed simple at the time. All I'd asked for was a busier social life and the opportunity to meet and date other men. Hot men. I was fairly sure I'd put that stipulation in place. Come on, I'd be stupid not to.

Of course, this happened before my experience with Nate.

Another tingle of anticipation skimmed across my skin. It made me think of the proverb, "May you live in interesting times." Most people didn't realize that was actually a curse and not a measure of goodwill. I couldn't help but wonder if I'd cursed myself. Or had I simply opened a new door, one that would lead to a bit of fun and some new experiences?

Maddie whistled. Startled, I pulled my attention back to her. "What?"

"You were in outer space somewhere. We still need to find out about our sweet older couple."

I glanced toward the table they'd been sitting at, only to find it empty. "They're gone."

As we made our way out of the mall, I thought about breakfast with Kevin. I smiled when my knees trembled.

A man who made my knees go weak—how cool was that?

Chapter Eight

Why were the tables at chain restaurants always sticky? I'd watched the waitress wash this particular table while Kevin and I were waiting to be seated, so I knew it was clean. It was just . . . sticky. And no matter how clean you knew something was, when it left some unknown residue on your skin, it seemed disgusting even if it actually wasn't.

The restaurant was busy, and the enticing scents made my stomach grumble for hot crisp bacon, scrambled eggs smothered in melted cheese, and a stack of pancakes covered in butter and strawberry syrup. That's what I wanted, but I didn't want to look like a pig in front of Kevin, especially after just sweating like one at the gym.

I figured I'd wait and see what he ordered. If he went for calorie and fat-laden food, I could do the same. My damp hair from the hastily taken post workout shower stuck to my cheek. I swiped it behind my ear. Naturally, I'd forgotten to bring a hair dryer with me that morning, so for a first date—if that's what this was, and I still had my doubts—I wasn't looking my best.

It didn't seem to bother Kevin. The morning sun cast a mystical-type glow over his features. With his golden-hued skin, he resembled a Greek god. He must have felt my eyes on him, because he looked up from his menu.

"You worked hard today, Elizabeth. If you keep it up, you'll begin to see the results soon."

"That would be nice." This exercise thing? I wasn't sure if it was going to stick. When my alarm blared at six that morning, I'd truly hated life. Even so, it turned out to not be so bad. There were very few people at the gym at that time of day, which meant I felt less like a fish out of water. "Thank you for meeting me on your day off."

"I enjoy helping my clients. And I would have been working out regardless. I wanted to see you, so it made sense to combine our workouts." His sincere tone surprised me, and my pulse ramped up a notch.

"You wanted to see me?"

Before he could answer, our waitress stopped at the table. "You guys ready to order?" She set a carafe of coffee (for me) and a pitcher of water (for Kevin) on the table.

Kevin closed his menu with a smack. "I'd just like a bowl of oatmeal and some fresh fruit with yogurt."

The waitress looked at me. I hesitated a beat. I wasn't a fan of oatmeal, but because my entire plan rested on whatever Kevin ordered, I said, "I'll have the same." Silly, really, that I wasn't confident enough to order whatever I wanted. But there you have it.

The waitress nodded and stuck her pen in her apron. "Got it. Shouldn't be long."

After she walked off, I poured myself a cup of coffee. Wrapping my hands around the hot mug, I inhaled the aroma. Life-affirming stuff, let me tell you.

"Coffee is dehydrating. You should compensate for your workout by filling your body with water," Kevin said, obviously not feeling the love for the bean.

"I drink water all day," I fibbed. "But I can't give up my coffee. I'd rather dehydrate."

"No, you wouldn't. Dehydration causes headaches, for one. And it's not healthy, for two. If that's not enough for you, the more water you drink, the better you'll feel."

"You won't change my mind about the coffee, Kevin."

Perfectly straight white teeth gleamed at me as he smiled. "Don't say I didn't warn you."

"Deal." Gathering my courage, I brought the conversation back to where it had left off. "So . . . you were saying you wanted to see me?"

He nodded, and my heart warmed. I wasn't used to spending time with such hunky men. Well, let me clarify—with such hunky *straight* men. Especially ones who looked like they'd stepped right out of a magazine. Now, it seemed they were falling out of the sky. I started to hum a few bars of "It's Raining Men," but when Kevin gave me a strange look, I bit my lip and stopped. Crazy should probably wait for date two, at least. I didn't want to scare the guy off.

"Tell me about yourself, Elizabeth."

Ugh. There was that question again. First from Nate a few weeks ago and now from Kevin. I hated this particular question, because I never really knew what to say. Did I tell the truth, which for the most part was boring, or did I make stuff up, which was lying, but at least I'd be interesting? "What do you want to know?" I finally asked.

"What makes Elizabeth Stevens tick? I haven't been able to figure you out. Most of the women I train talk nonstop. You're so quiet, I always wonder what you're thinking. It's mysterious."

I almost choked on my coffee. Out-of-breath-so-I-couldn't-talk was "mysterious" to Adonis. Good to know. I filed the information away for future reference. For the next time I wanted to be mysterious. "Well—you know, I figure I'm there to learn from you. Not talk your car off."

"I like that. It shows me you're serious. I'm glad you came today. I missed you. I thought you'd given up."

"I couldn't make it in. I had some family problems to deal with," I murmured. My mind was still stuck on the fact he'd missed me. *Me. Elizabeth Stevens.* I began to look at Kevin in a different light. Also, because I hadn't seen Nate since the incident at my sister's, I wasn't sure what was going on there. He'd shown up and comforted me in a scary situation, which was cool. And that had kept my worries at bay for a while. But now I was beginning to wonder—and yeah, worry.

I probably needed to bake some more muffins. Knowing my luck, gypsy magic came with some sort of expiration date I didn't know about.

But at that moment, right in front of me, sat a guy who

definitely seemed interested. My radar could have been off, but I didn't think so. Not with the attention he'd been giving me all morning. In fact, if I was honest, I could get used to that sort of treatment. In a heartbeat.

"You still haven't revealed anything about yourself. What do you like to do?" His eyes told me he was being truthful; he really wanted to know. "Elizabeth?" he prodded.

My brain blanked out. I tried to think of something interesting to say, something that would make me out to be more than a divorcée with too much time on her hands. When nothing else came to mind, I said, "I watch a lot of television and I'm into crafts."

Oh My God. Could you get more boring?

"Cool," Kevin said. "Anything else?"

Anything else? I needed to say something. Fast. Something desirable. Something he wouldn't expect to hear. My mind flashed through various topics, disposing of them as quickly as I thought of them. I latched on to the first semi-interesting one that came to me. "I also collect sex toys," I blurted.

Apparently, my voice was louder than I'd expected, because at least four tables of people turned to stare at me. Heat suffused my face. I scooted down in my booth. I wanted to disappear. And then, a bit too late, I remembered the *quiet-equals-mysterious* lesson. I should have just shook my head and smiled serenely.

A glance at Kevin told me all I needed to know. His tawny face had lightened a few shades. It appeared I'd shocked him, and not in a good way. "Um . . . well, that's nice," he said.

Great. Probably, he thought I was a sex-starved maniac. Or a pervert. "I don't really collect them," I murmured. "I just have a few."

He didn't say anything. After a sip of his water, a bit of color returned to his complexion. The air between us had changed and, suddenly, I was ready to go home. The waitress appeared, bless her heart.

"Here you go." Setting the food down, she said, "Enjoy! Let me know if you need anything else."

A moist blob of gooey beige cereal sat in front of me. At

least the waitress had also brought brown sugar and butter. Fat and sugar might make the liquid cement edible. And honestly, I needed to put something in my mouth other than my foot.

After I doctored my cereal, I pushed it around with my spoon. I wanted to put things back on an even-keel. Looking up, I said, "I'm sorry about that."

He ate a spoonful of oatmeal before answering. When he did, his voice was calm. "Intimacy is unique for each person. I guess it just surprised me. Let's just move on, okay?"

"That would be terrific." Probably, the timing was off. I mean, if we were alone, he'd probably like the sex toy idea a lot more. As far as I knew, most men were into a little creativity in the bedroom. At least that's what I'd heard.

I swallowed a bite of the now-too-sweet cereal and then asked, "Why did you decide to become a physical fitness trainer?" Being the asker of the questions was much better. It made it easier to breathe. Not to mention I was way less likely to make a fool out of myself.

"Nothing remarkable. I've always been into sports, and I like exercising. I also like to help people reach their dreams." He shrugged. "It's a good career for me, because I can do both."

"Wow. That's great. I kind of feel the same when I'm baking a wedding cake. It's the start of someone's marriage, and I get to be a small part of it." I was talking too fast. I inhaled a breath to calm myself.

"My brother is getting married soon. I wish I'd known you when they were planning their wedding, I'd have set you up."

"Have you ever been married?" I asked.

"Not yet. Came close once. But let's not talk about past relationships. I do have a question for you, though."

"Ask away."

"What are you doing next weekend?"

I didn't have plans, but I didn't want to go to the gym again at the crack of dawn on my one day off, so I answered carefully. "Other than working, I'm not sure. Why?"

"I have tickets to Blue Man Group on Saturday night. Would you like to go with me?"

And then I realized. He was asking me out on a date. An honest-to-goodness, real, go-out-on-the-town sort of date. Trembles poured down my spine like warm water. How many years had it been since I went out on a date? So long ago, I couldn't even remember, that's how long. "Sounds like fun," I said before I talked myself out of it. *A real date.*

"Good! We can grab some dinner first. Do you like seafood?"

I think I nodded. Anticipation strummed over me as I tried to plan what I would wear. I might even go shopping again. I'd eaten half of my oatmeal before I realized it. Funny how the sweetness of the moment made something as unappealing as oatmeal taste good. Hesitantly, I smiled at Kevin.

A date! I couldn't wait to call Maddie. She'd been pushing me to go out for months, so I knew she'd be thrilled. Plus, she'd help me figure out my wardrobe and makeup and everything.

This magic stuff was working better than I'd expected!

Today was turning out to be a really bad day. Alice had called in tears once already because of Troy. The enchanted cupcakes had seemed to even her out for a few days, but now she was just as upset as before. I wondered if the effects were ever permanent or if I'd continually be baking to keep a spell alive. *Mental note to self—check with Grandma Verda on that.* Though, on the good news front, it didn't appear as if my magic had hurt her, either.

Also, Jon's mood was far from bright and sunny, and I was mostly just trying to stay out of his way. On top of all that, I couldn't seem to get a hold of Maddie. Not at work, not on her cell, and not at home. I figured she was home, because whenever I called her, all I got was a busy signal. Which was odd, because as far as I knew she had call-waiting. If nothing else, I'd see her tomorrow for our normal Wednesday lunch, but I really wanted to talk to her today.

And I still hadn't seen Nate. I knew it shouldn't bother

me. I had a date with another man that weekend. But come on, Nate was the first guy to—well, to be blunt—make me come in forever. Plus, something about him had dug into my heart.

I felt a little weird about going out with Kevin while I had these unknown feelings for Nate, but it wasn't as if we were committed or anything. Like I said, I hadn't seen the guy since that afternoon at Alice's. Over a week ago. And that amazing night? Almost two weeks had passed. And yeah, I had to wonder if whatever interest he'd had in me had disappeared.

I hoped not. Probably, he was working ridiculous hours. Or maybe I just wished that. Because part of me worried that he thought my family was a bunch of lunatics, that with my gene pool he was better off staying away. Who could blame him? Between Grandma Verda and the encounter at Alice's, it made perfect sense to me. That didn't stop me from hoping I was wrong. I wanted to see him again.

"Did you place the order for fondant? We're almost out," Jon said, entering the kitchen.

"No, but I can place it today and express it."

His lips turned downward into a pout. "With what we'll pay, we may as well pick it up locally. Can you do that tomorrow before coming in?"

"Sure." After all, it *was* my fault. But it meant driving clear across town during morning rush-hour traffic. Not exactly the best way to start any day.

"Thanks. Just pick up enough to get us by, and I'll go place a normal order now. Say, two weeks' worth."

Nodding, I turned back to my batter bowl. No wedding cakes to bake, but I did have two birthday cakes and one baby shower cake to get out of the oven before I left.

"Lizzie?"

Now what? "Yeah, Jon?"

"Andy's going out of town this weekend on business. Want to share a movie and a pizza or something?"

A nuance in his voice compelled me to turn around and face him. "I can't on Saturday. Friday sounds good, though."

"Oh." Another pout. So unlike Jon. "Well, okay then. Maybe I'll see if Maddie wants to get together on Saturday."

Something was definitely off. "Are you all right?"

"I'm fine. Just didn't feel like spending the weekend alone. After we're done here on Saturday, I'll be at loose ends."

He said he was fine, but he wasn't. Jon's expression gave it away. The sadness in his eyes, the set of his shoulders . . . Trouble in paradise, maybe?

"What's going on?" I whispered.

He straightened his shoulders. "You know me too well, Lizzie."

I wiped my hands on a towel and went to give him a hug. He pulled me closer to him, and we stood that way for a minute. Then, leaning down, he gave me a kiss. This wouldn't be unusual, we kissed each other often. You know, not so much a kiss as a peck. This kiss, though, was different. Fluttery and soft, he held it a smidge longer than a friendly kiss dictated.

When he pulled back, he appeared startled, and then he grinned again. "Have I ever told you how adorable you look with your hair up?"

I shook my head. My hand went to my lips. "That kiss had a little more heat in it than I'm used to."

"Just a kiss for an enticing woman."

I didn't know if he was trying to avoid the conversation or if he really had no clue, but regardless, I decided to play along. But then, the magical brownies whipped into my thoughts. Hell. Is that what this was about? I never thought my wish would affect Jon. Grandma Verda had said the magic could be unpredictable, and this was certainly that.

Probably, I was overreacting. But if I wasn't, I'd have to do something to fix it. I'd think about it later. To get back on topic, I said, "I can change plans for Saturday."

His baby-blues lit up for a second. "Really?"

"Yep. If you want." My heart plummeted. Of course I'd be there for him. He'd been there for me over the past year repeatedly. But that didn't mean I wouldn't be disappointed.

"What were you doing on Saturday?"

"Oh, not much. Going out for dinner and to see Blue Man Group with a friend."

"As in a date? Or as in really just friends?"

Now who knew who too well? "It's cool, Jon."

A spark of a grin. "A date, huh? No, you keep your date. It's about time you went out and did something fun. I'll be able to occupy myself. We're still on for Friday, right? I can pick you up. I know you hate driving at night."

I probably should have argued with him, but damn, I really wanted to go out with Kevin. So, I took the chicken's way out and went with it. "Yeah, we could go see the new Willis flick." Jon adored Bruce Willis, if you get my gist. If that didn't brighten him up, nothing I knew how to do would.

A real smile and a chuckle. Yay me for being smart.

"I would love that."

"Cool! It's a plan."

Jon left, and my mind went back to the weight on his shoulders and the sadness in his gaze. I ran through all the possibilities and could only come up with one scenario that made sense. He and Andy were having problems. Of what sort and how badly, I had no idea. But I'd find out, and when I did, maybe I'd be able to help.

Glancing at the clock, I groaned. It seemed the day would never end, and I really wanted it to. I'd decided to stop by Maddie's after work to see if she'd discovered anything about Alice's jerk of an ex. I'd had an inspiration. One I definitely wanted to play with.

I couldn't think about it now. After all, Troy wouldn't be at any of the events these cakes were meant for. In thinking about the magic, I'd kind of deduced it might be best to conserve my energy. That way, when I used the magic it might be more powerful, stick around for longer, and give me better—and quicker—results. Thus far, I hadn't seen anything miraculous, other than that very first wish. You know, the one where I cursed Marc on his wedding night? My emotions that day were about as strong as they could get. Somehow, I knew that meant something. Besides discerning what it meant, I also needed to learn how to use that *something* to my advantage.

I forced myself to get back to work. Once the cakes were in the ovens, I cleaned up and then made my way to the office. Jon was seated at his desk with a pile of mail in front of him.

"Anything interesting? Or just more bills?" I asked, settling myself at my desk.

He didn't look at me at first, just fiddled with the letter he held. When he finally turned, a quiver of apprehension slid into me. Jon rarely got angry. Or if he did, he kept it to himself. So when I saw anger in his eyes, I knew something was up. And I knew I wasn't going to like it. "What is it?"

"You should read for yourself," he said, passing the letter on to me.

I skimmed the words quickly. Perspiration bubbled on my forehead. I read it again, slower this time. The letter was from Marc.

About a year before our separation, A Taste of Magic was experiencing some growing pains after its first year of business. Jon and I were going to take out a bank loan to help us get by. Marc had offered to loan us the money instead.

I'd liked the idea, because it was the first time Marc had ever shown any interest in the bakery. And the thought of keeping it in the family appealed to me. Jon, on the other hand, hadn't liked the idea. The only way Jon would agree was if we made it an official loan and not just a personal one from husband to wife. I got that. I mean, Jon was an equal partner in the business, so he wanted the loan terms spelled out clearly—and legally.

Papers were drawn up. Everything looked good, so we signed them, and we'd been paying Marc back ever since. The one caveat, which hadn't been an issue until now, was the loan made Marc a partner, albeit a silent one. Now it seemed he wanted to take on a more active role in running the bakery. In the letter, he stated it was to "protect his interest in the face of diminishing profits."

"Bullshit. He can't do this, can he?" I asked Jon.

"He can. At least until we pay the loan off. I wasn't worried about it when we signed the papers, because you two had been together for so long. I didn't see it as an issue." The light of anger I'd seen earlier deepened. "But now, I think it's his way of screwing with you. It hasn't been a great year, but it hasn't been horrible, either. Certainly not enough to instigate this."

"I'll talk to him. Maybe I can change his mind." The last thing I wanted—or needed—was Marc in my life. In any way. And yes, that most definitely included my business. The shock began to wear off. In its place, a tight wave of fury rode in. How dare he? I mean, really, who the hell did he think he was?

"Let's just take out a new loan and pay him off." We'd end up with a higher interest rate, but at least Marc wouldn't have any say over A Taste of Magic.

Jon shook his head. "We tried to do that last year, right after you and Marc separated. Remember? Things are tighter now, so if we couldn't get what we needed then, it's highly unlikely we will now. At least, not with terms we can realistically pay back."

Yeah, that was the problem. We were barely staying afloat as it was. "I'll talk to him," I said again. Probably, it wouldn't work, but it was worth a try.

And if that didn't do it, well, there was always magic.

I knocked on Maddie's door and tried to put my worries to rest. Between Marc, Alice, and Jon—not to mention Nate and Kevin—I had plenty to worry about. Hopefully, an hour with Maddie would raise my spirits. She was usually good for a few laughs.

When she opened the door, I pushed past into her apartment. "Where have you been all day? I've been trying to call you for hours."

She didn't say anything, just walked into the living room. Dressed in blue leggings and an oversized pink T-shirt, her face bare of cosmetics, she gestured for me to follow.

"Are you sick?" A bright multicolored quilt lay crumpled on the end of her couch. Discarded candy wrappers were on the floor, and a half-gallon of ice cream sat on the coffee table with a spoon sticking out of it. *Oh shit.* There was also a box of tissues and several wadded up ones strewn all around. This wasn't illness. It was heartbreak. "Problems in the new relationship already?"

"I'm fine." Maddie plopped down on the sofa and crossed her legs. She grabbed the ice cream container and swished the melted layer around with the spoon.

"If you're fine, then why are you wallowing in Kit Kat bars and"—I leaned over to read the letters on the container— "double fudge ripple mocha chunk ice cream?"

"There isn't a man in this world meant for me. That's why."

"Don't be silly. Of course there is. Did something happen with—crap, I forget his name—that has you this upset? You guys seemed to really click when we all went out."

"His name is Spencer. And yes, something happened." She dipped the spoon into the melting ice cream and licked it clean. "We were supposed to go out for dinner last night, but I didn't feel like dressing up. So I didn't. I also didn't feel like wearing makeup. So I didn't do that, either. And then Spencer got here and he thought . . ." Her voice broke off.

"He thought what?"

She slammed the ice cream container back on the table. "He thought I was sick. Wanted to stay in and take care of me. Thought we could order out and watch a movie." She sniffed. "As if I was so ugly, he couldn't bear to be seen with me in public."

"Um . . . Maddie, I'm sure he didn't mean that."

"I realize that. Now. But last night I was so hurt, I completely overreacted. And today, I can't get a hold of him. I've left several messages, but he hasn't called me back." She shivered. "I was a shrew. Seriously, Liz, he'll probably never talk to me again."

"Your phone has been busy all day," I pointed out. "Maybe he tried calling."

"It was off the hook earlier, but it's been back on for a while now."

"Oh." I sat down next to her and wrapped my arm around her shoulders. "Give him a chance. I'm sure he'll call back. And really, if he doesn't, then it's his loss."

Weak words, but what else was I supposed to say?

"It's more than Spencer. Something is wrong with me lately," Maddie whispered. "I've changed, and I can't decide if I'm happy or not."

"What do you mean?"

"I don't know how to explain it. At first, I was really content with myself."

Yes. That's exactly what I'd wished for Maddie. To be happy with herself. "That's good. Isn't it?"

She nodded, her blonde hair falling into her face. "Well, it was. Now, though, it doesn't feel real. And I'm jumpy all the time, and irritable. It's like I can't get the energy together to do anything, and part of me doesn't care. That scares me."

Oh no. Had my magic done this? My stomach twisted. Of course it had. Side effect number one was staring me in the face. "So, you're not content anymore?"

She cleared her throat. "I'm miserable, but I don't know why. I can't seem to relax."

This wasn't what I'd wanted for Maddie. I thought back to the wish I'd cast, and I couldn't figure out where I'd gone wrong. I'd have to fix it. And if my hunch was right about Jon, my fix-it list was getting longer and longer. My stomach cramped again. "It will get better. And Spencer will be fine. You'll see."

She sighed. "Don't get me wrong, because I know Marc hurt you, but I was so jealous of the two of you for so long. I think I still am. I want what you had."

My temper flashed. With everything that had happened that day, I couldn't stop it. I didn't give myself a chance to calm down. "Jealous? Of what? Being cheated on, lied to, and having my entire life screwed up because of him?" How could anyone be envious of that?

"Oh, stop. I know he was an ass there, probably for a few years. But you know as well as I do that what you two had was good for a ridiculously long time. You met in high school and never broke up. You just loved each other, and no one else could come between that."

I gasped. "Hello? Someone did—or are you forgetting Tiffany?"

She exhaled a long breath. "I love you, sweetie, but think about this. You say now you never dated anyone else, that your life was stolen by Marc. That's bullshit. And you know it."

I blinked. Tears welled behind my eyes, and I pushed them away. I would not cry. Not over this. "I don't know what you're talking about." I turned my head, so my gaze hit the wall.

"Shit, shit, shit. God, I'm sorry. That is not how I wanted that to come out."

"I should go." I aimed for the door. I didn't have any desire to hear what else she had to say. Not right now.

Maddie bolted off the couch and wrapped her arms around my waist. I stopped but didn't say anything. Couldn't say anything. Damn, this sucked—in a big way.

"Listen to me; then be mad and leave. Never talk to me again. Whatever. But you will listen to me, or I will never forgive myself." She inhaled a deep breath, and her arms tightened around my waist, as if she thought I'd run off at the first possible second. Smart girl.

"What Marc did to you was shit. You never cheated, you never thought about cheating, and he took your unconditional love and tossed it out the window. But all those years you *were* happy? Those were not wasted years. You were exactly where you wanted to be. You missed nothing. You need to see that, or you'll never move on."

I crumpled to my knees. Her arms were still around my waist, but instead of letting go, she crumpled, too. My breathing came too quick, so I settled myself before speaking. I couldn't be mad at her, not really.

"How long have you been keeping that in?" I asked.

Resting her forehead on my back, she said, "Forever."

"Is this because of Spencer? Are you lashing out because you're hurt?" That had to be it. This stuff she was saying caused way too much pain, so it couldn't be true.

"No. Yes. I don't know. It's how I've felt for a while, but maybe this thing with Spencer brought it to the surface."

"There is a man for you. Maybe it's Spencer, maybe it isn't. You'll find him, or he'll find you. You're too perfect for that not to happen." If Cupid's arrow didn't strike Maddie, I certainly didn't have much hope.

She snorted. "Perfect? I am so far from perfect it isn't even funny. I'm neurotic about my entire body. And now I've turned into a crazy person."

My tears let loose, but they mixed with laughter. "We're both a mess, aren't we?"

"Aww, Liz. Understand I'm not saying Marc isn't an ass. He is, he hurt you. That's enough to put him in the donkey department for eternity as far as I'm concerned. But please, don't trash what you once had together. Learn from it, sure. Pretend all those years were nothing but a mistake? No, don't do that. Because doing that will not help you."

"I don't know how to let go. And he isn't making it any easier." I told her about the letter from Marc and how he wanted to take a more active role in A Taste of Magic.

"Oh, sweetie, that bites. Do you think talking to him will help?"

"I don't know. I have to try. But seeing him at the bakery will make everything worse. I don't think I'll ever comprehend what went wrong." I shuddered.

"You might not. But you need to put it behind you. I miss the Liz you used to be," Maddie admitted softly.

Yeah, I missed her, too. "I have a date on Saturday," I confessed, more to change the subject than anything else. I didn't want to talk about Marc. Not now. Maybe not ever.

Standing, Maddie squealed. "The trainer guy from the mall?"

I pulled myself to my feet. "Yes. Kevin."

"That's so cool! Are you excited?"

A bud of warmth unfurled in my chest, melting the cold freeze. "I think I am."

"It'll be wonderful! This is exactly what you need." Taking her seat in the living room again, Maddie said, "Have some ice cream." Then, she wrinkled her nose at the container. "Yuck. This is gross. I wonder if I can refreeze it."

I followed her to the kitchen. Thank God we were good again. I hated fighting with Maddie. "Did you have a chance to investigate Troy?"

"Yeah, he's a jerk."

"I know he's a jerk. Did you find out anything else?"

"A little. I made some notes for you. He has his own website. It's filled with pictures of him, but other than that, there's not much there. It's like he's trolling for women or something." She put the ice cream away. "Is there anything in particular you wanted to know?"

"How to get a hold of him, for starters."

"Oh, that's easy. I have his address and his place of employment. He has both listed on his site. Not the smartest guy in the world, obviously."

My jaw dropped. "Where does he work?"

"The Brookhaven Sports Club. Isn't that where you said Alice met him?"

"Yep. He told her he lost his job; that's why he needed so much money." I shouldn't have been surprised. I'd already known this guy was trash.

"The woman who answered the phone said something strange when I asked about him. She asked if I was a member, and if I wanted to file a complaint. It seems he makes a habit of hitting on women and doesn't know when to take no for an answer."

My heart went out to my sister. She was a smart woman, but somehow she'd fallen for a loser. "Why is he still employed there?"

"No clue."

Crap. It looked like I might have to join yet another gym. I almost groaned at the thought. But then I realized I already had everything I needed. "Thank you for looking into this. I appreciate it."

"If you need any other help, let me know." She hesitated for a second. "Do you think I should try calling Spencer again?"

"Absolutely. But wait a couple of days. Give him the opportunity to call you back first." And that would, hopefully, give me the chance to fix Maddie's spell. Because this time, I really needed to get it right.

I also needed a copy of *How to Cast the Perfect Gypsy Spell*. Badly.

Chapter Nine

I slid my car into the parking lot at the grocery store and heaved a sigh of relief that I'd made it safely. I stepped out of the car, and my eyelashes froze to my eyelids instantly in the subzero temperature. Frosty white snow pummeled me as I raced toward the bright lights of Dominick's.

Yes, I was a crazy lady, rushing to the food store like everyone else because of a fast approaching late-winter storm. But hey, my cupboards were a little too bare for my comfort. Besides, how could I work the magic if I didn't have the proper baking ingredients? Exactly. I mean, what a perfect way to use a snow day. So here I was, on one of the worst days of the year, navigating the ice and snow for a box of baking chocolate and some flour. I should probably pick up some normal food, too, otherwise I wouldn't have anything to eat but brownies and cookies. On second thought, that didn't sound so bad.

The store was packed. People swarmed everywhere, and even though I was one of them, I still didn't get it. I actually needed food, but I knew there were plenty of people programmed to run to the store at the first sign of a snowflake. And all of them had chosen my store.

I wanted to hurry, but the crowd made it difficult. I was kind of hoping to see Nate later. A certain image refused to leave my mind—dinner, a movie, coffee, curling up together on the couch. Besides, I missed him. And based on the card I'd found taped to my door this morning—from Nate—he missed me, too. Plus, now I knew he hadn't been avoiding me. He'd just been stuck on the late shift. So yeah, I really hoped he'd be around that evening.

I pushed my cart fast, stopping to toss things in here and there. I didn't pay attention to the other shoppers. For one, making eye contact encouraged conversation, which I didn't want to do. For two, Chicago was so huge it wasn't likely I'd run into anyone I knew.

When the cart looked adequately full, I made my way toward the front of the store. The lines would be horrendous, and I needed to get on the roads before they became even icier. As I turned the corner out of the frozen foods section, I rammed into another cart. "I'm sorry," I mumbled, backing up so I could swerve around and continue on my way.

"Elizabeth?"

My heart stopped. I clenched the cart handle so tightly my knuckles turned white. Life so wasn't fair. Lifting my gaze, I drew in a deep breath.

"Hi, Marc."

He looked good. His dark hair hung longer than I'd remembered. It curled slightly around his cheeks, softening the harsh lines of his face. Dark brown eyes, almost black, centered on me. He wore the leather coat I'd given him on our last Christmas together. That bit in hard. Too hard. Why did he have to look so damn good?

My heart started beating again, only to crack in two all over, the pieces quickly being trampled on by grocery shoppers intent on getting by us.

"Some storm, huh?" he asked in a conversational tone, as if I were a neighbor or an old friend from college, not the ex-wife he'd cheated on and lied to. Just some acquaintance. No one special.

"Yep, some storm." I didn't have any words to say. And it didn't matter that I'd planned this moment a thousand times in my head, because now that it was happening, I had nothing.

"I'm surprised you're out in this," he said.

"I had to get some stuff. They're saying this storm could last a couple of days."

"That's why I'm here. Tiffany, well . . ." He broke off, as if he realized I wouldn't want to hear about Tiffany. I never said he wasn't smart.

"Why are you at *this* store? Your condo isn't anywhere close to here."

"We're renting it out. We bought a place not far from here just before the wedding. As it turns out, we're going to be needing the extra room." His gaze flitted away from mine. Could he possibly be uncomfortable? No, not likely. Not the amazing Marc Stevens.

"I heard about Tiffany's condition." Damn if I'd congratulate him. Sour grapes? Yep, a whole vat of them.

"You know we're having a baby?" When I didn't respond, he said, "News gets around fast."

Me and my big mouth. Now he probably thought I'd purposely searched for gossip about him and his lady love. Awesome.

"I was just thinking of you the other day," he said.

"I'm sure you were. After all, insinuating yourself into my business probably took a bit of thought, didn't it?" I snapped. Maybe it was good I'd run into him. If nothing else, it saved me a phone call.

His eyes narrowed. "That's business. A Taste of Magic isn't doing as well as it should be, and I do have a monetary interest. I just want to ensure that I don't lose any money."

Anger sizzled. "We haven't missed one payment to you. I don't want you showing up at the shop. You don't know a thing about running a bakery."

"I don't plan on learning how to bake. That's your job. I'm more interested in tightening costs and lowering your overhead. Have you thought about moving to a less expensive locale?"

"That's exactly what I'm talking about. Moving to a different locale would hurt business even more. The clientele we serve expect a certain address. And none of that matters. We agreed that you'd stay out of the running of A Taste of Magic. I expect you to live up to that agreement." Wow. I couldn't believe I'd said everything I was thinking for once.

"Sorry, I can't do that. Business is business. If you don't want me involved, then pay off the loan. It's that simple." Marc sighed. "I don't want to argue with you. I've been thinking about you lately, and not because of that damn bakery."

"Why? What could you possibly have to think about now?" The walls of the store closed in on me. I pulled at my coat and tried to take in another deep breath to push the sudden nausea away. Jon and I were going to have to find a way to pay Marc off. Fast.

"Remember those long talks we used to have before everything went crazy?"

I quickly looked to the side, so he couldn't see my face. All my anger receded, replaced with a pull of longing so strong I gripped the cart even tighter. I'd fallen in love with Marc during one of those long talks. Sure, we were thirteen at the time, but it could have been yesterday. Nice of him to remind me.

"I miss them. We had some great conversations over the years, Betty."

And that quickly, the anger was back. *Betty*. Just a name, right? Hearing it was like fingernails on a chalkboard. Marc was the only person who'd ever called me Betty. I used to like it. "Don't call me that. I hate it."

His jaw opened, and then he snapped it back shut as if I'd hurt him. Me, hurt him? Did he not remember the last conversation we'd had? The one where he told me I'd made his life incredibly unhappy? The one in which he very bluntly announced that he considered our entire marriage a mistake? "I should go," I mumbled.

"Wait." He grabbed my wrist tightly. He wasn't hurting me. He was just making sure I didn't take off before he finished with me. A favorite tactic of his. One I'd actually forgotten about, which kind of surprised me.

"I was thinking about calling you and setting up a time to get together for lunch. It would be nice to be friends again, don't you think?"

I twisted my wrist until he let go, and then I looked him straight in the eyes. This wasn't easy for me, but I managed it. "Are you insane? We can't be friends."

He shook his head as if he were exasperated with me. "I know the divorce was hard, but it's been over a year since we separated. You should be over it." He reached out to touch me. I stepped back so he couldn't.

"This isn't about the divorce." Okay, so maybe it was—partly, anyway, but it was also about my business.

"Betty, we started out as friends. I know you miss me. Don't try to tell me you don't. I know you better than that. I know you better than anyone." While his voice remained calm, the tone of it was oozy as slime.

He may as well have punched me in the gut. Before I could answer, he pulled his cell phone out of his pocket. Realizing he had a phone call, I relaxed. Saved by the bell. Thank God, because I had no clue what I was going to say to that.

My stomach threatened to revolt, and while throwing up on Marc certainly held some appeal, I far preferred to keep my cookies where they belonged. Another wave of nausea had me digging in my purse for a mint.

"No, I'm almost done here. Chocolate ice cream? Yeah, I can grab some," Marc said into the phone. He turned his body slightly away and murmured, "I love you, too." Once he'd replaced it, he faced me again. "Come on, Betty, one more chance at a friendship. What do you say?"

The longing to agree pulled at me. How stupid could I be? If I didn't get out of there immediately, that whole vomit thing might seriously occur. "Don't call me Betty. Oh, and by the way, I don't miss you at all. You don't know me nearly as well as you think you do. Good-bye, Marc," I said, in a giant rush of immature syllables. Hopefully, they made sense. If not, too freaking bad.

Without looking back, I pushed the cart away and got out of the store as fast as possible. He had the decency not to follow.

I loaded the groceries into my backseat as threads of sour emotion gnawed at me. Once in the car, I rested my forehead on the steering wheel, waiting for the car to heat up. I was proud of myself for telling Marc I didn't miss him, and I was proud I'd walked away.

Of course, I'd flat-out lied. While I didn't miss being his wife any longer, I did miss his friendship. At least, the friendship we'd had when we were truly in love. When we were partners. The two, for me, were inexorably combined. And even I knew that no amount of magic could ever bring that back to me again. Though maybe, just maybe, magic might help me end this once and for all.

What did I want more? Payback for the hellish way Marc treated me, or release from the pain merely thinking about him caused? Maybe I could get both. Maybe I couldn't. Maybe I'd have to choose one or the other. Or maybe I was just screwed. I'd have to think long and hard about that.

With a sigh, I put my car in gear and slowly backed out of the lot. Suddenly, the only thing I wanted for the night was a hot bath and my bed.

Two hours later I curled up on the couch with a quilt, a book, and a hot cup of cocoa. The incident with Marc remained fresh in my mind, so much so concentrating on the book proved difficult. Hell, who was I fooling? It was impossible. I snapped the book shut. Part of me thought I'd been a coward for running off the way I had, but how else was I supposed to act? Dealing with Marc, and my feelings about him—and our divorce—hadn't been easy to begin with; now, that difficulty reached an entirely new level.

I needed to do something. I thought about baking something new for Maddie, so maybe I could fix whatever I'd done wrong. But doing so in the mood I was in scared me. What if I was right and the emotions I felt could alter the spell I was trying to cast? That wouldn't be good. I could make everything even worse for her. Sharp fear turned my stomach. No, I decided, better to wait one more day and give it a go tomorrow, after a good night's sleep.

Sudden knocking on my door dragged me from my

musings. A quick glance through the peephole showed Nate and Sam in the hallway. Surprised, I unlocked the chain and opened the door wide.

Nate smiled, and my heart reconnected. It was as simple as that. He wore black jeans that had been washed so many times they were almost gray, along with a black turtleneck. I loved turtlenecks on men. I found it an incredibly sexy look. "Hey, what are you guys up to?"

"Sam's mom is in Ohio for a few days, so he's stuck with me. We were supposed to go to the movies tonight, but the snow ruined our plans," Nate said, hand on his nephew's head.

"We were gonna see a lame movie anyway. I'm too old for Disney," Sam said. Kinda funny, as the boy was wearing blue sweatpants and a *Pirates of the Caribbean* T-shirt. Disney á la Johnny Depp.

"You're never too old for Disney. Why don't you guys come on in? I just made some cocoa." I motioned for them to follow. "I don't have any coffee made, but if you want some, I can start a pot."

"Cocoa's fine. Do you have marshmallows?" Nate asked.

"Of course I do. Who drinks cocoa without marshmallows?"

"Ah, a woman after my own heart. That sounds great. I hope you don't mind us barging in on you. Sam was going a little stir crazy, and I thought a visit might help." Nate ruffled Sam's hair as he spoke. Then, his eyes met mine. "And I wanted to see you."

"I wanted to see you, too." A whisper of happiness settled around me.

"What's 'stir crazy,' Uncle Nate?" Sam asked.

Nate knelt down so he was eye level with his nephew. "You being bored out of your mind. And me, with nothing to occupy you. Which made both of us a little nuts."

"I told you, we should have brought my PlayStation. Then I wouldn't be driving you nuts. You should really listen to me. I'm a pretty smart kid."

Nate chuckled. "Oh, I know you're smart, kiddo. But your

mother likes the fact I don't have a PlayStation. It forces you to actually talk to me."

I loved watching man and boy interact. It made my heart go mushy. Nate seemed really good with kids—definitely a plus in my book.

Sam stuck his bottom lip out. "But it's boring!" Turning to me, he said, "Do you have a PlayStation?"

I laughed. I couldn't help it; he sounded so hopeful. "Sorry, Sam. No dice on the PlayStation. But maybe I can dig up a couple of board games to play. Will that interest you?"

"What do you think, Sam? Sound like fun?" Nate winked at Sam.

The boy scrunched up his face. "I guess so. What do you have?"

"Do you know how to play Monopoly? Or Sorry!? I know I have those." My heart zinged, and little flutters of excitement bounced around inside of me. I'd hoped to see Nate that evening, and here he was. Sure, not how I'd imagined it, but I'd take what I could get.

"Anything will be fine, Liz," Nate said, squeezing my hand. Such a simple touch, but it sent electrifying tingles over my skin. "Thanks for saving me," he whispered. "I didn't know how else to entertain him."

I wanted to tell him he and Sam were saving me as much as I was saving them. For some reason, though, I didn't. "I'll go grab a few games, and we'll see how it goes. Help yourself to some cookies, if you want. They're in the cupboard next to the refrigerator."

"Home-baked?" Nate asked with a grin.

Ha. If he only knew how dangerous it was asking me for anything home-baked. "Just Oreos, but I plan on baking tomorrow. I'll save you something."

After I returned with the games, we set up at the kitchen table. Over hot cocoa and Oreos, we battled out a game of Monopoly and then moved on to Sorry!, and all the while, I tried to think of something witty to say to Nate. Something flirtatious. Seeing as my last attempt (at the restaurant with Kevin) hadn't gone that well, I was more than a little gun-shy.

And I wanted to talk about *that* night. You know, that amazing moment on my couch? Yep, that one. But not only couldn't I bring it up around Sam, I wasn't sure how I would, even if I could. It bothered me, just a little, that we hadn't discussed what had happened between us. Did it mean something bad because we hadn't? Or was I just worrying too much? I didn't know.

Settling on a safe subject, I asked, "Why is your sister in Ohio?"

"Business. She was supposed to come home today, but her flight was canceled."

"What kind of business?"

"She's an attorney. Her firm has a branch in Columbus, so she's out there once a month or so."

We continued to chat while we played. I learned about Sam's school and that he was a sports buff, just like his uncle. The hours passed pleasantly, and before I knew it, Sam was yawning.

"I'm tired of this. Can I go watch TV?" he asked.

Stretching my back, I glanced at Nate. I hoped he wouldn't suggest they leave. I wasn't ready to say good night. Besides, I really wanted a kiss. I didn't know if that would happen with Sam in the room, but that didn't stop me from hoping.

Nate stood and then stretched his arms over his head. "Actually, it's past your bedtime." Turning to me, he said, "We should probably leave. But we'll help you pick up first."

I tried not to be disappointed. After all, it *was* late. But, dang it, I really wanted to spend more time with Nate.

After the game was put back together, I said, "Let me put these away and then I'll walk you to the door." Maybe, if I was really lucky, I'd get a good night kiss.

In my bedroom, I had just slid the games back on the shelf, when a pair of warm hands encircled my waist. "I wanted a moment alone with you," Nate whispered into my ear.

A shot of longing licked its way through me. Pivoting,

I reached my arms around Nate's neck. "I'm glad. I wanted to be alone with you, too." And then, his lips met mine, and everything else melted away. Everything I felt the first time we kissed came back in a rush. My body responded instantly, and again, all I wanted was Nate. "Where's Sam?" I mumbled.

"Watching television. He'll be fine for a few minutes." Nate stepped backward, pulling me with him. We landed on the bed, and his arms tightened around me. "I've really missed you. Did you get my card?"

"I did. Thank you for that. I was beginning to worry."

"About what?"

"Oh, I don't know." Suddenly, I felt extraordinarily shy. "What happened between us? That's not normal for me, so I guess I worried that—well—that it was for you."

"Normal? Not at all. I'm not sure what came over me that night, but I haven't been able to stop thinking about you. I'm sorry I haven't been around much."

"It's okay." But was it? I should have felt relieved that what we'd experienced wasn't the norm for him, but I didn't. I mean, I'd wanted to hear that. But now? My mind centered, once again, on the banana muffins and the brownies. On the magic. How would I ever know what was real and what wasn't?

He stroked my back. "I should probably take Sam home. I had fun tonight," he said, his attention focused completely on me.

I pushed my misgivings aside. Whatever was going on, I was enjoying it, and that's what mattered, right? Right. Better to just go with it. For now, anyway.

I stood up and then pulled Nate to his feet. He lowered his head, and I ran my tongue over his lips before we settled into another kiss. The taste of him was intoxicating. Each kiss left me wanting more. More than that, I wanted him to stay. I wanted to see where this could lead, and more than anything else, I wanted him to keep touching me. Unfortunately, the kiss ended too soon.

"I really should go. Before Sam runs in here to see what's

taking so long." Nate ran his finger along my cheek, the touch soft and gentle. Reluctance shimmered over his face, and the fact it did made me smile. "I'd love to stay."

"Maybe another time," I said.

We left the bedroom together, and Nate roused Sam from the couch. After they left, I locked up and leaned against the wall, waiting for the buzz in my body to recede. I brushed my fingers along my cheek, thinking of Nate's touch. My skin felt hot, flushed. Everything with Nate was a new experience for me, and I was enjoying every minute of it.

But, even so, I was sort of let down. Maybe it was my worries about the magic, or maybe it was the way the evening ended, because I certainly hadn't wanted it to end. As I thought about it more, I realized it probably had little to do with Nate and far more to do with Marc. Bumping into him at the store still sat inside me, swirling around like nervous energy I couldn't dispose of.

Meandering back into the kitchen for something cool to drink, I opened the freezer to get some ice. There I saw it, huddled innocently between a frozen pizza and a half-gallon of ice cream. I thought I'd buried it farther back than that, but there it was, front and center. Taunting me. Daring me to pick it up.

My chest tightened as I grabbed the Ziploc bag. Ripping the top open, I took out the foil-covered, decade-old, hard-as-a-rock slice of wedding cake. I held it for a few minutes. How could something so innocuous create such ridiculous emotions?

Without thinking, I put it to my cheek and closed my eyes. My arm became as frozen as the cake I held. Unable to do anything, I sank deeper and deeper, my mind numbing, almost as if the frozen cake had touched it. I tried to let go, but my hand remained clenched tight.

And then, my world flashed, turned upside down, and changed. Magic, I guess. My mind went blank, and everything became fuzzy and hazy. When it sharpened again, I was standing next to Marc at our reception, slicing into our wedding cake, smearing it on each other's faces. Remembered joy of the day flew back at me as if it were yesterday. Every emotion, every hope, every dream cascaded through me like a waterfall. I wasn't particularly afraid, just a little disoriented, a little out of whack. Dizzy, I stepped backward blindly.

Jazzy music played in the background. Tight, two-inch heels pinched my feet, and my dress swished around my legs. The imagined taste of the buttercream icing filled my mouth, the sweetness of it almost making me gag.

Joy at being Mrs. Marcus Stevens whooshed over me, just as it had on that long ago day. My future loomed bright and sure ahead of me. I felt it. I saw it. Right there. My heart overflowing with love, I reached out to touch Marc, only to find myself separated from my ghost self. I couldn't touch him, couldn't do anything but watch. It seemed I was nothing but a spectator.

My head pounded. My legs started to shake. I sank to the floor. Gripping the cake tighter, I tried to make sense of it all, tried to breathe normally. In. Out. In. Out. It didn't work. Whatever this was, it kept on, and finally, I just gave in.

The pressure of Marc's phantom arms tightened around my waist as we danced. The touch of his lips floated over mine, so close I'd have sworn he was standing in the kitchen kissing me. The sound of applause from our guests filled my ears. Everything just as it once was came alive inside of me, in front of me, all around me.

Frankly, it pissed me off.

No longer feeling the love, I wanted to walk up to this prior me and shake her. I wanted to tell her to get out and run away fast. I wanted to warn her that this man, her husband, was going to deceive her, lie to her, and hurt her beyond comprehension. I wanted to take the fairy-tale glaze out of her eyes and shove reality in its place. I wanted her to know. God help me, I just wanted her—*me*—to know.

My chest grew heavier, and I fought to end this. To stop it before I lost my mind. Again, the urge to yell and scream at the long ago bride overcame me.

The thing is—I knew better. My prior self would have

laughed at such comments. That other Elizabeth loved Marc so fully, so completely, that even if she'd been warned, she wouldn't, couldn't, have believed it.

"Help me," I sobbed. "Make this stop."

I needed to turn away. I knew this, but there was this gaping hole in me I can't explain. It grew and grew and, as it did, all the pain from the last year overwhelmed me, almost crushing me with its power.

Then, as clear as a bell, a voice spoke inside my mind, cutting through the images like a razor sharp knife. Female, soft, but with an edge, this voice said, "Elizabeth, let go. Just let go."

Tears trailing down my face, I stood, replaced the cake in the freezer, and stumbled to my bedroom in a haze.

I curled up on my bed and cried. When I finally stopped, I held my pillow tight to my chest. Staring at the wall, I forced my mind to remain empty. Not only didn't I comprehend what had just happened, I wasn't sure I even wanted to know.

The snow still billowed, fell, and blew outside. It was early, as sleep had continually evaded me throughout the night. I sipped my coffee, enjoying the punch of caffeine and heat. Last night had weirded me out. Actually, pretty much the entire whole of the previous day was a freaking mess better off forgotten. Well, except for my time with Nate.

I washed my hands and then reread the new magic list I'd written. This time, I tried to be even more exact in what I wanted to accomplish; I didn't want to make any more mistakes. Also, the fact that Grandma Verda had never been able to reverse the spell she'd cast on my grandfather scared me. What if I couldn't fix my mistakes? What if whatever I did lasted forever and that was that?

Because of this worry, I'd been trying to figure out the gypsy magic thing, what made it work and what didn't. I guessed I needed a lot of emotion and energy to get the desired results. I already knew the specific words and phrasing I used were also important. But, really, the only spell I'd cast that had the exact effect I'd wanted was Marc's limp dick, which was a complete accident. A fun one, but an accident nonetheless.

My mixer was plugged in, ready to rumble, with plenty of Post-it notes stuck to the mixing bowls stacked to the side. Six mini cake pans were greased and floured and resting on the surface of my kitchen table.

Into each of the six bowls, I dumped all the dry ingredients for each individual cake and then followed up with the wet ingredients. Not the best way, but for my purposes it would work just fine.

Time to play.

I set the first bowl on the mixer and then slowly beat the ingredients together. With a heavy swallow, I focused on my list, closed my eyes, and said, "Marc, you continually choose to hurt me, first in the way you ended our marriage, and now in trying to interfere with my business." My voice broke as the words left my mouth. Everything from the day before kicked in heavy and hard.

"My wish for you, Marc, is to experience deep and intense regret over your actions toward me, to stop interfering in A Taste of Magic, and for you to realize that the way you ended our marriage was wrong. Until you come to me and apologize for the miserable way you've treated me, you will find no relief from this turmoil."

The magic wrapped itself around me like a tight-fitting glove, comforting me in its weave. Just as before, lights danced and electricity zinged. All my thoughts centered on Marc until the dance of magic faded. I tipped the beaters back and moved the bowl to the side.

When bowl number two was in place, I said, "Troy, you've stolen money from my sister. My wish for you is to pay her back every cent you sweet-talked out of her. It will be a compulsion you can't ignore, and it will twist and turn in your belly like acid until you return the money to Alice." As soon as I said the words, the magic was back, stronger than before.

I let the tide of power ride over me until the light hit the batter. With the third bowl, I steadied myself before speaking. When ready, I said, "Maddie, you're a beautiful woman, inside and out. My wish for you is to find true happiness in yourself, however you want that to be, in the ways that truly sing to your heart and make you shine."

My kitchen became a kaleidoscope of colors swirling around me as if I were lost in a rainbow. Tingles sped up my arms, through my hands, and then to the bowl. This time, I didn't wait for the light show to end. I grabbed the fourth bowl, and put it in place.

"Alice, you will find peace in your heart and the greatest love of your life. This is my wish for you."

I took a deep breath. Tried to refocus. My apartment looked like a disco room; colors zapped everywhere, bouncing off the fixtures, the ceiling, and the walls. So much so, my eyes hurt from the vividness, the brightness of it. Switching bowls, I noticed my arms trembling from the power, from the energy.

"Jon, I can tell you're confused by something going on in your life. My wish for you is to discover what it is you are unsure of and to take the steps you need to fix it without being afraid but still remaining true to yourself and who you really are."

I grabbed the last bowl and tried to see past the dizziness enveloping me. Maybe this wasn't such a great idea, doing them all at once. My body was overflowing with energy, and I sort of worried I might have a heart attack or something. But I wasn't able to stop. The magic pulled at me, beckoned me to continue. I breathed in a mouthful of air and allowed my wish to flow through me. I wanted to feel it before I spoke.

Tipping my head back, I watched the colors bop around on the ceiling. "This wish is for me. My wish is to find the path that will lead me to forgiveness, to being able to truly let go of the past, and to find whatever I need to really move on with my life."

Instantly, the intensity of the swirling colors magnified. A surge of energy ripped through my body with such strength, such power, that I let go of the mixer and stumbled backward.

I closed my eyes and raised my arms as the magic thrashed through me. "I will be happy!" I yelled, lost in the strength of the moment. Wind swept through my hair, making it whip around my face, slashing at my skin. Yep—wind, in my freaking apartment. I kept my eyes closed as the power slowly bled out of my body.

"Excellent, Elizabeth. I'm impressed," a woman's voice, the same voice from the previous night, whispered in my ear. Yeah. In my ear. Her breath blew warm on my cheek, I swear. And then, I smelled flowers—everywhere. Opening my eyes, I fully expected to see the owner of this voice (Miranda, possibly?) standing in my kitchen. Only, no one was there. "Hello?"

No response.

Maybe if I closed my eyes again? What the hell, may as well try. "Hello?" I repeated.

No answer, but the scent of roses remained.

Shivers of apprehension tickled my skin. *The Twilight Zone* was back, and I wasn't sure how to handle it. I grabbed the phone. I needed to talk to Grandma Verda. Like, right this instant. Or, really, like yesterday. She didn't tell me Miranda paid personal visits to her granddaughters, something I kind of thought I should have known. I didn't know for sure if it was my great-great-great grandmother, but that made the most sense.

When I tried calling, Grandma Verda's machine picked up. With the snowstorm, she was probably at my parents', but I didn't want to have this conversation with eavesdroppers in the background. I'd try her again later.

Paying close attention to the labels on the bowls, I poured the batter into the individual mini-cake pans. I sprinkled different toppings on each so I'd be able to tell them apart. This was the simplest way I'd thought of to not mix them up.

I set the timer on the oven and began cleaning the mess up, but all I could think about was Miranda, and if it had truly been her voice I'd heard. I didn't know what scared me more.

Hmm. A visitor from beyond, or insanity?

Chapter Ten

I handed the box with the cake over to the receptionist at the Brookhaven Sports Club and steadfastly ignored my trembling hands. "He does work today, right?"

The blonde and way-too-perky girl behind the counter said, "Yep, Troy comes in at seven every night for his class. I'll leave this for him."

"Great, I appreciate it." Swiveling on my heel to leave, she halted me.

"Is there a note? You know, so Troy knows who brought it?"

"Oh, um, sure. Could you put, 'From a secret admirer?'" I really hadn't thought this through.

Her face blanched, and she gestured me forward. When I stood directly in front of her, she leaned over the counter. "Listen, he's not a great guy. There's been a lot of complaints against him." She whisked her gaze to the left and then to the right. "Are you sure you want me to give this to him?"

"What kind of complaints?" I asked without hesitation. Maybe, just maybe, I'd be able to learn something new about Troy the Creep.

"He's a womanizer. And there's even been a few rumors that he's stolen money from some of his conquests. He's really not a nice man."

"Why is he still employed here then?"

"Nothing's been proven. Besides, he's friends with the manager." She picked up the box. "You want this back?"

I shook my head. "No. I'll . . . um . . . just be careful. Thanks for the warning, though."

When she nodded, I escaped to my car. It should have been

a breeze dropping off something as simple as a magical cake, but it wasn't. I'd even phoned before driving over, wanting to make sure I wouldn't see Troy face-to-face, but I was still nervous. Luck seemed to be on my side.

I hoped it stayed that way. Marc's office was next on my list, and pretending to be a secret admirer was out of the question. Because his entire office knew me, I couldn't simply glide in and out. That meant for me to get Marc to eat cake, I'd have to eat crow first. Yech. And sure, with creative thinking, I could probably find another way to get it to him, but my ex was weird about food. A cake appearing anonymously on his desk would never make it to his mouth.

At least I didn't have time to fret over it, because the sports club and Marc's office were within a ten-mile radius of each other. Just a short drive, even in the busy noontime traffic. In no time at all, I'd parked the car outside of his office building. I mentally went over what I wanted to accomplish. I didn't want to get into an argument, and I didn't want to talk about the bakery. All I needed to do was be nice and get him to eat the cake. With luck, the magic would take care of the rest.

My legs wobbled when my feet hit the ground. Gripping the box, I rode up the elevator and focused on the moment he would come to apologize. If I could keep that thought in place, I'd have a much better chance of getting through the next fifteen minutes or so.

"Hi, Angie," I said to Marc's secretary. "Is he in?"

The brunette's eyes widened when she glanced up from her computer. "Oh, wow. Hi, Elizabeth. I haven't seen you in forever." Questions filled the air between us. I didn't answer them. I was just grateful Tiffany no longer worked there.

"I'm sorry for not calling first, but this won't take long. Is Marc in?" I asked again.

"Well, he is. Give me a minute. I'll see if he's free." With another curious look at me, she scooted out of her chair, lightly rapped on the door, and then let herself into Marc's office. Within seconds, she returned with Marc right on her heels.

"Betty? Twice in one week. It must be my lucky day."

"Do you have a few minutes?" I asked, taking in his appearance. Dark suit, tie loosened, hair mussed—but even with the frazzle, Marc Stevens was a handsome man. Irritation flickered, and I shoved it aside.

His eyes whisked over me with an appreciative gleam. I'd worn a dress he particularly liked. Dark midnight blue, it hugged my curves in all the right areas, swirling out slightly above the knees. The deep color gave my skin a creamy glow, and the neckline was cut just low enough to give a hint of cleavage. It was a dress that left far more to the imagination, but that's what Marc had always liked. I figured it was smart to go in with every advantage I could.

"Of course. Come on in."

Following him, I clutched the box tighter. The last time I'd been in this office was about two weeks before our separation. We'd gone out to lunch. Once again, I wanted to go back in time and kick the old me in the ass. Just to wake her up.

I sat down in the chair across from his desk. I was glad when he chose to sit behind his desk instead of in the chair next to me. I didn't want him to be too close. This was harder than I'd thought, probably because of the vision I'd had the other night.

"I'm really surprised to see you. You were angry with me at the store."

"I'm sorry about that. I wasn't prepared to run into you, so, well, I overreacted."

He tapped his long, manicured fingers on the surface of his desk. Opening a drawer, he removed a small picture frame and flipped it toward me so I could see the photograph. "Do you remember this day?"

It only took a glance to be able to say, "Yes." The picture was of me. Maybe at sixteen or seventeen. The smile on my young self's face turned my stomach. "That was taken at one of the school carnivals."

"You were the most beautiful girl in our school, and I couldn't believe you wanted to be with me." He set the frame on the desk and angled it toward him. "You may not believe this, Betty, but I do think of you with fondness."

Yeah, right. Fondness? Bite me, ya know?

"I didn't come here to rehash old days. You made your choice, Marc, and whether I agreed with it or not, it's the life we have now." I didn't know what he was doing, but no way did I want to be dragged back through the past in front of him. I did enough of that on my own.

"I thought that's what you wanted. You didn't come for closure? Tiffany said . . . never mind. What is it you want then?"

"Tiffany suggested I needed closure? How nice of her, but no, that's not why I came. I thought about what you said at Dominick's. And while I'm not sure we can ever be friends again, I don't want to be afraid of running into you."

"What do you have to be afraid of? I'm not trying to hurt you. I just want to talk to you every now and then."

"That doesn't make any sense. You left me for another woman who is now your wife. How can we be friends after that? You were the one who preached honesty on my birthday. Do you remember that? That's all I'm doing. Being honest." Hot anger eased into me. Swallowing, I set it aside. For now.

"I'm really busy this afternoon, Betty. If the purpose of your visit is to tell me how horrible I am, then it's better if you leave. I put out a hand of friendship and you bit it off. Trust me, I won't make that mistake again." Ice edged his words.

I was stunned. No guilt, no nothing, just anger, and somehow, it was all *my* fault. You know, why wouldn't I want to be friends with the amazing Marc Stevens? I must be crazy.

Not.

"Do you feel any remorse about the way you ended our marriage? Because honestly, from this side of the desk, it appears you don't. And that is the number one reason why we can't be friends." Ouch, I instantly regretted my words. A little too harsh when I was supposed to be playing nice.

His cold eyes narrowed. "What's there to be sorry about? You know my favorite saying. It's a dog eat dog world. I found something that made me happier, so I went with it. There is nothing to be sorry about."

See, told you he was a jerk.

He twisted a piece of paper between his fingers, which meant he was either nervous or angry. My bet was on anger. "Now that you're here, we should talk about your little bakery that's losing money hand over foot," he said in a condescending tone.

Little bakery? Up until to that point, I'd purposely kept A Taste of Magic out of our conversation, but no way was I going to let that comment slide. "My *little* bakery is doing just fine. Business hasn't been as brisk this year as we'd like, but we're not losing money. And if you think I'm going to let you come in and make all sorts of changes, you're sadly mistaken."

"You don't have any choice. Until you pay the loan off, I do have a say in how it's run. Whether you like it or not."

"Just because you're a financial planner doesn't mean you know how to run a business. It's much more than dollars and cents."

He looked at me as if I were an idiot. "It's all about the bottom line, Betty. How much you spend versus what you profit. And your profits are less this year than they were at the same time last year."

I forced myself not to argue with him. He was talking to me as if I knew nothing about the basics of business, which pissed me off. Besides, A Taste of Magic was about far more than the bottom line. It was about celebration, making dreams come true, and finding a way to balance that with the logistics of a profitable business.

I reminded myself what the goal of this meeting was. Sitting up straight, and with a calm voice, I said, "I didn't come here to fight with you. I want to apologize for running off the other night. So why don't we get back to that?"

"You're sorry? That's nice to hear."

"Here." I set the bakery box on his desk. "I know how much you like white chocolate and coconut. Consider it a peace offering."

His shoulders relaxed slightly as he picked up the box. Flipping the lid off, he peeked inside. "I miss your baking. It was nice of you to do this."

"It's not much, but I know you always loved my cakes. Besides, I really do feel bad about my reaction to you the other night." I squirmed in my chair at the lie. Well, I guess it wasn't really a lie because I did feel really bad. Just not the way I'd let on.

Yeah, I know I was rationalizing.

"It looks great."

"Taste it. I made it especially for you," I said in the sweetest tone possible.

Marc lifted the cake from the box and bit into it. Another bite, and then he replaced it. "I'll save the rest for later this afternoon." He brushed crumbs off his jacket. "It's great," he repeated.

Pleased I got to watch him eat the cursed thing, I said, "I need to get back to A Taste of Magic. My lunch break is about over." Besides, I didn't think I could sit there another minute. Not without taking the cake and smearing it into Marc's perfect face. While fun, and possibly empowering, it would also be counterproductive.

"I'm quite happy you came by, Betty. It's the first sign you're willing to be honest with yourself. I'll call you soon. Maybe we can do lunch."

I'm sure my jaw dropped open, because I distinctly remember snapping it back shut. I couldn't figure out what game he was playing. And, honestly, being in the same room with him raised all sorts of questions and emotions I didn't want to confront. "I need to go."

Escorting me to the door, his arms reached out as if he was going to hug me. Not in this lifetime, so I stepped out of his reach. Marc touching me was not a smart idea. I didn't trust how my body would react, and I wasn't prepared to find out.

Cocking his head, his mouth pinched tight, he said, "I'll talk to you soon, Betty."

"Seriously, Marc, stop with the 'Betty.' It's as if you say it on purpose, just to annoy me."

"You're being childish. It's what I've always called you. Anyway, we'll get together in a week or two. We have business we need to discuss. When you're a little less emotional."

I ignored the jab and made my way out of his office. The thought of him issuing commands about my business muddled together with everything else I was feeling. At the moment, though, anger took center stage. I hoped he was right—that we *would* be getting together soon. Because I kind of figured an apology would go a long way to setting me free. Even a magic-induced apology was better than nothing.

As I started my car, I wasn't sure what would make me happier: an apology or the realization that he'd suffered.

Who was I kidding? The suffering would win   hands down.

Dashing into my apartment, I ran to the phone. For some reason (call me crazy) I really thought a conversation with my grandmother was in order. Of course, she seemed to have a far more active social life than I did, so she probably wasn't home.

"Hello? Who's there?" Grandma Verda screeched.

Wincing, I said, "Hey, Grandma. It's Elizabeth. Are you busy?"

"Busy? I'm eighty-five years old. How busy can I be?" She cackled at her joke, as if it was the funniest one ever told in the world.

I played along and laughed. "You're busier than I am most of the time."

"I'm watching Judge Judy, make it quick. She's laying into a scammer and I don't want to miss anything when the commercial is over."

"Is anyone there with you?"

"Just Shirley. Why? You have a thing against cats?"

"No, Shirley is fine. I didn't want to interrupt you if Vinny was over."

"Nope. Not now. Dinner later. You want to talk to Vinny?"

"Grandma, no, I just need to ask you something."

"Well, quit wasting time then. Hurry it along. At my age, you have to talk fast and loud."

"Well, I was wondering. Have you ever spoken with Miranda?"

"Miranda? She died long before I was born. What are you talking about? Something happen?"

"I mean, since whenever you got, you know, the magic?"

"What's going on, Elizabeth? How in blazes could I talk with a dead woman?"

Yeah, that's what I wanted to know.

"Never mind, Grandma. How are you doing?"

"I'm good, dear. Why wouldn't I be?"

"Well . . . you know, the 911 stuff and leaving the stove on when you fell asleep."

"Not you too! Your mother calls me every blasted night to make sure I haven't burned the place down. I'm thinking of screaming 'FIRE' into the phone next time she calls. I'm fine, Lizzie. My show is on. I'll talk to you later."

"Bye, Grandma. Enjoy Judge Judy."

I hung up the phone and grinned. Grandma Verda was crazy, but I loved her. I changed out of my work clothes into a pair of sweats and sneakers. After seeing Marc that afternoon, I'd stopped by Alice's with her cake before returning to A Taste of Magic. Jon's remained on my counter. I'd give it to him tonight when we went to see the Willis flick.

Which meant the only delivery I had left to make was Maddie's. No time like the present, right?

I grabbed my keys and the cake and headed to the hallway. My eyes automatically went to Nate's door, and without fully realizing it I went there instead. Mentally shaking myself, I backed up to go to Maddie's as originally planned.

The door from the outside opened, cold wind pouring into the hallway before it slammed back shut. "Hi, Elizabeth, looking for me?" Nate asked, brushing the snow off his jacket as he walked. Sam trailed behind, his small frame covered in white.

I grinned. "Making snowmen?"

"How'd ya guess? We actually made three. You should go check them out."

"I will." Sam's cheeks were pink from the cold. "You look like a snowman, Sam," I said to him. "Go inside and have your uncle make you some hot chocolate."

"We're going to see a movie and then I have to go to my grandparents'," Sam said. "But Grandma has PlayStation, so it'll be fun."

Nate lifted a brow. "When did she buy that?"

"Last time I stayed with her."

With a chuckle, Nate pulled his key out of his pocket. "Does she play it?"

Sam nodded. "But she's not very good. She keeps forgetting what button does what."

"Wanna come in, Liz? We're going to get Sam's stuff together and head out, but I have a few minutes."

Gee, did I want to? Rhetorical question. "Sure, sounds good."

Once in the apartment, Nate helped Sam out of his winter gear. "Go change, kiddo, and get your stuff together."

Sam took off down the hallway.

"I have to work in the morning, and my sister isn't back from Ohio until tomorrow afternoon, so the folks are watching him."

"Your family must be close. Where . . . um, where is Sam's dad?"

"He lives in Colorado. Sam only sees him a couple of times a year."

"That's rough. It's cool he has you as a father figure." Ouch, should I have said that?

"Well, a male figure, anyway." His eyes dropped to Maddie's cake. "Hey! You didn't forget. What did you bake?" He removed his coat and reached for the box. Being completely lost in the green of his eyes, I handed it over without thought.

"It's a cake. Just a small one." His shirt was plastered to his chest from the outside exertion, and his hair was damp around the edges. I wanted to pull him down to the ground, rip his shirt off, and proceed with some serious indoor exertion.

"What kind?"

Dear God, what kind? *Any kind*. I could think of several types of indoor fun to be had. It wasn't until he set the cake down on the table and lifted the lid that my brain clicked in. Damn, he meant the cake. More's the pity.

"This looks great. Thanks!"

"No problem," I murmured, watching his hands. Strong, capable hands, able to bring a woman to immense pleasure . . . as they removed the cake from the box.

Shit! He was going to eat it. Maddie's cake! "Wait!" I said, just as his mouth closed around it in a bite.

Now, I was going to have to start over and bake her something new. At least the magic wouldn't do anything to Nate. I was very specific that it was meant for Maddie.

"Hmm?" Replacing the cake, Nate said, "You don't want me to eat it?"

"Oh, no. Not that. You should have it with coffee—or milk—that's all," I stumbled over the words. It's not like I could blast him for eating Maddie's magical cake. "Is it good?"

"Terrific. Thanks again." He closed the distance between us in a breath. "Come here."

He didn't have to say it twice. I stepped to him, his arms closed around me, and his lips touched mine. An entirely different type of magic eased into me.

Prodding my mouth open with his tongue, it slipped inside, and I tasted the sweetness of the cake and the hotness of Nate all at once. My body reacted immediately, and I leaned into the embrace, into the kiss.

"Eww. That is SO gross!" Sam's voice cut into the moment. Nate pulled back and tossed me a grin. You know the type: the "Oops, we've been caught," sort of grin. Completely endearing, that grin. I smiled back and wrapped my arms around myself. When I was with Nate, all thought of Marc evaporated. Instantly.

"You ready to go?" Nate asked Sam.

"Yeah. Can't we see the new Bruce Willis movie instead of Disney? Please?"

"It's rated R, so no. Grab your coat, Sam. I want to feed you before the movie." Turning to me, he said, "Hey, do you want to go? We're probably just going to hit McDonald's for fast food, but I'd love it if you joined us."

I so wanted to say yes. "Thanks for asking. I'd love to, but I can't. I have plans tonight with a friend."

He nodded as disappointment flashed over his expression.

"I really would love to, Nate, but I promised."

"That's cool. Maybe another time."

"Definitely another time." Yay! He wanted to go out with me!

"I get off work tomorrow at six. How about dinner?"

Wow, he moved fast. "Oh. I have plans tomorrow night, too." What kind of luck was that? Every weekend I sat at home with nothing to do but watch *Buffy* and play with latch-hook rugs, but the one weekend I was booked Nate asked me out. Not once, but twice.

"Oh, well, okay then." Shrugging, he said to Sam, "Let me go change and we'll get going."

"'Kay, I still want to see the Bruce Willis movie instead of Disney."

"Not happening. Get over it."

Sam frowned but went into the living room, picked up the remote, and crashed on the couch.

Nate's eyes returned to me. "We need to take off. Thanks for the cake. It's terrific."

"No problem. You guys have fun tonight." At the door, I turned back, only to find he'd followed me. "I'll see you later."

Bending over slightly, his lips touched mine in a quick kiss. "Enjoy yourself tonight." I felt his eyes on me as I walked to my apartment.

This totally stunk. Two possible nights out with Nate, and I had to say no.

I really hoped he'd ask me again. And what the hell was I going to do about Maddie now?

"The movie rocked, don't you think?" Jon asked as we pulled into my parking lot.

"It had a lot of action," I replied. Not that I really knew. I'd barely been able to pay attention. There was too much going on for me to lose myself in a movie. Jon didn't need to know that, though.

"How do you think I'd look if I shaved my head?"

"Nothing like Bruce Willis."

"Yeah. That's what I figured. Mind if I come in?"

"Of course not. I'd planned on it." I wanted him to eat the cake I'd made, and I wanted to talk to him about Marc. We needed to come up with a plan to keep my ex from throwing his weight around in our business. In case my spell didn't take hold.

In the hallway, I'd just unlocked my door when Nate exited his apartment. And, as always, I was happy to see him. When he reached us, I said, "Hi, Nate. This is Jon, the friend I told you about earlier."

After the introductions were complete, I asked, "Did Sam end up liking the Disney movie?"

Nate smiled, but his eyes were on Jon. "If you ask him, he'll say no. But he seemed pretty into it. Heck, even I liked it."

A cop who liked Disney. How cool was that? "Where are you off to?" I knew he wasn't going to work, as he wasn't in uniform.

"My sister got an early flight in. Just going to get her from the airport and run her to pick up Sam from my parents' house." He glanced at his watch. "In fact, if I don't leave now, I'll be late. Nice meeting you, Jon."

Jon nodded, and Nate took off. Once we were in my apartment, Jon whistled. "Where have you been hiding him? Methinks you have some 'splaining to do, Lucy.'"

"He's my neighbor. Your Desi Arnaz imitation is horrible." I hung our coats up in the closet. "I have coffee and cake. You want some?"

"Yes on the coffee, but I had too much popcorn at the movies for cake. Maybe later. But I want to know more about your neighbor. You're not telling me something, Lizzie," he said with a grin.

"There's nothing to say." Well, nothing substantial, anyway. I didn't know what was happening between me and Nate, and until I did, I was keeping my mouth shut.

"Pretty sure there's more to it than that, but I'll let it go. He didn't look happy to see me, that's for sure."

"What are you talking about?"

"He was giving me the eye."

Laughing, I said, "He's not into guys, Jon. No matter how cute you are."

"Dork. Not *that* kind of eye. The green eye of jealousy."

"Nah, I told him we were friends. There's nothing for him to be jealous of."

"Maybe you did, but it didn't sink in. Your Nate was definitely distressed to see you with me." Jon tucked his thumbs into his jean pockets. "And what do you mean there's nothing to be jealous of?"

"Well, let's see. We're business partners. We're best friends. And we've never been anything else. So there's nothing for Nate to be envious about."

"Maybe we could change that."

Before I could make sense of his statement, he walked over and put his hands on my shoulders. "Lately, I've been thinking a lot about you. About us. We've always been close, we never fight, and whenever we're together, we have a lot of fun. I think it's time to see if we can be more than just friends." With that, he tipped my chin up with his hand, lowered his head, and kissed me like he never had before. Not a simple kiss. Not a friendly kiss. A tongue in my mouth, halfway down my throat, kiss.

Unfortunately, or fortunately, depending on your point of

view, my body didn't respond. It was nice, but it wasn't right. Not quite like kissing my brother, but more like, "No, this just isn't how it should feel."

As soon as that thought hit my brain, I disengaged myself from his arms. Fast. I wiped my hand over my lips. Jon just stood there, frozen.

"What are you doing?" I asked. I mean, don't get me wrong, over the years, I'd definitely fantasized about Jon. It was kind of hard not to. He was sexy, sweet, and always made me laugh. But those were just fantasies. They were never meant to come true.

He shook his head, as if trying to clear a haze I couldn't see. "I don't know. You were standing there, and suddenly, I just wanted to kiss you." He ran his hand through his hair. "I'm so sorry. Lately, I've been feeling things that don't make any sense. Maybe I'm going through my mid-life crisis early."

And if I'd had any doubts before, I didn't any longer. Side effect number two was a reality. Thank God I'd baked that cake for him. "You don't have to apologize, but let's not go down that road again. You and Andy are terrific together. You don't want to harm that, do you?"

I figured if I got him talking about Andy, whatever he was feeling would disappear—at least for now. And then, later, I could get a few bites of cake into him. Once again, I had to hope that my magic would fix this. I was beginning to wish I'd never baked those damn brownies.

"Maybe I should leave," Jon said, moving toward the door.

"No! Don't be silly. Go have a seat in the living room and find something on TV to watch. I'll make some coffee." When he hesitated, I said, "Jon, I want you to stay."

He smiled and, thankfully, it reached his eyes. "Okay. Thanks, Lizzie."

After I made the coffee, I joined him in the living room. I'd brought the cake and a couple of plates with me. One way or another, he was going to eat some before he left.

A few hours later, I was yawning, but Jon wasn't. At some point in that time frame, the cake had mostly disappeared—

thank God. Now I had to hope it would work. We hadn't gotten around to talking about Marc, but I figured that would have to wait. I was more concerned about whatever the problems were between Jon and Andy.

In thinking about Jon's kiss, I realized that he'd seemed as uncomfortable as I was. And, when I thought about was happening with Maddie, the same truth existed there. It was like the magic worked, but because it wasn't right for them, they weren't able to be happy. This concept both relieved me and worried me.

Also, because of Jon's apparent unease, I wondered if the magic would have even worked for him if things were solid for him and Andy. So, with that thought in mind, I flipped the television off. "We should talk," I said.

Red blossomed on his cheeks. "I'm sorry about earlier. Really."

I shook my head. "No, not about that. I want to know what's going on with you and Andy."

"Ah, what brings that up?" Jon's gaze didn't meet mine but instead floated somewhere on the wall behind me.

"Give me a break, Jon. It's kind of obvious you've been miserable. You were completely there for me, so I'd like to return the favor."

"You're a sweetie, but it's not really a big deal. Andy's fine. I'm the one not sure about what I want."

"You've always known what you've wanted. When you met Andy, you told me he was exactly what you'd been looking for. What happened to that?"

Jon shrugged. "Like I said, it's me. That mid-life crisis thing."

"Is Andy really on a business trip?"

"Hell, is this conversation really necessary?"

A-ha. I'd stumbled onto something. "Yeah, it is. Spill it, where's he at?"

"He moved out temporarily. Said I needed to get my head straightened on what I really wanted."

"It's that bad?"

"I didn't think so, but obviously Andy does. So now I'm supposed to decide the rest of my life in the next week."

"Andy gave you a deadline?" That didn't sound like the Andy I knew and loved.

"He wants to adopt a child or hire a surrogate, and I'm not ready for that. So yeah, basically, he's ready to be a dad, and if I'm not, he's moving on." Jon's voice was a little too cavalier; his hurt hid there, underneath.

I doubted Andy had expressed it that simply, but I let this slide. Besides, it wasn't a stretch for me to realize how important having a child was. When you wanted one, you wanted one, there were no two ways about it. "What are you going to do?"

Jon shrugged again. "I don't know. I keep hoping it will come to me, whatever the answer is."

"Where's he staying?"

"With his sister. She has a million kids. Maybe the craziness of it will show Andy our lives aren't meant for a child. At least not right now."

Or it might reinforce his want. I bit my lip. Probably better to keep that thought to myself. The last thing Jon needed was something else to dwell on. "What can I do?"

"Nothing, but I do appreciate your asking."

"That's what friends are for," I replied.

He grinned and sang a few lines from the Dionne song. I joined in, and suddenly, everything felt normal again. Maybe, just maybe, my spell had already taken effect?

But then he leaned forward and grasped my hand. "Part of me wonders how it would be for us. If we tried."

"You and I both know it would never work. Give it a few days. You'll see I'm right. Besides, I really believe you and Andy are forever. You're just going through a rough patch."

"Maybe. Maybe not. But I need to get going. I might be late tomorrow," he said as he stood.

"I'll hold down the fort until you get there." Quick hugs, a normal kiss good night, and I was alone again.

The day, the night, and everything in between processed as I brushed my teeth and readied myself for bed. Weird, weird, and weirder. That seemed to be the tagline of my life. At least recently.

Oh, joy.

Chapter Eleven

"Thanks for coming over, Lizzie. I don't think I can handle seeing him alone," Alice said as she paced her living room. My sister was normally pale, as both of us were blessed with skin a tad warmer than a bottle of Wite-Out, but today, there was literally no color in her face. And the dark purple blouse she wore didn't help her washed out complexion.

"What did Troy say when he called?"

Clasping her hands together, she stopped in front of me. "Just that he needed to see me and to please not say no."

"Well, maybe this is a good thing." Could the spell be causing this? I didn't know. It sure seemed to be manifesting quickly. "I'm glad you phoned. Sit down, Alice, you look like you're going to fall over."

Sighing, she scooted into a chair and clasped and unclasped her hands repeatedly. "I don't know if I want to see him."

"Nah, it's good you said yes. Closure is important." Points to Tiffany for that. She'd nailed that one, even if I hated admitting it.

Alice snorted. "Yeah, right. Have you had closure with Marc yet?"

"Not completely, but I did go see him yesterday."

"Really? What brought that on?"

Glad to give her something else to focus on, I related the story of running into Marc at Dominick's Grocery and then visiting him at his office. I didn't mention the loan—or the magic.

"I don't understand why you apologized to him. You had every right to run out like that."

"Because I don't want him to think he gets to me that way.

It gives him too much strength." Close enough to the truth, at least as far as I was concerned.

"That makes sense. So, this is kind of the same thing, right? By agreeing Troy could come over, I'm showing I'm not afraid of him."

"Exactly. Plus, he can't pull anything stupid because I'm here with you."

A sharp knock snagged Alice's attention. "Shit," she whispered. "He's here."

"Calm down. I'll get it."

The man on the other side of the door didn't live up to my expectations. Instead of looking like the slimy dirtball he was, Troy Bellamy was average height, average build, average everything. If I'd met him under different circumstances, I'd think he looked like a nice guy. *Note to self: work on instincts.*

Though, he didn't appear to be comfortable. His brown hair was plastered to his head, and his skin had a glossy sheen to it, as if he'd been sweating—a lot—and his cheeks were a smidgen too red.

His dark eyes skittered over my shoulder. "I'm looking for Alice."

"She's here. I'm her sister. Come in."

He crossed in front of me and moved through the dining room. I followed him but stayed to the side, where I could see everything. I wanted to be there for Alice, but in a subtle way.

Alice stood and crossed her arms. Pride made me smile. So much better to stand up rather than let him tower over her.

"Hi, Troy. I was surprised to hear from you."

"Yeah, well. Look, this isn't easy. I want to pay you back," he blurted. "The money you gave me, I'm feeling sick about it."

"Money is the least of what you owe me," Alice said lightly.

"The thing is, I can't get it to you all at once." He grabbed a crumpled envelope from his pocket. "This is a third of it. It's a check, but I swear it's good."

Alice hesitated. "Is this going to take away from your kids?"

That's my sister. More worried about children she didn't know than she was for herself.

Troy ran his hand over his stomach and winced. "I can't stay. I need to go lie down or something. I just wanted to give this to you."

Alice still didn't reach for the envelope. "I don't want money if your kids need it."

"They don't. They're set. I promise."

"Your promises don't hold a lot of weight with me," Alice said. I wanted to cheer, but I kept silent.

Troy scowled. He looked as if he was going to say something, but instead, he bent over and groaned in pain. "Could I have some water?"

Okay, this piqued my interest. I hadn't expected to see visual proof of my magic. Not like this, anyway.

My sister looked at me, her eyes asking me to bring the water, and I nodded. I'd done this to the guy. The least I could do was get him a glass of water.

"Liz will get it. You should sit down."

I returned with the water and handed it to Troy.

After gulping some down, he said, "I've been feeling like crap since last night. I can't get this out of my head."

"Your wife was really pissed off. I don't want to take that check unless I know she's all set."

"What the hell, Alice? I'm paying you back. What do you want, a fucking note from my mother?"

Alice stepped back as if she'd been slapped. "You're so hostile. What did I do to you? I loved you and you stole from me. I should be the hostile one."

"Just take the money. I'll pay you some each week until the balance is paid in full."

Alice finally accepted the envelope. "Fine. I don't want to see you again. Mail it to me or drop it off at A Taste of Magic for my sister. She'll get it to me." She switched her focus to me. "Is that okay?"

"That's fine." I pulled a business card from my purse.

"Here," I said, giving it to Troy. "Just put my name on the envelope."

His eyes darted from me to my sister and back. "I don't know what's going on, but my mother was a witch. One of you did this, so yeah, I'll pay back the money, but take the damn spell off."

Alice gave a shaky laugh. "You're crazy. Maybe you're just developing a conscience."

Troy groaned again and wiped his brow. "Don't play stupid. I grew up around this stuff. You're mad, I get that. You want to punish me. That's understandable. But now that I know what you can do, I won't screw with you again."

My jaw dropped, and tiny pinpricks sped along my skin. I never expected anyone to figure out what I was doing. I couldn't decide if it was cool or not.

"Please. Take it off. I can't live like this. I'm in nonstop pain."

Alice frowned. "Maybe you should go to the hospital, Troy. You're talking nuts, and if you're really hurting, there's a medical reason for it."

Eyes wild, he stood and dropped the glass. Water splattered on the floor. "My mother did this to me when I was a teenager. The exact same damn thing, so I know better. Take the spell off, Alice. I'm begging you."

Alice paled even more, if that was possible. "You should go." She pointed to the door. "I want you to leave now."

"You're not lying, are you? You don't know anything about this." He advanced a step toward me, and then his face crumpled in pain again. "That means it's you. Take it off."

"You heard my sister. You should leave." I shuddered at the venom in his eyes, and yeah, I did feel bad. But the spell would go away on its own, once he repaid Alice. I figured he'd get the money together faster that way.

At any rate, I couldn't take it off unless I baked him something else. I doubted he'd eat anything from a stranger again. If he'd pinned it to the cake, of course.

"Fuck. You win." He reached into his jacket pocket and pulled out his checkbook and a pen. Scribbling fast, he wrote out another check and handed it to Alice. "There, it's all there. Go cash it now. I'll wait."

Alice glanced at me for confirmation and I nodded again. She took the check, looked at the dollar figure, and smiled. "The bank isn't open now, Troy. It will have to wait until Monday. I hope the money is there."

"It is. I swear." He ran his fingers through his hair. "Is the spell off now? My stomach doesn't hurt so much."

Alice sighed. Pointing at the door again, she said, "Just leave."

I followed him and, when he opened the door, I whispered, "If the money isn't there on Monday, you won't feel good for long."

His eyes popped open, but he didn't say a word.

I gotta say, I'd never seen a man move so fast in my life. And I felt damn pleased that for once my spell worked exactly how I'd wanted. Maybe I was learning something.

At the same time, apprehension gnawed at me. I rubbed my arms to calm the goose bumps. At first, I'd mostly considered the magic a game. Something to play at and have a bit of fun with. Something to help me get over Marc and find a new path in life. But now, between Maddie and Troy, I truly realized the magnitude of the gift. Miranda must have been one scary lady, and it seemed I was following in her footsteps.

I wasn't sure I liked that idea.

"What do you think, Maddie? Hair up or down?" We were in my bedroom, and I was fussing with my hair, getting ready for my date with Kevin. Maddie sat on my bed, mostly staring off into space.

When she'd arrived, she'd almost seemed like herself. I'd just about convinced myself that she'd actually been ill, like a cold, and that it hadn't been my magic after all. But now, I realized that was just wishful thinking.

Her glazed eyes centered on me. "Either will do. Whatever you want."

"What's wrong?"

"Hmm? Nothing. I'm just tired."

Frowning, I twisted my hair and clipped it. Using my fingers, I scrunched my bangs and pulled a few wisps toward the side of my face. Stepping back, I took in my full appearance.

After reading up on Blue Man Group online, I got the idea it was a casual, fun performance that could get really messy, depending on where you were sitting. With that in mind, I was wearing black jeans and a dark green sweater.

I thought I looked pretty good. Plus, the workouts were actually making a difference. My thighs felt tighter, and the denim hugged my legs perfectly.

Possibly, my mother was right on target with her gift. Of course, no way was I admitting that to her. Another glance at Maddie and my heart sank. "Come on, tell me why you're so out of it."

"I already did. I'm tired. I was on the phone late with Spencer last night."

"Oh! That's great! How'd it go?"

Pulling her knees to her chest, she sighed. "I don't know. Fine, I guess. We're going out next weekend."

"So why don't you sound happy about it?"

"I'm miserable, Liz. But what's worse, I can't put my finger on why."

"Not feeling any better at all?" Damn, I really wished I'd stopped Nate from eating Maddie's cake. I blamed it on his green eyes. Tomorrow, I promised myself, I'd fix it.

"If anything, it's worse. Before, I kind of liked how I wasn't so fanatical about every last detail of my appearance. But now, I don't care at all. And what's worse, I can't seem to make myself care. Nothing matters anymore."

I sat down on the bed next to her. I didn't know what to say. *I did this.* After seeing Troy, I had no doubts that Maddie's misery was because of me. My higher self wanted to admit it to her. My lower self wanted to run and hide. Regardless, I knew enough to stay quiet. Telling her at this point was a very bad idea.

"How about I cancel my date with Kevin? I'll whip us up some brownies or something and we can watch a movie. Have a girls' night." This shouldn't wait until the next day. Seriously—I needed to make it better. If my sister hadn't called me to come over earlier, I'd have already taken care of Maddie. But no way could I let Alice deal with Troy on her own.

Maddie shook her head. "My parents will be here soon, so I can't. You may as well go out and have fun." Her eyes gleamed, and just for a second she looked like her old self. "Besides, you look spectacular. Don't waste it on me."

"I can still cancel. You can come down when your parents leave."

Another shake. "Not tonight. They're staying over so I can drive them to the airport early in the morning. They're going to Hawaii for some insurance convention for my dad."

Well. Shoot. It would have to be tomorrow, then. "Let's hook up in the afternoon. I can tell you about my date, and you can feast on something decadent. What do you want me to make? Anything your heart desires."

She laughed, thank God. "Well, Brad Pitt, but if you can't serve him up, how about that mocha brownie thing you made once? With the mousse center?"

"Ask and ye shall receive," I replied.

"If I'm going to splurge, it may as well be on something luscious." She tucked her hair behind one ear. "I'm gonna run upstairs and clean up a smidge before my parents show. I'll see you tomorrow. What time?"

"Come on down after lunch, around one or two. And Maddie? Try not to worry too much. Everything will settle." It needed to, because my glamorous friend was long gone, and the girl that remained wasn't quite Maddie. More like a hollowed out carbon copy.

"I've never felt like this before. But yeah, you're probably right. It will blow over." She pointed at me. "But you—you have a great time tonight. Promise?"

After I closed the door behind Maddie, I made sure I had all the ingredients for the mocha brownies. I'd get up early and bake them first thing. Hopefully, that would be the end of that. I didn't think I'd be casting any other spells for Maddie again.

Another once-over in the mirror proved I was as ready as I could possibly get. Marc flitted into my mind, and I tried to shove him away, but I couldn't. It was as if he'd stepped solidly into my apartment with the goal to ruin my evening. Resolutely, I focused on Kevin, and slowly Marc—and the sour taste in my mouth—dissipated. When the phone rang, I gave myself a mental shake.

"Lizzie?"

"Hi, Grandma. What's up?"

"Why did you ask if I'd spoken with Miranda? Where did that question come from?"

Great. Because I hadn't heard the voice again, I sort of thought I'd imagined it. You know, the power of the moment and all that jazz. "Oh, I was just curious."

"Spill it. Why were you curious?"

"Seriously, Grandma, no real reason. I'm still trying to get my mind wrapped around the whole idea, and I wanted to know if she . . . well, communicated with you in any way."

Silence. Grandma Verda wasn't stupid, so I doubted she believed me, but hopefully she wouldn't push. Yeah, if it happened again, I'd probably tell her. But at that point I was keeping my mouth shut.

"Is that the truth, Lizzie?"

My buzzer went off. Perfect timing. "Hey, Grandma, my date's here, so I gotta go. I'll talk to you soon."

"Are you going out with Nate?"

"No. His name is Kevin, and if I don't go now he'll think I stood him up."

"Go. Have fun. But you should think about Nate."

"Trust me, Grandma, I have." *All the time.* After hanging up,

I went to put my coat on. As I left my apartment, I tried to reclaim my excitement.

I'd looked forward to this for most of the week, but now that it was here, I kinda wanted to stay home. Probably because I was worried about Maddie. Not to mention Alice and Jon.

All thoughts vacated my brain when I saw Kevin. Maddie was right. He was completely hot. Mouthwateringly, sinfully, wickedly hot. Suddenly, the evening ahead brightened.

I pretended I didn't hear the tiny voice in the back of my mind. The one that insisted I'd have a much brighter evening if it involved Nate. But settling down with one guy wasn't what I wanted. I did that once already. No need to go that route again.

This was what I'd wished for, what I'd blamed Marc for taking away from me. Choices. Adventure. Freedom.

My date was with Kevin; therefore, I intended to have an amazing time with Kevin.

Simple as that.

Walking out of the Briar Street Theatre, Kevin took hold of my hand, his strong fingers closing around mine. "That show was awesome. Did you like it?"

"It was great. I loved the music. I can't believe I've never gone to see it before. Thanks for taking me." The warmth of his clasp felt solid and real. I liked it, more than I'd expected.

"Feel like stopping and grabbing some dessert?"

I laughed. "You, the water-drinking, salad-eating, only-good-things-go-in-my-body, trainer of all trainers, want to buy me dessert?"

"Treats are good for you. You just don't want to eat that stuff all the time."

I stifled a yawn. "Actually, Kevin, I've had a really long day, and I have to work in the morning. I'm kind of tired. Do you mind if we call it?"

"Sure, let's get you home so you can get some sleep."

Wow, I loved that. He didn't try to change my mind. He

just agreed. Not able to hold it back any longer, I yawned as I slid into the seat of his car.

Bluesy jazz spilled from the radio. I leaned my head back against the cushion of his car and closed my eyes. Contentedness seeped into me as the sound of the engine and the hum of the road lulled me to sleep.

I don't know how much time passed, but I woke to Kevin's lips at my ear.

"Hey, sleepyhead, we're home."

Reaching up, I touched his cheek, felt the prickly roughness of his not-so-smooth shave, and murmured, "Okay."

He walked me in and we stopped in the hallway, in front of my door. "I'd invite you in for some wine, but I really am beat."

"That would be sweet, but I'm the water guy, remember?"

"Oh yeah, that's right," I teased.

"Hey, Elizabeth, I had an amazing time tonight. I'd love to take you out again. Maybe dancing. You're so incredibly easy to be around, and I really enjoyed myself." He smiled shyly. "I hope you did, too."

"I had fun, Kevin." This surprised me a little. But hey, part of what I wanted was to date different men, to regain what I never had when I was younger. Not such a hard choice. "I'd like to go out again. Dancing sounds great."

"We'll do it then." He eased toward me, so my back was against the wall. When he kissed me, it was different than kissing Marc, which made sense. But more pointedly, it was different than kissing Nate. My belly warmed, but I didn't have the tingles and the sparks shooting out all over the place. Not necessarily a bad thing. Just a different thing.

Kevin's body pushed me tighter against the wall as he deepened the kiss. Not quite the instantaneous combustion I'd gotten used to with Nate, but my body slowly came alive under his touch. While it wasn't mind-blowing, it was definitely nice, and more than I'd expected.

With a sigh, he stepped back. His dark chocolate eyes heated with desire, telling me what he really wanted. "I better go."

His husky voice rode over me smoothly. "You're far too tempting, Elizabeth."

"I'll, um, see you in a few days. At the gym," I murmured, the effects of the kiss, the strength of it, still surprising me.

"Let's plan something for next weekend, if you want. We can talk about it during training."

I nodded and pulled my keys out of my purse. Kevin watched me unlock the door before he turned away. As he did, I happened to glance down the hallway and my heart stopped. And then it floated upward, until it got stuck in my throat and I choked on it.

Nate stood at the door from the outside, police uniform on, so I assumed he'd been called into work. His gaze was on me, but he didn't say anything, just stepped out of the way to let Kevin pass, and then continued down the hall toward me.

"Hi, Nate. Did you have to work tonight?" I asked, trying to keep my voice casual. Maybe he hadn't seen the kiss. Not that I'd done anything wrong, but still. The thought he may have seen the lip-lock really bothered me.

"Yeah, they needed an extra body, and I didn't have anything going on." He stopped in front of me, his eyes definitely on my lips.

I bet they were red, swollen from the kiss.

I held my head high. I felt guilty. Maybe there wasn't a reason, but I did. That was dumb, because Nate and I hadn't even been on a proper date. We barely knew each other.

Yep. Rationalizing. Again.

"I didn't know you were dating someone," he finally said.

"I'm not. Well, I wasn't. First date." Brilliant, Elizabeth—just brilliant.

"Ah. Have fun?"

"Saw Blue Man Group, and yeah it was great. Have you seen it?"

His gaze kept darting to my mouth. I envisioned my lips as nearly bursting, giant red water balloons, marking me easily as a woman just kissed. I rolled my bottom lip into my mouth and scraped it with my teeth. It felt normal enough.

"A couple of years ago. It's a fun show. Will you be around tomorrow?"

"Should be. I have plans with Maddie." Then, I realized he probably didn't know her. "Hey, have you met Maddie? She lives upstairs."

"Nope. She's a friend of yours, right?"

I nodded. "Why don't you stop by? She's coming down in the afternoon. It'd be good for her to meet the law enforcement around these parts," I teased, hoping to ease the moment.

His gaze settled on my face. What felt like forever passed, but it was probably only a few seconds. "I'll see you then. Sleep well, Elizabeth."

Unlike the previous day, he didn't lean over and give me a kiss as a good-bye. Just walked to his apartment and let himself in without a backward glance. Selfish of me, because I'd just been thoroughly kissed, but it bugged me.

Yeah, he'd definitely seen the kiss. Now I had to decide how I felt about that. In my bedroom, I slipped out of my clothes and pulled my nightgown on, and thought about it. I really liked Nate. A lot. I'd also had had a great time with Kevin. And, while I'd certainly been more intimate with Nate, I knew a little more about Kevin.

Of course, I had a sneaking suspicion that Kevin was younger than me. I wasn't sure by how much, but I seriously doubted he was over thirty. Kind of cool, dating a younger man. Also a little nerve-wracking. What did he see in me?

"Why do you do that to yourself, Elizabeth?"

The voice hit me straight on. Jumping slightly, I turned my gaze toward the direction of the voice, but I didn't see anyone. And yeah, it was the same voice from before. I took in one long, slow breath and tried to relax. "Miranda?"

A bodiless giggle echoed in the room. "Who else?"

Every hair stood up on end with the answer, and I shivered automatically. I hadn't expected a response. Not really. "I don't know. You were my first guess."

I waited breathlessly to hear her again. Fear mingled with

excitement. When a few minutes passed with nothing forth-coming, I slid beneath my sheets and closed my eyes. Ghostly Grandma or not, I needed to get some sleep. Besides, some-how I knew if I allowed myself to think too much about it, I'd let the fear seep in, and then I'd be up all night.

When I was a little girl, on nights I couldn't sleep, my mother used to tell me to pretend I was floating on a cloud. That my cloud bed would whisk me anywhere I wanted to go, so it was best to sleep on the journey so I would be pre-pared when I arrived. Silly, but I still used this image to help me fall asleep. So, huddled in my bed, I willed my pulse to slow to a reasonable level and envisioned a white fluffy cloud. Curling up on the cloud, I breathed deeply. It took longer than normal, but I did relax. A few minutes later, I began to fall away.

I hovered, not quite descending off the precipice into deep sleep, and enjoyed the moment. My body seemed weightless; my mind was empty. I sighed, snuggled in, and then, some-thing pushed at me, pulled at me. It was like I'd become a ball, bouncing from one hard edge to another.

Bam. Bam. Bam.

Wide awake, I snapped my eyes open. A blinding light pul-sated throughout the room. Chills coated my skin. Sitting up, I exhaled and peered into the light. In the middle of it, the hazy shape of a figure stood, but I couldn't quite make it out.

"Can you see me, Elizabeth?" I heard Miranda say.

Squinting, I tried to focus past the haze, but couldn't, it hurt my eyes too much. Blinking, they watered and the wet-ness decreased my vision even more. "Hello?"

Another second passed, and my room returned to its nor-mal quiet darkness. No light. No form. No voice.

Cuckoo land . . . twilight zone . . . whatever I wanted to call it was gone. I sat up and stared at the room. I wrapped my arms around myself to chase the chill away.

"Miranda? Are you still here?"

While I didn't hear a reply, my room filled with the scent of roses. Ah. I was pretty sure that meant she was still there.

Knowing sleep was now out of the question, at least for a little while, I grabbed my pillow and quilt and went to the living room.

"I don't think I like this," I whispered. Well, duh, who would? And, it wouldn't do me any good to move out, because it wasn't like it was my apartment that was haunted.

Nope, it was me.

Chapter Twelve

"Why are you so jumpy?" Maddie asked over a bite of her brownie. While she didn't look as tired today, she still lacked her usual glow. Hopefully, this new magic would be as strong as the Troy magic, just in reverse.

"I'm not." At her disbelieving look, I said, "Nate is supposed to join us. That's all. I'm wondering what's taking him so long." Not the full truth, but close enough. Besides, I didn't think mentioning Miranda would help me in the sanity department.

"You're not trying to fix me up with this cop, are you?"

"Absolutely not. In fact, if you so much as blink an eye at him I'll have to take you down."

Her startled expression quickly gave way to humor. "It's like that, is it? Well, good for you. I'm happy to see you're playing the field a little." Another bite of chocolate disappeared into her mouth. "Dangerous, though."

"Dangerous how?"

"Dating two men at once when one of them lives right down the hallway. Most men, no matter what they say, don't like to share."

Leave it to Maddie. With virtually no knowledge of my experience the prior evening, she'd hit it right on the head.

"That's why I'm nervous. He saw me coming in with Kevin last night. Plus, he saw me with Jon on Friday night. I wouldn't have thought anything of it, but Jon seems to think Nate will take it the wrong way."

"He probably will." Her eyes flickered over me curiously. "Why haven't you mentioned Nate before?"

"There wasn't much to mention. We haven't dated yet. There's just this . . . I don't know, *thing*, between us."

"*Things* are good. Maybe he's uncomfortable about coming over after seeing you with two different men on the weekend. Go get him. I'll help you clean things up. At least as far as Jon goes." Clearing off her plate, she pushed it aside. "That was terrific, thanks for making it."

She'd hardly eaten any. I wanted her to eat more. Just to be sure. Not that long ago, she'd told me she missed the old Elizabeth. I missed the old Maddie. I wanted her back. "Have another slice and I'll go grab Nate."

"You talked me into it. Heck, it's Sunday. If I can't pig out on the weekend, when can I?"

"Exactly. Be right back." In less than a minute, I was rapping on Nate's door. When it swung open, I had my smile ready to go.

Only, it wasn't Nate on the other side. It wasn't Sam, either. Instead, a red-haired woman with large, bottle-green eyes stared at me. "Yes?" she asked.

"Hi. I'm Nate's neighbor. Is he here?"

"Yes. Wait one minute, please." The door closed in my face, only to be opened by Nate a scant few seconds later.

"Elizabeth, what's going on?" Exasperation colored his tone. Something I hadn't heard from him since the window night. I stepped backward before replying.

"Is this a bad time? I just wanted to see if you were still planning on coming over." At his blank expression, I continued, "To meet Maddie?"

"That's right. Sorry. I can't now. Something unexpected came up, so I'll have to take a rain check."

"Is anything wrong?" I scooted to the side, trying to see in past him. I wanted to know who the red-haired beauty was, but I couldn't come right out and ask, now could I?

"I'm fine. Sorry about today. We'll get together soon."

"Oh. Sure." Now I wanted to ask when he had in mind, but I couldn't do that, either.

"Have fun with your friend," Nate said before closing the door. I felt as if I'd been dismissed. It reminded me of Marc, and that made me feel worse.

I stared at the closed door for a few seconds, wondering what was going on behind it. Wishing that Miranda's magic came with a few of Superman's abilities, I turned on my heel and went back to my apartment.

"Well?" Maddie asked, wiping the chocolate away from her lips. I was pleased to see a much larger chunk of the brownie had disappeared from the pan.

"He's busy, I guess." Who knew I'd be this disappointed? Not me, that's for sure.

"You guess?"

"I don't know. Let's not talk about it. Tell me about your parents. Did they get off to Hawaii okay?"

I pretended to be involved in small talk with Maddie, but my focus remained firmly on Nate. And the mystery woman. And what was happening between them in Nate's apartment. To think I'd felt bad about his seeing me with Kevin. Stupid. Stupid. Stupid!

"Are you listening to me at all?"

"What? Oh. Of course I am."

"You're off in another world. Want to share why?"

"A woman answered the door at Nate's. I've never seen him around another woman, so it's bugging me," I blurted. "I don't know why."

Maddie's mouth split in a grin. "You're kidding, right? You know damn well why it's bothering you. The same exact reason it bothered Nate to see you with Jon and Kevin."

"Which is why it shouldn't mean anything to me. I'm not sitting here pining over him or anything."

Maddie snorted. "Baby, you most certainly are pining."

I opened my mouth in denial, saw her pointed look, and sighed. "Maybe a little. I didn't know he was seeing anyone else. It was weird, that's all."

"Was she dressed?"

"What?"

"This woman. Did she have clothes on?"

"She didn't answer the door naked, if that's what you're asking."

"What about her hair?"

"It was perfect." Long, red, and beautiful. Maybe I should dye my hair red?

"Makeup? Did she have lipstick on?"

"What's with all these questions?"

Maddie stood and shook her head, amusement glittering in her voice. "Answer. Did she have lipstick on?"

"Yes."

"Was it smudged?"

"No. Everything about her was perfect. She could have stepped off the cover of a magazine. If this is your way of helping me feel better, you're failing. Miserably."

"Dork," she said, laughing.

"What is so funny?"

"If she was dressed, if her lipstick and hair were perfect, then it stands to reason that no hanky-panky was going on behind closed doors."

"You can't know that."

"For sure? No. But think about it. If mystery woman and Nate were rolling around in bed together, you'd have seen the signs of it. Smudged lipstick, mussed hair, shirt unbuttoned."

"Good point, but it doesn't prove anything." It made me feel better, though.

"Nope, but it gives you something to hang on to." Using her fork, Maddie cut off a chunk of brownie. "Here," she said, lifting it to my mouth. "You need this more than I do."

Tasting the explosion of sweet chocolate on my tongue, I nodded. I certainly did. Unfortunately, the spell wasn't going to affect me.

But hey, the sugar couldn't hurt.

Jon's face creased in a grin. "We just got the Henderson gig. The entire thing! Shower, rehearsal, and wedding."

I looked up from the next month's planning calendar.

"Really? No way." The Henderson wedding was huge. They were Chicago's own version of the Kennedys, and if I'd understood Jon correctly, they'd just chosen A Taste of Magic for their nuptial baking needs. All my worries about paying off Marc evaporated. With a client like that, we'd be the hit of Chicago as soon as word got out. Business would be booming.

"Seriously, Liz. I just got the call from the consultant team. We're it. Mrs. Henderson and her daughter are coming next week to meet with us."

"You know what this means to us, Jon?"

He grabbed my hands and twirled me toward him. "It means we've made it. We can pay Marc off, and then, after we pull this off, we'll be the elite bakery in Chicago. Bigger store, higher-paying clientele, and the ability to create spectacular cakes without the worry of cost. You can be the artist you've always dreamed about! This is it!"

Pulling out of the dance, I smiled, but at the same time focused on the realities. I didn't want to burst his bubble, but this was not the time to get overexcited. "Yeah, and if we screw it up, we'll probably be out of business."

"Hush, you. Don't ruin this moment. We haven't screwed up one job yet. This will be no different. This is it! This is what we've been working toward."

"Jon, stop. What did the consultant say, exactly? Has Mrs. Henderson already hired us, or is this an interview?"

"Interview. But it's as good as in the bag."

I shook my head. "This is why I'm the practical one. It's not in the bag. Not yet. I know you're excited, and it's great news, but we have a lot to do."

"Aw, Lizzie, don't ruin this," he implored.

His tone got to me, just like a little boy pouting when his favorite toy was taken away would get to me. "I'm not. I'm going to do everything possible to ensure they do hire us. But you need to calm down."

Crossing his arms, Jon inhaled deeply. "You're absolutely right. This is why we're the perfect team. What do you need from me?"

I felt like crap, deflating his enthusiasm. "Can you finish up on the Walker cake? I'll start on some research so we can decide what we want to show Mrs. Henderson and her daughter. What day are they coming?"

"Next week. Wednesday, ten in the morning."

"Good. Plenty of time to work this out then. Do you mind dealing with the Walker cake?"

"No. Work your magic, and I'll handle the kitchen."

Work my magic. Bless Jon. What an absolutely tremendous idea. The excitement I'd dampened out earlier began building. And for the first time, I realized how perfectly named our bakery was, considering the circumstances of my heritage. "You're such a smart guy, Jon."

"That's a definite, but you're only now noticing?" he teased.

"What consultant are they using?" My mind was already sifting through the possibilities.

"Social Niceties."

"Doesn't surprise me. Do you know who's in charge?"

"Boss lady herself. You planning on calling her?"

"Yeah. I'll try to get some inside info on Mrs. Henderson and her daughter, and then I'll plan what we want to showcase."

"*We'll* plan on what we want to showcase."

"That's what I meant. We're a team."

"You're my perfect partner. In more ways than one."

"Have you talked to Andy? How's he doing?" I asked, knowing full well Jon didn't want to discuss Andy.

Jon frowned, but I saw the quick light of sadness hit his eyes. "I'm going to get started on the Walker cake. Let me know if you need anything."

"Wait. I didn't mean to upset you. I just don't want you to forget that what you and Andy have is unique."

"I used to think so. Now, I think it's over. Don't worry, you didn't upset me."

Jon closed his eyes. When he opened them, the sadness was gone or at least hidden well. I expected him to say something else, but he didn't. He gave me a halfhearted smile and left the office.

I'd seen him eat the damn cake I made for him. Why did my magic work on some of the people but not all of the people? And why did the brownie spell seem to affect Jon, which was an accident, but the one meant for him hadn't taken hold?

Not to mention Marc. What was going on with him? No apology yet.

It distressed me. Something else I'd have to discuss with Grandma Verda. Or maybe Miranda, if she talked to me again. Actually, Miranda would probably be best. Could I make her talk to me, or was I stuck waiting for her?

Hmm. I'd pretty much decided I was going to confide in Maddie. After she was back to normal, that is. I needed some help with all of this. And I missed confiding in her. Hopefully, I'd see a change in her soon.

On a whim, I went to the Google search page on my computer and typed in *Miranda Ayres*. I wanted to know more about her, because I couldn't figure out why she was paying me visits. Sure, I was her great-great-great granddaughter, but there had to be another reason. It was obvious, thankfully, that she wasn't trying to scare me. But what she wanted with me was a complete mystery.

Of course, there were no listings for her on Google. Chewing on my lip, I tried, *Gypsy Magic*. This garnered a couple of hits. Well, more like two million, so I scrolled through the first few. Unfortunately, nothing apropos to my situation popped up. A couple of stores, a website, and a psychic troupe for corporate entertaining (which might prove interesting, but was fairly useless to me) were the top three hits.

Clicking the X, I closed the Google page and flipped open my contact folder instead, as I might as well start the research for the Henderson job. Picking up the phone, I dialed the number for the Henderson wedding consultant. Time to get busy. The sooner we nabbed this client, the better.

Two hours later, I stretched the muscles in my shoulders. After speaking with Destiny of Social Niceties, I thought I had a handle on Mrs. Henderson and her daughter. It might not prove overly beneficial, as Destiny had said they were complete opposites and were butting heads on every step of the process.

Somehow, I'd have to find a way to make them both happy. I'd figure it out. I'd have to, what with so much at stake.

"I can't believe I've never been here before. It's so close to A Taste of Magic, you'd think I'd have eaten here at least once," I said to Kevin, pushing my plate back. "Thanks for asking me to join you."

Kevin's long wavy hair was pulled back tight, highlighting his high cheekbones and full lips. He'd phoned me earlier, asking me to dinner after I got off work. It had been a completely pleasant surprise. Even the healthiness of the vegetarian fare hadn't bothered me.

Come on, I'd choked down oatmeal for the guy—he was that luscious. Vegetables weren't close to being an issue.

"I'm glad you're enjoying yourself. They have great salads and amazing fruit smoothies chock full of vitamins and nutrients. You should check them out for lunch one day."

Right. Over my normal burger and fries? Not likely, but he didn't need to know that. "I'll keep that in mind." I glanced around the restaurant and noticed it had almost emptied out. "We've been talking awhile; I didn't realize we'd been here so long."

"Ready to go?" Did he sound disappointed?

On a whim, I said, "Why don't you follow me back to my place? I can make coffee, tea, or whatever you want and we can hang out." I gulped down a sip of my iced green tea to hide my nervousness. Why I was anxious about it, I had no clue.

When he smiled, I relaxed. He really was a nice guy.

"I'd love to. Actually, I need to make a quick stop, but I'll be right behind you."

"Oh. Okay." I didn't ask where or why. It was none of my business, but I *was* curious. "About an hour?"

"Probably less, but no more than that."

We walked out together, and he gave me a kiss on my

cheek before waving. "See you soon," he said. Nodding, I got in my car, watched him leave, and headed home.

Back at my place, I ran through my apartment trying to straighten it up as much as possible. When everything was as close to presentable as I could make it, I filled a pitcher with water and ice. I sliced up a lemon and tossed those into the water.

I kind of wished I had time to bake something. And, because I had no clue what I would wish for, it was probably best that I didn't have the time. The ringing phone startled me. Half-worried it was Kevin calling to cancel, I glanced at the Caller ID, something I rarely did.

It read: MARC STEVENS.

Oh. Was this actually it? My hand trembled as I picked up the phone. "Hello?"

"Betty. I'm calling to set up lunch, as we discussed. What day is good for you?"

And he didn't sound miserable at all, so likely the magic (once again) hadn't taken hold. Now it was even more important that we nailed the Henderson account. "This isn't a good time, Marc. I'm waiting for my date." Ooh, that felt good.

"Date? I didn't know you were dating."

The buzzer sounded. "He's here. I have to go."

"Wait, what about lunch?"

"What is it with you and lunch? Normal guys do not ask their ex-wives out for lunch all the time." When he didn't respond, I hung up without even a morsel of guilt. I knew he didn't want to meet for lunch to talk about the bakery. He'd just show up unannounced when he was ready for that.

I pushed him out of my thoughts. I couldn't deal with Marc. Not right now. But, I have to admit, I loved telling him I had a date. Pathetic? Probably. But also very, very cool.

When I let Kevin in, it was immediately obvious where he'd gone. Before, at dinner, he'd come straight from the gym. Now his hair was damp from the shower, and I could smell the clean scent of his shampoo when he walked past me.

"You didn't have to change," I said. Instead of the worn T-shirt and stretchy gym pants of earlier, now he wore tight denim and an orangey-red button-down shirt. On anyone else, the color would have been ludicrous and overly bright. But on Kevin the trainer? Absolutely gorgeous.

"I wanted to," he said. "So this is your place." His eyes roamed the small confines of my apartment, and a little frown appeared on his face. Yet again, I wished I'd taken the time to decorate. And unpack.

"It's a mess," I said.

"Just moved in?"

Yeah, definitely time to make some changes. "No. Just lazy."

"You should make the time to get it done. Where we live reflects a lot about who we are. Your home is also your sanctuary," he said, as if he were a teacher at some Zen spa. "You'll have to come by my condo sometime and see what I've done. If you like it, I'd love to help you out here."

"That's very thoughtful of you." I hadn't lied; it *was* thoughtful of Kevin to offer his help. But that other stuff he said? It sort of rubbed me the wrong way. I'd get to decorating. When I was ready.

Anxious again, but not entirely sure why, I nodded toward the living room. "You can come completely in. I won't bite."

"You can if you want," he teased.

That little tiny statement made me quiver, and the annoyance I'd felt seconds ago vanished. Another emotion hit me full force. Anticipation? Want? Nah, straight out needy desire. I called it like I saw it, and let me tell you—it had been way too long since I'd had sex. Come to think of it, even my toys hadn't seen the light of day for a while. They'd remained tucked away in my nightstand drawer ever since the last time Nate was over. Images of Nate kissing me, touching me, whipped into my thoughts. And then, a pain of longing hit me so quick I almost doubled over.

I must have looked kind of odd, because Kevin reached across and pulled me to him. "I'm teasing you."

"Oh. I know." Pressing my palms to his chest, I stepped back. "Do you want something to drink?"

"Water would be great."

I felt his eyes on me as I walked away. Once in the kitchen, I settled myself. I wanted to enjoy myself with Kevin. With that thought in place, I poured us each a glass of water. Heck, with the lemon slices, it sort of looked appealing.

"I'm rubbing off on you," he said, accepting his glass when I returned.

"I don't always drink coffee." Though, close.

After we situated ourselves in the living room, a strange sense of semi–déjà vu hit me. Yep. Same place (my apartment), same woman (me), different drink (water, not coffee), different man (Kevin in place of Nate), and similar yet somehow different emotions. Weird, but there you have it.

Kevin reached behind him and grabbed one of my latch-hook kit rugs I'd only half-completed. "What is this?" He turned it around, obviously in an attempt to find up from down.

I choked down a piece of ice that was caught in my throat. "A craft. When my ex and I split up, I needed to keep my hands busy. Somehow, it helped in keeping my mind busy, too. I never finished any of them." I waited for him to ask me about Marc. The question was going to come up sooner or later. I preferred later.

A wide smile broke. "Is this a unicorn?"

Heat flushed my face in embarrassment. "They only make those in so many designs. So yeah, it's a unicorn."

"There's nothing wrong with unicorns." Setting it back down behind him, he said, "My sister used to do these. Actually, I think she had a unicorn."

"Probably the same picture."

We chatted for a bit about nothing in particular. Family, work, Chicago, just the normal stuff and nothing terribly exciting taken as a whole but still enjoyable, I think, for both of us. Even so, I couldn't completely relax around him. Probably, it didn't mean anything. Because we were still in the getting-to-know-each-other stage, I wrote it off to that.

After a while, I summoned up the nerve to ask the one question that had been on my mind. "How old are you?"

He laughed. I squirmed. "I wondered when you'd get around to asking."

"Are you going to tell me or are you going to make me guess?" I knew it shouldn't matter, and I already knew he was younger than me, I just wanted to know how much younger. What if I was way off base and he was barely over eighteen? I squirmed again.

"Guessing sounds like a good idea to me. How old do you think I am?"

"You're in your twenties, I think."

"Twenty-what?"

I went low, figuring it would be easier to go up than down. On me, that is. "Twenty-two?"

"Not quite that young. Guess again."

"Twenty-five?"

"Close. Twenty-seven. See, not as young as you thought."

Still. Kevin was *eight years* younger than me. Did I like that idea or not? I couldn't decide. While it was cool he was interested in me, eight years is a lot. It made me a little uncomfortable. "Kevin, do you know how old I am?" In case he thought somehow that I was his age, I needed to make sure.

"I do. You filled out your birth date with your paperwork at Steel Bodies."

"So you don't think I'm too old for you?" I hated asking that question, and honestly, felt really stupid the second it left my mouth. But I really wanted to know.

"Age isn't so much a physical thing as a mental thing. Or maybe even a spiritual thing. Actual years mean nothing. It's the experience we generate from life that ages us. I've met people younger than me in years that were far older than me in spirit. And vice versa, too."

The Zen teacher was back, but he hadn't actually answered my question. I tried again. "I can buy in to that. At least to a certain extent, but do you think I am too old for you, regardless of how you judge age?"

His chocolate eyes melted, and his face softened. "I think we're the perfect age for each other. I'm completely interested in you, and I hope you feel the same about me."

Warmth tickled my cheeks. "I'm interested, but—"

"No buts, Elizabeth, interested is all I need to hear." He stood, pulled me to my feet, and wrapped his arms around me. "Let's dance," he said.

"Dance? There's no music."

"But there is. Close your eyes. You'll hear it."

I stepped into his embrace and closed my eyes. My head resting against his hard chest, his arms tight around me, our bodies moving together to silent music, all combined to start a gentle warmth in my belly.

"Can you hear it?" Kevin whispered, his breath hot against my ear.

"Weirdly enough, yes, I can."

And so we danced. I'm not sure for how long, but long enough for the warmth to climb from my belly into my limbs. Slowly, it traveled through my body, until every inch of my skin blushed from it. I didn't have to look at a mirror to know I was pink all over.

I didn't care.

Kevin's lips began at my ear. One small kiss, and then another. My eyes remained shut. His hands moved down my back until they squeezed my bottom, pushing me closer.

Oh, he was hard. No doubt about that. His teeth bit at my earlobe and then my jawline until his mouth met mine. I dragged my fingers through his hair and opened my mouth to his.

Warmth gave way to heat, and I lost myself in it, in his touch. We stopped dancing and sort of toppled backward to the couch, Kevin on top, his weight comfortable and hard all at once. I wrapped my legs around his hips and arched my back, so the pressure of his hardness was right there, right where I wanted it.

My mind quit functioning. All thought processes completely

shut down. I opened my senses and let myself feel, taste, and listen to everything happening.

Kevin stroked his fingers along the edge of my jaw. "I want—"

The ringing of the phone interrupted his statement, which was really a pity. I'd have loved for him to finish his sentence. He lifted his gaze to mine, filled with questions and heat. I was tempted to let the phone ring, let it go to voicemail; after all, what could be important enough to step away from this? I needed to feel desirable. I needed to feel wanted. And right now, I did.

But by the third ring, the daze began to clear, and I wasn't as comfortable. I wasn't totally sure why I was doing what I apparently had been about to do. Happy for the reprieve, I scooted out from beneath him. "I should get that. Sorry."

"No problem." He rolled off me into a stand. I leapt up and ran to the kitchen and grabbed the phone off the wall. I kept meaning to buy a cordless, but always seemed to forget.

"Hello," I said, not looking at Kevin, who had trailed after me into the kitchen.

"Elizabeth? Have you talked to your grandmother today?" It was my mother, and she sounded upset. Great.

"Today? No. Why?"

"No one seems to know where she is. She didn't answer earlier so I sent your father over, but she's not there."

My first instinct was worry, but then I thought of Vinny. "I bet she's with Vinny. Do you have his number?"

"No. Do you?"

"Nope. When did you talk to her last?"

"Last night. She usually tells me if she's not going to be home when I call. I'm really worried. What do you think we should do?"

My mother was asking me for advice. That worried me almost more than my missing Grandma Verda. "Check in with Alice and the boys. Maybe they've heard something."

"I already did. No one has talked to her today at all."

"Whose day was it?"

"Mine, but she hasn't been home."

I glanced at the clock. Concern skittered over me, but I set it aside. "It's only eight, Mom. She maybe went to the movies or to Bingo or something. I'm sure she's fine. Give her another hour and try her again."

"That's what your dad said. Maybe I'm worried about nothing, but she's not herself lately."

"Mom, really, listen to Dad. If she's not home in a couple of hours, let me know."

"I will, but what can you do?"

"Remember Nate? You met him at Alice's. He lives next door. I can ask him what we should do if she's not home by then." It was the only thing I could think of. But honestly, Grandma Verda had a more active social life than I did—at least normally—so most likely, she was out having fun. I tried to hold on to that, but I'd be lying if I said I wasn't worried at all.

"Thank you, sweetie. I'll call you either way and let you know."

After I hung up, I turned to Kevin. "I'm sorry about that. My mother is upset because *her* mother isn't at home, safely tucked in for the night. It has to be strange to suddenly feel like the parent to your parent."

He smiled and pulled me to him. "It's not a problem. You're here. I'm here. Where did we leave off?"

Before I could say a word, my phone trilled again. Startled, I grabbed it, thinking it was probably my mother again.

"Are you busy?"

"Um. Kind of. What's up, Jon?"

"Just wanted to talk, but if you're busy, you can call me back. Or I can call you back later. Whatever you want."

"Is there a problem?"

Silence, which meant there was, but Jon wouldn't say so—not if he knew I was busy.

"Just call me back when you can."

The telltale beep of another call buzzed through. "Hey,

Jon, I have another call coming in. I'll get back to you soon. I promise."

Clicking over, I swung an apologetic smile to Kevin. I noticed he was backing up toward the living room. Poor guy.

"Hello?"

"Troy was here again, Liz." My sister's panicked voice came over the line.

"Again? What did he want?"

"I don't know. I pretended I wasn't home, so he ended up leaving."

This bothered me. A lot. "The check was good, right?"

"Yeah, the money is in my account, all is squared up now. At least financially. But I didn't want to answer because he was so weird when he was here last time. All that mumbo jumbo stuff about witches and spells."

"It's good you didn't answer the door. Did you see him through the peephole?"

"Yeah. How else would I have known it was him?"

"Did he look sick? He was sick before; that's why he thought there was a spell."

"I don't know. He looked angry. So I sort of just backed up and went into the bedroom and watched the parking lot until I saw him leave."

"You did great, Alice. Exactly what I would have done." Heaven help me if the spell hadn't ended with the payback of the money. How would I convince him it wasn't on purpose? Even more worrisome, how would I take it off? "Do me a favor, though. If he comes back, call me. I'll take care of it."

"Really? It's not your battle, sis."

"Let me handle it, Alice. I'm not emotionally involved with him like you are."

"Only if you're sure."

Grandma Verda popped into my thoughts. "Hey, Alice, have you seen Grandma today?"

"Not you, too. Mom already asked me that. I haven't. Is she really missing?"

"I don't know. Probably not, but I figured I'd ask since we

were on the phone." Hanging up once again, I said to Kevin, "I'm sorry, but my family is all nutso tonight."

He smiled a wholly relaxed smile at me. "It's cool." He stepped toward me and—you got it—the phone rang. *Again*.

"Shit," I muttered. I grabbed the receiver. "Yes?"

"What's wrong? You sound ticked."

"Oh. Hi, Maddie. Not angry, just one of those nights."

"You think you could come up here for a few minutes? I want to show you the dress I bought."

"Um, actually, I'm waiting for both my sister and my mom to call me back."

"I'll just come down. See you in a few."

"Maddie? Wait." All I heard was the dial tone. It looked like I'd have the chance to think about what had almost happened with Kevin. Maybe good. Maybe bad. Sometimes, it was nice to just roll with it.

"Kevin, I have bad news. My friend Maddie is coming over. Right now. She hung up before I could answer."

A loud rap on the door announced her presence. Man, she's fast. "That would be her," I chuckled.

Kevin smiled and squeezed my hand. "Things come up. I should get going, anyhow. I have an early morning at the gym tomorrow."

Personally? I kind of felt pummeled by all the information that had been dumped on my head in less than ten minutes. I didn't know if I should be disappointed or relieved. Happy or sad.

Sighing, I let Kevin out and Maddie in.

Chapter Thirteen

For the first time since hearing about Grandma Verda being missing, my skin itched with anxiety. My mother called again to inform me Grandma still wasn't home and no one had heard from her. It seemed somewhat silly to notify the police when we didn't really know what was going on, but something proactive needed to be done.

Which is how I ended up knocking on Nate's door at a little after eleven. I was uncomfortable at the possibility of waking him up. Hell, I was uncomfortable simply talking to him at that point. But for my Grandma, I'd get over my nerves.

I only hoped Nate was actually home. A cop's hours were not exactly of the nine to five variety, as I already knew too well. When the door whipped open, I was partially relieved and partially frozen in my tracks.

Sleepy green eyes and a pillow-creased cheek told me I had, indeed, awakened him. "Is something wrong?" he asked, voice scratchy. It was yet another indicator of my intrusion.

"I don't know. Maybe. Honestly, I'm not sure what you can do, but thought maybe you'd at least be able to tell me what *I* should do." I heard myself ramble on and immediately snapped my jaw shut.

"Come in," he said, grabbing my wrist and gently tugging me inside. "Tell me what the problem is." He closed the door behind us, and I leaned against it for support.

"My grandmother is missing. Or maybe not. I guess we don't really know, not for sure. But she's not home, and my mother is upset. Anyway, we don't know if we should file a report or what."

"Verda?"

"Yeah. I thought maybe asking you would be a good idea because you said you knew her and, well, also because we didn't know what the normal protocol would be."

Nate ran his hand over his face. "Give me a second here." He disappeared into the kitchen and returned with a glass of juice an instant later. He gulped a swallow. "How long has she been missing?"

I realized, suddenly, he was wearing boxers and a tank. Strong legs, muscular legs, but I couldn't focus on them at the moment. Even though I would have liked to. "Not sure. None of the family has seen or talked to her since last night."

"Did your mom check with area hospitals?"

"Oh, God. I don't think so. Should we?"

"If for no other reason than to rule it out, sure." He set the juice on the table and murmured, mostly to himself, "I wonder if she called 911."

My brain clicked in. "That's how you know her! You've responded to those calls before, haven't you?"

"Yeah, but she didn't want me to say anything. Your grandmother is one feisty lady, so she probably doesn't want to be seen as vulnerable. Especially by her family."

Wow. He *got* her. That was cool. "You know her pretty well already." I laughed, trying to hide the fear that was beginning to grow. "Wait a minute. Are you one of the cops who brought her beer and Cheetos?"

He choked on his juice, wiped his mouth, and said, "What are you talking about?"

"My grandmother. She said the cops bring her beer and Cheetos after she calls 911."

"Are you serious?"

I nodded.

"Trust me, no police officer brought your grandmother beer. She's just messing with you. Let me put some clothes on and we'll go back to your place. That way, you can call your mom and we can start checking the hospitals." For a brief moment, uncertainty passed over his face. "That is, if you want me to come with you."

"Yes. I do. Thank you for offering."

A few minutes later, we were standing in my kitchen instead of his.

"Do you want to call your mom before we start checking the hospitals?" Nate asked.

"No. She'll get more upset if we put that thought in her head. Let's start with the major ones, and if Grandma Verda isn't at any of them, I'll call my mother then."

"Sounds good. Where's your phone book?"

"In the closet." I started to walk out of the kitchen, but he stopped me.

"I'll get it. Why don't you make some tea or something? To calm your nerves."

I nodded. When he left the room, I turned the water on and grabbed a mug out of the cupboard. I was about to fill it when I realized a little plastic cup I'd left in the sink was now sitting in the garbage disposal. Probably, the force of the running water had pushed it down.

"Did you say the coat closet?" Nate called from the other room.

"No. In the hallway," I replied. I turned the faucet off and plunged my hand into the half-filled sink. The damn cup had blocked the drain. I pried at the plastic edges with my fingers, trying to force it loose. It didn't budge. Maybe if I stuck my fist in it, I could pull it out?

It was worth a shot. I shoved my hand into the cup and gave it a good yank.

And then I realized how stupid an idea it actually was. Now my hand was wedged tight in the cup, which had pushed down even farther into the disposal. I pulled back as hard as I could, and the thing still didn't move. *Crap.* Now what? I stood still for a second, trying to decide the best action to take. I needed to figure this out.

Preferably before Nate returned.

I wanted him to see me as sexy, and trust me, there was absolutely nothing sexy about a woman stuck to her sink. With my other hand, I opened the silverware drawer and retrieved a butter knife. I slid it in between the cup and drain, hoping to pry it up some. This position? Awkward as hell. Ambidextrous I was not, so maneuvering the knife with my left hand was agonizingly difficult.

I gave it the best go I could, but all I managed to do was bend the knife from the pressure I was exerting on it. *Great.* Why hadn't I bought sturdier flatware? Who knew how important 18/10 stainless steel could be? Not me, that's for sure. Of course, I never thought I'd be in a position like this.

I tossed the knife on the counter and gave my fist another hard pull. Still no dice. Giving up and swallowing my embarrassment, I yelled, "Nate? Can you come here?" I mean, I guess it was good he was even there. What would I have done if I'd been alone? I couldn't reach the phone from where I stood. But come on—like I wanted Nate to see me like this?

"I can't find the phone book. Are you sure . . ." He broke off. "What's going on?"

I pivoted at my waist so I could see him. I tried to stand up straight. I tried to look poised. I'm sure I failed. "I'm stuck. Can you help me?" I tugged my arm again.

His lips quirked into a grin. "What is it with you getting stuck in small spaces?"

I shrugged, but because one arm was pulled tight, only one shoulder lifted. "Really, it doesn't happen that often." God, I wanted out of this sink. "Help me? Please?"

He came next to me and rolled up his sleeves. "What did you do, exactly?"

"There's a cup wedged in the disposal. I was just trying to get it out." Oh. Wow. He smelled really good. I scooted closer so I could smell him better.

He looked at me curiously. "What are you doing?"

"Um. Nothing." And then I maneuvered myself so I was even closer. I leaned in more. I wanted to kiss him. Just once. But before my lips made their way to his, he'd turned back to the sink. I didn't know if he'd purposely avoided my kiss, or if he just hadn't seen it coming. I still wanted to kiss him.

Plunging his hands into the water, he grabbed my wrist. And then, he twisted it slowly back and forth. I felt some of the pressure bubble away, and then—bam—the suction released and my hand came free. Why hadn't I done that?

"Thank you." I dried my hands off on a towel. "But the cup is still stuck."

"Why don't you go get the phone book, and I'll work on that?" He was still grinning.

Before I could answer, my phone rang. My embarrassment fled. Worry slammed through me as I thought of Grandma Verda. "Maybe they have news." I picked up the receiver. "Hello?"

"Your grandmother is at the hospital with her friend Vinny," my mother said. "He had a heart attack, so she's been waiting for word on how he's doing."

Relief poured into me, and the weight sitting on my shoulders disappeared. "She's okay?"

"She's upset. We're going over there now to pick her up. Do you want to meet us there?"

"Are you taking her back to your place?"

My mother snorted. "If she lets us. She'll probably argue."

"Why don't you go ahead, and I'll call Alice, Scot, and Joe and let them know Grandma is safe. How's Vinny doing?"

"He's stabilized."

"Well, that's good. I know how close Grandma is to him. Let me know if she needs anything and tell her I'll come see her tomorrow after work."

After I informed my siblings of Grandma Verda's whereabouts, I closed my eyes and sighed.

"You look exhausted," Nate said. When I opened my eyes, he was standing directly in front of me, the plastic cup in hand. He set it down on the counter.

"How did you get that out?"

He shrugged, but another glimmer of humor lit his eyes. "You must have loosened it. So Verda is safe?"

I nodded.

"Good. I'm glad."

"Me, too. Thanks for being so great. I completely appreciate it." I realized he'd played my hero four times now: the window saving incident, my sister, the sink, and now my grandmother. God, my family really was crazy.

"That's what neighbors are for."

I truly hoped he thought of me as more than a neighbor, but I wasn't sure how to broach that, so I kept my mouth shut. You know, the "silence equals mysterious" thing? Better late than never, right? But he didn't say anything, either. Maybe *he* was trying to be mysterious? Finally, I said, "I'm really sorry I woke you up."

"I'm a cop. It's normal. Nothing new there." He hooked his thumbs into the belt straps on his jeans. "At least tonight it was a pretty face that broke into my dreams."

The teasing quality of his voice made me smile. "What kind of dreams?"

"Oh, something about a woman stuck in a window and having to rescue her."

"Sounds like an amazing dream," I teased right back.

"It was, Liz. It definitely was." His arm reached out and hooked around my waist. One good yank and I was right there. "I've missed you the last couple of days."

"I've been around."

"But busy."

I refused to explain anything, so I just stood there watching him. Maybe, just maybe, if he fessed up about the red-haired chick from the other day, I'd explain who Jon was.

Nate already knew about Kevin.

He angled his head downward, and I knew he was going to kiss me. I couldn't wait for him to kiss me. Closer his lips came. Closer. Tilting my face upward more, I closed my eyes, breathed to the beat of my heart, and waited.

His lips rested on the tip of my nose, moved to my forehead, and then he unhooked his arm. "I'm going to get some more sleep. You're all set now, right?" Whipping open my eyes, my gaze on my feet, I swallowed frustration.

"Yeah, I'm fine. Thanks again for your help." And then, my stupid phone rang again. He stepped backward. Coldness at his absence surrounded me. I answered the phone.

"I thought you were going to call me back?"

"Sorry, it's been a crazy evening." I glanced at Nate. "Hey, Jon? Can you give me a second?"

"Sure," Jon replied.

I hooked the receiver over the top of the phone base. "I need to take this."

"Alrighty then. Get some rest."

I lifted my chin and met his eyes with mine. "You too."

After he left, I willed my racing heart to slow down and tried to convince myself I wasn't really disappointed. That I didn't really care Nate's kiss reminded me of a kiss you'd give a child. Of course, that didn't wash. I recognized myself for the liar I was. Not only did I care, I cared far more than I should.

Picking up the phone once again, I said, "I'm back. What's up?"

"I'm nervous about the Henderson gig. I wanted to go over a few things with you."

Sighing, I plopped into a chair. Knowing Jon, I figured he mostly wanted company to take his thoughts off his domestic issues. "What's worrying you? Let's start with that." I settled myself into friend mode, all the while trying to expunge Nate from my mind.

This? Not an easy task, I assure you.

"She's gonna drive you crazy. You know that, don't you?" Scot asked, as we assessed my bedroom. "Are you sure you want her here?"

"Yes and yes." At his doubtful grin, I chuckled. "Fine. I'm not sure. But she's coming." After the scare with Vinny, Grandma Verda, for some reason, had finally decided to move in with me. Temporarily, she claimed. But seeing as it was her idea, I wasn't so sure.

Regardless, for the time being anyway, she would be my roommate. She and her cat. While we could certainly share my bed, I preferred not to. I move when I sleep—a lot. I figured we'd both be more comfortable if we had our own bed to sleep in.

Luckily, even though my apartment was only a one-bedroom, that bedroom was huge, so it was easy to fit in two beds. Even more fortuitous, Scot had an extra bed he'd hauled over for me. Gotta love big brothers. Sometimes they come in handy.

"Let's move the smaller boxes into the closet and the larger ones can be stacked over here, by the bed," I said. Mainly, I was trying to clear the far corner of the room so there'd be a spot for the bed Scot had brought over on his truck.

"Why don't you unpack everything and throw the boxes away?" my brother asked with a smirk. "Rather than just find another spot to stack them?"

"I don't have time to do that; she'll be here in the morning. So, help me or leave, but quit being a butthead."

He put his hand over his heart. "Ouch. You wound me, baby sister. I shall cry a thousand tears at your hurtful remark."

"Not likely. How did you get an extra bed, anyway?"

"It's my old one. It was still sitting in storage. You may as well use it for now."

"I appreciate it. You know, your place is bigger than mine. Grandma could stay with you easier than with me."

"No."

My brother, the one-word wonder. I actually didn't mind Grandma moving in, but teasing Scot was just so much fun. "Aw, come on. Think about it at least."

"I'll think about it." He picked up the box closest to him and stuck it in the closet. "Thought about it. No."

"She stayed with you before. When her condo was painted."

"Uh-huh, which is why I'm saying no. You'll find out why soon enough. If you really don't want her here, call Alice."

"She'd probably be good for Alice, but she wants to stay here. You and I both know there's no talking her out of something once she makes up her mind."

"Then quit haranguing me."

"Whew, that's a big word for you! Is that your word-of-the-day?" I grinned to soften the insult. "Sorry, couldn't resist."

"Bite me. Are we doing this or not?" Scot asked, gesturing to my room.

"What? You can't talk and move silly little boxes around at the same time? It's called multitasking."

Scot crossed his arms over his blue T-shirt. "I'm going to leave, and you'll be stuck sharing that bed with Grandma."

"Doesn't bother me."

"And her cat. The cat likes to crawl on your face when you're sleeping. You'll wake up with hair in your throat and the taste of the litter box in your mouth."

I shuddered. "Gross. You've made your point."

Once the room was rearranged appropriately, I asked, "Hungry? I can make something if you are."

"No thanks. I'm going out tonight."

Something in his voice startled me. I'd always been fairly attuned to my siblings. Well, all except for Joe. I'd never figure him out. Scot and I were close, being the two eldest, and we'd always had an especially strong connection. "Out to dinner with whom?" I watched him closely.

His eyes shot downward and he brushed his hair off his forehead. "Did I say I was going out with anyone?" If there was a picture next to the word avoidance in the dictionary, it would most definitely be one of Scot. Trust me. He was, beyond a doubt, hiding something.

"You'd like me to believe you're eating at a restaurant by yourself? Come on, bro—I know you better than that. You despise eating in public by yourself."

"Not true. I eat out by myself all the time."

"Where? McDonalds?"

"And this is important to you why? You sound like Mom."

"Ouch. Don't ever say that to me again."

He didn't speak, just shifted a few more boxes around in the closet—which was totally unnecessary, by the way.

"Don't tell me, then. Whatever."

"You're such a whiner. I've been meaning to talk to you

about this anyway." He hesitated for a second and then continued, "I'm meeting Marc for dinner tonight." It was way too evident he didn't like admitting it to me. We were both silent for a minute while I took it in. I wasn't completely sure how I felt about it.

That's a lie. It bugged the hell out of me.

"Marc? My ex-husband Marc? Why in the world would you be doing that? You hate me that much?"

"Give me a break, Liz. He's my financial consultant, you know that. You hooked us up." Lifting his gaze from the floor, he said, "He does a good job with my money."

Silly, but I wanted to scream "Traitor!" at him. I wanted to stomp on the ground like a three-year-old. Basically, I wanted to be an obnoxious brat. Obviously, I didn't. Because while I didn't like it, I did understand. I hated that I understood. Sometimes, being mature sucks. "Well, okay. Marc is exceptional at what he does," I grudgingly admitted.

"You're not going to cry or anything, are you?"

I laughed at the expression on Scot's face. As soon as I did, all the tension in the room evaporated. Poor guy. "Of course not. It's up to you who you hire. I won't say I'm happy about it, but it's your call."

"Don't think I didn't lay into him after he left you. I did. Hell, I even gave him a black eye." Scot grinned at that statement, and my heart warmed. Like I said, sometimes, older brothers rock. Even better, I remembered Marc showing up at the house with a shiner. I didn't bother asking him about it because that would have shown I cared. And you don't want to show a man who's just left you for a Barbie doll bimbo that you cared. "That was you?"

With a sheepish grin, Scot nodded. "And then, we just got back to business. That's how it is with guys. I showed my respect for you, he took it like a man, and we forgot about it."

Ha. I wished I could forget about it so easily. Maybe I should punch Marc in the eye. I almost told Scot that Marc was sticking his nose into my bakery business, but really, what would that have solved? Absolutely nothing, that's what.

With a smile as bright as I could make it, I said, "Let's go haul the bed in so you can head out for your date with Marc."

"Brat."

"Snot."

An hour later, after we'd finished setting the bed up, Scot took off. I wondered if he'd ever give up his bachelorhood. I kind of doubted it. Years ago, I'd tried to fix him up with Maddie, only it hadn't clicked. For either of them. I was tempted to remedy that with a magical batch of cupid cookies but quickly decided against it. After all, I'd be ticked off if I was magically coerced into falling in love with someone. Besides, it was unlikely it would work anyway. The result would probably be something entirely unexpected. Not to mention, something entirely disastrous.

Yeah, I caught on quick.

What I could do was go check on Maddie. I'd only seen her a minute the other night, so I was really curious if she was back to normal or not. Then, I had a mile-long grocery list of Grandma Verda's to fill.

I tucked my keys in my pocket and took the stairs to Maddie's. She answered the door with a smile on her face. "Oh. I thought you were Spencer."

"Don't sound so disappointed." *Wow.* Points for me and for Miranda's magic. "You look amazing," I said, taking in her shining hair, rosy cheeks, and sultry-shaded eyes.

"Thank you! I'm feeling so much better."

"Can I come in? Or is he going to be here at any minute?"

"Oh, of course you can. Want to join us tonight? We're going to check out a new comedy club Spencer's all excited about."

She stepped aside, and I walked past her. "Nah, I don't think Spencer would be thrilled with an add-on." Before she could argue, I said, "Besides, I have plans with Dominick's tonight."

"Oh! If I give you a list, could you pick me up a few things? I know that's awful of me, but I've been so miserable lately I haven't even bothered shopping."

"Sure, that's cool. So, you're really feeling back to normal?"

"Better than normal." She grabbed a notepad out of her desk and wrote a few things down. Handing it to me, she said, "This will do until I can get to the store. I really appreciate it."

"It's the least I can do," I said without thinking.

"What do you mean?"

"Oh, well. Hmm. We need to talk, but this probably isn't the best time with Spencer showing up soon. Tomorrow, if you can, let's get together."

I needed to share the weight of this with somebody, and Maddie was my best friend. And now that she was feeling better, I didn't have to worry about her reaction. At least, I didn't think I did. Before, well, who knew what she might have done. Visions of a girl fight flashed in front of me. Trust me, she'd win, hands down.

A curious light glinted in her eyes. "You want to come here, or should I come to your place?"

Good question. Grandma Verda would have moved in, lock, stock, and barrel by then. It could be a good thing, since she knew the story better than I did. Or, it could go the other way, if she decided I should keep my mouth shut. Making a decision, I said, "Here. I'll come up here." Later, if Maddie wanted to talk to Grandma about it, she certainly could.

"What's this about?"

"Nothing to stress over. Something I want some advice on. That's all."

A knock on her door brought another smile to her face. "How do I look? Tell me the truth."

"Breathtaking," I said. "I'm gonna take off. Have a great time tonight!"

"I plan on it. In more ways than one." She opened the door. Spencer, a blond cutie with glasses, smiled in appreciation as his gaze flitted over Maddie. I couldn't blame him. She was a knockout.

"Hi, Spencer. Bye, Spencer." I walked to the hallway and waved behind my head as I took the steps. "You guys have fun!"

At my place, I found the list from Grandma, jotted Maddie's items on it, and went off in search of delicacies such as Spam and Wonder Bread.

Yep, my thoughts exactly. Absolutely disgusting. If nothing else, living with Grandma Verda would be a culinary experience I wouldn't soon forget.

Chapter Fourteen

"Grandma, what is that smell?" I asked, coming into the kitchen. The move-in over, I was trying to adjust to having a roomie. Already, I recognized I'd have to relax on a few things.

Shirley meowed and rubbed herself between my legs. The giant orange tabby had waltzed into my apartment as if she were a queen, inspected the entire place, and then pounced on top of the TV. More often than not, she was there, soaking in the warmth.

"Hi, honey. I'm making dinner for Shirley."

It took a minute for that to sink in. "You're cooking the cat dinner?"

"Well, of course. You don't like to eat cold food every night, do you?"

Um. Okay. But I wasn't a cat. "What is it you're heating up?" I probably didn't want to know. Not really. But a strange compulsion overtook my senses, and I asked anyway. Dumb, huh?

"She really likes Spam mixed in with some tuna and a little of her moist food. Don't you, baby?" Grandma sing-songed to the tabby.

"Wait a minute. You actually put canned cat food in my Calphalon pan? Grandma, no."

"What? Your pan is too good for my Shirley? I hardly think so. Don't be silly, Elizabeth. It will wash."

I really wanted to point out to her that I wasn't the silly one. Most people would be as grossed out as I was at the thought of heating up cat food on the freaking stove. But. She. Is. My. Grandmother. I must show respect.

"'Kay, just don't use any other pan. That can be Shirley's pan. Lucky cat."

Mental note to self: replace cat pan with human pan as soon as possible. Oh, and don't use cat pan for soup or any other human food.

Well, unless I had a reason to cook for Marc again.

"I'm going to take a bath and get ready for bed. I'm meeting Maddie tomorrow for lunch, so I won't be here. Will you be okay?" Maddie had spent the previous night at Spencer's so was unavailable for our planned talk. I figured a Saturday afternoon was better anyway. More time to explain I wasn't crazy.

"Joe's coming by to take me to the hospital to see Vinny. I'll be fine." Grandma Verda spooned the absolutely disgusting mash of weird food into a bowl and set it down for Shirley. And, I have to admit, the feline pounced on it as if it were a feast for a king. Or, in this case, a queen.

You know how certain cooking smells just linger and never really dissipate—like, cabbage? Well, that smell would likely never leave this apartment. Probably, I'd have to find a new place when, and if, Grandma moved out.

An hour later, I was tucked into bed. Grandma had insisted that the bed Scot brought over was sufficient, that she didn't need my larger one. This, as silly as it sounds, made me happy. I loved my bed. It was the only valuable piece of furniture I'd purchased when I moved in.

"Good night, Grandma. I'm glad you're here," I said into the dark.

"'Night, baby. Thank you for having me."

My eyes closed. I stuck my nose into my pillow. I'd sprayed it liberally with my peach-scented body spray to douse out the cat-food stink. I had a feeling I'd be sleeping like this for the remainder of Grandma's stay.

And then, out of nowhere, a warm breeze touched my cheek, and the heady fragrance of flowers overtook the peach. I squeezed the blanket tight around me, curling my fingers into a fist. Excitement and apprehension mingled as I waited.

"Elizabeth, can you see me this time?"

My eyes popped open. Yep, she was back. No way could I ignore her, either. The entire room swirled with a kalei-doscope of light as Miranda's voice hit my ears. It was if a

million rainbows were in my bedroom, shooting off in a zillion different directions.

Great. Now Grandma would know about Miranda. I hoped
like hell it didn't scare her to the point of a stroke. Or a heart
attack. "No," I whispered, squinting through the colors.

"What? Lizzie, did you say something?" asked Grandma
Verda.

"No, Grandma." Keep your eyes closed, I prayed. Just keep
them shut.

"I need you to see me. It has to be you. No one else has
been as strong as you are. You're the only one I've really been
able to connect with."

"I can't see you," I whispered. And what did she mean
"connect with?"

"What the hell is this? Lizzie, what's going on? Who else is
here? Are you on the phone? What's with all the damn color? Is
this some disco thing?" My grandma's voice flooded the room.
She wanted answers, and she didn't sound scared at all.

"Can you hear her, Grandma?"

"Verda, can you see me?" Miranda asked, ripples of excitement floating off each word.

Wait. Could ghosts get excited? Apparently, they could.

"Who is that? Who's talking to me?" *Now* Grandma
sounded nervous.

I sighed. There really was no way around it. I really, really
hoped she was strong enough to handle this. "It's Miranda.
She's come to pay a visit," I said carefully, ready to rush to her
bed if need be.

Miranda laughed. "What a delightful girl you are." Every
time Miranda spoke, the lights in the room pulsed and increased in brightness.

"Miranda? Well, it's about time," my grandmother said.
"I've waited for this for far too long."

Huh?

"Magic?" Maddie laughed. "Sure. Okay, honey. Whatever
you say."

"I'm serious. Everything I've told you is the truth."

She arched a waxed eyebrow in disbelief. "And you say this . . . Miranda is trying to appear before you and your grandmother?"

"Well, it was just me. But with Grandma moving in, she caught the show last night."

"And what did Miranda say last night?"

I ignored the disbelief in Maddie's voice. "Not much. She left almost right away again. It's as if she can't stick around for very long. And for some reason, I think it's important we see her. She just kept asking if we were able to."

"And could you?"

I shook my head. "No. The room fills with color, and sometimes I think I see a shape in the middle of it, but it's more like the suggestion of a shape than it is an actual shape."

"Oh. I see. A *suggestion* of a shape." Maddie grabbed her purse from the dining room table. Opening her wallet, she sifted through business cards.

"What are you doing?"

"I have a card for a psychiatrist I was going to see. I think you need it more than I do. Aha, here it is!"

"I don't need to see a shrink. I'm fine. Well, okay, not fine. But not crazy, either. What I'm telling you is the truth, so unless your psychiatrist is also a medium, it's not going to do me much good."

She returned to the couch and put her hands on my shoulders. "Look me straight in the eyes and tell me you're not making any of this up."

"I am not making any of this up."

Letting go, she sighed. "You're serious, aren't you?"

"Yeah." Silence loomed between us as she let the information absorb in.

"So—you cast a spell on me?"

I nodded.

"Assuming I believe you, that's why I was so miserable?"

"I think so. It was the first spell I cast on purpose, and I thought I was giving you something good. I didn't do it right, so yeah, pretty sure it was my fault you were miserable."

"That spell almost ruined things for me and Spencer."

"I know. I'm so sorry."

"Are you positive the second spell isn't going to screw me up in some way?"

I fiddled with a loose string on the hem of my shirt. "Well . . ."

"Well, what?" She frowned. "You're *not* sure?"

There really was no two ways about it. I'd chosen to confide in her. Mistake? Maybe, but nothing I could do about that now. I might as well say it all. "No. I'm not positive. But you're feeling better, right?"

She crossed her arms. "Now? Yes. But I felt good with the last spell, before everything went crazy."

"I fixed it as soon as I could."

Another raised brow. "Did you? I was pretty unhappy for a while."

"Well. You see . . . Um."

"Spit it out, Elizabeth."

Oh, she was ticked. Maddie almost always called me by nicknames. "Nate ate the first fix before I could stop him," I blurted.

"Can you prove it to me?"

"What? That Nate ate the cake? Just ask him."

She sighed. "No, that you . . . put magic, or whatever, in your baking."

"Yes!" Why hadn't I thought of that? "Do you have a cake or a brownie mix? Muffins? Anything?"

Instead of answering, she beckoned me with her hand and marched to her kitchen, shoulders set. I didn't know if proving it was such a good idea, after all. I mean, yeah, I wanted her to believe me, but I also didn't feel like getting clubbed.

I heard the slamming of cupboard doors before I even reached the kitchen. A box of muffin mix, a mixing bowl, and the muffin tin was already sitting on the counter. She moved in a blur, so intent to get me all the ingredients I needed to make her believe.

Or to prove I was a fake.

She put her hands on her hips. "There you go, Elizabeth. Will this do? Is this enough for you to cast a spell?"

Whoa. Definitely not a good idea. "Look. If you don't believe me, you don't believe me. Even if I do this, you'll find a way to ignore what you see."

"I swear I won't. Unless you're afraid?"

I'm not ashamed to admit her taunt worked. Nodding, I grabbed the muffin box, read the back quickly, and ripped open the top. "We need to decide on a spell. What am I wishing for?"

"How about your heart's desire? Getting Marc back?"

"I don't want Marc back. Besides, I already spelled him. One worked. I'm waiting on the results from the second one."

"Oh?"

"Let's do this. And then when you see I'm not a liar or crazy, I'll explain then."

"Fair enough. Okay, um, wish for world peace."

"My grandmother says it doesn't work that way."

"How exactly does it work then, Elizabeth?"

Holy cow, she was pushing all of my buttons. Clamping my mouth shut, I tried to think. "Never mind. I know what I'll wish for."

I dumped the contents of the box into the mixing bowl, cracked two eggs, and measured in the oil. Before I began, I focused on Maddie once more. "Are you sure about this? Sometimes it can get a little overwhelming."

Tapping her foot, she replied, "I'm one hundred percent positive. Just do it."

I ignored the electric mixer and picked up the wooden spoon. This way, she wouldn't be able to blame anything on electricity. Besides, I preferred my muffins dense and rich. There was no reason for shoddy muffins, even if this was only a test.

Scraping the sides of the bowl to start, I fashioned the exact words to say. Because I wanted this to be a powerful show for Maddie, I was casting the only spell I could think of that meant anything to me at the moment. The one I still couldn't seem to get right.

I closed my eyes and started stirring the contents together. I focused on what I wanted, poured my heart and soul into it, and whispered, "This wish is for me. I wish to be able to see my life with clarity, to know what I truly want, and to find the courage to go after it. No matter what it is, my wish is to never hide from myself again."

The familiar energy began at my toes and climbed up my body like a vine, stronger and stronger. It reached my hands and flew out of me into the spoon. Instantly, the weighted zap of electricity sung through the air, bright colors flared from the spoon into the bowl. I kept stirring, repeating the wish over and over. Wind blew, and I heard a crash behind me, but I didn't stop. My body pulsated with power, with magic, and I mentally grabbed hold of it and pummeled it out of me, straight into the batter.

I opened my eyes and saw the entire bowl was alight with myriad colors, shining, darting, glowing, jumping around as if someone had set off a miniature firework show. Laughing, I tipped my head back and repeated my wish one last time, with force, with all the emotion I could wring into it. I shuddered, let go of the spoon, and dropped to my knees. Slowly, very slowly, the energy faded, and Maddie's kitchen returned to normal.

With a deep inhalation, I centered myself, ascertained I could stand without falling, and then pulled myself to my feet. Turning, I looked at Maddie. "That proof enough for you?"

"Damn, Lizzie. What the hell are you? A witch?"

I felt her then—Miranda. I knew she was there, with me, inside me, around me. My heritage. My gift. Who I truly was. "No, Maddie. Not a witch. I'm a gypsy."

I fed Jon a bite of the new cupcakes I'd baked for him. Instead of trying to fix anything, I'd cast a spell to remove the effects of all the other spells. Maybe, just maybe, that would work.

He grinned at me and swallowed the bite I'd shoved into his mouth. Wiping crumbs off his lips, he said, "Enough. We need to focus. They'll be here soon."

Happy he'd eaten some of the cupcake, I tossed the rest in the trash. If it worked on him, I'd bake another batch for Maddie. Just to be sure. I mean, yeah, she seemed okay, but I was still anxious about it. "We're going to ace this. Quit flipping out."

"Aren't you the person who bluntly told me not to get too excited?" Jon asked, pacing the length of the lobby at A Taste of Magic. "You know we need this. Not just to pay off Marc, but to get everything back on track. I don't want to screw it up."

We were expecting Penelope and Grace Henderson at any moment. I no longer worried about getting the job. I'd put the time and my magic into the samples they would taste test, so success shouldn't be an issue. Well, I hoped not. And no, I didn't feel guilty—use what you got, that was my new motto. Besides, we'd give them their money's worth, and they'd be thrilled at the results. I was positive of that.

"Yes, but now you can't be nervous. Now, since they'll be here at any second, you need to be persuasive, charming, and sure we are the best in the business."

He stopped pacing and thrust his hands into his pants pockets. "I can do that."

Smiling reassuringly, I said, "Of course you can. You're the most charming man I know."

The bell on the door jangled, and the well-dressed politician's wife and her daughter strolled in. Penelope Henderson was tall, almost six foot, with ash blonde hair cropped close to her head. The effect was one of aged beauty and almost larger than life eyes.

Grace, in contrast, was barely taller than five foot and had long sweeping hair and a pixyish face. Unlike her mother, who wore a fashionable jewel-toned tea-length dress, Grace was dressed simply. Jeans, a T-shirt, and sneakers. Of course, I'd bet money that her ensemble, as casual as it was, cost more than most of my wardrobe put together. That's the way it was with high society.

"Mr. Winterson and Ms. Stevens, I presume? I am Mrs. Henderson, and this is my daughter, Grace."

Moving forward I stretched out my hand in greeting. "It's a pleasure to meet you both. Please, come in. We have some samples for you and some ideas to share for your wedding." I directed this last comment toward Grace, which earned me an icy glare from the mother. Apparently, the bride wasn't in charge.

The door jangled again, and I glanced over. As soon as I saw who'd entered the shop, my blood turned cold. This wasn't a scenario I'd considered. And suddenly, I wasn't nearly as sure of our success as I'd been just a few seconds earlier. Troy Bellamy stood at the shop entrance, straight as a rod, angry eyes focused on me.

"Jon, why don't you escort our guests into the backroom to show them the samples we've prepared? I'll take care of our new customer." I spoke calmly, and my smooth voice didn't betray my nerves. Not sure how I managed it, I pulled it off. Troy walked closer, stopping somewhere between the front door and the counter. What was he doing there?

Jon glanced at me and nodded. "Please, come with me. I know you'll love what A Taste of Magic can offer your daughter's wedding."

Mrs. Henderson stiffened her back. "I'd prefer to discuss matters here, where the sun is shining in the windows."

"It's plenty light enough. I assure you." I sent a pleading look to Jon. The last thing we needed was Troy creating havoc with the client of our career. Losing this job would hurt. Big time.

Jon, bless his soul, with no clue at all to the severity of the situation, took it in stride. "Let me show you. If you're still uncomfortable, we can bring everything out front."

The mother didn't look convinced, but Grace stepped in. "We have an appointment with the caterer in an hour, Mother.

Let's not make them move everything out here. That will just waste time."

Nodding briskly, Penelope Henderson said, "True. So very true." With her hand on her daughter's elbow, Mrs. Henderson guided Grace toward Jon. "Let's get this over with then."

I told myself to breathe. Once Jon had escorted the Hendersons out of the lobby, I pulled myself up straight. Facing the interloper, who'd stayed quiet thus far, I said, "Troy. What a surprise." An unpleasant one, but still a surprise. "What can I do for you?"

He sneered. "I figured it out. It was the cake, wasn't it? You hexed me with a cake."

Stiffening, I looked over my shoulder. If the Hendersons had heard that, there was no way A Taste of Magic would get their business. And that would ruin everything. I waited a pause, but luckily, it seemed okay. They weren't running from the shop yet.

"Don't deny it," Troy said. "Like I said before, my mother is a witch. You can't fool me."

My mind ran through all the possibilities of each answer I could give him. I chose to stay on the side of safety. Keeping my voice low, I said, "I don't know what you're talking about, Troy. You look like you're feeling better."

He nodded. "Yeah. After your sister cashed in my hard-earned check, all the symptoms faded. Funny that, don't you think?"

His shirt was clean and tucked in, his pants freshly pressed; he could have been on his way to a job interview. Add in the fact that he wasn't a terribly big man and I didn't understand my anxiety. But then I looked into his eyes again, and I saw danger there. This man would do whatever he could to get whatever he wanted. Once again, I wondered how Alice had missed that.

"What can I do for you?" I repeated.

"I want my money back. It was never a loan. Your sister just gave it to me. I figure you owe it now." His voice was loud—too loud—and I shot a glance over my shoulder. How could they *not* hear him?

"You figured wrong. I'm not paying you any money, Troy."

"Hey," he said good-naturedly, all charm and sweetness. "You can pay me in installments. I'm cool with that. It seems to me you have a pretty sweet deal here with this fancy bakery and all."

And that's when I knew this man was a lot scarier than I'd given him credit for. Yeah—he'd frightened me before, but to be able to hide your true nature in a blink? That terrified me.

In two steps, he was right in front of me. I stepped backward. He moved up again.

"No." I pushed the word out, but a ball of fear unraveled inside.

"Oh, you'll pay me all right. I figure you can't hurt me again because damn if I'll be stupid enough to eat any of your concoctions a second time."

The coldness of his gaze struck deep in my belly. I thought, for just a second, about giving him the money. He was a scary man, and it *was* just money. But on the other hand, what he was doing wasn't right. I mentally weighed all this in my head while trying to determine how I could get him out of the shop before he did something crazy. Plus, his voice was sure to carry to the back room if it got much louder. Something I definitely didn't want to happen.

The quickest and safest way was giving in. I hesitated, but then I thought about what he did to my sister. What he was trying to do to me. And you know what? Giving in wasn't an option—at least not for me. I tried to walk behind the counter to give myself more room, but he grabbed my wrist. And that reminded me of Marc.

"You're not going anywhere."

Something happened then. I don't know what, exactly, but he pissed me off. Raising my gaze to his, I said, "You will get your hands off me now."

"Aw, whatcha gonna do?"

I took my other hand and placed it on the hand that still held mine. In a controlled voice, I said, "I don't need a cake, Troy. Whatever gave you that idea?"

"You're bluffing."

Forcing myself to remain calm, I remembered the power of the magic, how it felt when it rushed through my veins. That added to my courage. "Try me."

Something in my eyes must have scared the hell out of him. Dropping my hand, he backtracked until I could breathe again. His eyes darted around the shop and then back at me. I could see he was trying to decide if I was serious or not. He needed to believe, without a doubt, that I was utterly serious. Mentally, I called to Miranda. *If there was ever a time for you to help me, Great-Grandma, this would be it.*

A brush of feeling passed through me. I didn't know if that meant she was there or if I was just overly hopeful. But I grabbed this feeling with both hands. Metaphorically, of course. I straightened myself, put one foot in front of the other, and then laid my palm on his chest. "Want to see what I can do, Troy?"

Closing my eyes, I decided to fake him out. I moved my lips as if I were casting a silent spell. He ripped my hand off his chest and swore. "Fuck. No money is worth this."

"Smart man." I opened my eyes. "Leave me and my family alone, and I'll leave you alone. That's a promise. But if you bother me or my sister again, you'll wish for the rest of your life you'd stayed away. I won't make this same offer again."

Dots of color popped up on his face. He swiped his hand over his forehead. And then—thank God—he exited A Taste of Magic without looking back. All the trembles I'd hid surfaced. That man? He scared me like no one ever had.

I gave myself a few minutes to calm down. Hopefully, we hadn't been loud enough to be heard in the back room, but I needed to settle myself before I could find out. If I'd screwed up this job for us, I'd never forgive myself.

I didn't know if Miranda had actually shown up or not. Probably not, because I kind of thought if she had, I wouldn't have to guess about it. She was pretty good about making herself known. Regardless, I didn't think I'd be dealing with Troy again. The fear in his eyes told me he'd stay away from me and Alice.

Since I felt better, I went to help Jon with the Hendersons. It wasn't necessary. Jon had it under control, with both Penelope and Grace smiling and chatting amiably. Like I said before, Jon was a master at charm. He could schmooze with the best of them.

I was fairly sure we'd be getting the Henderson job. And if we did, our business life would be right where we wanted it to be.

If only Jon and I were able to do the same with our personal lives, we'd be all set.

Chapter Fifteen

"Why are we doing this?" I asked Grandma Verda and Maddie. "Remind me, please."

Maddie shrugged as she set the Ouija board in the center of my kitchen table. "I just want to see what happens."

"I don't know. These things scare me. A lot."

Grandma Verda chuckled. "Miranda in your bedroom doesn't frighten you, but a piece of wood with some numbers and letters on it does?"

"Yes. Besides, she doesn't seem to have any problems talking to me whenever she wants." Though, she never said very much. That didn't mean a Ouija board was the answer.

"My mother said Miranda tried to connect with her, but she never did with me. I always wondered about it," Grandma Verda said.

Ah, that's what her statement was about the other night. I'd never gotten around to asking, and she hadn't volunteered the information before now. "Why do you think she's trying to talk to me? I can't figure that out."

Grandma tipped her head as her gaze hit mine. "I've been thinking about that. Maybe because you both experienced heartbreak? The loss of a man, of a relationship, you loved?"

"Maybe," I said, considering her words. "But even so, what happened to me with Marc is very different than what happened to her. I'm not pregnant, for one thing."

"It's just a guess. But if this works . . ." Grandma nodded toward the Ouija board. "Maybe you can find out for sure."

She had a point. That didn't mean I was on board with it, though. "I'm not convinced this is the right plan. Can't we just wait and see if she comes back again?"

"Quit worrying. There are three things that can happen. One, nothing. Two, Miranda talks to us. Three, someone else talks to us," Maddie said.

"Exactly. It's number three that's freaking me out." I mean, come on, now that I knew magic existed, what's to say there weren't a bunch of creepy things out there that were also true? Like vengeful spirits and poltergeists? I shivered. "I really don't want to do it."

"Humor me, Liz. You brought me into this. I'd like to see what Miranda has to say with my own ears. Or eyes, I guess, in this case. We used to play with these things when we were in college. You never seemed afraid then," Maddie said.

"Oh, I was. I just kept my mouth shut."

"If you don't want to try it, we don't have to." Maddie tapped her fingers on the board. "It's just an idea. Verda's right. Maybe direct questions will give you more information. Or maybe you'll find a way to contact her when you want to, instead of always being surprised when she shows up."

Grandma Verda slid me a look. "Let's give it a go. I'd sure like to know what Miranda wants. She disappeared the other night almost immediately."

"That's normal for her." Hesitantly, I sat down and placed my fingers on the plastic doohickey. Maddie and Grandma Verda did the same. "Now what?"

"I think you should try first, Elizabeth. She seems to be attached to you," Grandma Verda suggested.

Sighing, I nodded. "We're trying to reach my great-great-great-grandmother Miranda Ayres. Miranda, are you there?"

Even though I'd hemmed and hawed about it, I really didn't expect anything to happen. I mean, why would Miranda choose a Ouija board to communicate when she could elicit a light show whenever she wanted? So, yeah, I was more than a little surprised when the damn planchette moved over YES. And then, the scent of fresh-cut flowers filled the room. I breathed a sigh of relief. At least I knew it was her.

"Um, wow," Maddie said. "Ask her something else."

"Grandma, did you move that?"

Shaking her head no, she said, "Maddie's right. Ask another question."

"Miranda, is there a reason you want me to be able to see you?"

YES.

"Why?" My hand trembled. I tried to hold it steady.

I–T

W–I–L–L

M–A–K–E

O–U–R

C–O–N–N–E–C–T–I–O–N

S–T–R–O–N–G–E–R.

Hmm. "Is there anything I can do to help?"

YES.

"What? Spell it for us."

B–E–L–I–E–V–E

"Believe," Maddie announced.

"Yeah, got that. I do believe. Kind of hard not to, so I don't understand."

Grandma Verda said, "What do we need to believe in?"

The planchette didn't move, so I repeated Grandma's question. Still nothing.

"Miranda? I'm confused. Could you help me out?"

NO.

"Geez, thanks," I said sarcastically. "This is a waste of time."

Y–O–U

"Shh, Lizzie," Grandma whispered.

M–U–S–T

"You must. You must what?" I asked.

B–E–L–I–E–V–E.

"Obviously, I do believe or I wouldn't be doing this, would I? No, I don't think so." Stubborn ghost.

S–A–R–C–A–S–M

W–O–N–T

H–E–L–P.

Maddie laughed. "That's awesome. She has your attitude, Lizzie. Or maybe you have hers."

"Oh hush," I said. "What will help then?"

J–U–S–T

B–E–L–I–E–V–E.

"This isn't telling us anything more than we knew before. Ask her something else," Maddie said.

"Oh. I know." This was actually kind of fun. In a weird bonding with your long-dead-relatives sort of way. We could have been in one of those Maxwell House commercials. "Miranda, were you with me at A Taste of Magic when Troy came in?"

NO.

That was all me? I scared Troy off all on my own?

YES.

"What did she say yes to? No one asked a question," Grandma said. "And who's Troy?"

"Um, I did. Well, I *thought* a question. I'll tell you about Troy later." *What do I need to believe in?*

Y–O–U

N–E–E–D

T–O

F–I–N–D

T–H–E

A–N–S–W–E–R.

"She went too fast. I couldn't figure it out," Grandma said. "What did she say? What did you ask, Lizzie?"

"I asked her what I needed to believe in."

"She said, 'You need to find the answer,'" Maddie replied.

Frustrated, I dropped my hands and stood. "That's enough. At least now I know where the women in our family get their mule-headedness from."

Grandma Verda laughed and removed her hands, too. "I could have told you that without Miranda."

Maddie tossed me a glance. Her skin, normally a golden hue, was pale white. "How can you two be so cavalier about this? This is totally insane." Clasping both hands around her glass, she shook her head. "I don't know. It's just completely unreal to me."

"Well, I didn't exactly take it easily the first time Miranda spoke to me. I'd be worried if you weren't nervous," I said.

"Lizzie. Maddie. *Look*," Grandma said.

The triangle was moving by itself. Really fast. My stomach jumped, and perspiration bubbled on my forehead. "She shouldn't be able to do that, should she?"

"What's it saying?" Maddie asked.

"Start over, Miranda," Grandma said.

The triangle stopped, moved to the center of the board, paused for a second and then started over.

M–A–G–I–C

I–S

G–E–T–T–I–N–G

S–T–R–O–N–G–E–R

U–S–E

I–T

W–I–S–E–L–Y.

The triangle hovered, circling the board but not stopping anywhere in particular. "I know it's getting stronger, Miranda," I whispered. Finally, it rested on GOOD-BYE.

Instantly, the flower scent vanished. I picked up the little plastic triangle. It felt warm in my hand. "I guess she's telling me to be careful of what I wish for."

Sound advice, even if it had come from a ghost.

Shirley jumped onto Grandma Verda's lap and meowed.

Grandma Verda nodded. "She never warned me when I used it. You must be really powerful, Lizzie."

"She is. You should have seen the light show in my place the other day," Maddie interjected. "Not to mention the wind. It knocked over my plants it was so strong."

"Wind? Light show? I never had lights or wind—just a tingly feeling that filled me. That's how I knew whatever I'd cast had taken hold."

"Really?" This interested me. "I wish Mom had experience with this, too. I'd like to know how it's differed for each of us."

Grandma Verda snorted. "Your mother, as much as I love

her, never believed in magic. She's the picture of your grand-father, through and through. Now, tell me who Troy is."

My grandmother never let anything slip between the cracks. Apparently, my mother hadn't filled her in. I hesitated. How much to tell her? "Alice's ex. He's a jerk. He came by the shop to talk to me."

Grandma didn't press. She just nodded and stroked her cat's head. Shirley meowed again, louder this time. "It's your dinnertime, isn't it sweetie," my grandmother murmured. "Girls, this has been a lot of fun for an old woman, but I need to feed Shirley and go see Vinny."

Ugh. I couldn't bear to smell the cat food again. "Do you need a ride to the hospital, Grandma?"

"No, dear. Your father brought my car over yesterday. I can get myself there."

"Just drive carefully." At her nod, I turned to Maddie. "Feel like going out to eat?"

"Sure. Let me run upstairs and check my messages and we can take off."

I gave Grandma Verda a kiss. "I'm going with Maddie. I'll see you later tonight."

Following Maddie into the hallway, I couldn't seem to stop myself from glancing at Nate's door. I missed him.

Oh, hell. Why not? "Maddie? I'm going to ask Nate to come with us."

She grinned. The color was slowly returning to her cheeks. "Sounds good. I'll be right back."

Knocking on the door, I crossed my fingers. Even though I knew that didn't really work, some habits were hard to break. Besides, if I could contact my great-great-great-grandmother via a Ouija board, anything was possible. Right? Right.

When he opened the door, he looked surprised. Not in an unpleasant, what-the-hell-do-you-want manner, but also not in a where-have-you-been-all-my-life way, either.

Nate's green eyes swept over me. "Hey, Liz. Is everything okay?"

"I don't only come to see you when something is wrong, you know."

He grinned, and my heart zipped. "I know. I just like to ascertain there are no problems right off the bat. Must be the cop in me."

I wouldn't mind having that. You know, a cop in me. Well, one in particular, anyway. I know, naughty, huh? I couldn't seem to help it. "Maddie and I are going to get some dinner. We wondered if you'd like to join us."

"We?"

Warmth crept over my skin. "Okay. *I.* I wondered if you'd like to join us."

"I would love to, but I have plans tonight."

Disappointed at the turn of events, I tried to keep a smile on my face. Last minute thing anyway, ya know? It shouldn't bother me. "Maybe another time?"

Nate leaned against the doorjamb and opened his mouth. Closing it again, he combed his fingers through his short hair before answering. "I've been wanting to talk to you." He hesitated again. "I'd like to go out. It's always nice to hang with friends. Just give me some notice next time."

"I thought . . ." I broke off, not sure what to say. Or rather, if I should say it. I certainly had more than friendly feelings toward Nate, and I definitely thought he had more than friendly feelings for me. "Are you involved with someone?" I blurted.

"I like you, Liz. You just seem to be in a different place than I am right now." He reached over and tugged my hair. "But I can always use another friend."

"Yeah, friends are great," I mumbled. *Different place?* "I'm going to get Maddie. I don't know what's taking her so long."

Before I was able to escape, the door to the building slammed shut, and the red-haired beauty from the other day approached us. She glided down the hallway. Seriously, it was as if she floated on air. I didn't know how to walk like that. Most days I was lucky if I didn't trip over my own feet.

And then I realized. If Nate had given her a key to the building, he must be serious about her. That hurt. Maybe it shouldn't, but it did. "Your plans are here," I said.

"Liz—"

"Hi, sweetie," Ms. Beauty Queen said when she got to us. Standing up on her tiptoes, she gave Nate a kiss on his cheek. "You're ready, I hope?"

"I should go. You guys have a . . . good time." It was obvious Nate was uncomfortable, and, hell, I wasn't exactly thrilled. I couldn't stand there any longer, and Maddie hadn't made an appearance yet, so I'd go to her. Backing up, I almost ran to the stairway.

"Elizabeth, wait," Nate called after me as I took the stairs two at a time. I figured he probably wanted to introduce me to his girlfriend, but honestly, why bother? Even if she wasn't his girlfriend, he'd already brushed me off. I didn't need to cry in front of him. That would make everything so much worse than it already was. Obviously, the magic of the muffins had long since dissipated. Which meant everything we'd experienced together was false.

I knew it was my own fault, but it still sucked. The only good thing about the whole damn situation was I hadn't become any more involved with Nate. Plus, seeing as I hadn't fed Kevin anything magical, I suddenly appreciated him a hell of a lot more. Though, there was the wish I'd made with the brownies. So. Maybe that wasn't real, either?

It seemed I'd learned a lesson. Lessons are supposed to be good, right?

Why, then, did it feel as if I'd just lost something incredibly important?

"It's time to change your workout," Kevin said, wrapping the measuring tape around my waist. "We'll switch things around a bit on Monday."

"Do we really have to?" I groaned, but my heart wasn't really in it. Not only did I no longer mind exercising three days a week, but I was seriously considering adding in a fourth day. Between trying to grab Miranda's attention, forgetting about Nate, and revving up for spring at A Taste of Magic, I needed a way to alleviate my anxiety. And yeah, as much as I hated to admit it, exercise was a great stress reliever.

"You're doing great! A full half-inch off your waist. That's awesome, babe." He wrote the number on my fitness chart and tossed me one of his sexier than sin grins. "I wouldn't have thought it possible, but you're getting hotter and hotter."

I flushed. "You *have* to say that."

"Why? Because we're dating?"

Oh. *Dating.* Actually, that wasn't what I'd meant, but he looked so darn sweet when he said it, it took me by surprise. Were we dating? Was I dating someone? I smiled. I guess I was. How about that? "Well, that's not exactly what I meant, but that, too."

"Speaking of, are you busy on Saturday?"

"I have a couple of hours of work in the morning, but I should be done by early afternoon."

Kevin dropped the clipboard on the counter and, placing his hands on my waist, pulled me toward him. "I know you deal with weddings all the time, but my brother is getting married on Saturday. I'd love it if you could come."

"Oh. Sure." A family gathering. A wedding, no less. "Will your family mind?"

"Only if you give them a hard time about not hiring you for the cake," he teased. "They can't wait to meet you."

He'd told his parents about me? Oh, wow. "All right, sure," I repeated, a little stunned. "I'd love to go."

Kevin accompanied me to my car, his arm loosely wrapped around my waist.

"You can either go with me or meet me there. I have wedding duties, so I'm going early. It won't hurt my feelings if you'd rather come later."

"What time is the ceremony?"

"Four o'clock. The reception is immediately after."

My mind flipped through Saturday's schedule. "Yeah, I'll meet you. I'll probably be at work until two or so. Easier if I go home, change, and then hook up with you at the church."

Leaning over, he kissed me, causing a quick fluttering in my chest, and ushered me into my seat. "Drive safely. I'll call you tonight and give you directions."

Putting the car into gear, I aimed toward home. I have to admit the date with Kevin lifted me up a bit. Which was nice, seeing as I'd been pretty miserable since the encounter with Nate. And that, I knew, was entirely stupid. But there was something about the cop that had gotten to me. Hell, who was I fooling? He *still* got to me.

Also, I sort of worried that this thing between me and Kevin was getting more serious than I wanted. I liked him, and yeah, I could even say he turned me on. But I didn't want serious. I couldn't be serious. We weren't right for serious. But hey, he was sweet, and fun, and he made me feel really good about myself.

There was absolutely nothing wrong with that.

Beyond that, though, something had changed inside of me. I wasn't sure exactly when it started, but I was beginning to value the time Marc and I were together. Not the way he left, never that. And not the way he'd acted since. But those early years? Maddie had been right on target. They *were* good. They had to mean something.

Now, instead of anger, I mostly just felt sad about our marriage. About the girl I'd been and the woman I'd become.

"Enough," I whispered, pulling into my parking lot. Driving slowly, I scanned the lot for a place to park. Shit. There was Nate. *With her.* He was holding Sam's hand, and they waved as the red-haired woman got into her car.

Quickly, I found a spot in the back and pulled my car in. I waited until I saw the woman drive off and Nate and Sam return to the building. Then, I waited some more. I didn't want to chance running into him. Didn't want to play nice when my heart remained bruised from our last encounter.

When I finally stepped from my car, the cold March wind

lew like ice on my face. Surprised, I lifted my hand to feel
he tear rolling down my cheek.

"No fucking way," I said softly.

How could this man, this cop I barely knew, make me cry?
t reminded me far too much of Marc. Sure, not the same,
1ot as powerful, not as real, but, damn, way too similar for
my liking.

I purposely pushed my worries about Kevin aside. He
vouldn't hurt me like Marc had. He wouldn't bruise me like
Nate did. Therefore, I decided as I entered my apartment, he
vas about as perfect a man for me as any could be.

A tiny voice inside (not Miranda's) reminded me that possibly it wasn't that Kevin *wouldn't* hurt me but closer to he
ouldn't. Ignoring the voice, I called out to see if Grandma
Verda was home. When no reply came back at me, I curled up
on my bed. Raw from my emotions, chilled from the weather,
nd tired from the workout, I just laid there and tried to get
varm.

Inside and out.

Saturday morning at A Taste of Magic proved to be busy. With
everal cakes to finish and deliver, Jon and I didn't have a second to waste chit-chatting. After a quickly gobbled lunch, we
ent the last of the cakes off with our weekend delivery service
nd collapsed in chairs in our office. I wished for a nap. A long,
blissful nap.

"I've been waiting for a calm moment to give you the
good news," Jon said.

The tone of his voice should have clued me in, but honestly?
t was all I could do to not fall over. I hadn't been sleeping well,
nd that, combined with how hectic our day had been, had left
me fairly out of it. "What good news?"

"Destiny phoned last night. After you left. About the Henderson job."

It took a minute for his words to beat their way into my
head. But then I sat up straight. "Oh my God. We got it?"

A wide grin broke out on Jon's face. "We did! It's official!

We should receive the deposit check next week! With that
and what we have in the account, we'll be able to pay off
Marc. It might leave us a little tight for the rest of the month,
but we'll be able to manage."

"Are you sure? I don't want us to end up in a worse position because we run out of operating funds."

"We'll be fine. I'm overcautious, so really . . . we'll only be
tight in the worst circumstances, but even then we can pull
through."

Relief flooded me first, followed by excitement. It was
perfect timing, because Marc's attorney had contacted us earlier in the week. We'd put him off, hoping the Henderson account would come through. And now it had! "Thank God,"
I said.

"Great news, huh? I'm glad I could surprise you with it.
You've seemed a little down today."

I shrugged. As quickly as it had arrived, my enthusiasm
fled. Don't get me wrong, I was thrilled we'd be able to pay
Marc's loan off and get him out of our hair. But now that I
didn't have to worry about the business, my personal life took
center stage. "Just a busy day," I said.

"We're going to get busier," Jon said. "I think we need to
talk about hiring some more bakers. And permanent delivery
drivers, instead of using the temp service."

"We don't have room for that, Jon."

He grinned again. "Yeah, I'm thinking we can finally upsize. We're already decently booked through the fall, and the
Henderson event will bring us more work than we can handle on our own. It's time, Lizzie."

All of it sounded too overwhelming for me at the moment.
I slumped in my chair. What the hell was wrong with me?
"Okay."

"That's it? *Okay?* You've wanted this longer than I have."

He was right. This was something we'd waited for. Planned
for. Talked about. Dreamed about. And at that moment, not one
iota of excitement hit me. Forcing a smile, I said, "I'm happy

about it. Give me a few days and I'll be driving you crazy with new ideas."

"Promise?"

"Promise."

Jon, the sweetie that he was, poured me a fresh cup of coffee and hand-delivered it.

"There's something I need to say to you." His nervous tone registered in my exhausted brain. Enough to propel me to set my precious cup of coffee down.

"Shoot."

"I'm sorry about that night at your place." Shoving his hands in his pockets, he leaned against the desk, his eyes on the floor. Or his shoes. Somewhere other than me.

"Oh, that? Jon, it's fine. No need to apologize. I haven't worried about it." A little white lie, but well worth it.

"Andy and I were going through a really tough period, and I was questioning everything. I don't know what made me come on to you, but thank you for not letting it go any further."

"You were very tempting," I teased.

Raising his gaze to me, he grinned. "Well, come on. I know that."

Ah, back to normal. Was it because of that last batch of cupcakes I'd made? The ones where I'd canceled all previous spells? I'd probably never know. But in this case, it really didn't matter.

"You and Andy figure anything out?"

"Sort of. We've compromised. I agreed to give the family idea serious consideration. We've signed up to be big brothers, and we're going to start volunteering once a week at the children's hospital." He shook himself as if startled by the revelation. "Andy agreed to give me the time to give it some time."

Hmm. Volunteering at the children's hospital might be something I'd enjoy. It might take some of the loneliness away, too. Definitely a thought to keep in mind. "Are you completely opposed to having kids?"

"No, it's not that. I just want to be sure it's what we both really want. That we can be good parents. My relationship with my father stank. If Andy and I have kids, I want to be sure I can handle it." Jon blinked as if he were surprised at his admission.

I wasn't. I knew his father was a deadbeat. "Well, honey, I think you're making perfect sense. But you're not your father."

"That's what Andy says. Anyway, I'm excited, nervous . . . hell, scared to death about it. But I love him, and I love the *idea* of parenthood. So, we'll see." Jon finished speaking abruptly, as if he came to the end of his speech and forgot the tag line.

Standing, I gave him a quick hug. "I knew you'd work it all out."

"Wish you'd let me in on it," he said with a chuckle. Glancing at the clock, he swore. "I need to go. We're taking our new little brother out to the movies this afternoon."

I smiled. Probably the first true, honest to God, from the depths of my soul smile I'd had in days. Months. Hell, years. "Go. Have fun and try to relax. I'll close up."

"Thanks, Lizzie."

After he left, I chugged the rest of my coffee and shut the shop down. Even though I didn't know for sure if Jon's newfound happiness was because of those cupcakes, I still thought it might be a good idea to bake some for Maddie. You know—just in case. Of course, this time, it would be up to her if she ate them or not. She still seemed to be fine, but I worried.

As for me? I, wonder of all wonders, had to meet a very sexy man at a wedding. I refused to consider the man I wasn't meeting. My only fear was I'd fall asleep during the ceremony. I could imagine it plain as day: "Mom, Dad . . . I'd like you to meet the woman I've been dating, only she's snoring right now, so we'll have to do it later."

Ha. I figured a venti cappuccino with two extra shots of

espresso would do the trick. Lucky for me, and for Kevin's family, there was a Starbucks—with a drive-thru—right on my way home. I felt like a little kid on Christmas.

Yes, Virginia, there really is a Santa Claus.

Chapter Sixteen

The bride wore black.

I kid you not. Apparently, Kevin's brother and his betrothed were not into the traditional. I wouldn't have known this until she began her march down the aisle, because everything else so far had appeared pretty dang normal.

But the bride? Formal gown, lots of lace and beadwork, long train, but the entire dress—every inch of it—was black. Not just your standard run-of-the-mill black either, but pure ebony. It seemed I wasn't the only shocked one, as glancing around the church I saw many mouths hanging open. And honestly, she looked beautiful. In a sacrilegious, I'm ignoring centuries of tradition, it's my wedding so I'll do what I want, sort of way.

I kind of admired her. Not that *I* would want to wear a black dress if I were ever to be married again. But it took some guts to pull it off. There were at least two hundred guests in attendance, so this wasn't a small-potatoes/on-a-budget wedding.

Guests were squirming in an attempt to get a better view. The bride continued up the aisle and, as she got close to me, I could see her eyes were wide and happy. What made me smile, though, was the fact that her lips were twitching.

Oh, my. There was a story here.

Swinging around, I glanced at the woman I assumed was Kevin's—and therefore, Kevin's brother's—mother. She looked unhappy. Okay, huge understatement. The tight pinch of her lips and the iciness of her stare told me she was seriously ticked.

Leaning back in the pew, I saw the groom, and he didn't seem surprised. At least the bride had let him in on it. Now,

I'd been to tons of weddings, but none of them started off with this sort of a bang. I truly hoped I'd get the full story later, because I was dying to know.

The ceremony itself was rather short, but the vows were sweet and meaningful. Kevin, by the way, was absolutely gorgeous in his silvery grey and white tux. Later, at the reception, before we'd even spoken, I noticed many appreciative (and smoldering) looks directed at him. And not all of them by women.

When he finally sat down next to me, I was relieved. I'd begun to feel a bit out of place not knowing anyone.

"You are stunning," he said. "I'm sorry it took so long to get to you. My mother is livid."

"What's with the black dress?"

"Rachel didn't want a formal wedding. Neither did Keith, my brother. My mom pretty much pushed them into it. This was Rachel's way of standing up to her."

I chuckled. "Harsh. She'll always have the pictures from this day as a reminder. It must have cost a fortune to have the dress made that way."

Kevin leaned in close and whispered, "My mom paid for the dress. She approved the design, just not the color. In Rachel's defense, my mother never actually asked her what color it was going to be. Rachel said it was the only thing she didn't ask about or try to control."

Controlling mamas are not such a cool thing. I laughed anyway. "I'm sorry, but how absolutely brilliant of your sister-in-law. Keith knew about it ahead of time?"

"Yeah. Rachel was going to choose a pale color, like lavender or something. Keith talked her into black."

"That's hilarious. Will your mom forgive her?"

"Someday she'll laugh at it. My mom's pretty cool, usually. This was the first wedding in the family, so she went overboard. When I, or my sister, get married and she has the perfect wedding, she'll cool down."

I seriously was having difficulty containing myself from congratulating the bride on a job well done. If I were to be in a similar situation, there's no way I'd be able to pull the same thing off.

"Enough about Keith and Rachel. Did I tell you how beautiful you are?"

"Yes, but you are more than welcome to say it again." I wore a sheath-style dress in purple, which skimmed my body like flowing water. I felt sexy as hell in it. Judging by the expression on Kevin's face, he agreed. Score for me.

"Want a drink before they serve dinner?" Kevin asked, his hand on my knee.

"I'd love one."

The drink went down well. Well enough, in fact, I followed it up with several more. After dinner, when Kevin pulled me onto the dance floor, my legs wobbled. Just a little. His arms came around me, and we danced—this time to actual music. The spicy scent of his cologne, the feel of his embrace, and the buzz from the alcohol all mixed together, leaving me with a happy, fuzzy feeling.

"I want to kiss you," Kevin whispered. "But if I do, my mother will start planning *our* wedding."

"Then you better not kiss me."

"I can save it for later. But, Elizabeth? You are interested in getting married again someday. Aren't you?"

Ah. What was the best way to address a question I didn't even know the answer to? "Maybe. It depends. I'd like to have children at some point." Heat rushed my face. An uncomfortable silence settled in around us, but we continued dancing.

"I'm not sure I want kids," Kevin admitted. "But I know I'd like to find my life partner. Someone I can laugh with, you know?"

I nodded. "Laughter is good."

"Come closer," he whispered.

His breath in my ear, on my neck, caused a trail of goose bumps all the way down my spine. I shivered and tightened my hold around Kevin, allowing myself to lean against him, resting my head on his chest. The uncomfortable moment passed, and I realized—suddenly—how good it felt, dancing with Kevin.

His arms wrapped tight around me, the firmness of his body next to mine, and the sound of his heart beating in my ear. It was real. It was solid. And hey, the guy did turn me on. Maybe not fireworks and explosions, but there's absolutely nothing wrong with a nice steady burn.

When the music ended and the deejay announced the bride was about to throw her bouquet, I followed Kevin off the dance floor.

"Sure you don't want to join in?" he asked, nodding toward the women falling in for the toss.

"Nope. I'd rather stay with you."

He smiled, and while I can't say it lit off sparks, it did warm me.

In a way, I felt stupid. Most of the single women at the reception would love to be in my place. Hell, most of the single women in the known universe. Kevin was easily one of the nicest guys—through and through—that I'd ever met. Not to mention that hot-and-sexy thing he had going.

Yeah. I decided I was definitely stupid. Another drink or two (or three) would fix that. "I'm going to get another drink," I said. I wanted to relax. I wanted to have a good time. And if I was completely honest with myself, I wanted to stop thinking about Nate.

"You sit here and be beautiful. I'll get it. You want the same thing or something different?"

"The same, please." I watched the bride grin and turn her back to the anxious women. Honestly, this was one tradition I'd never really understood. Why get so fired up about possibly catching a bouquet?

A young lady, maybe around twelve or thirteen, leapt into the air when the flowers went flying. She caught them easily. The grin on her face made me smile. And that helped me remember being a teenager and wanting—desperately—to catch the bouquet at a cousin's wedding. What made me laugh, though, was the sour expression on some of the women's faces who'd missed the catch this time.

"Here you go," Kevin said, returning with my drink. "We'll

have to work this off on Monday, you know. Alcohol plays havoc with the body. Lay off the coffee tomorrow and drink lots of water."

"Sure," I said.

"You have no intentions of laying off the coffee, do you?"

"Since when do you know me so well?"

"I'm learning," he teased. His hand found its way to my knee, and he rubbed my skin slowly. Every now and then, his fingers would slide under the hem of my dress, just a little.

Remember the slow and steady burn I mentioned? Kevin was definitely stoking the fire. I sipped at my drink, the sweet tang going down easily, adding to the heat in my belly. I felt myself begin to relax. Finally. Maybe I'd have some fun now.

The next two hours were more of the same. Drinking, dancing, with Kevin touching me. Softly, secretly, like a perfectly planned out seduction. By the end of the evening, I only wanted one thing.

"You can't drive. You've had too much to drink. And actually, so have I. Let me call you a cab so I know you get home safely." His fingers found my lips, and with a gentle brush he said, "Unless you want to share a cab. To my place?"

"Yes. Yes, I do," I whispered. I wanted a warm body, hot sex, and arms to hold me all night. No. I didn't just want it. *I needed it.*

Kevin's eyes darkened as soon as I spoke. "Let's go," he said.

Standing, I smoothed my dress down. "I need to use the restroom and get my coat. I'll meet you at the door."

"Don't change your mind." His husky voice slid into me like melted butter over freshly popped popcorn.

"I won't."

Thirty minutes later, I followed Kevin into his condo. It was striking. He'd used a minimalist focus in decorating, which agreed with the type of man I'd found him to be. While simple, the pieces of furniture he'd selected merged together to deliver a perfect blend of laidback masculinity.

The floors were all light wood—oak, possibly. But the deep red area rug added a dash of color. He'd used glass, brass, and black leather for his furnishings. Above his sofa hung the only painting in the room: a mash of vibrant colors, as if someone had emptied every hue of paint onto the canvas and swirled them together.

"This is really nice," I said. "Did you do this or did you hire a decorator?"

"I did it. My sister helped at first, but she kept trying to add knickknacks and pillows and other clutter I didn't want." He unbuttoned my coat as he spoke and slipped it off my arms.

"I'm impressed, Kevin. And a little embarrassed you saw my place."

"You should fix it up. I'd love to help you. Just say the word." He removed his jacket, tossed it aside, and then pulled me into his arms. "I'm really happy you decided to come home with me."

Then, without another word, his lips were on mine. I eased into the kiss, tried to relax, and willed myself to regain the feelings from earlier.

Rubbing the small of my back, he deepened the kiss, pulling me even tighter to him. "I've wanted you for so long," he murmured, breaking contact with my mouth. "I've thought about you almost every day since we met."

And I'd thought about . . . well, for the most part, Nate. Not something I could say, of course. "You've been really great to me," I replied. "It's been weird for me, joining the dating world again."

Where were the sparks? Where was the heat? Where the fuck was the want?

"You're so hot," Kevin said huskily, the same tone as earlier. Only now, it didn't have the same affect on me.

Screw this. I came here willingly. I wanted this. Possibly, the cold outside air had numbed my senses. Probably, I just needed to work a little harder at it.

I wrapped my arms around his neck, pushing his head toward me. "Kiss me again." It had been there before; I could get it back. I had to get it back. Otherwise, it meant—no, I refused to focus on what it meant. "Just kiss me, Kevin."

I opened my mouth to his. He groaned and plunged his tongue inside, tasting me as if he couldn't get enough. Tugging his shirt out of his waistband, I slid my hands underneath and ran them along his muscular back. Warm skin grew warmer at my touch, but even that didn't do anything. I felt dead inside.

Abruptly, I stepped back, ending the kiss.

"Did I do something wrong?"

What a sweet, sweet man. "No, you didn't. It's me." How to explain what I didn't understand? "Um, can I use the restroom? All those drinks," I said. Lame excuse, but maybe, just maybe, I'd be able to get myself together if I had a few minutes to myself.

"Through the bedroom," Kevin said, pointing to a closed door to the right of his living room. "You'll see it right away."

The heat of his stare followed me as I made my way into his bedroom. Another masculine room—all done in dark earth tones. His bed was massive. While I knew it was probably a standard king-size, it appeared to be larger than life. So large, in fact, its very presence almost mocked me.

Which was completely ridiculous. Because, come on, how could a bed mock anything or anyone? It was an inanimate object. I ran by it as if it would reach out and pull me to it, like a monster-bed in a really bad horror movie.

In the bathroom, I splashed my face with cold water and then leaned against the counter, looking in the mirror. The woman staring back looked miserable. Unhappy. And trapped. That scared me most of all. It didn't take me long to realize what that meant.

The charade was up. I couldn't sleep with Kevin. I couldn't date Kevin. And possibly, after tonight, he'd prefer to never see me again, which would be a shame. I truly liked and appreciated the guy. I just knew I couldn't continue on with him.

What I didn't know, or wasn't ready to comprehend, was why.

When I returned to the living room, he'd put a pillow and a blanket on the couch. In his hands was a long T-shirt. His face gentle but his eyes sad, he said, "I'm a smart guy. You've changed your mind." He held his hand up. "Wait. No excuses. Maybe it's too soon. Don't worry about it."

My heart broke. This man was damn near perfect, and here I was throwing him away. And for what? A man I barely knew yet somehow recognized? Crazy. "Kevin, I'm sorry. I don't think we should date anymore."

"I was worried you'd say that. Just my luck to fall for a woman who doesn't want to be with me."

His smile lessened the edge, so I didn't feel quite so horrible. "I just—I'm learning who I am without my ex, and I thought maybe we could make it work. Or at the very least have some fun. You've been so incredible to me." Tears filled my eyes.

"Elizabeth, stop. I'm just a guy like any other guy. It's better to end this now before I completely fall in love with you. I'm glad you're being honest."

"I like you so much," I said.

"Good, because I like you, too." Pulling me into his arms again, but for a hug, he whispered, "And don't think this gets you out of the gym. No one else gets to train you, got it?"

I laughed softly and stepped back. "Got it."

"Who's the lucky guy?"

This startled me. "What? No—"

"Ah, I see." He smiled again, and this one reached his eyes.

"There's no other guy," I said again. Even if I wanted there to be, there wasn't. "I should go home."

"No. I set up the couch for you. It's late and, this way, we can grab a cab in the morning to pick up both of our cars."

"Are you sure? It's not too awkward?"

"Of course not. You're a friend! And this way I can pump you full of water in the morning."

I could do this. Kevin offered me friendship, and that absolutely rocked. Besides, it's not like staying the night would hurt anything.

Yawning, I rubbed my hands over my eyes before unlocking my door. I wanted to catch some sleep in my own bed. While

Kevin's couch was certainly comfortable enough, I'd kept waking up throughout the short night. At least we'd left things on a positive note.

He'd been great all morning and, before going our separate ways, he'd given me another hug. Yeah, we'd be okay, and I'd gotten one hell of a friend out of it. But I wondered about the choice I'd made. Was it based on anything other than fear? I thought so, but I stressed over it. I also worried that my magic brownies had made him feel more for me than he normally would have. Which meant, just in case, I'd have to straighten that out sometime soon.

Pushing the door open, I kicked my heels off. Shower, bed, and then later some food. Maybe a Tylenol or two.

"Where have you been, Lizzie?" said my grandmother. "We've been worried sick."

We? Turning on my nylon-footed heel, I opened my mouth to respond and then promptly shut it again. My parents, my brothers, my sister, Maddie, and Nate were all in my living room, watching me with sleep-deprived eyes.

"Um. What's all this?" I managed to mutter.

Grandma Verda pointed a finger at me. "We thought you were lying dead in a ditch somewhere. There are police out looking for your car, young lady. Where in blue blazes have you been?"

My father crossed his arms. "Your grandmother was worried. We came to keep her calm. You should have called her, Lizzie."

My mother whisked over to me and gave me a tight hug. "Glad you're safe. Being safe is all that matters."

"Welcome home," Maddie said quietly, stifling a yawn.

"I still want to know what you were up to," my grandmother said. "You should know better than to go gallivanting around town all night. We tried your cell phone and everything."

"I . . . well. I had a date last night and um—" I broke off as I caught Nate's dark expression. "I'm sorry," I mumbled. "I turned my cell phone off for the ceremony. I went to a wedding . . . and forgot to put it back on. I should have phoned." Damn. It's not like I was used to having a roomie to stay up and worry about me.

Nate stood. "I'm glad you're safe," he said, mimicking my mother. His gaze didn't meet mine, wandering somewhere just to the side of my face. "I should go. I had a few friends unofficially looking for your car. I need to call off the search."

My stomach hurt. I wanted to say something to him, but I didn't know what. He nodded to everyone and left—very quickly, I might add. I frowned at my family but tried to keep my temper somewhat at bay. "Don't you think you all jumped the gun? Just a bit? I wasn't even gone twenty-four hours. You could have given me just a little more time before involving Nate."

"Grandma contacted him first. He had her call us. No one knew where you were, sis. We didn't know you had a date. Jon said you didn't say anything about going out. Grandma didn't know. Maddie didn't know." Scot's words were sharp and pointed. "It's not like you to disappear without telling anyone."

My sister still hadn't said anything, but her face was blotchy, which meant she'd been crying. Joe's shoulders were set. Wow, I'd really lived like a nun if one miserable night out brought everyone to my apartment in fear.

On one level, I got it. But on another . . . it just annoyed me. I mean, yes: I'd behaved in an unpredictable manner. And in doing so, I'd managed to scare and then piss off my entire family plus Maddie, Jon, and Nate. But come on; it was *one* night.

Everyone was staring at me. The walls closed in around me. I breathed, hoping to relieve the suffocating pressure I felt, but it didn't work. "I'm sorry," I said again. "I should have called. I just didn't think of it."

My grandmother stared at me with watery blue eyes. She was holding back tears, and that realization curled in my belly like acid. I felt like dog-doo on the bottom of designer shoes, but my family would get over it. So would Jon and Maddie. I knew this. Nate, on the other hand?

Probably not. And that was just something I'd have to deal with.

"I'm really sorry," I said to my family, to Maddie, for the third time. I wanted to run and hide. Go somewhere else. Anywhere else. So I took a clue from Alice's playbook.

"I'll be right back." I went to my bedroom, closing the door behind me, and burst into tears. I'd hurt one man, alienated another, and scared my entire family. It was just too much.

My mother's voice came through the door. "Honey? We're leaving now. I'm sorry we upset you. We were just worried."

"I know, Mom. You can come in if you want."

She did and gave me another hug. Brushing my tears with her hand, she said, "Just get some rest. Maddie said she'd call Jon and tell him you're home."

"That's nice of her." I'd have to thank her later.

"But Lizzie? Don't do that again. No matter how old you get, you're still my baby."

"I know."

"Good. I'll call you tomorrow."

"Thanks, Mom."

A few minutes after everyone left, my grandmother came into the room. She perched herself on the edge of my bed and glared at me. "You scared everyone. Poor Nate was beside himself. He's a good man. You should be focusing on him and not this other person you were with all night."

Leave it to Grandma to say what she thought. "Stop. It's not what you think. I slept on the couch."

She snorted.

For some reason, that made me cry all over again. "You know what? I'm tired of this. I'm sick of being a mouse."

"What? What are you talking about, Elizabeth?"

"You know, a mouse. Mousy. For once in my life, I'd like to be the snake. I thought I could do it, I thought it was working out okay. I thought I'd found the snake. But no, I'm still just a mouse." I blurted everything out in one garbled mess of words.

Gotta give my grandmother credit. Her granddaughter was making zero sense, sounded like a blithering idiot, but she patted my leg and said very calmly, "Well, if that's what you want, that's what you'll have."

Ha. Did she have an instruction book on finding your inner snake? If so, where the hell was it?

I rolled over and punched my pillow. "I'm going to sleep now, Grandma."

"You do that, dear."

Chapter Seventeen

I hesitated before going into my apartment. A week after my infamous night out and, while I'd made my peace with everyone else involved, I'd yet to speak with Nate. Glancing toward his door, I envisioned walking over, knocking, and apologizing.

I couldn't do it.

"Coward," I whispered, deciding on trying the next day. Don't let this fool you, as this was the exact same decision I made every single day. You'll notice I hadn't lived up to my promise yet.

Inside my apartment, I immediately started a pot of coffee and went to change. Apparently Grandma Verda was out, because Shirley meowed loudly at my heels, probably hoping I'd heat her up some Spam-special cat mix. No. Not happening.

I tugged my sweater off as I entered my bedroom. Tossing it to the hamper, I unbuttoned my pants, glanced toward my bed looking for my pajamas, and caught a flicker of color to the left. Pivoting my gaze to see what caught my attention, I sucked in a deep breath. Then I did what any normal woman in the same situation would do. I screamed my ever-living heart out.

Oh my God. It couldn't be. I took a step forward and then backed up again. No way. She didn't. She couldn't have.

"Grandma Verda, what have you done?"

I blinked. I blinked again. Honestly, I was really hoping I was hallucinating.

Sitting along the wall next to my bed was a rather large glass tank. That wasn't what scared me, but inside the damn tank was a huge, coral-colored snake. The thing had to be— oh, I don't know—eight-feet long.

A freaking snake in my bedroom.

Grandma Verda was crazy. I mean, it had to have come from her. Who else?

A snake. In my bedroom.

I moved a little closer. The snake slithered to the other side of the tank, its blood-red tongue flicking in out in out. My stomach turned upside down, and I shivered. Really, what was she thinking? That I'd curl up with it and pat its head?

"Lizzie? I'm home! Did you see my gift?"

I flew out of my bedroom and told myself to remain calm. You know, because she was old. "Grandma, why is there an eight-foot snake next to my bed?"

"Why, honey. You told me clear as day you wanted a snake. It took a little longer than I wanted because I had to research to find the perfect one. And it's not eight feet long. Closer to five." She wrinkled her nose. "There's a lot to buying a snake. I also bought you a book on snake care."

"No. I never said I wanted a snake. Never. I despise snakes."

"Lizzie, yes you did. That morning. You said you didn't want a mouse, you wanted a snake. Now, I don't understand why you'd want something scaly instead of soft and cuddly, but it's your pet." She turned to hang her coat up and said, "You're half undressed. Go put something decent on."

"Grandma. I don't want a snake. You misunderstood me. I said I wanted *to be* a snake. Meaning . . ." Oh, hell, I sounded like a freak.

"Meaning what? Why would you want to be a snake? What a ridiculous notion."

"Oh, never mind. Where did you get it? It needs to go back. I can't sleep with a snake in my room. Why is it in my room, anyway? Right next to my bed!"

"I bought it from a very nice man. It was his son's, but his son just got married, and the new wife refuses to keep it. It's a caramel corn snake. I thought that was perfect, because you love caramel corn. Oh, and he's almost fourteen years old. Isn't that remarkable?"

"Remarkable." I would never be able to eat caramel corn again. "Well, call whoever you bought it from. I'm not keeping it."

Grandma Verda huffed. "I spent days arranging this for you." She picked up a book with a whole bunch of disgusting slimy snakes on the cover. "Maybe you need to read up on them and then you'll want to keep him." She flipped the book open. "Corn snakes can live for thirty years, Elizabeth! Sometimes more."

"I appreciate the thought, but listen. Snakes scare me. I don't want to own one, I don't want to feed one, and I can't imagine changing his cage. I am a bad person to own a snake because he wouldn't get the proper care."

"That's why I bought you this book. Feeding him is easy! I bought you plenty of frozen rodents."

Did she say what I thought? "What?"

"Frozen rodents. I didn't think you'd want to feed him live ones."

Ugh. "And they are where?"

"In your freezer. Where else would they be?"

She'd probably heat one up for him in my Calphalon pan, too. I gagged at the thought. Of course she wouldn't; I mean, cat food was a far different thing than frozen rodents. But still. "Um, do you feed it to them frozen?"

Grandma Verda slapped the book on the table. "Read the book. Find out for yourself."

"Give me the number, Grandma."

She pouted but dug in her purse and handed it over. Of course she frowned at me. I didn't care.

I dialed the number, all the while trying to calm myself. When the man answered, I said, "Hi. My name is Elizabeth Stevens. My grandmother purchased a snake from you? Well, it was a mistake and, honestly, it needs to go. I can't keep it."

When I finished my conversation, I sighed in relief. "He doesn't want it back but had another person interested in it. He's going to have him call me."

"Fine. I was trying to make you happy. Don't ask me for

anything ever again if you're not going to keep what I buy for you."

I ignored the pout in her voice. I mean, really. A snake! It was like my worst fear come to life. Why do you think I wanted to *be* a snake? Because I was scared to death of them, that's why.

"We need to move it out of my bedroom. I can't sleep with it in there. And when does it need to be fed again? I'm not doing that."

"Oh, for pity's sake. Calm down. He doesn't need to be fed for five to seven days. You'll have to move him yourself if you want him moved. I had Scot bring him over and set everything up."

"Scot? As in my *brother* Scot?"

"Yes." Grandma Verda shook her head slightly. "I worry he's on drugs. He laughed the entire time he was here."

Of course he'd laughed. He got to be part of the greatest joke in the world. I was going to kill him. "I'll call him. Right now."

I darted a glance toward my bedroom. Damn. A snake?

Maddie peered into the snake cage. "He's kinda cute. You sure you don't want to keep him?"

"You're serious? You think he's cute?"

"His colors are gorgeous. I always wanted a snake when I was growing up. My mother had a ridiculous lifelong fear of snakes, so she always said no."

Let me tell you, this boggled me. How could I be friends with someone who wanted a snake as a little girl? That's just— weird. "Maddie, you're one weird chick." I went to open the freezer, then remembered what was in there. "Can you get the ice out?"

She looked at me strangely but pulled the ice out, apparently not noticing the box clearly labeled as disgusting dead rodents. "When was Scot here?"

"Earlier today. But he made me wait five whole days before coming. The jerk. He thinks this is just too funny for words."

"You really slept on the couch?"

"Um. Yeah." I shivered. "I really want the snake gone. Do you want him? If this guy doesn't come through?" I'd never visit her again, but she could come here, right? Right.

"Hmm. Maybe. I'll think about it. You're all alone to-night?"

I nodded. "Vinny is home from the hospital, so Grandma's been spending all her time over there."

Maddie knelt down in front of the snake. "Hey, what's with the white stuff in his mouth? Is that normal?"

"No clue. Don't care. He won't be my problem soon."

Hands on hips, she said, "Yeah, but he is now. So, you should find out about the white stuff."

She had a point, as much as I hated to admit it. "All right, I'll call . . . someone, in the morning."

She sipped the lemonade I'd poured for her. "Good. So, have you heard from Miranda recently?"

"Not a peep, which is strange. Of course, I haven't really done any magic lately, so maybe it's connected."

Flipping her blonde hair behind her shoulder, Maddie grinned. "Maybe you should tonight then!"

I shrugged. The magic thing? I don't know. It had kind of lost its appeal after all the setbacks. "Hey, why don't we get a movie tonight or something? Or go out for one?"

"Can't. Spencer is taking me to his parents' for dinner. I'm a little nervous. What if they don't like me?"

"What wouldn't they love about you? You're beautiful, smart, funny, and you like snakes. They'll adore you."

We were silent. Maddie watched the snake slither around and do whatever snakes did. You know, snakey stuff. I, on the other hand, devoutly ignored the beast. I knew I was being stupid about this, but I couldn't help it. Pictures of snakes made my skin crawl, and while I knew there was nothing wrong with having a snake as a pet, I was flat out uncomfortable with every single aspect of owning one. Tomorrow I'd call around to some pet stores to see if they'd take him. Whoever had wanted him apparently didn't any longer, as they hadn't contacted me.

"Have you talked to Nate yet?"

I'd told her about Kevin, and while I hadn't said anything about Nate, she wasn't stupid. I shook my head. How could I miss him so much? I hadn't figured that one out yet.

"Why not?"

I set my glass in the sink. "Not sure what to say, I guess."

"How about you're sorry for upsetting him, but nothing happened between you and Kevin. Tell him the truth. You care about him, and you're not dating anyone else." Maddie pointed at me. "You're going to stay unhappy until you deal with it."

"*I* am not dating anyone else, but I'm fairly sure Nate is. So, what's the best that can happen? He accepts my apology and kindly informs me he's involved with someone else?" I shook my head again. "It would suck, and I'd be putting myself in the line of fire. Not doing it."

"You owe him an apology, if nothing else. You should have seen him that night, Liz. He was totally freaked out. I'm not so sure he *is* involved with anyone, because he definitely looked like a man who had feelings." She paused a moment. "For you."

Hope bubbled up, but I quashed it. I knew what I'd seen, and the expression on Nate's face when he'd looked at the red-haired woman had been filled with love. I'd bet money on it. "No. You're wrong. I wish to God you weren't, but you are."

"Well, you'll never know for sure unless you take a stab at it." She winked. "You could always whip up something magical."

"No, that's what got me into this in the first place. I don't want to be with anyone because of a spell." I mean, there wasn't any doubt now. That amazing night on the couch? Yep, it had to be the result of the banana muffins. Only, for me, everything I'd felt was real.

Too real.

"Yeah, I get that. I was joking, anyway."

Wanting to change the subject, I asked, "You want some cookies? I baked them yesterday."

She looked at me like I was crazy. "Don't get me wrong, but, um . . . I'm a little wary of eating anything you bake at this point."

I stuck my tongue out at her. "No reason to be. The cookies are clean," I teased. "Word of honor." I hesitated. "But there is something I've been wanting to talk to you about. I think I should bake you something new—"

"Absolutely not. I'm not going through that mess again," she interjected.

"Just listen to me before you say no. I'm thinking it might be smart to bake something to take off the effects of all the other spells. You know—just to be sure. I don't want you getting so miserable again."

She shook her head. "I'm feeling terrific. I don't want to screw with that. You fixed whatever was wrong, so let's just leave it alone."

"Are you sure?" It made me happy to get something right, but I didn't want to leave anything to chance.

"I'm positive. But if I start feeling weird again, I'll let you know. Deal?"

"That works. Just don't wait too long if you think something has changed. Promise?"

"I promise." Then, she checked her watch. "I need to take off. Spencer will be here soon, and I bought a gift for his parents I want to wrap." She put her glass in the sink and gave me a hug. "Try to have a nice evening. Take a bubble bath, read a book, relax. It's the weekend, ya know?"

After Maddie left, I roamed around my apartment, not sure what I wanted to do. I briefly considered going to see a movie on my own, but it didn't appeal enough to put forth any real energy.

Switching on the TV, I sat on the far corner of the couch, where I couldn't see the snake. Boredom clawed at me. It had been a while since I'd sat there, alone, on the weekend.

On a whim, I ran to the kitchen and tried phoning Jon and Andy, thinking they might want to hang out, only no one answered. I thought about calling Kevin but couldn't do it. It wouldn't be right. Not yet. Maybe in a few months we'd become hang-out buddies. And then, I noticed my answering machine was blinking its new message light, so I pushed the button.

"Betty, it's me. Give me a call back. On my cell."

BEEP.

"Hey Betty, it's me again. Still waiting for your call."

BEEP.

"Are you screening me? Come on, I just want to talk to you. It's important."

BEEP.

"Elizabeth, this is Marc. I've called you three times over the last three days. Please—call me back."

The light went out, indicating there weren't any other messages. Was I desperate enough for company to call my ex-husband? No. But I had to admit, he'd piqued my curiosity. If it was due to the magic cake, it certainly had taken long enough to work.

Though, Marc was definitely stubborn and possibly had held out that long. But what if it was something else? And, why did I care? Would I take him back? Now?

Shoot. I seriously didn't know what to do. Making a decision, I hit the delete button and returned to the living room. I picked up my half-finished unicorn rug, plopped down on the couch, and began latch-hooking.

Nice. Somehow, I was right back where I'd started. Miserably alone, crafting something meant for kids in my crappy apartment with absolutely nothing else to do.

Interesting, really, how the exact same place could mean so many different things. This same living room I sat in depressed had been the scene of three different men kissing me. Three different men, all handsome, all desirable in their own ways, interested in me. Nate on the couch, hands all over my body, inside my body, eliciting responses from me I didn't think were possible. Jon, bewildered, confused, and his sweet kiss. And Kevin, dancing with me to silent music, confusing me even more.

I'd also cried many tears on this couch over Marc and our marriage. Our divorce. Spent way too much time feeling sorry for myself. For my life. God help me, for the person I'd become. I remembered promising myself to change. To not do this self-pity crap again. But it seemed, at least for tonight, that's exactly what I was doing.

"No. I'm not going to," I whispered. Sudden energy propelled me to run around my apartment, grabbing every single latch-hook rug I owned. Why the hell I'd bought so many of them when I never finished any, I had no clue. Yanking open a drawer in the kitchen, I pulled out my scissors and stacked the rugs on the counter, one on top of another.

"You're history, Mr. Unicorn," I muttered, choosing that one first. The scissors cut through the plastic and the yarn, the tearing sound oddly gratifying, and slowly, I dismantled the rug, dumping the pieces into the garbage as I did.

Bits of yarn floated in the air, and I sneezed. Weird, but the simple act of destroying crappy home craft projects was extremely pleasurable. When I finished demolishing the final one, I shoved the trash can under the sink and slammed the cupboard door shut.

"Better." But strangely, still not enough. My eyes whipped around, trying to find something else—anything else I could do to prove to myself I'd changed. That I was a different woman now than I was a year ago.

You see, it was suddenly of extreme importance that I wasn't the same person Marc had abandoned for someone else. Misery pulled at me, but I shoved it away.

"No more. No. No. No," I cried. Loneliness surrounded me. It came in a giant wave, almost suffocating me with its strength. My breathing hitched in my throat, the air pushing out of me in short, fast gasps. I gripped the counter. This was going to stop tonight. It *had* to stop tonight.

"What am I supposed to do?"

She arrived then. All at once, a fragrant rush of roses permeated the air. My skin tingled. And then, oddly, the air changed. It was as if someone had turned my AC on full blast.

"Miranda? Talk to me. Tell me what to do!"

No response. Didn't she know I needed her?

"I know you're here. I can smell you. You have to be here for a reason, right? Why else would you keep returning? I'm thinking it's to help me. But you're not really helping and, trust me, I could use the help."

Still no response. Damn. What good was a ghost grandmother if she refused to talk? Then, the weirdest sensation came over me. It was as if someone placed their hands on either side of my face and applied pressure. I allowed it to happen, I stopped resisting, and my head turned until my gaze rested on my refrigerator.

"What? You're hungry?"

Of course, no response. I flipped my gaze around the room again, only to have the hands force it back. And just like before, I was staring at the refrigerator.

"Okay, okay." Walking to it, I swung the door open and examined the contents. "Juice. Milk. Leftovers. Condiments." Nothing that jumped out at me. Nothing that made any sense. Nothing that would make this agony go away.

A hand grabbed the back of my hair and forcibly pulled down. Hard. My neck yanked backward with the tug, and my head jerked upward. Now, my eyes rested squarely on the freezer. Ah. *That.*

"Got it. Thanks." Opening the freezer, I closed my eyes and reached around and past the disgusting dead rodent box until I found it. Pulling it out, I sat down on a chair and unzipped the bag. I turned it upside down . . . and the foil wrapped cake fell to the table.

I picked at the foil, not quite ready to unwrap it. The last time I'd seen the actual cake inside had been over a decade ago. When I believed in love.

When I believed in forever.

When I believed in . . . Well, when I believed.

I wanted to throw it away, like I'd done with the rugs. But somehow, I knew that wasn't enough. I needed to open it. I needed to look at it. And then, I needed to get rid of it.

If I did that, would I be throwing my dreams away with it? Well, yeah, that made sense. In a stupid life-altering, change your destiny, new-age sort of way. My hand shook as I gently peeled back the foil. I'd been smart enough to put the cake in plastic wrap before covering it with foil, so nothing stuck.

There it was. White on white. Crushed icy pink roses, smushed a bit, but still recognizable. Oddly, it didn't look as if it were a decade old. It didn't appear to hold the key to my future. It was a hunk of frozen cake. Nothing more. Nothing less.

I made the mistake of picking it up. As soon as my skin touched it, everything changed. Instead of sitting in my kitchen, I was once again at my wedding, then at my reception, various scenes flipping by speedily, like a DVD on fast-forward. Just as before, my real world bled away. It was as if I had stepped into the past. But as a ghost. It felt real, but I knew it wasn't.

After the reception came our honeymoon. Then our first home. Then our second. And then, finally, the one we'd built together. While all of this was happening, emotions were zipping around inside of me. At first they were amazing. Love. Happiness. Fulfillment. But negative emotions soon followed. Frustration. Sadness. Wanting a baby and Marc's refusal. No longer cuddling together on the couch at night. Fights. Recriminations. Guilt. More fights.

Guilt? I tried to grasp what was being shown to me. I tried to understand *why* it was even happening. And then—suddenly—everything slowed down. No longer on fast-forward, the vision in front of me was of *that night*, in heart-wrenching slow speed, flickering before me. My thirty-fourth birthday. Except this time, I watched Marc's face as he spoke to me. His hand shook when he gripped the chair. He told me he was leaving me. And then, when my prior-self turned her back on him, cursing him, I saw regret shimmer over his expression.

It was there. The regret I didn't think he felt, so obvious in his eyes as he stared, frozenlike, at the back of my head. But when my old self pivoted, angry words flying from my mouth, the regret instantly vanished, shielded by that ice cold glare I'd spent the last year remembering.

The tears came then. No way in hell could I stop them. I sobbed, and while I'd cried plenty in the past, never like this. Never this all-consuming explosion of tears that just wouldn't stop.

My chest hurt from it, my soul ached from it, but strangely— my heart? It felt free, light, and whole. Still crying, I dropped the cake on the table and sat there, waiting for the trembles to stop, the tears to cease.

They didn't. Standing, I grabbed the cake again, thinking I'd drop it into the garbage, or maybe the disposal, when my eyes fell on the snake. *Oh God*. That was something else I needed to do. I'd had him for a week, which meant he needed to eat. Still crying, I maneuvered the little door for feeding and dropped the cake in there. Fast.

Every pet I'd ever owned had loved people food. Snakes couldn't be any different, could they?

Besides, it seemed a fitting end to the cake. To the old Elizabeth. To me and Marc. Being digested by a snake.

Locking the hatch again, I didn't wait to see if it ate it. I was going to take a hot bath and then go to bed and, hopefully, when I woke in the morning, it would be a brand new day.

Hell. If I was really lucky, it would be a brand new life.

Chapter Eighteen

"Do you think he's dead?" I asked Scot as he drove. "He looks dead. But do you think he's really dead?"

"Yes. I do. A vet isn't going to help him," Scot said, slowing the van to make a left turn.

I killed the snake.

I'd woken up that morning weirdly at ease; even the rain hadn't bothered me. I was going to talk to Nate. I'd decided it was time, so I was nervously excited, strangely hopeful. But after my shower, I realized the snake wasn't moving. *At all.* I naturally couldn't touch him (ew), so I'd knocked on the glass, but he'd stayed all curled up tight. I'd considered sticking something in the tank to prod him, like a wooden spoon, but couldn't deal with the actuality of it.

Frantic, because somehow the thought of a dead snake in my home was even more horrifying than a live one, I'd begged Scot to come over immediately and haul us to the veterinarian's office.

I am a horrible person. I disliked the snake, but I hadn't meant to murder him. Probably, it was the cake. Even though it didn't look as if the snake had actually eaten any of it, what else could it be?

But still, he was dead or faking it really well.

That was an idea. Maybe? "Scot, can snakes be trained? Like dogs? Maybe he's just playing dead."

"Why do you care? You couldn't wait to get rid of him."

"I just feel bad," I murmured, eyes on the road.

Two hours later, I didn't feel any better. The vet assured me it wasn't the cake that killed my snake. Though, he did give me a strange look when he saw the cake in the tank. Oh wait, not a tank. It's a *vivarium*.

Luckily, he didn't ask me to explain, but he did firmly vocalize I shouldn't consider owning a snake again. Ever. For my entire life. Yes, he said those exact words. Seeing as I wholeheartedly agreed with him, I didn't argue or point out how rude he was. Nor did I point out it wasn't my idea to own a snake in the first place.

Apparently, the fourteen-year-old snake had been riddled with some weird disease that would have been treatable months ago but wasn't dealt with, so he died from it. I still thought the cake pushed him over the edge. You know, vapors can be deadly.

"When we get back to my place, will you do me one more favor?" I asked Scot. "You owe me. You knew I'd freak, but you helped Grandma anyway."

"Come on, Lizzie. You gotta admit it was hysterical. I wish I could have been there the first time you saw him."

"Don't be a jerk," I snapped. "I'm late for work, and I need you to take any remaining snakey stuff out of my apartment."

"Snakey stuff?"

"Dead rodents," I huffed. "In my freezer."

"Chicken."

"Yep. But you'll do it?"

"Yeah. I have a friend who has a couple of snakes. I'll take them to him."

"I have some wrapping paper if you want to gift wrap it," I suggested.

"Or I could leave them there. For you to deal with."

"I should have called Joe," I muttered, glancing out the window as we pulled into my parking lot.

While I felt terrible about a living creature dying, I was really happy—no, ecstatic—that he was not in my home any longer. Plus, I'd learned something. Never, ever, no matter what, tell Grandma Verda anything that could be misconstrued to such disastrous results, ever again. Oh yeah—I also learned I didn't really want to be a snake. They were entirely too, um, reptilian for my peace of mind. Plus, that tongue thing? Creepy.

I sipped my coffee and basked in the sun that shone through my windows. Spring was in the air, with the bite of winter's chill softened by buds of warmth. And I just knew the second I stepped outside I'd be wrapped in the unique scents of the season. Fresh, breezy, the promise of hot summer days in every whiff. Normally on Sundays, I'd sit around most of the day. I'd catch up on chores, maybe watch a movie or read a book. Not today. Today, I was going shopping.

I hated my furniture, but beyond that, I wanted the black gone. No wonder I'd been depressed for a year. I was living in an apartment of mourning.

Brushing the crumbs from my morning toast off my hands, I considered hauling Maddie out of bed and insisting she come with me. But I sort of wanted to do this on my own. After the vision sequence with Marc, I was finally ready to move on. I didn't need to see him now, and I didn't need to hear an apology. Visualizing his regret was enough.

Yeah, I still needed to talk to Nate, but for some reason hesitated. If he wanted to talk to me, he knew where I lived, right? Right. Which meant, if I was honest with myself, he didn't want to talk to me. I figured I'd focus on something I could do rather than on things I couldn't. No matter how much it hurt.

After checking the Sunday advertisements, I mapped out my day. Several furniture shops were having spring sales. If I could save money *and* redecorate my apartment, even better.

I jotted a note for Grandma Verda, who was still spending the majority of her time with the recovering Vinny, grabbed my purse, locked my door, and then headed into the sunshine. Right away I realized filling my apartment with new furnishings wasn't going to be as easy as I'd thought. Let me tell you, these furniture shops? Tons of choices for someone who didn't really know what she wanted. Deciding to browse, my eyes scanned the store I was in.

"Excuse me," I mumbled as I passed an older couple who were discussing the merits of a La-Z-Boy recliner.

The woman glanced up and smiled. "If you don't mind me asking, what do you think of this chair? We're considering buying it for my granddaughter, but we're not really sure if it's young enough for her."

Her striking white hair pulled at a memory, and I took a closer look as I answered. "It's nice. But without knowing the décor of her home, it's hard to say."

The man said, "Sit down in it, will you? We're getting too old to get in and out of chairs in public. We'll embarrass ourselves." He grinned. They seemed like a really sweet couple.

And then, I remembered who they were. The couple from Starbucks. The ones whose history Maddie and I tried to guess but who'd disappeared before I could ask. How weird was it seeing them again?

"Sure," I answered. Sitting down in the chair, I pulled the leg-rest up and sighed. "Oh yeah, this is relaxing. Maybe I'll consider buying one."

"So if your grandmother purchased this for you as a wedding gift, would you be happy or annoyed?" the woman asked. "We're not sure if she'll think our tastes are too old for her."

"Um. My grandmother? A chair would be great. It's the snake I couldn't handle."

"Snake? How interesting," the lady said with a smile. "I bet that's a great story."

I shuddered. "Not really. But she meant well. Your granddaughter is getting married?" I pulled out a business card and handed it to her. "I own a bakery that specializes in wedding cakes. If she hasn't chosen anyone yet, have her come in."

Accepting the card, the woman nodded. "Thank you. Could we have another, perhaps? So I can give one to her and keep one for myself?"

"Definitely." I gave her another card. "Please feel free to give it to anyone you want."

"Oh, it's for us. We're finally getting married. After twenty years together, we decided to make it legal," she said with a nervous chuckle.

"Twenty years?" So Maddie and I were both wrong. Interesting. "That's amazing. Congratulations!"

The old man's eyes twinkled. "I asked her to marry me on our second date. It's taken her this long to say yes."

Her cheeks turning pink, the woman tucked both business cards into her purse. "Sometimes it takes a while," she said softly. "But you waited for me, and I came to my senses."

"You're just stubborn," the old man teased.

"Can I ask a question? If it's too personal, I'll understand." At the woman's nod, I continued. "Did you ever doubt in those twenty years that you were supposed to be together?"

"Oh no. I fell in love with him the moment I met him. Like a romance story."

"Then why so long to get married?" I realized I was being rude, but I needed to know.

Her frail shoulders moved upward in a shrug. "Bad first marriage. I guess it took me twenty years to see what was in front of me the entire time. That just because my heart was broken once, it didn't mean it would happen again."

The elderly man reached over and squeezed her hand. And then, a look so intimate passed between them that I felt as if I were intruding. After a few more minutes of chit-chatting, I said, "Congratulations again! I hope to see you and your granddaughter soon."

Imagine. Twenty years with someone without a wedding ring. Twenty years to get over a bad first marriage. Sure, they certainly appeared happy, but I was smart enough to understand they'd probably argued about it over the years. Honestly, it spoke volumes that they'd managed to stay together to reach the point of getting married. Most relationships probably wouldn't.

Stopping midstride, I thought of Nate and a rush of dizziness hit me. Reaching out, I steadied myself by grabbing onto a chair. It was time. I needed to talk to Nate. Regardless of what he said to me. Regardless of how he reacted. It was time.

My heart jumped in my chest. Hell. Now or never, right? Right.

"Hey, Elizabeth. I'm surprised to see you." Nate shook his head. "That didn't come out right. I'm glad to see you. How are you?"

"Can I come in? I won't take long. I promise." My skin prickled with nerves, and my legs threatened to collapse. This was brand new territory for me, and I hadn't even given my-self a chance to prepare what I was going to say. I was too afraid I'd chicken out if I didn't come to Nate immediately.

"Absolutely. Come on in."

He opened the door wider, and I stepped into his apartment. I didn't see his girlfriend, but that didn't mean she wasn't there. Possibly she was sleeping off a night of amazing sex. Yeah, I just had to put that image in my mind.

"Do you want anything to drink? I have juice, soda, wine, whatever you want," Nate said, gesturing toward the couch. "I even have coffee."

Taking a seat, I exhaled. "No. Thank you. If I don't say this straight-out, I'm not sure I will."

Apparently he'd just gotten out of the shower, because his hair was wet. His white T-shirt tightened across his chest, cling-ing to areas he must not have dried properly before answering the door. Even knowing he had a girlfriend, I still wanted to rip that shirt off. I know. Hopeless. Completely and utterly hopeless.

Instead of sitting next to me on the couch, or across from me in his chair, he sat on the coffee table in front of me. So close, our knees were almost touching. Shoot. He smelled re-ally good.

"I'm listening. What's going on? Everything okay with your grandmother, your sister, and all other assorted family members?" he asked with his trademark twitchy grin.

I loved that twitchy grin.

"Um. You're too close to me," I blurted. "I can't think when you're this close to me. All I want to do is kiss you. And I can't do that, so you should probably move." Tell me I didn't just say what I think I said.

Yeah. I know. I did.

"You want to kiss me?"

"I'm sorry. I know you have a girlfriend. I shouldn't have said that. So, let's forget I did and I'll say what I came to say instead." I fidgeted in my seat.

"I'm much more interested in following this kiss line of discussion. Why stop at wanting to kiss me? Why not lean over and kiss me? Do I need to be closer?" He scooted closer. "Is that better?"

What was happening? I didn't think he was the type to cheat. Maybe I was wrong about the girlfriend thing? A blossom of hope eased its way through me. "Do you have a girlfriend?" I blurted.

His green eyes narrowed. "What makes you think I have a girlfriend?"

"I've seen you with her. Or at least with a woman who I thought was your girlfriend. I know you love her and that's good. Well. Not good for me. But good for you, and it's not that I don't want you to be happy, because I do. If she is your girlfriend, that is. You know, it's just, well . . . for a while I thought maybe we could be happy together."

This was, without a doubt, absolutely not going as planned.

"Why don't you start from the very beginning and tell me what you came to say. Then we can work through this addled idea of yours and come back to the kiss."

Addled? Did he just call me addled? That's something my grandmother would say. And yeah, maybe I was a little confused, but who could blame me? With him sitting so close and smelling so good and all. I twisted a few strands of hair to give me a few seconds to compose myself. "I came to apologize to you for that night you thought I was missing."

"You're a big girl. If you want to stay out all night, you don't have to ask permission from anyone." His gaze skittered away for an instant before returning to me. "That being said, you really scared a lot of people who love you. And your grandmother was really upset. I'm just surprised you forgot to call her." While his voice was genial enough, it held a thread of coolness. I hated that.

He ran his hands over his face. "I thought . . . Well, it doesn't matter what I thought. Once you were home and I realized you were with your boyfriend, I thought it best to give you some distance." Leaning over, he brushed my nose with a finger. "But I was worried about you. I can't tell you how relieved I was when you walked through your door."

"Kevin isn't my boyfriend, Nate. I mean, I was dating him. But that night? Nothing happened. I'd had too much to drink, so I crashed on his couch." I cleared my throat. "We're not seeing each other anymore, either. In case that's important to you." It probably wasn't. But I had to toss it in. You know, just to be sure.

He raised an eyebrow. "What about that other guy I saw you with? Jon?"

I laughed, trying to cover my nerves. It came out sounding like a noise a drunk hyena would make. Don't ask me how I knew this, I just did. "He's going to love the fact that he was right. Jon is happily involved with someone else, and even if he wasn't, he wouldn't be interested in me."

I so wanted to kiss Nate. His lips were way too close.

"You two seemed really tight. I'm pretty good at judging people, and it was obvious that you and Jon know each other very well."

"Well, yeah. We do. Jon and I went to college together and we own A Taste of Magic together. Other than Maddie, he's my best friend." Nate didn't say anything, so I said, "He's like my brother. He's my family."

Understanding flooded Nate's expression and, I have to say, the fact it did made my entire world brighten. Every color in his apartment became more vivid. Especially the green in his eyes.

"So you *were* dating Kevin. You're not now, and you were never dating Jon? Do I have this correct?"

"You sound like the cop you are. But yes, you do. And I am sorry I didn't call my grandmother. She'd just moved in, so I wasn't used to someone waiting up for me."

"Are you dating anyone else I don't know about?"

"No."

"Are you *considering* dating anyone else I should know about?"

"No." I laughed the hyena laugh again. "But you haven't answered my question. That woman I've seen you with? Who is she?"

"I do not have a girlfriend, Lizzie. Who is this woman you're talking about?"

"You're not lying to me, are you? Well, that would be stupid, wouldn't it? Lying, I mean. But this woman—you two seemed close. And she called you sweetie." Yeah, I was blubbering incoherently again. I snapped my mouth shut and promised myself to not say another word.

But then, he did the totally unexpected. He grabbed my hands and cradled them in his. The heat transferred from him to me, and tingles erupted all over my body. Not unlike the magic when I baked.

"What are you doing?"

"Describe this woman to me," he coaxed.

"Tall. Gorgeous. Red hair. Green eyes." Pulling away from his grasp, I said, "She answered your door one night when I came to see you. I saw her the night I invited you to dinner with me and Maddie. And I saw you and Sam in the parking lot one day waving to her as she left." Closing my eyes, I willed my heart to calm down. "You love her. I know you do. I saw it in your face. And, I know we haven't exactly known each other that long, and I'm not saying I love you, because heck if I know what love is anymore, but I do care about you and I did hope we'd—"

"Stop," Nate said, interrupting, his deep voice easily drown-

g out mine. "Open your eyes, Liz." His fingers brushed across
my lids as he spoke.

Opening them, I forcibly held my lips together. At this
point, I'd pretty much said everything I'd wanted to say, plus
several things I didn't. Better to keep my mouth shut and let
him do all the talking.

"You're right. I do love her. Her name is Julie, and she is
one of the three most important women in my life."

"So she is your girlfriend." Even though I'd guessed this,
even though I knew he loved her, even though I knew there
was nothing in my future with Nate, other than possibly
friendship, hearing her name, hearing him make absolute fact
what I already knew made it so much worse.

Standing, I said, "Thank you for talking to me. I think it's
best if I go home now. I hope you have a great day." What the
hell? I sounded like a customer service rep.

Before I could make it to the door, Nate's arms swung
round me, stopping me.

"You didn't let me finish."

Fine. Finish me off. We'd barely gotten started, so stopping
shouldn't be that difficult, right?

"Go ahead," I said, resigned to hearing more about the
wonderful Julie.

His lips touched my hair and his arms tightened. "Liz, I already told you I don't have a girlfriend. Julie is my sister. She's
Sam's mom. And you, with all your strange ideas and crazy
ways, have become one of those three most important women
in my life. All I want is the chance to get to know you better.
To see where that might lead."

"Your sister?" Now that he mentioned it, her eyes were a
matching set to his. Wow, I'd reached a new low. Stupid, relieved, embarrassed, and gloriously hopeful—all at once. Was
there a medal for that?

"My sister."

"Who is the third important woman?"

He chuckled. "My mother." Dropping his arms, he turned

me around to face him. "Come here. I'm ready for that kis now."

"You are?" I teased, still wrapping my mind around every thing he'd said.

"One thing, Liz. Honesty between us from now on. N misconceptions or assumptions. For either of us. Deal?"

"Deal. That sounds great," I said. I had no clue where i would lead. If anywhere. But at that moment, we were at th beginning. And with all beginnings there was always a chance always a possibility. And you know what? Nothing sounde better than that.

"Come here," he said. And I did. I walked into his arm and his lips came down to meet mine and the world disap peared. Heat flashed instantaneously and, well, everything fla out just felt right.

How cool was that?

Chapter Nineteen

"The little line turned pink."

Confused, I looked up from the menu. My sister and I were eating at the veggie restaurant I'd been to with Kevin. "What are you talking about?"

Alice closed her menu, her brown eyes wide with shock. "The little line. It turned pink."

Call me stupid, but I had no clue what she was going on about. Of course, this was likely due to the fact that Nate and I had patched things up. My mind—stubborn as it was—refused to stop thinking about him. "Alice, what line?"

Reaching into her purse, she dragged out a small white plastic rectangle and pushed it across the table. "That line. And seven others. All pink."

One glance at the test kit and I knew. "You're pregnant? Are you sure?" My baby sister was having a baby? I didn't know if I should jump up and down for joy or cradle her in my arms and cry. Simultaneously, I wanted to do both.

Her pale cheeks flooded with color. "Yes. Eight tests have given me the same results. What am I going to do?"

"Troy?"

She nodded. "Do I tell him?" The fear in her voice made me want to find the jerk and spell him all over again.

"No." Oh shit, was that good advice? I mean, jerk or not, he had rights. While I preferred she didn't say anything to him, it wasn't my decision to make. "I don't know. You don't have to now. At least, not until you know what you're going to do. Even then, it's up to you. I'll stand behind you, whatever you do."

I thought of the road ahead of her, the decisions she needed to make, and it boggled me, overwhelmed me. And seeing as

I wasn't even the pregnant one, I couldn't imagine how she felt.

"I'm keeping the baby, Elizabeth."

Of course. I would do the same. "Yeah, okay. That's great. You're going to be a mommy, and I'm going to be an auntie." Did my happiness sound false?

Her cheeks paled again. "Mommy. God, that's scary. It's a huge responsibility. What if I'm not up for it?"

"You have nine months to get ready. I'll help you. Mom will. Grandma Verda will be ecstatic."

"Um. No. I have about seven months. I've ignored the signs for a while."

"You've been under a lot of stress, so that makes sense. Don't beat yourself up about it."

"What am I going to do?" she asked again.

"You've already decided, honey. You're keeping the baby right?"

"Yes. I know that. I just don't know what else I'm going to do. It seems . . ." She shrugged. "Unimaginable."

"We'll start taking steps. We'll find you a doctor first, then get all the information we can, and before you know it, it won't seem so frightening."

"Part of me wants to tell Troy," she admitted softly.

"Why? Do you want him back?"

"No!" She shuddered. "I just think he should know, I guess."

"But then he'll be in your life forever. He's not a good man." When she didn't say anything, I said, "You already know he's a horrible father."

"That's why I haven't told him yet."

I leaned over and grasped her hand. "Just wait. Let yourself get accustomed to the idea first. And then, if you still want to let him know, we'll talk about it."

When she nodded, relief flooded me. No way, no how, did I want that man in her life.

The waitress came by and took our order. After she left, Alice said, "What's it like living with Grandma?"

Happy to see some color return to her cheeks, I answered, 'She's not been around a lot lately. She's with Vinny most of the time."

Alice's gaze slid to the side of me. "Someone's heading this way," she said.

"Hi, Elizabeth!"

I pivoted my head toward the familiar voice and saw Kevin approaching our table, an attractive woman I remembered from the wedding next to him. When they stopped at my chair, I forced a smile. "Hey, Kevin. How are you?"

"I'm great. This is my sister, Kathy. Kath, this is Elizabeth, a friend and one of my clients. You guys didn't actually meet at Keith's wedding."

I introduced Alice, who barely responded, but come on, who could blame her? I noticed Kevin glance at Alice with interest. Under other circumstances, I would have maybe set them up. He was a great guy. But I didn't think Alice would be in the mood for a date.

He smiled. "Thank you for the granola bars. I really enjoyed them!"

"I'm glad you got them. I'm sorry I didn't see you when I dropped them off, but you were busy with a client." The night Nate and I made up I'd put together a batch of home-baked granola bars, with a little magic, for Kevin. I'd used the same spell I'd used for Jon. You know, to erase any after-effects from the brownies. Just to be sure. I should probably do the same thing for Nate, but something kept stopping me. Things were good. Happy. And part of me didn't want to know if it was only because of magic. I'd have to deal with it at some point. I knew that.

But not yet.

After a few minutes of chit-chatting, Kevin said, "We should get to our table." He bent down, as if he were going to hug me, but then stood back up. "It was great seeing you! I hope you're not giving up on your workouts."

Well. "I wasn't sure. Because of, you know."

His eyes softened, and I remembered all the great things I'd seen in him. But even with that, I didn't doubt my decision for a second.

"Just come on in. It will be great."

The waitress brought our food, and Kevin and his sister went to their own table. I turned back to Alice. "Honey, how are you feeling?"

"Sick. Scared. Miserable. Excited. Freaked out." Biting her lip, she said, "Does that answer your question?"

Clasping her hand in mine again, I tried to instill as much positive energy into my words as possible. "We'll figure it out. You're not alone."

"Then why do I feel so alone?" The tremors in her voice made my heart crack in two.

"I don't know. I don't know." But as I sat there, across the table from my sister and her unborn baby, a glimmer of an idea whisked through me. For the moment, I set it aside.

"You'll be terrific, Alice. You'll see." Eyes filled with doubt met mine, but she didn't argue, just pulled her hand free.

"Wow. I'm really going to have a baby." Alice shook her head, as if clearing cobwebs, and her body rippled with a shiver. "You don't seem nearly as surprised as I feel. How can you be so calm?"

"I don't know," I said again. Probably, though, it was because of everything I'd experienced lately. Once you knew ghosts and magic were real, there wasn't much left to surprise you.

Quietly, we picked at our lunch, neither of us in the mood for further conversation. When we went our separate ways, me to work, Alice to start looking for doctors, I hugged her as tightly as I could.

"I love you. I'll stop by later tonight," I murmured. And then, I watched as she shuffled to her car, head down, looking about as lonely and pitiful as a person could get.

Me? I just wanted to make her world a better place.

Nate and I stood at the last furniture store on my list. We'd been shopping for a good part of the day, and I'd already found almost everything I needed. Now, I was after the perfect couch.

"What about this one?" Nate asked, plopping down on a bright orange one similar to my parents' Naugahyde version but in leather.

"Orange leather? Not in this lifetime. I kind of like that one, though." I pointed to a soft camel-colored sofa against the back wall of the furniture shop.

"I thought you wanted color."

"I do. But not orange."

"Well, let's go take a peek, then."

As soon as I sat on it, I knew it was *the one*. Envisioning morning coffee and the newspaper, afternoon novels, and evenings curled up with a blanket, I nodded in satisfaction. "This is it. I love it." Glancing at the price tag, I winced. Today was taking a huge bite out of my wallet. But after a year of mourning, it was worth it.

"What else do you need?"

"Aren't you getting tired of this? I can come back another day." He'd tolerated my wandering from store to store like a champ, but I didn't want to push it. You know, that whole men and shopping thing.

But then he surprised me. "I'm having a good time. Besides, it's cool I'm helping you. What's next?"

My stomach twirled at the affection in his gaze. A little secret here: I was falling hard and fast. God help me. Biting my lip, I said, "Actually, that about sums it up. Other than a few pictures, maybe."

"Didn't you say your sister was an artist? You should have her paint you something."

"She's stressed right now. Maybe later." I'd seen Alice several times since that day at the restaurant, and she seemed to be doing better. She wasn't her old self. Not yet. But I was happy to see her moving forward. Even better? She hadn't contacted Troy yet. Thank God.

After I purchased and arranged for delivery of the couch, we headed out into the early evening. Excitement at all the changes in my life put a bounce into my step. Within a few short weeks, my apartment would be furnished, painted, and decorated. I couldn't wait.

And me and Nate? Things were good. I didn't allow myself to question if maybe—just maybe—they were *too* good. That question? I wasn't ready to answer it. So I didn't.

Procrastination? Maybe. Denial? Probably. Whatever you wanted to call it, I was in it up to my eyeballs. Again, I let the worries slide away. At the moment, the only thing I wanted to concentrate on was the evening ahead of me.

After Nate unlocked the door to our building, I followed him in. We still hadn't had mind-blowing, crazy, hot, make-my-knees-melt sex, but I planned on remedying that situation as soon as possible.

"Want to come in?" I knew Grandma Verda was at Vinny's, so I had the place to myself. At least for a few hours.

"I was hoping you'd come to my place. I have the night off." He brushed a kiss across my lips. Soft. Sweet. But with the promise of more.

"I didn't think you'd ever ask. Let me go in and leave a note for Grandma, and I'll be right over."

Fifteen minutes later, I waited for Nate to answer my knock. Only he didn't. He couldn't have changed his mind already. Could he? I knocked again and waited some more. Still no answer. Maybe he'd been called in to work? But you'd think if that was the case, he'd have let me know. I mean, he had to pass my apartment door to even get outside.

Finally, because I didn't know what else to do, I tried opening the door. It opened. Ha! I'd have to razz him about leaving his door unlocked. I stuck my head inside and yelled, "Nate? I'm here."

I heard a *thump thump*, followed by, "Liz? Can you come back to the bedroom?" Weird. His voice sounded muffled and far away. But hey, if he wanted me in the bedroom, who was I to argue? I wondered if he was lying on his bed, waiting for me. Possibly naked. Anticipation and a tiny bit of nervousness tickled their way through me.

The few steps to Nate's bedroom only increased the tickles. And then, right before I crossed the threshold, a hard shiver rolled its way down my body, from my head to my toes. But he wasn't on his bed. And I didn't see him anywhere else in the room, either.

"Nate?"

More thumping. "In here! Let me out. I'm . . . um . . . stuck."

I swiveled my head, trying to decide where *in* was. "Where?"

"The closet. Let me out of the closet."

My nervousness fled. Humor replaced the anticipation. I approached the door. "You're stuck in the closet? Really?"

"Rescue me," he said, laughing.

"I'll need to see some ID. To ascertain you are who you say you are." Oh my God, this was just too much fun!

"Normal protocol for this sort of situation is a strip search. I'll expect nothing less." The hot, sexy drawl of his voice ignited a slow burn deep in my belly.

"A strip search, huh? I'll see what I can do." Kind of cool—getting to play hero for the cop. I twisted the door handle slowly, barely noticing the dampness on my palms. When I swung the door open, I laughed. Poor Nate was squashed in the closet. With about a dozen boxes stacked around him.

Disentangling himself, he held the crush of boxes back while stepping out. In a quick move, he shut the door. I heard a few boxes tumbled behind the door, and I laughed. "I thought you were all unpacked?"

"I am. Well, sort of. Most of that stuff needs to go into storage." He wrapped one arm around my waist. "Thank you for rescuing me."

"You're so very welcome. I'd say we're even now. You'd have been stuck in there a long time if I hadn't come over." I tried not to laugh again. "How'd you get in there anyway?"

"I was cleaning up before you got here, and some of the boxes fell out. Apparently, the doorknob is broken on the inside, because the damn thing wouldn't open again." He kissed my nose and then my forehead.

"But how'd the door get closed to begin with?"

A sheepish grin hit his face. "I was trying to keep more boxes from falling. I was just going to ease my way out. That didn't work so well." He tucked a strand of hair behind my ear. "I'm glad you're here. In more ways than one."

"Me, too. And I was thinking . . . if it's okay with you, I'll stay the night tonight. I told Grandma in the note not to expect me home until morning," I whispered. His arm tightened around me immediately, so I had to assume he was on board with the idea.

And then, in one swoop, he picked me up and strode to his bed, depositing me gently in the middle. Curious, I sat up and glanced around his room. I hadn't paid much attention earlier, as I was intent on finding Nate. Dark colors and no frills. Just what I would have expected.

"Like what you see?"

I focused on him, letting my eyes skim the length of his body. "Very much. Why don't you join me here so I can get a closer view?"

There was that naughty grin again. Can I say yum?

He slid on the bed and, kneeling in front of me, grasped my face gently with his hands. Lips brushed against mine. "Isn't it time for that strip search?"

"Yes. I think it is." I yanked his shirt toward me, and we both fell backward on his bed. Let me tell you, I was ready *just like that.*

Nate plunged his tongue into my mouth, and I groaned. He smelled so good. We rolled so we were face-to-face but on our sides. He wrapped his leg over mine, dragging my body closer to his. Evidently, he was also ready *just like that.* And that made me groan again.

"I have wanted you for so long," he whispered. His mouth scorched my skin as he kissed me from earlobe to earlobe. He paused at my neck, kissing me in tiny, slow increments. This

was an excellent thing, by the way. My neck is a total eroge-
nous zone.

"Okay, Nate?" I mumbled.

"Hmm?"

"You can keep doing that as long as you want. But I should
warn you."

"Warn me?"

"I can't be held liable for my actions if you do."

He laughed—a warm, husky hum that did nothing to cool
the building fire. "Promise?"

"Uh-huh."

His hands were on me in a blink, tugging at my shirt, my
pants, helping me get everything off. I figured since he was
being so gentlemanly, I should help him disrobe also, correct? Besides, there was still that strip search thing to contend with.

Happy to oblige, that was me. I unbuttoned his denim shirt
and struggled with removing it from him, but finally it slid off.
My breath caught, and I had to remind myself to push air out.
And then back in. The taut muscles of his chest and the tight
ripples in his abs begged to be touched. So I did. I started at his
chest, his warm skin growing hotter as I moved my hand down
to his stomach.

I worked to unclasp his jeans. He helped me, but I stopped
him from taking them completely off. Instead, I tugged the
denim down, just a bit, so his hips eased out above the waist-
line, his bright red briefs barely showing. And then I had to
remind myself to breathe all over again.

This look? I loved it. There was something about the smooth
line of a man's firm stomach leading into the angular line of his
hips that turned me on. Not that I wasn't hot already, but this
was the icing on the cake. I wanted to taste him—so very badly.

"Are you licking your lips?"

Another type of warmth flushed my skin when I realized
I was, indeed, licking my lips. "Well. Yeah. Got a problem
with it?"

"Sweetheart, you can lick your lips all you want. As long as it's with me."

Together, we removed the rest of our clothing, stopping here and there to kiss. To touch. To taste. To experience each other the way we wanted. His hands stroked me everywhere. First my stomach, then my breasts. But he didn't stop there. Nate seemed to instinctively know what I liked, what I wanted, and he strove to please. And yeah, pretty freaking amazing, right? Right.

"My turn," I whispered, wrapping my arms and legs around him and rolling so that he was beneath me. Straddling him, I leaned over, running my lips over his neck, his collarbone, his chest, his glorious stomach, before his hands gripped my waist and pulled me back to him.

"Now. I want you now," he murmured.

I couldn't talk, so I nodded. As soon as I did, his hand reached out to the nightstand, fumbled with a drawer, and returned with a condom. I took it from him and ripped open the package. His hand joined mine, and in a heartbeat we were ready to go.

"I want to be on top," I said. "I never have before."

He blinked as if surprised. "Never?"

"No." Marc hadn't liked the idea, but I didn't want to explain. Not now, anyway. "Do you mind?"

A shudder whipped through his body. The green of his eyes turned almost black. "What do you think?"

"I think we've wasted enough time." I situated myself on top of him. Raising my hips, I said, "Ready?" Every part of my body zinged, his body rippled below me, and I felt him jerk upward. How's that for an affirmative response?

"You're teasing me." He rubbed his thumbs over my nipples, and as he did, I found where I wanted to be. Slowly, so slowly, I sank down. He pushed his hips up, and then, just like that, he entered me.

My breath came out in a rush. Everything I thought I knew before this moment evaporated into thin air. All I knew was the feel of him pumping into me and my body meeting his. Thrust for thrust. Nothing, no toy on Earth, could come close to this.

The waiting was worth every damn second.

"Oh. Wow."

"My thoughts exactly. You feel so good, Liz."

"So do you. Oh. Wow."

Nate gripped my hips and thrust into me again. Over and over, and then some more, until, all at once, everything exploded. Lights danced in front of my eyes, my body trembled and shivered from the energy between us, and finally I collapsed on top of him in a pile of loose muscles and melted joints.

His hands stroked my back and then my hair. An overpowering sensation of contentedness washed over me, around me, through me. I lifted my head, so I could see this man who'd so completely taken my breath away.

He smiled at me, and his arms tightened around my body. I put my head back on his chest and tried to ignore the worry that was beginning to overtake my happiness.

Sex with Nate? It wasn't what I'd expected. It wasn't what I'd thought it would be. It was more—so very much more than I ever believed possible. And with circumstances such as they were, what the hell was I supposed to do about that?

Chapter Twenty

"Lizzie? Someone's here to see you," Jon said, entering the kitchen at A Taste of Magic.

I placed the nested set of mixing bowls in the cupboard and swung the door closed. Thinking it was the elderly couple I'd met at the furniture store, I said, "Tell them I'll be out in a minute."

I rolled my shoulders back to stretch out the kinks, happy the long day was almost over. Before meeting with them, I wanted to duck into the restroom to be sure I didn't have powder on my nose. Sometimes, after a full day of baking, I resembled a ghost with the layers of flour that coated me.

"No, Lizzie. Not *them*. *He*." The abrupt, staccato beat of Jon's voice should have clued me in. Sadly, it didn't.

"He? Exactly who is here?" Maybe Nate had stopped by? My pulse sped up at the thought.

"Marc. 'Dickhead' is in the house. Want me to shoo him away?"

Okay, not such a nice surprise. What could he want? You see, it didn't matter that I'd made my peace with my failed marriage. I still didn't want to see him.

But then, I realized it was probably about the bakery. Most likely, Marc had decided it was time to make some changes at A Taste of Magic. I'd planned on mailing his check on my way home that night, but now I could give it to him in person. "No. I'll be out in a few minutes. Have him wait in the office."

Jon put his hands on his hips and narrowed his eyes. "Are you sure? You don't have to talk to him. I can easily give him his check and send him on his way."

"I'd rather give it to him. So yeah, send him back."

After a quick onceover of my appearance, and with a fresh cup of coffee in hand (you know, for strength), I let myself into my office.

"Betty, thanks for seeing me," Marc said. He was standing in the corner, hunched against the wall, his eyes following me. Dressed in a dark grey suit, he was as polished as ever. The spitting image of success.

"Didn't leave me much choice, did you?" Sitting down at my desk, my mind ran through all the different possibilities. He had to be there about business, because even when we were married, Marc rarely visited A Taste of Magic. While he never said it out loud, I was fairly sure "his wife, the baker," had been another sore spot.

Yeah. Anyway, water under the bridge. "What did you want to see me for?"

"You're not taking my calls, and you sure as hell aren't returning them. *You* didn't leave *me* much choice."

The nerve in my neck began to throb. "Last I checked, we were still divorced."

"Last I checked, we were still partners in this place," he said, his gaze taking in the office with one full sweep.

I opened a file on my desk and retrieved the envelope I'd addressed earlier. "Here you go."

"What's this?" He walked toward me.

"A check. Business is doing well enough, so we've decided to pay the loan amount back in full. As of now, you no longer have any interest in A Taste of Magic." Yeah—I have to admit—saying that felt pretty damn good.

He ripped the envelope open and pulled out the check. After glancing at the dollar amount, he folded it and slipped it into his pocket. "Thank you. But it's not why I'm here."

That startled me. "Why are you here, then?"

He put his hands on my shoulders and knelt down so we were nose to nose. "I just want to talk to you. I miss you, Betty."

"I'm expecting clients soon. This isn't the best time for me." I stood and walked to the other side of the room. One of Marc's tricks was to enter your physical space to show you he was the predator and you were his prey. I used to put up with it. That was the old me.

"This isn't the best place to say what I want to say, anyway. Can we get together for lunch? Dinner?" My expression must have displayed my distaste at the idea, because then he said, "A drink?"

The pleading quality of his tone surprised me. It shouldn't have gotten to me, I knew this, but it still did. "What's going on? You have me at a disadvantage here."

He stood, his perfectly pressed pants straightening over his long legs. "I think I made a mistake." I saw him struggling for words—odd for my ex. "I want to discuss reconciliation," he blurted.

Did I hear that right? "Leave it to you to make getting back together with me sound as formal as a business arrangement. 'I want to discuss reconciliation,'" I muttered.

Breathe, I instructed myself. Luckily, I listened to myself and sucked in air.

"It's not like that," he said. "It's—" He ran his hands down the sides of his pants. Could he be nervous? Scared? Of what?

And then, in a flash, I knew. He was scared of his new life. Which meant he wanted his old life back. Which meant— yep, you got it—me. Not only did I not want to discuss reconciliation, I truly didn't believe he did, either. Not after the way he'd left me. And not after all the conversations we'd had since then. Even so, I couldn't ignore it. I wanted to, sure, but part of Marc's reaction could be because of the magic cake. Part of this could very well be *my* fault.

Sweat beaded on my forehead. Who was I kidding? It *was* my fault, no two ways about it. I made a snap decision. "Why don't you come for dinner Friday night? We can talk then. Privately."

Marc's eyes lit up, and I felt a tiny, teeny, smidgen of guilt for not saying straight out I wasn't interested in reconciliation. But I needed to get him to my place so I could fix this mess. Or at least try.

"How about Saturday? Friday is an early pregnancy class 'iff and I are taking. She will not believe I have a dinner meet-
g that night."

Prick. Prick. Prick. Since when did I feel sorry for the imbo? I plastered a fake smile on my face. "Sure. Saturday at
·ven."

He advanced, and I was pretty sure he was going try to kiss
e. Um, yuck. I opened the office door and stepped outside.
'll see you then, Marc. My clients should be here shortly."

He nodded, disappointment settling in his eyes, but he was
nart enough not to push. "I'm looking forward to it, Betty."

And then, miraculously, he was gone. Sweating like a con-
ruction worker on a hot summer day, I returned to my of-
ce and collapsed in my chair.

I mentally rehashed the entire conversation with Marc.
Iausea curdled in my stomach. Most of the magic I'd cast had
ven me undesirable results. What was it Grandma had said?
Magic is unpredictable." Other than Troy—whose spell I was
ill happy I'd cast—I'd had to play fix-it for almost everyone
se I'd baked for.

Meddling with other people—with their thoughts and
notions—wasn't what I'd wanted when I accepted Miranda's
ift. But somehow, that's what I'd done. From the very first
ell, even. I thought of Nate, and my heart quickened and then
ropped inside of me like a lead weight. I'd been trying to ig-
ore what nagged at me. I'd tried to set it aside, to not think
out it. But now, after seeing Marc, I couldn't do that.

I wanted to be with Nate. I wanted to see where it would
ad. And yeah, a huge part of me hoped it would lead to
mething wonderful. But what if the only reason he remained
terested in me was because of magical coercion? Could I live
ith that? Could I go on, wondering if what we had together
·as real? The answer hit me straight on, and I gasped from the
rength of it.

No. I couldn't. Which meant, besides taking care of Marc,
d have to face my fears and do the same with Nate. And then
d have to live with the results, no matter what they were.

Because, let's face it, if my magic was powerful enough to bring Marc back to me, asking for a second chance, it was certainly powerful enough to make Nate experience emotions that weren't real.

I thought of our night together, the words we'd said to each other, the kisses we'd shared, and the electricity between us. Was all that false? Just a wish-induced experience? Possibly. And I wouldn't know unless I did something about it. Once I did, we might never have another night together again.

The bell jangled on the shop door, announcing the arrival of my new clients. As I left my office, I focused on getting through the next few hours. Later, I'd deal with the rest of it. I couldn't hide behind the magic any longer. I refused to.

I was ready for this to be over. One last bit of magical baking—maybe two—and I was done. Forever. Grandma could have the gift back.

I didn't want it.

It seemed to be my day for surprises. When I got home after work, Grandma Verda, in black leggings and a long gauzy hot pink shirt (where did she buy her clothes?), was packing her belongings. In *my* boxes. After dumping the contents all over the floor. Oh well, they needed to be dealt with anyway.

"What are you doing?"

"I'm moving in with Vinny," she announced. The look she gave me bore no room for argument. I didn't argue.

"Cool. When?"

"Early next week. He needs help, and I'm already there all the time. And you're all set now. You don't need me any more."

Is that why she'd moved in? "Maybe I do. Things aren't exactly settled. And I love you, Grandma." Other than a few minor incidents, I enjoyed living with Grandma Verda. I wasn't so sure I was happy to see her go.

"I love you too, Lizzie. But Shirley isn't comfortable here and you should have your freedom."

"What are you going to do with your condo? I can find you a real estate agent if you want to sell it."

"I'm giving it to Alice. She could use more room and a rent-free place to live."

"Um. Grandma. Do you know something?"

"I know nothing for sure. Just call it a hunch. Why?" She looked at me curiously, but I saw the glint in her eyes.

Crafty old lady, my grandmother.

"What kind of a hunch?"

"Miranda came to me in a dream. I don't know. It's kind of hazy, but I'm operating on instinct. Why are you asking?"

"No reason." Wow. Miranda was invading dreams now? Anyway, it wasn't up to me to tell Grandma. It was up to Alice.

I helped with the packing, which didn't take long, seeing as she didn't have that many belongings with her. When we were done, I said, "I'm running to the store. Do you want to come?"

"Not tonight. I'm going to take it easy."

She sighed, and for maybe the first time ever, I saw fatigue in her movements, in her gaze, and it worried me. "Are you sure you should be doing this?"

Her watery blue eyes focused on me. "I am. He's a good man, and I'm at the end." I opened my mouth to object but snapped it shut when she continued. "Don't look at me like that. I'm not planning my funeral. I've lived a long life, and I'm tired. I want to be somewhere I'm needed, and I want to be with someone who makes me laugh. Moving to Vinny's accomplishes both."

"Okay, Grandma. As long as you're sure."

And that was the end of that.

Later that night, me, Nate, and Grandma were ensconced in my living room. Nate's head rested on my shoulder as we watched *Buffy the Vampire Slayer*. Earlier, when we'd been discussing our favorite TV shows, he'd expressed disbelief that any show with the phrase "vampire slayer" in it could possibly

be a worthwhile way to spend time. This was a circumstance
that needed to be changed. Immediately. So, I'd pulled out my
DVD collection to expose him to the truth of all things Buffy.
We held hands like teenagers on their first date, and it was
incredibly, amazingly, blow-me-away intimate. Who knew
something as simple as hand-holding could elicit such strong
responses?

Not me, that's for sure.

Maybe it was because I worried it would be one of our
last nights to cuddle, to be together. I hoped not, but until I
reversed the effects of the other spells, I wouldn't know. So
yeah, I was taking full advantage while I could. As soon as
he left that night, I was going to bake. My decision, and not
being sure what would happen, had left me with a strange
melancholy feeling the entire evening. I squeezed Nate's hand.
He squeezed back.

Grandma Verda perched in the chair across from us,
meticulously knitting something in baby pink yarn. Booties,
she claimed. Alice still hadn't shared her news with anyone
else yet, supposedly, so I wondered what Grandma knew. If
anything.

When episode three rolled to a close, she set her knitting
aside. "I'm taking Vinny to a few appointments in the morning, so I'm going to bed." After saying our good nights, and
right before entering the bedroom, she said, "Have you heard
from Miranda lately, Lizzie?"

"No. She's been strangely quiet." It wasn't a lie; not really.
I hadn't exactly *heard* from my ghostly grandma. Think about
it. Not one word was spoken that night with the wedding
cake. Besides, the entire encounter was intensely personal and
for me alone.

"We should try to contact her again. Maddie should be
here because she was last time," Grandma added before closing the door to the bedroom.

Nate sat up, stretched his arms behind him, and yawned.
"Who's Miranda?"

Avoiding the question, because, come on, how in the hell

did I explain that one, I said, "Have I made you a Buffy fan yet?"

"Nice try, sweetie. But I can see avoidance from a mile away. Who's Miranda?"

Damn. I hadn't planned on explaining this. I still didn't think it was a good idea. The show *Bewitched* came to mind, and I remembered the premiere episode. You know the one, when Darrin first discovered Samantha was a witch? Yeah, he didn't react very well, did he?

Nah, better to not share this with Nate.

"Miranda is a touchy subject. It's probably better if I wait to talk about it until things have calmed down some." Ha! Complete truth. Many points for me. And really, I had no way of knowing if Nate would even be around in a few days, anyway.

"Fair enough." His fingers brushed my cheek, the warmth of it sweet but sensual and causing havoc with my ability to think coherently. "What's going on for you Saturday night? I thought we could go out for dinner. Maybe catch a movie."

Disappointed, I pulled back from his touch. "I have plans. I meant to talk to you about it earlier, actually."

"What type of plans?"

"My ex-husband is coming for dinner. There's a few areas we need to clear the air on so . . ." I grappled with the right explanation, the right words. "Closure. He's looking for closure and, honestly, we never really had it, so it's something that needs to happen."

"Didn't you tell me he was remarried? And expecting a baby?"

"Yes. And that's why it's important I talk to him. He's just going through some doubts, that's all. He won't be here long, Nate, and I don't want to be with him. This just, well, I have to do it."

Nate's eyes gripped mine. "I guess I'm supposed to be the big man here and not let this stress me, right?" He frowned, and I saw worry cross his features. "Are you sure you have no interest in patching things up?"

"I'm positive. You're the only man I'm interested in." Wow, that was easy to say. And it only scared me a little bit. Probably, if things didn't work out the way I wanted, I'd wish I hadn't said it. "I don't even expect him to be here more than a couple of hours, so if you want to come over later, we could watch a movie."

"You're filled with complications, aren't you?"

"Me? No complications here." Yeah, I know. A little lie. Because, come on, if being a gypsy and being able to cast magical spells isn't a complication, then what is?

He seemed to make a decision, and he smiled. "I'd like that, but I still want to take you out this weekend. Is your schedule clear for tomorrow night? Or do you need to check your appointment book?" he teased.

"Ha, you think you're cute, don't you? Tomorrow sounds great, and I don't need to check. I'm free."

"Good." Leaning over, he kissed me gently. "I work the early shift tomorrow, or I'd invite you over."

The timbre of his voice made me shiver.

After Nate left, I shut the TV off and busied myself straightening up, all in an attempt to shake the want from me. My body screamed for release, and I pretty much had to ignore it. That sucked. While in other circumstances I might have found a way to alleviate my blood-pumping desire, with Grandma Verda in residence, I only had one choice.

Turning the kitchen faucet on full blast, I splashed cold water over my face. When I felt more normal, I pulled out the recipe and the spell I was going to use for Marc and Nate. Two different cakes for two different men. Hopefully, I'd see two different results. For Marc, I wanted his feelings to revert back to normal, so he could focus on his new life. And Nate, I wanted the spell to prove Nate's feelings for me were real. I wanted that more than anything else.

After getting the ingredients measured and ready, I made sure the bedroom door was closed tight. Grandma Verda was a heavy sleeper, so I doubted she'd hear me, but I didn't want to chance waking her. I knew she'd had a difficult time sleeping with worrying over Vinny, Miranda, and, well, me.

Switching on the mixer, I began.

"My wish is simple! I've cast spells in the past that might have altered people's emotions and actions. This wish is to erase any of these effects on anyone who eats these cakes, but most specifically on Marc and Nate. I want the truth to come out, and only the truth. I wish for all previous enchantments to be removed!"

I repeated the wish a couple of more times as the magic bounced through me, around me, creating a maelstrom of colors, wind, and electricity. This time, I felt everything explode from the center of me, from my heart, like I never felt before.

All the anger of the prior year, the fears, and the desperation flew out of me. Quickly following, all the hopes and dreams I'd begun to have for Nate filled me, surrounded me, and pushed me forward. My knees trembled, and my arms shook. I sucked in air but held on tight, my body rippling with energy.

The power of it almost brought me to my knees, but I forced myself to remain upright until it all slowly died down. Then I released my grip on the mixer and, folding my arms on the counter, cradled my head in them. Raw emotion from letting go of the last of my fears and anger collided with my worries and hopes over Nate, of what would happen.

"Liz? What the fuck did you just do?"

Oh no! I turned to face Nate, my heart in my throat. "Er, that's a long story." I tossed him a weak grin, the trembles beginning all over again. He stood in the entry of the kitchen, his body ramrod straight, his eyes narrowed. But what scared me was the frigidness of his expression. "Why are you here? How did you get in?"

"I left my pager here. When I knocked on the door, you didn't answer, but I heard you yelling. I got scared, tried the door, found it unlocked." His gaze swung around the room.

"And found you doing something that I, no matter how hard I try, can't find a reasonable explanation for. I need you to explain this to me. Now, please."

"Chill out, Nate, she's not a devil worshipper. There's a reasonable explanation, and you'll hear it," Grandma Verda said, emerging from the bedroom. She focused on me. "Sweetie, that was incredible. Now I understand why Miranda tried to connect with you. Even my mother's power wasn't that strong."

"Power? What? Hell, do I even want to know?" Nate backed up against the wall.

Me? I had no clue what to say. My mouth was glued shut. Yeah, I know. A new concept for me.

"If you're interested in my granddaughter, you do. If you're not, because of something like this, then she's too good for you, young man. And if that's the choice you make, I'll have severely underestimated you." Grandma Verda pointed a finger at Nate. "I thought you were a pomegranate, not a lemon. Don't let me down."

I was seriously going to have to talk to her about her fruit thing.

And then, while I was still trying to figure everything out, a kaleidoscope of color washed the room. Goose bumps coated my skin, like before but also different somehow. The scent of flowers filled the room. And I knew, from the bottom of my toes to the top of my head, that I was finally going to meet my great-great-great-grandmother.

The swirl of colors grew brighter, pulsating to the beat of my heart. Then, seemingly out of nowhere, a woman stepped out of the rainbow. She wore a brightly hued dress. Her long dark hair cascaded around her face like perfect, flowing silk. But what amazed me most of all, I think, was the remarkable resemblance she had to my sister.

Miranda turned to my grandmother first.

"Give him a chance, Verda." Her lilting voice floated over me, through me. She wasn't completely see-through, but she wasn't completely, wholly there, either. What she was, however, was amazingly beautiful. Like Alice, but still different.

Every hair on my body stood up on end. I never actually expected to see her. The room hummed with energy, myriad hues sparkling softly all around us like raindrops of every color in the world. Grandma Verda smiled at the apparition and then sagged against the door, probably so she wouldn't fall to the ground.

Who could blame her?

I tore my eyes off Miranda and searched out Nate. When I found him, I walked to his side. I'd never seen his skin so pale. I grabbed his hand, felt the iciness of it, and tightened my hold. He didn't break free.

"What is that?" he uttered in a gravelly, what-the-hell-is-going-on-now sort of voice.

"Not what. *Who*," I whispered. "And her name is Miranda. She is my great-great-great-grandmother. And yes, Nate, she's very real."

His eyes zipped around the room. But then he drew in a deep breath. Glancing at me, he said, "Really?"

At my nod, he focused on Miranda. "It's—ah—nice to meet you. I think. Wow. Okay. Even I'm a little startled here, and I've seen a lot of wild things in my life. Maybe I'm losing my mind?"

Miranda laughed. A sound not unlike tinkling bells. "You're adorable. He's a good choice, Elizabeth. You did the right thing."

Nate coughed. He cleared his throat. "Is this normal for your family?" he asked me.

"It's becoming normal," I answered.

He shook his head, as if to clear himself from a daze. "Then I might as well get used to it, huh?" He looked at Miranda again, and I saw something—acceptance, maybe—shimmer in his eyes. "I think I'm falling in love with your great-great-great-granddaughter. So I'm glad you think I'm a good choice."

Falling in love? With me?

Miranda laughed again. "I won't have the energy to stay long. But my granddaughters will fill you in." She faced me. "Elizabeth, I need to tell you a few things, but I need to be quick about it. Don't pass the gift on until you know who it should go to. Who it goes to is as important as the gift itself. You'll know, soon, who the right person is."

I nodded mutely.

"We're a lot alike, you and I. This is why you were able to sense me in the very beginning, and this is why I've been able to connect with you. Your emotions pulled me to you, and now . . . your decision to take control and be strong allows me to even be here. There's more coming. More you'll need to know. But not now. Think about what I've said and listen to your heart. Do you understand?"

But then, before I could even answer and tell her, no, I had no clue what she was talking about, she reached her hand toward my grandmother. "Verda, I did try to come to you. To connect with you. When you struggled so much with your marriage and the wish you made. I'm sorry I couldn't reach you, but I did watch over you. Always. I'm proud of all the women in my family. Never think otherwise."

My grandmother nodded as she wiped the wetness away from her eyes. "I think I felt you then, when things were so difficult." She smiled softly, as if she'd finally made peace with something. "I'm glad to see you. My mother spoke of you often."

"I'll see you again, Verda. I'll see all my granddaughters again." With that, Miranda's form shimmered slightly, becoming more transparent. "I have to leave now, but remember what I said, Elizabeth."

And then, as quickly as she'd arrived, she was gone.

I thought of everything she'd said, but honestly? My mind wouldn't let go of the *falling in love* statement from Nate. What kind of power was that?

My grandmother tugged at her nightgown and then wiped more tears from her cheeks. "Let me go change, and then we'll explain everything to your young man." She disappeared into the bedroom and tightly closed the door behind her.

Nate grasped my shoulders and turned me to him. "I don't know what happened here. Not really. But it won't change that I have serious feelings for you. Please don't be afraid to tell me everything."

I straightened my shoulders. "I'm a gypsy, Nate. It's in my blood. It's who I am."

"And you get visits from a long-dead relative often?"

"I wouldn't say often. But every now and then, yes. Usually, her visits aren't like this."

He thought about that for a minute, and then asked, "When I walked in, what were you doing? All the lights, wind, and other stuff I saw . . . what was that?"

Here we go. Like it or not, it was truth time. Nervous jitters danced through me, but I pushed them away. "I was casting a spell." And then, I explained to him what had happened with some of my other spells. I told him why it was important I nullified the prior enchantments from Marc. When I'd run out of words, I snapped my mouth shut.

"And did you ever spell me?"

Of course, he had to ask that. I'd ask in the same situation.

"Just once directly. And it was an accident. It was before I knew about the magic. Remember those banana muffins I baked you?" Warmth tickled my cheeks. My stomach somersaulted. "And that, er, night on the couch? I think that night was the result of those muffins. So maybe . . . what you think you feel for me, you really don't."

He prodded my chin upward, so I'd look into those amazing green eyes of his. "Everything I feel for you is very real. I never ate those muffins, Lizzie. I'm allergic to bananas."

I took a breath. "Allergic? Seriously?"

"Seriously."

I wanted to grab on so badly it almost hurt. But I couldn't. Not yet. There were still the brownies to deal with. "Well.

There was one other spell. It wasn't meant specifically for you. But it might be affecting you."

"And that was?"

"Right before I saw you that night, I'd baked a batch of brownies for me. The spell I cast was for me to date . . . um . . . well . . ."

"Go on. It's okay."

"Hot men. And you're pretty hot."

He laughed again, humor glittering in his eyes. "I've been interested in you since the beginning. So, no, Liz. It had nothing to do with any brownies. You're stuck with me."

Everything was real? As much as I'd hoped it would be true, I hadn't allowed myself to think this moment would really happen. I tried to temper my happiness, my excitement. "Well. If you don't mind, I'd still like you to eat the cake I was making when you walked in on me. Just so I know. For sure."

"Absolutely. I'll stay here tonight until it's done. I don't want you worrying about this. *I* know how I feel about you." He bent down and kissed me lightly. "Now I just need you to believe it, too."

More heat flushed through me, but I didn't care. If I hadn't gotten stuck in my window, would I have even met Nate? Thank God I'd gone out that night and lost my keys. Fate, every now and then, knew exactly what she was doing.

"Are you ready to hear everything, Nate?" my grandmother asked, striding from the bedroom. I could tell she thought it was going to be a problem, convincing Nate not to end things based on gypsies and magic and ghosts.

Nate released his grip. "Actually, I think we're all set here, Verda. I wouldn't mind hearing all the details, but it isn't necessary."

A cop. Practical to his core, from everything I could see, and he was willing to accept this part of who I was at face value. Oh, that didn't mean he'd buy into all of it, I knew that, but still.

I said, "We'll be waiting for a cake to bake anyway. So,

eah, let me make some tea, and we'll tell you Miranda's tory." I mean, really, if we did end up together, like in narriage someday, and had children, he had a right to know verything, didn't he?

Exactly.

Chapter Twenty-one

Nate and I entered my apartment, just returning from our night out. While the evening had been fun, I couldn't completely relax. And probably, neither could Nate. I asked him about every fifteen minutes or so if his feelings had changed. Luckily for me, he hadn't gotten annoyed with me yet.

Even more important? Each time I asked, his answer remained the same. And it was the "all things are wonderful" answer I wanted to hear.

I kicked my shoes off and headed for the couch. He followed, sitting down next to me. He opened his arms, and I scooted into them. With my head on his chest, my cheek rubbing against the softness of his shirt, my body finally began to unwind. Weird or not, whether it made sense or not, this man affected me in a way Marc never had. And I never would have known these feelings if we'd stayed together. So yeah, in a screwed up, backwards sort of way, it was a blessing he'd left me.

"So—are you still sure?" I had to ask again. It was almost impossible for me to believe that something this awesome wasn't the result of magic.

His arms tightened around me. I couldn't see his face, but I heard his deep intake of breath. All at once, the calmness that had started to seep into me evaporated. "What? It's happening. Isn't it?"

He answered, his voice low and serious, "Yes, Lizzie. I think it is."

Oh God. I knew it was too good to be true. I pulled out of his embrace. Sitting up straight, I tried to swallow my disappointment. My sorrow. "It's okay. None of this is your fault. It's mine. And you've been so terrific."

"Lizzie—"

I held up a hand. "No. It's fine. Really." If he tried to explain, if he tried to be nice just to make me feel better, I knew I wouldn't be able to hold back the sadness that was pushing in on me. I hated this, but come on, I knew it was a possibility.

A light of something hit his eyes. Probably, he felt bad.

"We can still be friends, right? You said yourself you can always use more friends," I babbled. I tried not to, but there you have it.

"Of course we can be friends. But you should let me finish what I was going to say." He reached over, grasped my wrist, and tugged me back to him.

Suddenly, I wasn't so sure what was happening.

Cupping my face with his hands, he tilted my chin upward so that we were eye to eye. The warmth of his touch settled my nerves. A crawl of hope began deep in my belly, branching out bit by bit, until all of my anxiety fled.

"What I was going to say," he said, his lips touching mine in a quick, sweet kiss, "is I'm becoming more enraptured by you every minute we spend together. *That's* what's happening."

"Really?"

"Really."

And then, as quick as a heartbeat, everything was right in my world once again. "You scared me," I said in a rush. "I thought . . . well, you know what I thought."

"I will tell you if anything changes, when it changes. I won't hide that from you. Trust in that. Trust in me. Please?"

I thought about that for a minute. And you know what? Nate wasn't Marc. He wouldn't show up one day, with virtually no clues, and tell me he was finished with me. So yeah, trusting Nate? "I can do that," I whispered. "I'm sorry I've been a little nuts today."

"Nuts I can handle. I don't like seeing you doubt me. Or us. So have some faith, Gypsy Girl."

Gypsy girl. How cute was that? "Faith. I can do that," I repeated.

We curled up again, with my head on his chest. We didn't watch television, and we didn't really talk. Mostly, we just enjoyed being with each other. I thought about the prior day and everything that had occurred. Nate had taken to the whole Miranda story fairly well, considering the circumstances.

After he'd asked a bunch of questions, he pretty much just held up his hands and went with it. Kind of cool, really. Of course, he also admitted that if he hadn't witnessed the magic and seen Miranda materializing in front of him, it might have worked out differently. And, while he'd probably have more questions at some point, I was just relieved he was willing to accept.

After a little while, Nate asked, "Where's Verda at? She hasn't moved out yet, has she?"

"She's staying at Vinny's tonight. But no, she's not officially moving out until Monday. I think she's busy rearranging his stuff to make room for hers."

Nate chuckled. He kissed the top of my head. "I was going to ask you back to my place, but if Verda isn't going to be here . . ."

"Yes. I'd love it if you stayed here tonight." After all, I'd wanted him in my bed for a ridiculously long time.

Standing, I grasped his hands and pulled him to his feet. "Follow me," I said in my best husky-voiced drawl.

In a blink he was behind me. In my bedroom, he reclined on my bed, his long legs spread out straight. His gaze whisked over me. "Come here."

"Not yet. Just relax." I went to my closet and pulled out a couple of boxes. Somewhere, there was a little silk something I'd never had a chance to wear for Marc. Tonight I wanted to wear it for Nate. I dug through one box, and then another. Finally, I found it.

I dangled the red hot negligee in front of me. "I'm going to go change." And when his jaw dropped open (yes, literally) I wiggled my hips. "Be right back, cutie."

"Baby, you don't even need to put it on now. Just come here," he groaned.

"Nope. You're a big boy; you can be patient. I *am* wearing this, Nate. Entertain yourself until I get back." I rushed into the bathroom and stripped off my clothes, and then slipped into the negligee. I brushed my hair until it shined, sprayed some perfume on, and then stood back to appraise myself.

Okay, exercise sucked, but the results? Totally worth it. I sizzled. Tugging my robe on over the negligee, I pushed back the nervousness. It's not as if Nate hadn't seen me, well, naked, but somehow I felt more exposed in the negligee. Weird, I know.

Stepping into the bedroom, I heard a vibrating sound and instantly realized what it was.

My entire body flushed with heat. It had to be as red as the negligee. "What are you doing?" I managed to choke out.

Nate, sitting upright on my bed, naked except for his briefs, had three of my toys laid out in front of him. He also had one in his hands, lights running up and down the shaft. Grinning devilishly, he said, "I found your stash. Strobe lights? Interesting, Liz. But what I really want to know is which one is your favorite?"

Mutely, I pointed to the bright purple one laying to the right of the other two toys. He set the flashing toy down and picked up the Bunny Rocket.

"Yes, that's it."

"Well, sweetie, why don't you come here and we'll see what we can do with this?"

Untying the belt on my robe, I let it fall to the floor. His gasp hit me in the stomach and, somehow, I wasn't nervous or embarrassed any longer. I stuck one of my hips out. "Why don't you come and get me?"

Oh my. I'd never seen a man move so fast.

Within the next several hours, I had more fun than I'd ever had before. And let's just say this: Battery operated sex toys? They're not only for solo use. Definitely not. Not when you find the right person to share them with.

"Liz?" Nate's husky voice murmured in my ear. His arms were crushed tight around me, our legs weaved together in a tumble.

"Yes?" I melted into him, on the verge of blissful sleep wondering how in the hell I'd lived before I met him.

"Are there catalogs for these things?"

"What? The toys?"

"Uh-huh."

"Yeah. And tons of Internet sites."

"Excellent. Let's buy some more." He kissed me, and I immediately felt the burn of heat begin once again.

This magic? The one we created together? It beat the hell out of anything gypsy magic could accomplish.

I wrapped up the remainder of the dark chocolate cake I'd baked for dessert and put it in one of the boxes from A Taste of Magic. I entered the living room and handed it to Marc, who was still sitting on the couch.

"Here, you should take this home. I won't eat it," I said. Besides, I had most of the second cake sitting on my counter. The one I'd made for Nate.

Really, though, I didn't think Marc was going to need to eat any more of it. The evening had started out rough with him making advance after advance. He'd said words to me that a year ago I would have loved to hear. But everything had changed. Thank God for that.

I'd rushed us through dinner, trying to hold him at bay. But then, soon after dessert, things had settled down. When he'd started to pace, I knew the magic was working.

I'd never seen my magic work that quickly, which, to me, meant he loved Tiffany and he'd love his baby. He just needed to get over his fears and not repeat his mistakes, not try to use me as a crutch. And dispelling the other magic pushed all that along.

He rose to his feet and accepted the box. "I want to say one more thing, Betty."

Enough was enough. "Seriously, Marc. Please don't call me Betty. Ever again."

He paused, the dark brown of his eyes deepening ever more. Nodding his head in acceptance, he said, "Got it. Sorry.

seem to have ignored a lot of what you've asked of me over the years."

I shrugged, just wanting this over with. Plans with Nate were calling, and I didn't want to waste another second. Tonight he'd talked me into watching *Star Wars*. "It's time to move on. For real. For both of us."

"I agree. I . . . I was kind of a dick at the end. I am sorry about that."

"You're right. You were a dick," I agreed. Hey, it was the truth.

He combed the fingers from his free hand through his hair. "I deserve that." He paused a moment and then said, "I did love you." He ran his hand over his eyes. "But then I stopped. I don't know why. I didn't know how to deal with it, and I was stupid. I should have handled everything better than I did. It's always bothered me, but ever since seeing you again, it's been worse. I really want you to know I'm sorry. Truly sorry."

Prickles of pain poked at my eyes, like tiny little needles. And because the new cake had reversed the delivered-to-his-office-cake's magic, I had to believe his apology was real. That it was heartfelt. And that meant more to me than a magically induced apology ever would.

"Well," I said. "I made mistakes, too. I pushed you too hard to start a family. I got angry with you for working so much. But the worst thing I did was trying to make you be the man I thought you should be, instead of allowing you to be who you are. We both grew up, and you changed, and I didn't know how to handle that."

He opened his mouth as if he was going to argue with me, but I put my hand on his shoulder to stop him. "We both made mistakes. Probably because we married too young. Let's just call it even, and both of us can be happy from here on out."

"I'd like that, Liz." Walking stiffly toward the door, he stopped abruptly. "No chance at being friends?"

Sadly, I shook my head. "We can't be friends. But we can be friendly. If we run into each other somewhere, we don't have to be enemies."

He put the cake box down and reached out a hand. Just like the old days, way back before we'd stopped loving each other. For some reason I didn't want to dwell on, I met his hand with mine.

Grasping it tightly, he tugged until I stood in front of him. "You are an amazing woman, Elizabeth Raymond Stevens. I hope whoever you end up with treats you much better than I did."

I blinked, and tears dripped out of my eyes. Silly, really, being this emotional. He leaned over, his lips touched mine, and this was *not* like the old days.

It was a simple kiss, yet it spoke volumes for me. This kiss was one of good-bye. The good-bye we'd never truly said. I stepped back and wiped the tears away.

For the very last time, thank you God.

He picked up the box, tossed me a smile, opened the door and walked away. Went home, where his wife and unborn child waited for him. Exactly where he should be.

As for me? I was in for a night of lightsabers and spaceships. But really, it was spending more time with Nate that put a smile on my face.

Well, that and, you know, that hot, crazy sex thing.

Chapter Twenty-two

I stood in my kitchen arranging another tray of hors d'oeuvres, listening to the chatter of my friends and family, feeling warm and solid. To celebrate my new life, and the decoration of my apartment, I was hosting a party.

And, if I did say so myself, a terrific party at that.

"Want some help with that?" Scot asked, nodding toward the tray. "And I wanted to ask you what's going on with Alice. She's really quiet."

I plastered on a smile. "She'll be okay. And yes, I'd love some help." Alice hadn't confided in anyone else yet, but she'd have to soon. Another month had passed and, while others may not have yet noticed the small bump her tummy had become, they would before too much longer. Regardless, it was her call when to say anything.

Breathing deeply, I opened the fridge and picked up a plate with a slice of lemon meringue pie. It was my sister's newest craving. "I'm going to take this to Alice," I said to Scot. "If you could just put the tray on the dining room table, I'd really appreciate it."

"Hey, where were you hiding that? Do you have more?"

"In the fridge. Bottom shelf."

Before I actually made my way to Alice, Maddie stopped me, waving her hand in my face, a huge diamond blinking brightly in the light.

"Oh my God, congratulations! When did this happen?"

Maddie's smile widened. "Last night. I really never thought this day would come."

"I'm so happy for you!" And I was. My friend was in love

and realizing her dreams. Major kudos for her. "But isn't this a little fast?"

Pink blossomed on her cheeks. "We're going to have a long engagement. But we wanted to make a commitment to each other."

"I think that's wonderful."

"I want you to be my maid of honor. Please? Oh, and if you promise no magic, I want you to bake my cake." Her grin told me she was teasing, and I laughed.

"Promise, no magic; and I would love to be your maid of honor." Glancing around, I didn't see Spencer. "Is he here? I want to congratulate him, too. He's a lucky guy."

"He'll be here soon. I'll bring him over when he arrives."

I gave her an awkward hug, because I was still holding Alice's pie, and said, "I'll be back in a minute. I want to hear all the details. But I need to talk to Alice."

"Go," she said, shooing me away. "I'm just gonna ogle my ring some more."

My eyes darted around the room, trying to find my sister. Jon and Andy sat on the couch, talking animatedly with my mother. Next to them, Joe was gabbing on his cell phone. Nate and his sister, with Sam in between, were playing cards at the dining room table. His eyes caught mine, and he grinned. My stomach flipped, and my heart warmed. This, you see, always happened when he smiled at me. I blew him a kiss and turned still trying to find Alice.

My dad had pulled a chair up to the television and was watching something. God knew what. Grandma Verda and Vinny were in the side by side La-Z-Boy chairs, sweetly holding hands. Everyone was accounted for.

Everyone, that was, except for Alice.

This worried me, because my apartment was not that big. On a hunch, I went to my bedroom and slipped inside. She was curled on my bed, her hands on her stomach, rubbing the tiny bump that was her baby.

"Hey, sis, you feeling all right?" I asked, quietly closing the door behind me.

"I get tired easily. Overwhelmed easily. It's okay if I rest for a while, isn't it?"

Sitting down next to her, I set the plate on my nightstand and then rubbed her belly. "Of course it is. How's my niece or nephew doing?"

"Fine. Healthy. Everything is good, so my doctor says."

"Then why do you look so sad?"

"I'm scared. Moving into Grandma Verda's place will be good, because of the room, but I don't know anyone there. I still keep thinking I should tell Troy, Liz. Should I?"

The danger in his eyes came back to me, chilled me, frightened me. "I don't want you to. But it's your choice." I hadn't yet told Alice about his visit to A Taste of Magic, but maybe I should. Just not tonight. "Hey, do me a favor? If you decide to talk to him, tell me first, so we can hash it out. Deal?"

She nodded. And when her eyes welled with tears, I pulled her into my arms.

"Tell me what you want," I whispered. "Tell me what you wish for."

"I want to figure out how to do this. I want to know I *can* do this. I wish I wasn't feeling so scared. So powerless. I want to be in control, but I'm not. The world is spinning around me, and I just want it to slow down. So I can catch a breath, figure things out, and be strong." It all came out in a huge rush of words, and even though our situations were starkly different, I recognized a thread of unity.

Control. Strength. Finding courage in the face of fear.

All of this helped finalize my decision. All of this told me I was doing the right thing. I'd given a lot of thought to what Miranda had said to me. And deep inside, I knew what I was about to do was, somehow, exactly what I was *supposed* to do.

"Sit up." I reached over and picked up the plate of pie. "Here, I made this for you. Pie makes everything better."

"You sound like Mom," Alice said through her tears. She accepted the plate, and I watched, curiously, as she took the first bite. And the second. I rubbed her belly as she ate it, and when nothing but crumbs remained, she handed the plate back to me.

Weird. I didn't feel any different.

"Thank you. Silly, but I feel better already."

"Told you," I said lightly. "Pie makes everything better."

"I'm going to go wash my face and get something to drink." She kissed me on my cheek. "Thank you for being my friend and not only my sister."

"Always and forever," I said. After she left, I set the plate down again and wondered if it had worked. If I'd passed the gift to my sister or not.

And then, flowers scented the air, and I smiled. A gentle light grew in the center of the room, turning into a pale rainbow. Energy hummed around me, and I focused on the colors, waiting. Entirely at ease with what once completely freaked me out.

And then, suddenly, there she was. *Miranda.*

"Hello, Grandmother."

Her smile, so like Alice's, made the rainbow pulse brighter. "You made the right choice, Elizabeth. I couldn't tell you to give the gift to Alice, but it's what I wanted you to do. Because she has it now, I'll be able to connect with her. And that will be vitally important."

"I didn't tell her about the magic, though. I need to."

My great-great-great-grandmother held up a ghostly finger. "Not yet. She wouldn't be able to understand just yet. Let her come to you with questions, because she will." She laughed again. "And I'll be there, to help her along, when the time is right."

I nodded, somehow understanding her meaning if not her actual words. "I don't feel any different. Shouldn't I feel different?"

She gave her tinkling laugh. "The magic stays with you now forever. You are the first in our line, so far, to have the strength to keep it *and* to pass it on."

Keep it? I still had it? I shivered. "We both have it now?"

"Yes, and hopefully this will continue. Alice's child, it's a daughter, and she has the potential to be the strongest of us all. Stronger than I was, even. This is why I'm still here. This is why it was so important I connected with you. I will be there for her as she grows, to learn what she can do. To teach her."

A fairy ghost grandmother. What child wouldn't want that?

Miranda continued. "But it was important for you to believe in order for you to pass the gift on to who it needed to go to."

"You said this before. That I should believe, but I've believed from the beginning."

Another laugh. "No, Elizabeth. Not the magic. You needed to believe in *yourself*."

And then, instantly, the energy dissipated, the colors vanished, the scent of flowers disappeared and I was all alone.

My sister was having a daughter. Possibly a little girl who would be born with magic more powerful than anything I could imagine. Tingles coated my skin as I stood from the bed. While my mind wasn't yet ready to accept everything Miranda had passed on, my heart and my soul knew it to be true. The next year, and beyond, would prove to be enlightening, interesting, and probably more than a little freaky.

Opening the door, I stood at the threshold. My gaze once again took in everything, everybody, but as always, it ultimately rested on Nate. The sweet, sexy cop I'd met so unexpectedly.

He beckoned to me. Smiling, I stepped toward this incredible man I'd found. My future might or might not be weaved together with him, but regardless, I knew one thing for certain.

I wrapped my arms around him. "I love you."

"Yeah? That's good, because I love you, too, Gypsy Girl." As his lips touched mine in a soft kiss, his eyes promised me more heat, more everything, later, when everyone went home.

And you know what?

Not only did I believe in love.

Not only did I believe in magic.

But, yes. Finally, I believed in me. And with the amount of points I get for that, there's no stopping me.

Tracy Madison

A Stroke of Magic

You know how freaky it is, to expect one taste and get another? Imagine picking up a can of tepid ginger ale and taking a swig of delicious, icy cold peppermint tea. Alice Raymond did just that. And though the tea is exactly what she wants, she bought herself a soda.

ONE STROKE OF MAGIC,
AND EVERYTHING HAS CHANGED

No, Alice's life isn't exactly paint-by-numbers. After breaking things off with her lying, stealing, bum of an ex, she discovered she's pregnant. Motherhood was definitely on her "someday" wish list, but a baby means less time for her art and no time for recent hallucinations that include this switcharoo with the tea. She has to impress her new boss, the ridiculously long-lashed, smoky-eyed Ethan Gallagher, and she has to deal with her family, who have started rambling about gypsy curses. Only a soul-deep bond with the right man can save her and her child? As if being single wasn't pressure enough!

Available July 2009!   ISBN 13: 978-0-505-52811-7

LINDA THOMAS-SUNDSTROM

Time to go wild.

Barbie Bradley was swept off her feet—literally. One moment the twenty-something was traversing Forest Lawn Cemetery in the dead of night with her best friend, the next she was thrown like a sack of potatoes over a man's shoulder. True, she and Angie had come to this odd locale for a singles party, but this wasn't quite how she'd planned to get picked up.

Darin Russell found "Ms. Right" at work, which was surprising because girls in the cemetery were usually a tad, in a word, stiff. Not that this one couldn't stand to loosen up. She seemed particularly sensitive about being named after the Mattel toy, and before he popped the question he had to know how she'd react to his furry little secret. You see, though he had a tuxedo and a Porsche, he had more in common with the residents of the Miami Zoo than Ken. And if things went according to plan, Barbie was going to see his animal side.

$\mathcal{B}$arbie & ᵀᴴᴱ BEAST

ISBN 13: 978-0-505-52813-1

☐ YES!

Sign me up for the Love Spell Book Club and send my
FREE BOOKS! If I choose to stay in the club, I will pay
only $8.50* each month, a savings of $6.48!

AME: _____

DDRESS: _____

ELEPHONE: _____

MAIL: _____

☐ I want to pay by credit card.

☐    ☐ MasterCard.   ☐ DISCOVER

CCOUNT #: _____

XPIRATION DATE: _____

GNATURE: _____

Mail this page along with $2.00 shipping and handling to:
Love Spell Book Club
PO Box 6640
Wayne, PA 19087
Or fax (must include credit card information) to:
610-995-9274
You can also sign up online at **www.dorchesterpub.com**.
*Plus $2.00 for shipping. Offer open to residents of the U.S. and Canada only.
Canadian residents please call 1-800-481-9191 for pricing information.
under 18, a parent or guardian must sign. Terms, prices and conditions subject to
ange. Subscription subject to acceptance. Dorchester Publishing reserves the right
to reject any order or cancel any subscription.